HENRIETTA GEORGIA

My Dusk, My Dawn

Brotherhood of El Book One

First published by Lyrical Poetry Co. Publishing in 2017

Second Edition

ISBN: 978-0-6480389-6-2

This book was professionally typeset on Reedsy.
Find out more at reedsy.com

Contents

DEDICATION

I dedicate this book to everyone that has loved and lost, everyone that has wanted to start over but could not, and everyone that has fought a battle and lost, but survived to tell the tale.

ACKNOWLEDGEMENTS

Thank you Jesus for going before me and for looking out for me always.

Thank you to my family and friends.

Thank you to the very talented and exceptional cover designer Stefanie Fontecha at Beetiful Book Covers for bringing my creative vision to life.

Thank you to all my fans, who love and feel the characters I've created as though they were real. They are as much a part of me as a part of you.

A very special thank you to T.S. who encouraged me to put pen to paper and write again.

Thank you to all The Beautiful Ones. You know who you are.

PROLOGUE

Nothing could stop us the way we were. Ours was not the great love story written in the stars. Our story was greater. It was fated, he for I and I for him. When we first met, I did not know this. I did not know all this. I did not know that we would end up like this. Nothing could stop us the way we were, except life itself. Only love had other plans at the time. At that time.

1

SOMETHING WICKED THIS WAY COMES

Duayne drove for what seemed like hours. The silence was deafening. I knew better than to further aggravate him, so I said nothing. It was cold. The pickup truck's leather interior against my bare skin felt cold. I pressed the heater on. He switched it off. I sat with my hands folded across my chest, my knees crossed. My feet bare. I closed my eyes and prayed. I felt a sense of foreboding. That this was the end. I prayed.

At moments, he sped, and the view outside the truck's tinted windows was a blur. The dream relocation to Austin, Texas was a nightmare. I had hoped for so much, but this was it. He would never change. He could never change. I had come to that realization too late.

He pulled into a filling station. Gas was running low and he'd figured it was time to refuel. Eyeballing me as he locked me in the car, I knew better than to try to escape. But I needed to escape. I had to escape.

He kept his .45 in the glove compartment. All I had to do

was get it. As he refueled, I faked sleep. When his head was turned, I opened the glove compartment. It was empty. He suddenly unlocked the door from the outside, startling me. My nightdress got caught on the edge of the compartment's door as I rushed to slam it shut.

"Looking for something?" he asked, lifting his shirt to reveal his handgun, tucked neatly in a holster beneath an untucked shirt. "This isn't the only thing I've got." Sliding in closer to me, he flicked open a penknife. Waving the blade in front of my face, he stated, "If I wanted this to be over, it would be over. Don't ruin this for me. You don't get to choose how this plays out. This isn't over by a long shot." The blade shone silver in the moonlight.

My heart leapt. I fought for words but none came.

"Cat got your tongue?" he asked. Suddenly, he held the blade beneath my chin. "Don't fucking try anything else with me."

I held back tears.

He held the blade there for a moment, before dropping it and putting it away. Tears rolled down my face and I turned away from him to face the window.

He started the car and drove. The black sky, peppered with stars, a blanket of calm in the chaos of my predicament. I found reassurance in the fact that the day would eventually break. This darkness would not last forever. I held back tears, wishing I could drift into an endless sleep, or a sleep with end that would see me waken from this nightmare.

No such luck. Somewhere between that thought and the car coming to a screeching holt, I jolted up from sleep. Duayne hopped out of the driver's seat, came over to my side, yanked the door open and gruffly grabbed me by the wrist. I tried

2

fighting him, but this was no use. He tightened his grip on my wrist and dragged me forward. "What are you doing Duayne, enough is enough!"

"Yes, enough is enough!" he yelled, his emerald green eyes glistening with disdain and contempt. Despite the hostility and anger reflected in his face, his mocha skin and beautiful face was as perfect as it was when we first met. Back then, I saw him as a protector. Now, he embodied all that I feared and loathed. "Enough is enough, and that's why I'm leaving you here," he explained.

I didn't recognize where I was. My heart skipped a beat. *He was leaving me in the middle of nowhere.* The only thing in sight was a local dive bar. I desperately tried to get out of his grip. The scuffle angered him further and in response, he shoved me against a nearby brick wall.

Towering over me, he stated, "Let's see you get out of this one you bitch." He spat on the ground in front of me, turned, walked away then drove off.

I froze, motionless and helpless to do or say anything. I had no fight left in me so I let him walk away and leave me there. For many years, I had hoped to get away from him. This was the moment he let me go and walked away from me.

It was cold and dark. I didn't know where I was. I dropped to my knees, in tears, as I glanced around me and at the dark skies above. For a moment I prayed. Prayed that where I was would lead me to a better place than where I'd been.

I don't know how I got here.

Country music played softly in the background. The saloon bar looked dingy but busy. *One of those places where one could get all you can drink Lone Star beers*, I figured. I was alone. Me myself and I in the middle of nowhere, in the middle of the

3

night. No shoes on, dressed in a barely-there night dress. Heart in my throat, I tried not to panic.

I don't know how I got here.

All the smarts that got me through law school couldn't help me now. All the foresight in the world could not have seen me here. Or maybe it could have. If only I had been more aware.

A man stumbled out of the saloon heading my direction. He'd clearly had too much to drink. Hoping he hadn't seen me was unrealistic. He had.

"Well look at what we have here!" he exclaimed loudly, slurring his words. "Dark berry, sweet juice!"

I got to my feet and stood there, waiting for the right moment to bolt. Drunkenly staggering towards me, he lunged at me. A wisp of air graced my face as I ducked from his grasp and bolted towards the door of the saloon.

The bar fell silent. "Well look at what the cat dragged in," said a man in the crowd. Other patrons chimed in, mumbling and casting dirty looks my way.

I tried to gain my composure. Lifted my head to appear confident though I didn't feel it. I resolved to ask the bartender for a glass of water and walked over to the bar counter.

Surely being inside here was better than being outside there, I reasoned. A lone man in a black and white checkered shirt, blue denim jeans and cowboy hat sat on a barstool at the counter, to my left. He tipped his hat at me, acknowledging my presence. I nodded in response. Hands trembling and pressed out in front of me on the countertop, I stood there, waiting to catch the attention of the bartender.

"A glass of water please," I requested, when I caught his

4

eye.

"That'll cost you," the bartender said, leaning back in a stance that indicated he was unwilling to serve me.

"Don't worry about it then," I replied, having no way to pay. *A glass of water was supposed to be free anyhow.*

The man at the bar who'd tipped his hat at me stated, "If the lady wants her a glass of water, give her that glass of water." He stood up, cool and collected. His wavy hair was a tawny brown hue, his eyes a deep ocean blue. The hat he wore shaded his ruggedly handsome face. A prominent longhorn belt buckle and cowboy boots with spurs completed the look. Standing there firmly, he didn't seem inebriated. Though my instinct had been off being with Duayne, oddly, I felt a sense of calm and peace in this man's presence.

"What can I get you lady, apart from that glass of water?" he asked, the kindness in his eyes apparent. "Daniel," he said, stretching a hand out to greet me.

I felt nothing like a lady, as I took his hand, and shook it. "Just a glass of water," I stated. I didn't offer my name in response, though it would have been the polite thing to do at the time. Then again, I hardly knew him, so being secretive and wary of him was the way to go.

"Gaitor Bait," the bartender retorted abruptly.

"Excuse me?" Daniel questioned, with disbelief, facing the bartender directly.

"Gaitor Bait. I see you're into it," the bartender stated, slamming a glass down on the countertop.

"Enough of that," Daniel responded. "That's no way to talk to me and there's no need for you to get all bent out of shape. All the lady's asking for is a glass of water. All I'm asking is for you to give it to her."

Another man sought to throw his two cents in. "Lady? She ain't no lady. See what she's a wearin'!"

Daniel turned to me, gave me a quick once over, then said slightly above a whisper, "I know there's gotta be some perfectly logical explanation as to why you're here, dressed like this. But we're not going to worry about explaining that to anyone. I'm fixin' ta get you out of this here mess. Trust me."

"Trust is a loaded word," I whispered back.

"Trust me," he said again, this time untucking then lifting his shirt and flashing a police badge which was hanging off his belt holster. "Here. 20 dollars," he said coolly, handing the money over to the bartender. "A bottle of mineral water, and a Coke. An ice cold Dr. Pepper." The bartender raised a brow at him and took the money. "Keep the change," Daniel added.

Clearly not amused, the bartender slammed another glass on the bar top, motioned towards me and stated, "Get this jungle bunny out of here." By this time, a few patrons had made their way to the bar, surrounding us.

"Chevy Monte Carlo '79. Black. To the left of the bar's entrance. Can't miss her. Find her, get in. Lock yourself in. Wait for me," he instructed, handing me the keys.

I took the keys, and for a moment, thought about how easy it would be to get into his car and drive without looking back.

"I'm trusting you," he said, in a deep and knowing voice, as though he'd read my thoughts. "I need you to trust me. When I say go, go."

Someone broke a bottle on the edge of the countertop. Another patron lunged for him. Daniel ducked. "Go!" he commanded.

I darted past the crowd and ran outside, my bare feet cold against the tar road. It wasn't long before I found his car. I did as he said. I got in, locked the door and waited. There was a blanket in the back seat. I wrapped it around me, comforted by that little bit of modesty. Moments later he was there, and rapped hard on the window. The fight had spread to the car park.

I unlocked the car, he quickly got in, assessed the surrounds before revving the motor, ready to go. "How's that for an exhilarating night," he joked, flashing me a dimpled smile. "Fancy meeting a beautiful lady like you in a place like this!" he exclaimed, taking off his hat and tossing it onto the back seat.

I sighed in response. "I don't feel like much like a lady at the moment," I replied.

"The situation you're in doesn't determine whether or not you're a lady. You just are," he stated as he drove swiftly away from the parking lot.

Silence ensued before he spoke again. Sensing my unease, he changed subject. "Dr. Pepper? Mineral water?" he asked, two bottles in hand. He'd managed to get our drinks in spite of the drama. I chose the mineral water.

As I sat there next to him in the car, I felt heavy inside and sad, but smiled all the same to be polite, and to avoid getting on the wrong side of this man who'd come to my aid. "Where are you taking me?" I asked as he manoeuvered the car out of the parking lot.

"The question should be, where am I *not* taking you," he replied, wincing slightly as he quickly glanced at his face in the rearview mirror. He'd copped a hit on his chin from the bar fight. He caught me staring. "Part and parcel of the

7

work I do," he explained before changing topic. "You must be cold," he assumed, turning the car heater on. "There's another blanket in the back."

His kindness, after everything I had been through was overwhelming. I couldn't hold back tears any longer.

"Hey, hey, hey. Come now. Don't cry," he pleaded. "I'm sorry for whatever's got you down. I understand you might not want to talk, and you might not want to trust me. But trust me, please make sure you do. I'm not taking you anywhere near where you've been tonight," he promised. "I'm heading South tonight. Whatever it is you're going through, I can help make it better. Lie low with me for a few days," he insisted.

I knew him but a minute, and yet I took comfort in his words. Maybe this was a prayer answered after all, a hero sent to rescue me at the most inopportune of times. Or maybe this was a further descent into darkness, a new story with an anti-hero at the helm. I shuddered at the thought, not wanting a repeat of Duayne or the situation that came with him. I prayed that where he was taking me was better than where Duayne had left me.

"I didn't catch your name," he stated.

"Temwani," I said. "Teme for short," I added.

He nodded in acknowledgement. "Pleasure to meet you Temwani," he said, not struggling with my name at all, as was the case with most people. "Did I say that right?"

"Yes, you did," I replied.

"Temwani, I'm sorry you had to hear that nonsensical talk back there at the bar. The attitude around some parts is if you don't understand it, it must be bad. Ignorance is all it is. Don't let it get to you," he suggested.

8

I nodded in reply, feeling too tired and overwhelmed to say anything. I'd heard enough racial slurs and insults to last me a lifetime. The man before me, helping me out was clearly above all that and was kind and compassionate.

"You got somewhere to be right now?" he asked.

"No... I should be at home but I won't be safe there now."

"Any friends you can call on?"

"No," I said firmly, shaking my head in response. The thought of calling Shania crossed my mind, but I didn't want to burden or worry her. I couldn't call my family, nor could I call anyone at the office. No one knew about the dynamics between Duayne and I. Besides, who knew what he'd be telling everyone right now. It would be his word against mine.

"Someone'll be missing you I'm sure," he stated, as though it were a given. "You'll be safe with me, 'til then," he promised.

I was grateful for his kindness but felt there'd be strings attached.

"I'm a former defence attorney," he suddenly announced. I immediately felt a sinking feeling in my stomach at the mention of the word *former*. Sensing my unease, he clarified, "I'm on a leave of absence, working part time as a P.I. right now."

My earlier anxiety dissipated. "Why did you show me a badge then?"

"Would you have come with me if I hadn't?" he asked.

"Probably not," I replied. "So you're not a cop?"

"I used to be, before I became a lawyer," he replied.

"Once a cop, always a cop some say."

"So they say," he said in response. "What about you. I

don't know anything about you?"

I wanted to tell him more about me, about the fact that I was a lawyer, star prosecution attorney for the Department of Justice, but I felt embarrassed about the situation I was in. He'd find out in due course, if at all. I was horrified that my position would bring the profession into disrepute. Duayne had held so many threats over my head as it was, the mere possibility of any of them coming to light would've killed my career right then and there.

"You alright?" he asked, concerned at my silence. "Don't feel pressured to tell me anything you don't want to just yet. I'm sorry I omitted to tell you the truth. It was for the greater good."

"That remains to be seen," I muttered under my breath.

"Don't be like that, beauty. I don't mean you any harm. How could anyone possibly mean you any harm?"

Beauty, he'd said. With every moment that passed, I found myself giving him a second look. His skin was smooth but slightly rugged, suggesting he spent much time outdoors. His physique strong, he was otherwise of average build. Though he wasn't the muscle Duayne was, he carried himself tall, and commanded respect in his demeanor. He'd stood up for me in that dive bar, and had gotten me out of harm's way. Despite the fact that my instinct had been off of late, I decided to trust him. It wasn't as though I had a choice anyway. I was in his car, and he was driving wherever he chose to drive, with me in it.

"You want to get out along the way, just say the word," he stated, as though he'd read my mind. "I'll take you wherever you want to go. I can turn back now if you want me to." One hand on the steering wheel as he searched for a radio station, he added, "The offer still stands for you to lie low with me for a few days. A few days to figure out what your next move will be. Wherever it is you've been, you can't go back there now. Not without reinforcements anyway."

Reinforcements, I thought to myself. *That was one way of putting it.*

"What kind of music you listen to?" he asked.

"RnB, soul, jazz, some country and rock and roll..."

"*Some* country and rock and roll?" he asked. "Should be country and rock and roll all the way, baby!"

I smiled, nearly breaking a laugh. "I listen to good music. Across all genres," I stated in finality.

He nodded in response. "Well, it's strictly country and rock and roll for me," he advised, turning the dial on the radio. "Nothing on the radio," he muttered under his breath before turning the dial and searching again. The intro to the Isley Brothers' *Take a Ride* came on and he let the dial rest on that song.

He hummed along momentarily before nudging me slightly. "Get some sleep if you can. Another hour and we'll be there."

"Okay," I said in response. Ron Isley's voice was soothing and comforting. I found myself relaxing somewhat in the presence of this man who I'd only just met. When the chorus hit, Daniel sang along. His voice was so beautiful and soulful, I couldn't help but smile.

"So, you don't listen to RnB but you listen to, and can sing along to the Isley Brothers?" I asked.

"Classic rhythm and blues slash rock. Of course I'm a fan," he confirmed, flashing me a dimpled smile, yet again.

"I love the Isley Brothers too."

11

"Guess we got something in common then," he said, allowing his eyes to briefly leave the road and sneak a quick glance at me. "Do you want me to crank up the heat a little more for you?"

"Okay," I replied, grateful for everything he was doing for me in stark contrast to everything Duayne had done to me.

"Look, I don't know who did this to you, but I can guarantee you it's only up from here on out," he said with certainty. I felt compelled to believe him, despite the cloud of doubt that had followed me around since the disaster that was my relationship with Duayne.

A few miles into the journey, Daniel stopped at the filling station for gas, some snacks and a toilet stop. For him. I needed the toilet but I didn't dare get out again in what I was wearing and not wearing.

"You sure you don't need the bathroom?" he asked again.

"I'll be alright to wait," I replied, out of the car now, stretching my feet. I didn't fancy walking into the public restroom without any shoes on – the floors would probably be drenched in urine. Plus, I needed to preserve whatever dignity I had left.

"Okay," he replied, as though he knew it would be pointless to argue otherwise. "I've just gotta make a phone call," he said. Keeping an eye on me as though I'd somehow disappear, he leant against his car and dialled a number on his mobile. Whoever he was calling this late clearly didn't mind. "Collen. I need to call in a favor," he said. After a slight pause, he stated, "Southern route, San Antonio....okay. I'll ask her." Putting the phone on mute, and turning to me, he asked,

"You okay for us to stop in on an old friend of mine? Currently on the force?"

"Do I have a choice?" I asked.

"You do... then again, not really. I'm concerned that you just gon' let this blow over. Whoever he was, he can't hurt you like this and leave you for dead."

"I hear you," I replied. "I appreciate what you're trying to do for me, but the best thing for me to do right now is to keep a low profile. I can't lay any charges on him. I still have to deal with him."

"You don't," Daniel stated. "A restraining order will help."

"It won't go far enough. I've tried it in the past. Didn't work."

"I hear you. But if he's hurt you tonight, and forced himself on you, that ain't right. At least let me introduce you to Colleen. She'll give you some options," he said. "Besides, it's on the way, we can grab a bite to eat, you can get a change of clothes..."

"Okay," I said quickly, not wanting to change my mind. I knew that rape needed to be reported. I knew that evidence had to be gathered after the fact. I knew that safety planning had to happen. I just never knew I'd need to do it for myself someday. I sighed deeply, suddenly overwhelmed.

"All good. See you soon," he spoke into the phone, before hanging up. Turning to me, he stated, "The only way is up." Observing me from a safe distance, standing next to his car in the moonlight, the reflection off the metallic black paint on his car gave his silhouette a light glow, angelic almost. "It'll get better," he promised, his words reassuring, his voice firm and kind.

I felt the tears roll down my face again, and I trembled

slightly from the cool night air. The tar road felt like ice against the soles of my feet. "A change of clothes would be nice," I managed, in between tears.

He nodded in response. Arms outstretched towards me, he offered comfort in the form of an embrace. I walked towards him and melted in his arms for a brief moment. "Better days ahead," he said firmly.

We hit the road again moments later. Turning the dial to find a suitable station, he suggested I put in a CD. "Have a look in the glove compartment," he said.

A brown leather bound Bible lay on top of a few CDs in the glove compartment. I randomly took some CDs out. Bruce Hornsby and the Range, Kiss and Queen.

"Which one – Bruce Hornsby and the Range, Kiss or Queen?" I asked.

Taking his eyes away from the road momentarily to glance at the CDs, he stated, "Your pick."

Bruce Hornsby's *Mandolin Rain* would make me cry but I put the CD on anyway. Daniel lightly squeezed my shoulder when the opening song on the album commenced. "Try to get some rest."

Taking his suggestion, I sank back into the seat and closed my eyes, wishing I could undo and wish away the things that had happened before I met Daniel, but then realizing that had things not happened the way they had, Daniel and I would probably not have met.

We got to Colleen's not long after. Colleen was tall, impressionable and beautiful. With raven hair cascading down her back, her pearl skin was striking, as were her chestnut brown eyes. In blue jeans and a flannel shirt, she was the picture-perfect country girl next door, except this girl next door had an armory full of ammunition, and served on the drug unit of the local police force. Despite it being early in the morning, she was wide awake and ready to problem solve. I instantly recognized her from a case I'd worked on, not so long ago. She recognized me too, but initially acted as though she didn't, preferring to examine the dynamics between me and Daniel before saying anything.

"I have a rape kit here, but I recommend you go to the hospital," she stated. "Help yourself to a spare set of clothes or two, some food, anything else you need. Resist the urge to shower and clean up, your body contains the evidence we need to hang this creep," she said. "Emphasis on internal evidence," she added.

Giving Daniel the once over, she asked, "You need me to come with? South Texas Medical ain't far from here."

"Should be okay," he replied, suddenly reserved.

"You're a long way from home, Counsellor," Colleen stated, turning back to me. I'd hoped that she wouldn't recognize me. No such luck.

I nodded in response, noting Daniel's puzzled look.

"Don't worry, this stays here," Colleen stated. "You might not recall but we met on the Murphy case. Diminished responsibility. You've got a knack for delivering killer closing arguments. 99.9% conviction rate," she stated. "They love you at the unit. Pity we can't send all our files your way."

"You're a prosecutor?" Daniel asked, the look on his face priceless, part awe, part shock. "I now understand your reluctance to press charges," he stated.

"Good," I replied. "I'm glad you do understand. I just want

this to be over and done with. I can't go back to mine tonight. Can't..."

"The offer still stands for you to lie low with me," Daniel reminded me. Colleen raised a brow then gave him a stern look.

"So long as you're helping, not hindering," she said. "You're welcome to stay here for a few days too," she offered, as though it were a competition.

"Thanks," I replied. "Both of you. Thanks."

"Time's getting on," Daniel said abruptly, suddenly anxious to leave. "I'll take you up to the Medical Centre now," he offered. "Coll, thanks for everything. I'll either loop back 'round and see you later, or I'll see you on my way back from South Texas, Tuesday."

"Might be earlier if an APB is put out," Colleen warned. "I don't suspect anyone will let her go missing for long."

"You won't..." Daniel started.

"I won't, someone else will," Colleen confirmed. "I can guarantee it. A good prosecutor won't go missing for long. Either way, I'll know where you'll be."

"Alright then," Daniel said, slipping his cowboy hat back on his head. "When you're ready," he said softly, turning to me. "Soon as you get what you need, we can hit the road."

Colleen led me to the bedroom to get some spare clothes. Her house was relatively bare, indicating that she spent a limited amount of time there. "You're a size 10?" she asked, giving me a once over. "How about some jeans and a blouse or t-shirt or two, for now?"

"Whatever you're willing to part with for now, would be appreciated," I told her.

"Good," she said, taking some blouses off the clothes

rack and folding them over the bed. She took out a pair of stonewashed jeans and deep blue denims from one of the drawers, along with a floral dress. "I'm not much into flowers. This'll look good on you," she said. She grabbed a small tote and put all the clothes in it.

"Thanks for everything," I said, grateful for her generosity.

"You're very welcome," she replied. "I just hope you'll be able to move on after this, make a clean break. Men like the one that did this to you ain't good for nothin'."

"Hope so too," I replied, not fully knowing what my next step would be, knowing only that I needed to get away for some time, and let things blow over.

Leaning against the bedroom wall, she advised, "About Daniel, you want him to leave you be, just be firm with him. He's got a heart of gold – loves putting himself into things, but he can get too involved if you let him," she started. "He's got a bit of a saviour complex," she clarified.

"I hear you," I replied, heeding her words. I'd sensed that already.

"He's like a brother to me. Wouldn't harm a fly. Just has a tendency to go into saviour mode and look for easy ways to solve things when there ain't no easy solution."

I nodded in response. I felt reassured by her words, but silently wondered about Daniel's firm insistence on me going to South Texas with him. I didn't allow myself to wonder for long. After everything I'd been through, I just wanted to escape, and he'd offered me that route.

"Now, for shoes...," she started, contemplating what to give me. "Love my boots, as you can tell," she stated, motioning at the collection of boots lined up against the wall of the walk-in wardrobe.

"In other words, you're not parting with them," I stated.

"You got it," she said, with a wink. "I've got a pair of ballet flats and some sandals though..."

"Either would be perfect," I replied. "I appreciate all you're doing to help. I need to use your toilet though, may I?"

"No," she said suddenly. "I mean, not until you've had a sample taken."

"Okay," I stated, not sure how much longer I could hold for – I was busting to go.

"Tell you what. I'll take a sample now, you can use the toilet, and they can take another sample at the hospital." Colleen suggested. "Ask for Doctor Edwards," she suggested. "Tell her I sent you."

"Okay," I replied.

"Let's do it now, get you out of your misery," she suggested.

The sterile white sheets, privacy curtain and white walls at the hospital did nothing to allay my anxiety at having samples taken.

Dr. Lorraine Edwards was polite but firm. I answered her questions hurriedly, not wanting to linger on any one detail. The nurse that worked with her took pictures of the bruises and contusions on my body. As a precaution, I was started on a course of post-exposure prophylaxis and antibiotics - tablets to be taken daily for 28 days, to help decrease the likelihood of acquiring a sexually transmitted infection. Questioning complete, I was free to shower and clean up in the private bathroom adjoining the examination room.

Grateful for the myriad of hot beads of water falling on my skin in the shower, I found myself overwhelmed with emotion. As I stood in the shower, I realized that apart from being in Daniel's car, it was the first time I'd been alone since Duayne had left me in the middle of nowhere. A flood of tears filled my eyes and fell, mixing with droplets of water. *I don't know how I got here.* I watched the shower floor turn red; a crimson red at first then rose, to a barely there blush.

He said he'd never hurt me, but he had. I'd prosecuted many for the crime of rape, but never did I believe it would ever happen to me. *He said no one else would ever want me, I was damaged goods.* Part of me believed him.

The nurse rapped on the bathroom door. "Everything alright in there?"

"Yes," I replied, my voice faint and hoarse from crying. I needed to get out. The hospital probably needed the bed. I needed to get away. Daniel was waiting.

He didn't touch my face. All the same, I avoided making eye contact with myself in the mirror but looked long enough to ensure my hair was not out of place. The warm droplets of water in the shower had curled my locks, which would make for easy maintenance on the road. I planned to hit the road hard. For as long as I could.

Out of the shower, I dried off and put on the deep blue denim jeans and red blouse Colleen had given to me. The nurse had left a jug of ice water on the tray beside the bed, along with an egg salad sandwich. I bit into part of the sandwich, placed it back down, then poured myself some water. I wondered after Daniel. No sooner than I had wondered, than I heard rapping at the door. "Come in," I called out.

19

Daniel stepped in. "Howdy," he said, taking his cowboy hat off his head and cradling it in his hands. "Was just about ready to call out the search party," he started, giving me a brief once over and a smile. Standing there for a moment, he held back saying something, and asked instead, "How are you feeling?" His smile vanished slightly when he noticed I'd been crying.

Outwardly I felt better, inwardly I felt worse. I struggled to find words to explain. "I feel so..."

"It wasn't your fault," he said, walking up to me, until we stood face to face. "However you feel now, it wasn't your fault," he assured me. "Just tell me what I can do to help, and I'll do it," he promised.

"I'm so tired," I told him. "I feel so tired but I'm afraid of sleeping. I feel I'll see him in my dreams, but I need to rest."

"Okay, so you stay here, overnight?" he suggested. "They can't make you leave if you're not ready to."

"I can't stay here. I can't have anyone recognize me," I said. "I need to take you up on your offer to lie low with you for a few days."

"You certain?" he asked.

"So certain," I replied.

"Be gentle with yourself," he advised. "Don't worry about judgement, worry about getting back right with you."

"Thank you," I said. "I truly thank you. You could be anywhere else, but you're here with me, thank you."

"Don't mention it," he said, offering to take my bag. "You eating the rest of that?" he asked, motioning towards the partially eaten sandwich.

"No," I said.

"You mind if I helped myself to it?" he asked, famished.

20

"Go ahead." He wolfed it down immediately. "You should probably get something more substantial to eat before we go any further," I suggested.

"Most definitely," he said, clearly still hungry. Taking a sip of water from my cup, he stated, "Okay. So, we leave now. As I mentioned before, you want me to take you back or anywhere else, you let me know."

"Agreed," I said, as though it were some sort of a pact. "I'm not going back to Austin tonight."

"Forget tonight, there's still tomorrow. I'll show you. Something beautiful this way comes," he said, boldly offering me his hand, which I took. I followed him out the door without hesitation, and without looking back. There was no going back now.

2

DOWN SOUTH

"I say we stop over in Alice for a little while, rest, then head for Edna," he suggested. "I can't keep my eyes open for much longer, I'm afraid," he said, sounding tired all of a sudden. It had been a long night. "Any objection to that?"

"No, I'm with you. When in Rome," I replied, feeling extremely exhausted myself.

We reached Alice around 3 am. Checked into the Sundowner Hotel, which was basic, sparsely decorated but clean. Daniel took the single bed closest to the door, while I took the one closest to the window.

"Try to rest," he suggested, kicking off his boots with reckless abandon and sinking into the bed for some much needed sleep.

After downing a glass of water, I slept but I tossed and turned relentlessly.

Thoughts of Duayne pervaded my mind as I slept, and I fought him off in my sleep. I cried in my sleep, only to find those same tears on my face as I woke.

When I opened my eyes, I found Daniel kneeling at the edge

of my bed. Staring into me, his ocean blue eyes were full of concern. "You slept fitfully," he noted, concerned.

Wiping the tears off my face, I told him, "I'm hoping it'll get better in time."

"It will," he said firmly, before leaning in to embrace me. "Maybe you're experiencing a few side effects of the medication you took as well?"

I nodded in response. The nausea and light headedness I was feeling definitely was.

The watch on his wrist read 5 am. We'd gotten to Alice around 3 am. Hardly any sleep had been had by either of us.

"Why don't you just get back to bed and try and get some more sleep?" I suggested. "You've done a lot for me tonight, get some sleep, don't worry about me, I'll be fine."

He sat on the bed next to me. "As much as I want to get some shut eye, I don't want to miss a moment with you. My arms are all yours if you want me to hold you," he said boldly.

I pondered for a moment at the sudden overture. Ordinarily, the last thing I would want was be to be embraced by another man. A man I hardly knew. At this time. But he was gentle and kind, and he was what I needed.

"Okay," I said, leaning into him, grateful for the comfort. He squeezed me with such fortitude I felt I would melt in his embrace.

"Take your own advice and get some sleep. It's still dark out," he said. "Sometimes it helps to try and sleep with a bit of white noise. Try and get some sleep."

I nodded in response, believing him. He switched the television on. *White noise.*

My stomach churned when I saw Duayne on the screen, giving a most sensational screen performance. "I just hope

MY DUSK, MY DAWN

we can find her in good enough time. It isn't like her to up and leave like this," he said, his emerald green eyes brimming with tears and feigned concern. "If anyone knows where she is, please get her to get in touch. I need her to come home."

"There's that APB we were tryin' to avoid," Daniel interjected. "...and I guess that's Duayne," he said. "Somehow he looks familiar to me," he thought out loud. "What does he do for a livin'?"

"He's a lawyer and an architect. Works for Saunders and Co.," I told him.

"They handle a few of the housing developments in the Austin and Dallas area," I explained.

"I see," he said. "I must've seen him around in the course of business."

I shrugged in response. He could've met Duayne in any number of ways and in any number of places. Duayne was everywhere and nowhere, as I discovered much too late.

"This is a mess, and that's putting it mildly," I announced, somewhat stating the obvious. "I can't lay charges on him now, it'll be his word against mine, no one'll believe me..."

"No," Daniel started. "You can. You've got enough evidence to do so. I believe you, others will."

I shook my head in response. I could just see it all. Me being cross-examined and Duayne's legal team crucifying me on the stand, casting doubt on my character, saying anything and everything they could to tarnish my reputation and my career. The decision to charge him would be at the expense of my career. I wasn't prepared to do that now, and risk losing everything.

"Talk to me," Daniel urged, not liking my silence.

"I can't go back right now."

24

"Okay," he acknowledged. "You don't have to. Call work, tell them you're okay."

I didn't even want to do that, but I knew I had to. Didn't want Daniel to be implicated in anything untoward.

"Jensen, isn't it? The head of the Department?" he asked.

I nodded in response.

"Okay. How about you call her, we get something to eat, and keep headin' south. My property in Edna's not too far away, we can hang there for a while. If you prefer somewhere more secluded, we can take the houseboat out to my shack on the edge of Lake Texana, after Edna."

A lot of options, too many almost, but I was grateful for all possibilities he put forward. "That all sounds good," I said.

"Alright then," he replied, suddenly abuzz with energy and optimism. He motioned towards the phone in the room. Scrolling through his mobile phone, he located the number of the State Prosecutor's office. I made my way over to the phone, flipped on the desk lamp and lifted the phone off the receiver, ready to dial. Daniel stopped me.

"Withhold Caller ID," he advised, dialing a few numbers before dialing the number he'd retrieved from his phone. "Make it quick. Don't give them enough time to trace the call," he suggested, pressing the speaker button on.

The phone rang out initially, before it rang into another line. "Jensen's office, Carla speaking."

"Carla, this is Teme." Silence greeted me on the other line. Eventually she spoke.

"Temwani? Star Prosecutor?"

"Yes..."

"Right, right! You're missing!" she exclaimed.

"Just out of town for the moment," I told her.

"Where are you, what's happened to you – your fiancé's been on the news..."

Fiancé. That we'd almost gotten engaged made me feel sick to the stomach.

"Just tell Jensen I'm fine," I told her. "I'll be in touch. Taking a leave of absence for now."

Daniel motioned for me to wrap up the conversation.

"...but the Skyler Brief, the trial starts this week..." she started.

"Thanks Carla, tell Jensen I'll be in touch. Tell everyone else I'm fine," I said, hanging up, keeping it short as Daniel had suggested.

"That was dramatic, hanging up on her. You could've ended it on a good note," Daniel stated, half laughing.

I shrugged in response. "You told me to wrap it up," I confirmed.

"Yes, but not like that," he said, laughing lightly. "Anyway..." he said, flipping the desk light off. "Fiancé?" he questioned not long after.

"Apparently. He's obviously running around town telling tales – we were not engaged to be married." I hadn't accepted his proposal, which was part of the reason why I'd ended up where I did.

"I see," Daniel said softly. After a brief pause, he stated, "Well, he's cruisin' for a bruisin' if he keeps this up. I can think of a few boys I can round up to give him a good ass whoppin', show him who's boss."

I laughed at the suggestion.

"Glad I can make you laugh," he said, in a serious tone, though he was part smiling. "But I'm being serious. He can't just go around doing what he's doing. Lawyer or otherwise."

I nodded in agreement, but somehow I knew with Duayne, things wouldn't stick. Not for long anyway. I sighed heavily at the prospect of having to deal with him at all, again. Before I could dwell on the thought, Daniel interjected, "Look, I'm really sorry you have to go through this. I don't mean no disrespect, but I don't believe this all happened for nothing," he said. "This isn't how your story ends. You'll see. I'm here with you now. You're safe with me."

I fell into his arms again and slept deeply this time, to the sound of his heart beating in his chest. His words echoed in my mind. *This isn't how your story ends.* With him holding me, it felt as though my story was just beginning.

Half an hour out from Alice, we stopped at a diner along the way, and had pancakes for breakfast. While I was hungry, my stomach didn't feel settled enough to eat much. I ate enough to allow me to take another dose of the PEP medication and antibiotics without feeling too sick.

Daniel on the other hand ate heartily, pouring an almost too generous amount of syrup onto the stacked pancakes on his plate. I smiled, thinking about how food would be one way to this man's heart. *One taste of my cooking and he'd be sprung,* I thought, but my own thoughts caught up to me. *Don't get ahead of yourself. You've just gotten away from Duayne. You hardly know Daniel. That may be true,* I thought to myself, *but you know how he makes you feel, and that's real.*

"A penny for your thoughts?" he asked after a long silence between us while we ate.

"I'm just thinking about everything there is to think about right now. Thinking about how lucky I was that you found

27

me when you did."

He dabbed his mouth lightly with a napkin before he said, "Luck's got something to do with it, but not everything to do with it."

"Meaning?" I asked.

"I'll tell you in the car," he said, raising his hand to get the attention of the waitress, so he could settle the bill. She turned slightly and smiled. He'd gotten her attention, though she was busy tending to another patron. He wrote on the back of the bill: *Thanks for the breakfast, keep the change.*

Slipping a fifty dollar bill into the bill holder before closing it, he got up, offered his hand to me which I graciously took. *This is becoming somewhat of a habit*, I thought. As we walked out, he caught the eye of the waitress, tipped his hat at her, and mouthed, "Thank you." I knew not long after, in his absence, she'd be thanking him for the generous forty dollar tip he'd left after a ten dollar breakfast.

Heart in my throat, once we were in the car I asked again, "What did you mean?"

"Before I tell you, know that I'm here with you because I want to be here with you. Know that the obligation side of things ended the moment I had you in my car," he started.

"Daniel, just say what you have to say," I insisted, suddenly on edge.

"I got a message the night I met you. The message was to rescue a young lady of your description and to get her to safety. The instructions were vague yet precise enough for me to recognize you when I saw you."

I tried to hide my surprise but I couldn't. "And?"

"As I said, the obligation and the job ended for me when I got you in my car."

"Who ordered the job?" I asked.

"Beats me. All I know is they gave me an advance for the job, and left no name or number to return the call on."

"Pretty mysterious if you ask me," I said.

"Someone's looking out for you," he stated.

"Why you?" I questioned. "Whoever it was, why did they choose you?" I asked.

"Lady, your guess is as good as mine," he said, "...though I've done some retrieval work in the past, so that could be something to do with it."

"Oh," I said flatly, feeling slightly discouraged. "I guess this is where we part ways then? Job's over, I can get back to whatever's waiting for me back in Austin, while you can go back to whatever it was you were doing before you felt obligated to help me and got roped into saving me?"

"No," he said firmly. "As I said, the obligation part of things ended the moment I took one look at you and realized that I wanted to be a part of your story. So even before I got you in my car, I ... well, I couldn't help but fall for you. So, please. Lie low with me until this tempest in your life blows over. Let me weather this storm with you."

I felt passion rise within me, and in his eyes I saw hope, compassion and to my surprise, love.

"So what d'you say?" he asked.

"You're such a believer," I stated. "Yes, I will lie low with you until this all blows over."

"Good," he said, starting the ignition. "Thank you for putting your trust in me. You won't regret it."

We hit Edna a few hours later. Daniel parked his car under

the house by the lake shore, and we decided to stay there for a few hours before heading out onto the water.

His house was sparsely decorated but felt homely. Pictures of boats, rivers and mountains peppered the walls, and a sole picture of a middle aged, beautiful blonde haired woman rested on the mantel. Before I could ask, he answered. "Jolène," he stated. "My mom."

"She's beautiful."

"Yeah, well, don't tell her that when you meet her, it'll go right to her head," he said jokingly.

"She lives here in Edna?"

"No," he replied. "She lives in Austin."

He didn't mention anything about a father or siblings so I didn't ask. I figured there'd be plenty of time to find out.

On the living room wall, a Swiss wall mantle clock caught my eye.

"Switzerland?" I asked.

"Yes. I partly grew up there."

"Français où Allemande? French or German?" I asked, excited at the prospect of a Swiss connection. Though it had been many years since I'd been back, Switzerland held a special place in my heart.

"Français," he replied. "I see we've got something else in common now."

I smiled in response but not for long. Suddenly, the house phone rang, startling us both. "Strange," he said, letting it ring out. "Unless someone's seen us drive out here, no one knows I'm here."

His mobile rang not long after. We stared at the screen together. Private number. He picked up, only to be met with a dead line.

"Strange," I said this time.

A text message came through moments later. *Job done? Have you seen the news? Is she safe?*

Daniel gave me a knowing look and we spoke without saying words. He dialed the number, only to be met with a service unavailable message, in German. "I'll text back," he said aloud. *Job's done, she's safe,* he texted.

A few seconds later, a reply came through. *Thank you.*

Heart in my throat, I searched for an explanation and perhaps a clue.

"This is coming from Germany," Daniel said. I nodded in agreement, recalling the out of service message in German, and the number the text came from. "Job's done. Let's hope this is it," he said in conclusion, not wanting to hear from whoever it was, again.

I silently echoed the sentiment, though I longed to know who cared enough to have hired him to ensure my safety.

Slightly spooked from the odd interaction with someone neither of us had met before, presumably, that was, we decided to head out onto his house boat and onwards to his cabin on the lake. Sleep would come later, and in safety. At least this was what we hoped.

The river lapped at the base of his shanty style house boat, as it coasted steadily in the dark, deep waters of Lake Texana.

"So, you've lived in Texas most of your life, apart from your time in Switzerland?" I asked.

"Yep. Born and bred in Texas," he replied. "I would've thought my southern drawl would have given it away?"

I shrugged in response.

"I guess I'm the last to learn that you're quite popular in

Austin. Lead Prosecutor?"

"Yep," I replied. *Not for much longer*, I thought. Not unless I managed to keep what happened between Duayne and I, a secret.

"How long you been in Texas for?" he asked.

"Two years now."

"And where were you before then?"

"Georgia."

"And before that?" he asked.

"The UK," I replied.

"And before that?" he asked again.

"Switzerland. La Suisse."

"Where? Où exactement?," he asked.

"Commugny, Canton de Vaud," I replied. "Daniel, why don't you just ask me where I'm from?" I suggested.

He smiled in response. "Would you prefer another line of questioning, Counsellor?"

I smiled back. "Perhaps."

"How are you feeling?" he asked.

"Okay," I replied. "You know, you don't have to ask me how I am every minute. I'll be fine."

"I'm just concerned, is all," he said. "You're barely eating, you've avoided talking about what happened last night, and I feel somewhat responsible for getting you happy again."

"I didn't ask you to take responsibility for my happiness," I replied, curtly.

"Sorry, that came out wrong," he said. "I meant to say, I wanna be the one who makes you happy."

"I'm damaged goods," I told him, regretting the words as soon as they left my mouth. I'd said those words in my mind many times over since Duayne had left me in that carpark.

"I can fix you," he said, leaving the helm of the boat to join me on the boat's shoulder. "I can't take away what happened to you, but I can make your life from here on out, better. I can at least try to," he said. "I can help put the pieces of your life back together again."

"How do you propose to do that, Counsellor?"

"Let me love you," he beckoned. "Let me show you what love can be."

I sighed in response. *Words, and promises.* I'd had enough of those to last a lifetime.

"You're not feeling me," he concluded. "Am I not your type?"

Slightly taken aback, I stated, "I didn't say that."

"What are you saying, then?" he asked, reaching over to take my hand. I let him. The weight of my hands in his felt comforting and reassuring.

"I'm just not too hot on words and promises at the moment."

"Right," he said in response. "That's understandable, given what you've just been through. How about I show you?" he asked. "Just agree to be with me on a trial basis, and if you don't like what you see, we can part ways."

I mused at the thought of such an offer, one which had never been made to me before, by anyone. *Boy was he bold*, I thought to myself.

"Care to share?" he asked. "A penny for your thoughts?"

"You're bold."

"As bold as love," he replied, reminiscent of a Jimmy Hendrix song.

"I've never been propositioned to this way."

"This isn't a proposition. It's a proposal," he said. Holding my hands in his, he stated, "Last night, I held your hand but for a moment. I'm asking you to let me hold your hand for more than just a moment in time. I want to be here for you, carry you through whatever you're going through. I have the feeling you were meant to be in my life for more than just a moment," he said, raising one of my hands to his lips, for a kiss. "No pressure," he added.

His argument was very persuasive, but I decided to remain on guard. I hardly knew him, he hardly knew me.

"I don't expect you to tell me how you feel right now. Matter of fact, I don't expect anything from you except for you to tell me what you need. And I can work at getting you what you need. I can..."

I leaned forward and gave him a full kiss on the lips, in a move that somewhat stunned him and me equally. "I'm saying yes to your proposal," I said, certain the kiss was more than he wanted and expected, but less than he desired and needed.

"That was...unexpected," he said, clearly chuffed that it had happened. "So, the possibility of us being an item – we give it a shot?" he asked, gently tracing the outline of my lips with his index finger.

"Yes," I agreed, my head reeling slightly from the kiss. I'd kissed him, and he'd taken me in whole and fully, as though he never wanted it to end. I had to reel things in before they went too far.

"Talk to me," he said, sensing I had something else to say.

"I just have a few ground rules I'd like to lay down, before we go any further." I started.

"I'm all ears," he replied, listening intently.

"Sex. I lost my virginity by force, but I still don't believe in sex before marriage," I told him. "So, no sex."

"I can deal with that," he said quickly, surprising me. "Anything else?"

"Honesty. Please be honest with me. Please tell me exactly how you feel, when you feel it.

"I can dig that," he replied. "Anything else?"

"Just one more. Respect. I need you to respect my choices, respect my wishes, respect me."

"Got it," he said. "Now, I've got some ground rules of my own," he started.

"Okay, I'm listening," I replied, noting how his eyes had suddenly lit up.

"Acceptance," he stated. "I'm not the easiest person to get along with, but I try. I just ask that you accept me in all that I am and for all that I am."

That sounded simple enough. "I can handle that," I told him.

"Exclusivity," he mentioned. "I'm not a fan of multiplicity. I want you and you only, and expect you to want the same," he said firmly.

"I hear you. I can give you exclusivity. Anything else?" I asked.

"I'm a man of faith, so I've got certain expectations tying into what I believe in," he said.

"Care to elaborate?" I asked, intrigued.

"I believe in church on Sunday, praying together, modesty, convention. I'm not perfect, but I try. I need you to under-stand that everything I do is dictated largely by what I believe in. If I don't believe in it, I won't do it, and I won't allow it. Not for me and not for you."

"Fair enough," I responded, intrigued by his openness.

"Though, being so strict about everything doesn't allow much room for flexibility, now does it?"

Caught off guard, he paused for a moment. "Within reason. Flexibility within reason."

"I hear you," I replied.

"I think we'll do alright then," he predicted, kissing my hand again. Getting up suddenly, he asked, "You finally ready to eat, Counsellor?"

"If it'll please you, Detective," I joked.

He raised a brow in response. "I'm off duty until further notice."

"Good. And yes," I replied. "I'm famished."

"Awesome," he replied, hurriedly throwing the white bass he'd caught earlier onto the barbeque plate, along with the vegetables I'd cut.

I watched him from a distance, considering his knack with all things to do with the outdoors. He turned sharply to meet my gaze. "You were saying?" he asked.

"I wasn't saying," I replied, laughing lightly. "You're too perceptive."

"You're too gorgeous," he replied.

Such a charmer, I thought, forgetting my earlier anguish and sadness. I could learn to forget and move on with him. At least this was what I hoped.

We cruised along the lake for a while longer after dinner.

Stepping away from the steering wheel he motioned for me to join him on the corner settee. I did. The water was clear and tranquil. A few mosquitos were abuzz. "Should probably head inside soon," he suggested. "There're enough mosquitos out here to swarm us out."

I smiled at the exaggeration and nodded in response. Despite how beautiful it was out on the water, the thought of being swarmed by mosquitos held no appeal.

"We're also gonna be out of range soon," he mentioned. "Did you want to call anyone before we head out?"

"My sister Kyela. She's in France at the moment. I'll send a quick text to her, and she'll let everyone else know I'm fine. Other than that, I don't have anyone else to call." I didn't want to risk dealing with Duayne again, and I needed time to consider my next move.

"Hey," Daniel said, getting me out of my thoughts and back to him. "You're not doing this alone. I'm here with you."

I half smiled in response. "There's still Duayne I need to contend with when I get back."

"Easy. Police escort to your property. Change the locks, install security cameras, get a restraining order out on him," he suggested. "Consider charging him with rape."

"I'm not sure I can do any of that," I told him. "He'll deny the charges, say it was consensual, draw it out, and try to destroy me in the process. He'll..."

"Hey. He can't hurt you any longer. He can try, but he won't succeed." Slapping a mosquito off his arm, he motioned for us to go inside.

Inside, I avoided the topic of Duayne, opting to shift the focus on my developing romance with Daniel instead. "Tell me more about you, tell me about your boat and why you love being on the water so much," I said.

"I had the external custom built, did the interior myself. Boating's a passion of mine, nothin' says freedom like getting out on the open water. I find it very liberating getting away from it all...," he replied.

"When do you find the time to do all you do? Your work in law, investigations and all?"

"Always plenty of time for work," he said, tight lipped about his line of work. "I've been single for a while too. That in itself gives me a lot of time to do whatever I please."

"Why did you quit law?" I asked.

"I didn't exactly quit. I'd like to say I walked away from it, but truth is I found myself in contempt of court over a contentious issue in a case. State Board recommended I take a leave of absence. Had to eat, and the Force and private parties were looking for an investigator at the time, so I made the leap."

"Sounds like you didn't have a choice but to. Sorry to hear that you had to walk away from practicing law," I said.

"Don't be. If I wasn't doing what I'm doing now, we might never have met," he reasoned.

"True," I said in response.

"Plus I enjoy being an enforcer of the law so to speak. Having a background in law gives me the edge in gathering evidence. I can visualize how it will all play out in court, and to a large extent, this helps determine the outcome."

I nodded my head in agreement. "Did you work solo or with a partner?"

"I worked with a partner. MacCauley and Brennan's the name," he announced.

"So, your partner, MacCauley, he or she still running the firm?"

"Yep. He – Craig still runs the firm," he said. It seemed I had touched a sore spot. "Still trading as MacCauley and Brennan."

"Oh okay," I said, putting the topic to rest. "So, you've been single for a while now?" I asked instead.

"Yes, though not anymore I'm not," he corrected.

"Right. Okay. Before you were with me, you were single. No girlfriend, no long term relationship?"

"My life was too full with work to make room for that," he said abruptly, contradicting himself. He obviously had time for me now.

"But you're here with me?"

"What we have here is different. I've been waiting for the right person to come along. You've only just come along," he explained. "Plus I wasn't the most sought after bachelor back in college. I kept to myself mostly, except when I needed to compare notes or do group assignments, and boy did I hate those," he recalled.

"You and me both," I laughed, the memory all too clear.

He took a swig of his Dr. Pepper then leaned forward as though he were letting me in on a secret. "So, in college you've got your jocks, your beauties, your geniuses, your nerds and your weirdos. I was one of the weirdos," he said plainly. "Now I'm a qualified lawyer, women want to be with me. For all the wrong reasons."

"I'm not sure I buy that," I told him. "I'm sure you've made many a woman swoon and I'm sure there's no shortage of women trying to be with you for all the right reasons," I stated, remembering the looks he would get when we were out. Looks he was seemingly unaware of.

"Money talks...," he replied.

"True," I said. "So how do you know that *I'm* not into you for all the wrong reasons?" I asked.

"Lady, I have the uncanny ability to know what someone

is about when I first meet them, and I know your intentions are good. Real good," he stated with conviction.

"Well, then. We're both off to a good start."

"You bet," he said, planting a passionate kiss on my lips.

Living in t-shirts, jeans and summer dresses was a welcome change from the usual suit and formal wear I wore daily when at work. Being outdoors was a welcome change from being in and out of court, to and from the office.

When we ran out of supplies we headed back into town, mostly under the cover of night. One of the local shop owners who was already familiar with Daniel took to packing us up a bag of the things we usually bought, with a few extras. Blue Bell Ice Cream, Best Maid Pickles, and extra bottles of Dr. Pepper.

Daniel and I got along like a charm, which shouldn't have come as a surprise. We were born under the same star, with our birthdays being only days apart. At times, he seemed to know me better than I knew myself. At times, I knew him better than he knew himself.

The five year age difference was but a number. His maturity infused me with a sense of responsibility and a sense of longing for permanence and a sense of belonging. To him. In our time together, I encouraged him to dream, encouraged him to surrender while throwing caution to the wind, and I encouraged him to love. We had found each other at a pivotal moment in time, and there was no going back to what either of us had known.

In the time away, I opened a new bank account, transferring funds out of my old one, which I suspected Duayne had access to, though it was not a joint account. When an address was needed, I used Daniel's address. I also worked out a safety plan for my return. The plan involved cutting Duayne out of my life completely. A clean break. In the two weeks we spent at the lake house in Southern Texas, I maintained very little contact with the office. The third week we were away, I was offered a brief relating to the possible disbarring of a lawyer who'd allegedly misappropriated client funds and had missed crucial deadlines. Trial was not to commence for another four weeks, so I planned to hold off on concentrated work on the brief, at least for a few days. The appointed lead prosecutor on the case was Ernesto del Vasta, a sharp, unapologetically rigorous lawyer with a track record of securing convictions each and every time. Without fail, he managed to ensure that maximum penalties were imposed regardless of the defendant's circumstances.

It was towards the end of that third week, one late afternoon on the drive back to the lake house, that Daniel suggested we head back. "I really enjoyed the time we shared, but we should be getting back. We can always do this again sometime?"

"In a heartbeat," I told him.

"So, how do we do this?" he asked. "Go back to yours?"

"No," I answered quickly. I was reluctant to go back to mine, under police guard or otherwise, fearing I would run into Duayne. I just wasn't ready yet.

"We could change the locks?" he suggested.

"No. I'll see if I can stay with Shania for the time being, then I'll find myself someplace else to live."

"Where does Shania stay?" he asked.

"Round Rock," I told him.

"I see." After a pause, he boldly suggested, "You can always stay with me. My place in Cedar Park has room enough for the both of us."

"Sweet of you to offer, but no, you've done a lot already," I told him.

"If not my place, *we* can go back to yours. Change the locks, set up a security system..."

"No," I told him. "I'm not living there any longer. I'm not sure I can get over the fact that it was where things went down."

"I see," he replied softly. Reaching out for my hand, he stated, "So, there's only one option now. You come stay with me."

"Two other options actually," I argued. "Staying at Shania's or getting another place. Getting another place is probably the way to go," I told him.

"Look, I know you want your independence and all, but with getting another place, you'll probably be at my place most of the time or I'll be at yours most of the time, so why don't you just come and live with me?" he proposed.

I smiled in response. "That's very presumptuous of you, Mr. Brennan."

"What, the prediction that you'll be at my place all the time?" he asked, grinning widely.

"Yes, that and then some."

"Well, it isn't a presumption if it's true now, is it?" he questioned.

"I guess not," I replied, a little excited at the prospect of me spending more time with him.

"Plus, you're not getting rid of me that easily."

"Who said anything about getting rid of you?" I asked.

"Anything's possible, what with you being mysterious and

all," he joked.

I smiled, feeling so deeply in love with this man, but not wanting to let on how much. *A little mystery wouldn't hurt the relationship*, I told myself.

3

THE RETURN

Daniel drove me in to work on Monday morning. "Call me when you're done," he insisted. "Try not to miss me too much."

"Daniel. My world doesn't revolve around you."

"It should," he joked.

"Yeah, yeah," I replied, planting a full kiss on his lips. "Keep yourself out of trouble."

"Trouble's my middle name," he announced.

"Oh is it now? I thought your middle name was Josiah."

After a pause where he presumably reflected on my statement, he stated, "You killed it."

I threw my head back in laughter. "Sorry Daniel, you know I love you," I said, words escaping my lips long before I intended them to.

"Do you now?" he asked. "Guess what. I love you more," he declared.

Love. My heart fluttered at the thought. This man, this life, this love. A far cry from where I'd been before, where I had to beg for the affection of a man who never intended to give me more than crumbs of loving.

"Okay, better get in there quick before you give them something else to talk about," he advised. "I miss you already," he said, squeezing my hand as I stepped out of the car.

"I'll be back in your arms before you know it," I promised, blowing him a kiss before turning and heading into the office building I'd last seen weeks ago.

Pete, the security guard at the front desk greeted me as he usually did, as though I had not been away. His brown hair was slicked back as it usually was, his uniform crisply ironed. Time had stood still for me, yet things here had gone on without me.

I didn't have my swipe card on me. It was with all the other belongings I had at my place.

"I haven't got my card," I advised.

"Rules is rules," he stated. "But I'll let you in this time, like every other time, which is like never. You always have your card with you. I'll let you in today. Just because." He smiled broadly, a twinkle in his chestnut brown eyes as though I'd made his day just by talking to him.

"Thanks Pete," I said.

"Good to see you're alright," he said as a side note. "Just have to clear security here and I'll let you through," he promised.

"Thanks Pete. Appreciate your concern," I replied as I put my belongings on the security scanner's conveyor belt.

My bag went through fine, but Rochelle, the guard on the other end asked if she could search it.

"You've got a bottle of some sort in there?" she asked.

I'd forgotten the glass bottle of sparkling water in my bag. "Oops, sorry, I forgot I had it."

"Don't worry about it," she said. "It'll be here waiting for you on your way out."

Pete scanned open the glass doors and I thanked him. I made a mental note to myself to get another security pass made up for me before the end of the day.

"See you next time," he stated. I gave him a quick wave in response.

As I walked down the corridor I heard brusque footsteps behind me before I felt a firm hand on my shoulder. *Jude.*

"Temwani. Nice of you to join us today. Where've you been?" he asked, his cockney English accent sharp and direct. His dark brown hair slightly tousled, the grey suit he wore brought out the same color in his eyes.

"Indisposed," I replied.

"Care to share?" he asked.

"No," I said firmly.

"Alright then," he replied. "You either tell me now, or I find out for myself soon enough."

"Leave well enough alone, it's none of your business Jude," I reasoned. The last thing I wanted to do was to talk to him about what had happened that night with Duayne. Jude was a born prosecutor. He wouldn't let it go, even if any action pursued was for my benefit but at my expense.

"You know Duayne came 'round here, looking for you," he claimed, leaning against the wall a little too casually.

My throat felt tight at the mention of Duayne's name. "Really?"

"No, not really," he said. "But now I know your disappearing act had something to do with him."

I kissed my teeth in response. "Jude, I wish you'd quit getting into my business. This hasn't got anything to do with the job I have to do and my performance in this job."

He took his prescription glasses off, his stone grey eyes serious and concerned all at the same time. "Teme. I've known you all of 5 years, I've mentored you, I consider you to be a close friend of mine, and this is the best you're gonna give me?"

"Jude, it's complicated. The less I tell you the better off I'll be, and the better off you'll be."

"How'd you figure that? How about you let me reach that determination on my own?" he suggested.

"No. The less I say the better," I resolved.

"Okay. Guess I'm going to have to find out what happened on my own." Annoyed and suddenly restless, he added, "Jensen wants to see you. Sooner rather than later," he warned. "I'll catch you later," he said as we parted ways by the lift. He took a left turn, heading towards the client conference room, while I headed right.

I decided to stop by my office before I went up to see Jensen. The mountain of files that greeted me on my desk was a welcome distraction. I looked forward to being busy, and in my busyness I hoped I'd forget Duayne and all that he'd done.

My office was the same as when I'd left it last, save for the new files that had been left there, likely by Ernesto or Jude. I flung my jacket over the chair and immediately started perusing the file on the top. A dangerous driving under the influence charge resulting in manslaughter. The defendant was a 17 year old girl. Trial in eight weeks. I'd barely sat down at my desk when I heard a knock on my door.

"Come in," I said.

Ernesto. He walked into the room with his trademark swagger and legendary presence that some would say could move mountains and cause oceans to swell. As senior prosecutor for the Jamieson County District Attorney's office, Ernesto was a force to be reckoned with.

"You're back. Where have you been Cariño!" he asked, approaching me and giving me a hug and a kiss on either cheek. "I told you a long time ago the man was bad news," he added, not giving me a chance to reply on where I'd been. "How are you."

"I'm fine Ernesto."

He shook his head in response, his perfectly coiffed black curls shaking along. "I can tell when you're lying. Don't lie to me. Nunca me mientas. *Never* lie to me."

"I can't talk about this Ernesto. Not with you. Not now." If he found out what Duayne had done, he'd be out for blood. After all, he'd made a career out of prosecuting the worst of the worst, and doing so successfully. Duayne was one of the worst.

"Okay," he said, sharply turning from me and pacing the room as he did when he was preparing pleadings in a case. "So, if you *won't* talk, shall we get the police to bring him in so he *must* talk?"

"No," I replied, almost breaking down in tears. "No más Ernesto. Let it rest. I can't do this right now."

"Okay," he replied, clearly disappointed at my decision to not lay charges on Duayne at this time.

"At least you're safe," he stated, the pacing coming to an abrupt halt.

I nodded in response.

"You been back to your place?" he asked sharply.

"No. I don't plan to go there for a while. Not for now anyway."

"How did you get here?"

"Daniel..."

He looked at me with a trace of disbelief. "Perhaps I should screen this man before you go any further?"

You're too much, Ernesto. "No. That won't be necessary. Daniel's alright."

"Daniel Brennan?" he asked.

"Yes. You know him?" I asked, surprised.

"Yes. Do you remember that case I had where the two sisters were accused of murder and the defense attorney was successfully able to argue diminished responsibility?"

"Yes." I vaguely recalled it.

"Daniel was the defense attorney," Ernesto stated. "Brilliant wordsmith. One of the finest legal minds. Then he got suspended."

My stomach did an unexpected cartwheel at the mention of Daniel's suspension. While I'd never seen Daniel in action as an attorney, I suspected his arguments would be on point. That coupled with his charm and way for words, I could only imagine how persuasive he could be. Ernesto never lost a case. Daniel must've been good.

"Be careful," he warned.

I hated Ernesto's warnings. He happened to be right most, if not all of the time.

"Okay. Next time you're in a bind, go to a bar. Any bar in the State of Texas, Louisiana or Georgia. Ask for a friend of the Brotherhood."

"The what?"

"The Brotherhood. The Brotherhood of El."

What?

"Whatever situation you're in, ask for the Brotherhood of El. They'll know what to do. They'll fix whatever situation you are in," he promised. "Just don't say you heard that from me."

I didn't know whether to thank him or harp on him for presuming I'd be in a bind again, but I thanked him in the end. The thought of a group out there to help had me hopeful but a little scared. Who were they and why did they do what they did? What exactly did they do to fix things? Why was Ernesto insisting on secrecy? I wondered. Apart from Daniel, could I have been helped that night? *No. You didn't even know they existed.*

"No need to thank me now. Thank me when that ex of yours is behind bars where he belongs," Ernesto said, his deep tenor voice as unforgiving as the look in his eyes. "He didn't deserve you," he added. "Jensen needs to see you by the way," he reminded me. "Don't delay."

"I'll see her as soon as we're done."

"Great," Ernesto said, absently examining some of the files in the pile on my desk. "I'll be in my office if you need me. I won't be needing you this afternoon, so you can take the afternoon off if you wish," he advised.

"I'll be fine to make it through the day," I responded. "No te preocupes Ernesto, I'm fine."

"You say you're fine, but I feel you're not fine," he stated. "Come back when your soul's ready," he said, in such a way that my heart fluttered. He genuinely cared about what happened to me. "Anything you need, I'll sign off on it," he offered. "Jensen does not conduct my matters, I do. If Jensen has an issue with you, call me." Placing the last file he perused down, he squeezed me lightly on the shoulder then left my office.

I went through a few more files for an hour or so, then made the move to go and see Jensen, the District Attorney. By the time I got up to see her, she was ropeable. The expression on her face told me from the outset that our conversation was not going to be pleasant.

I somehow knew what she was going to say before she said it. Heart in my throat, I held back tears and listened to her scathing remarks on process and reputation.

"Your story was blown out all over the media. Your personal life should be just that. Personal. I don't give a rat's tail about who, what, when or why, I just care that you come in here, perform, and do your job. You have just one job, and generating unwanted media attention isn't a part of that job. I hope I've made myself clear," she fumed.

"Yes, you have," I replied.

"I don't want a repeat of this," she stated. "Next time..."

"There won't be a next time," I quickly interjected.

"Good," she stated. Looking me up and down, she added, "You look well."

Don't pretend you care, I thought. "Thank you. Was there anything else?" I asked, eager to get away.

"No."

"Alright then. I'm onto that brief Ernesto has carriage of. I won't disappoint you. I'm sorry for any inconvenience caused to your office."

"Good," she replied flatly. "I'm glad we have an under-standing."

Turning to go, I couldn't wait to leave her presence. I

walked away, softly closing the door behind me. As I stood there in the hallway, I wanted to retreat and be alone and cry, but I couldn't. The mountain of files on my desk would see to it that I didn't, and for that, I was grateful.

The lift couldn't come fast enough as someone approached to queue up with me.

"Temwani! Long time!" I turned to see Malik, a prosecutor I'd worked with closely in my junior years. I'd come to regard him as a big brother. He was originally from Sudan, and stood a neat 6 feet 10 inches. His warm brown eyes reminded me he was someone I could confide in.

"How are you?" he asked, genuinely concerned, in stark contrast to Jensen's attitude.

"I'm doing okay," I lied, trying desperately to hold back tears.

"No phone call, no nothing...," he noted. "You know, you could've called to let me know how you were. I could have smoothed things over with Jensen for you."

"I hear you, but I just didn't want to burden anyone with the weight of my problems."

"And I hear you," he replied. "You wouldn't have heard any complaining from me, but I guess you didn't know that."

I sighed and shrugged in response.

"Do you want to talk about what happened?" he asked, his deep brown eyes imploring me to say more.

"No," I quickly responded.

"Okay," he said, stepping back as the lift had finally arrived. "After you," he offered as the doors opened.

Jude was in that lift. *Not again - twice in one day.*

"Temwani," he stated, "I've got a bone to pick with you."

"It can wait," I told him. I'd heard from Toni that he'd been saddled with a lot of my files in my absence. He wouldn't have been happy. Then again, he might have been. He loved sinking his teeth into interesting files.

"Okay," he said begrudgingly. I knew I would have to make time to see him specifically. I just couldn't do it today.

"Welcome back," he stated, giving a quick wave without turning as he exited the lift and walked on, presumably to Jensen's office.

"I told you Duayne was no good," Malik said as the lift closed.

"Tell me about it. Seems I was the last one to know," I said regretfully.

I was relieved to be back in my office again. It would soon be time for lunch, but I planned to barricade myself in and get through as many files as I could before calling it quits for the day. As I sat down at my desk, the fragrance of fresh flowers caught my attention first, before my eyes focused on the bouquet of white peonies and beautiful cornflowers in a square vase which rested on my table. My heart swelled. *Daniel.* I opened the greeting card and read the note:

Keep your head up,
D. xxx.

I immediately picked up the phone to call Daniel. He picked up on the first ring.

"Baby, thank you for the flowers," I started.

"What flowers?" he asked.

"Oh, so it wasn't you that sent me the flowers I have sitting on my desk?"

Silence met me on the other end of the line. "Babe, I do have flowers waiting for you here at home, but I haven't sent you any flowers at work."

"Oh, okay," I said, somewhat disappointed. "I just assumed it was you who sent me these... the card was signed off with the initial D."

"Duayne?" he asked.

My heart sunk. "No. I doubt it. Duayne never bought me flowers. Plus the message said, "*Keep your head up.*" Doesn't sound like anything Duayne would say."

"Well, I'd like to take credit for having sent you those flowers, but I can't. When I do sign off with my initials only, I use D.J., J being the first initial of my middle name."

"Hm. I thought your middle name started with T?" I asked. "As in?"

"Trouble. I thought you said Trouble was your middle name?"

Silence ensued then, "Oh, you killed it, babe," he said, laughing gregariously as he recalled the conversation we'd had earlier.

"Got you." I chuckled at the mere fact that I'd made him laugh so hard. "How's your day been so far?" I asked.

"Good, nothing to report. Yours?"

"I don't know where to begin," I told him.

"Sounds like you've had a tough one. How about I take you out for lunch?" he proposed. "Or perhaps I could pick you up earlier than planned?"

"You read my mind," I replied. "I'll work through lunch, and we can have an early dinner."

"Sounds awesome," he stated.

We said our goodbyes then I hung up the phone. He would

be picking me up in a few hours. I swiveled in my chair and gazed at the beautiful floral arrangement. If it wasn't Daniel who'd sent them to me, and it wasn't Duayne, who had taken the time out to send them to me?

After such a taxing day, it felt wonderful to come home and melt in the embrace of a man who loved me so much. Who wanted me so much. Who seemed to stand to bear the weight of the world on his shoulders. It felt as though we were fated, he and I.

"I've got just the perfect thing for you," he announced. "Take a seat," he commanded, motioning towards the arm-chair. "Put your feet up," he ordered, kneeling and slipping my feet over onto the foot stool. "I'll be back in a moment," he promised, walking away with a spring in his step.

I sat back and felt my body mold into the chair. I didn't realise how exhausted I was until then. I closed my eyes for a brief moment. In the distance I heard the shaking of ice and drink in a handheld mixer. He was doing up a cocktail.

Trying not to drift into sleep, I sat up and reflected on the day. As much as I hated interacting with Jensen of late, I enjoyed work as a lawyer. I enjoyed being a lawyer and mingling with other lawyers, I enjoyed being a part of the administration of justice. For a moment, I felt a pang of sadness when I wondered how Daniel felt, having had to give up the practice of law momentarily following the suspension of his license.

He returned with two Mojitos which he placed on the side table to the right of me. In an abrupt move, he straddled the footstool, swept my feet up into his lap and offered me a foot rub. Conveniently, a small towel and some lotion lay on the floor, in a wicker basket next to him. Everything had been prearranged. He whisked up the bottle of lotion and quickly poured a generous amount onto his hands and my feet.

I initially resisted, but he insisted. "Tell me about your day," he implored, smoothing the lotion into my skin and rubbing it in, in a circular motion. His hands were strong and firm, making the touch that more heavenly.

I filled him in on Jensen's tirade, to which he replied, "Pay her no mind. She's probably acting the way she is as she might think you're gunning for her job."

"Right."

"I'm being serious," he replied. "You've got enough experience behind you, and your success rate speaks volumes. Also, oftentimes when you're down, there's always someone there trying to keep you down. She's starting to sound like that someone."

"True," I agreed. He knew what he was doing with the foot rub.

"How does this feel?" he asked, tenderly rolling my foot from left to right and right to left, before kneading the palm of my foot.

"Amazing." I was going to have to get him to stop eventually, as amazing threatened to turn to sensual. "How was *your* day?" I asked.

"Nothing to write home about," he replied. "I did make some headway on a tough case I've been working on though. Not to give too much away, but I've found a link to Australia. It seems the perpetrator in question's been flying under the radar for a while now. Managing to evade the authorities."

"What kind of matter is this?" I asked, curious.

"I'd rather not discuss it with you," he said, tight-lipped.

"Not right now anyway."

"I see," I replied, enjoying the massage too much to care about what he did and did not share with me.

"I'll tell you more in due course," he promised. "There is something I do want to discuss with you though," he said. "Mom's wanting to meet you asap."

He caught me by surprise. "Oh? Why all of a sudden?"

"You ask too many questions for your own good, Counsellor," he stated. "Point is, *I* want you to meet my mom," he said, smiling gingerly.

Next level stuff, I thought to myself, not sure whether I was ready to get any more serious than we already had, just yet. Still, he hadn't given me any reason to be apprehensive.

"So, what d'ya say, we go see her over the weekend? She's only 30 odd minutes away. Just thought we'd stop in so I can see her, and so you can meet her."

"Sure," I replied, despite my misgivings. He traced his fingers along the inside of my leg, stopping at my knees and the back of my knees. I'd never been touched there before, and his touch had me feeling all kinds of things, but mostly beautiful and loved.

"How does this feel?" he asked.

"Wonderful."

"I *bet* it feels all kinds of wonderful," he stated, touching me the same again.

The pleasure I felt was overwhelming. "Daniel..."

"You're so beautiful," he stated, interrupting me. "What you see in me I don't know. All I know is you're beautiful and I'm so glad you chose me as I was choosing you."

"Daniel, you're too much," I replied. "I think you're beautiful too."

He smiled. "Teme, you're so beautiful the thought of you sets my body alight. So beautiful I quietly envision us in a future time yet unknown and yet to come, enjoying each other."

I shook off the sudden arousal that overcame me and tried to remain composed.

"I'd kiss those beautiful lips of yours right now, but we had an agreement. Doing that now will only lead us down the path we agreed not to go down." With that, he stood up, gently placed my feet on the footstool and advised, "I'll be back."

He came back with a wrapped, boxed gift which he sat in my lap. I took pains to unwrap it, trying to not rip the beautiful gold and blue fleur-de-lis wrapping paper. It was a red and gold cloth bound copy of The Complete Works of Shakespeare. My heart soared.

"Daniel, you shouldn't have. Thank you!"

"You're very welcome, babe. I know how much you love Shakespeare, and I figured you must have his many works at yours, but it's time you made yourself at home here. So there you go," he said.

"You're amazing Daniel."

"Glad you think so," he replied, flashing me a toothy smile. "What d'ya say we get some dinner organized, hey?"

"Let's," I agreed, getting up, suddenly invigorated and full of energy. He had that effect.

We dined outdoors on the patio enjoying another Mojito, some sautéed salmon, steamed rice, grilled bell peppers, zucchini, Portabello mushrooms and eggplant, with a Caesar dressing lightly drizzled over the lot. As we engaged in small talk, the Texan sky changed from a deep orange and pink to purple, and then dark blue. Evening would be upon us soon.

Daniel's phone lay on the far end of the dinner table, to his left. A message came through. He glanced at it quickly, frowned slightly then set it aside. A while later, another message came through. I could sense the hesitancy in checking his phone the second time.

"Care to share?" I asked, startling him.

"Not really, but I guess I should," he replied. He immediately showed me the messages.

The first one read:

You were supposed to rescue her, not fall for her.

The second message stated:

Falling in love with her was not part of the deal.

"What the...?" I questioned.

"Hm...my thoughts exactly," he said. Suddenly on edge, he ran a hand through his hair, rendering it slightly tousled. "I know I've asked you this before, but are you betrothed to someone else? These messages sound an awful lot like they're coming from a jilted lover."

I side stepped his question. "Have you tried calling that number?" I asked.

"I've tried, but it's a dead end. Whoever it is, they're using a remote server somewhere," Daniel said. "Whoever it was, I'm guessing they're tied in to the job I took up the night we met."

"How so?"

"Instructions were to rescue you and keep you out of harm's way," he explained. "I did just that," he stated. "And then some. Whoever it was, they didn't count on me fallin' for you," he acknowledged. Nervously biting his bottom lip, he recalled, "I had nothing else to go on apart from the location and a description of you."

"Okay. Are you able to retrieve the job details and we can backtrack from there?" I asked. "It worries me that whoever this is, they are following our every move. And no, I'm not betrothed to anyone else so that makes this even more complex."

"It does," he agreed. "The job was literally a one sentence text." He scrolled through his messages until he found the one:

Rescue a subject, beautiful black female, en route to San Antonio, black Chevy Cherokee - get her out of harm's way.

"Payment was pre-wired to me, details of the payee were withheld," he recalled. "And a pretty penny that was," he stated. "Fifty large."

I felt my jaw drop. "Fifty thousand dollars?"

"Yep. Fifty thousand dólares."

"That's outrageous," I replied.

"Guess you could say so, but your life is obviously worth much more than that," he stated.

"You're such a sweet talker, Daniel," I declared.

"Well that *is* the truth. Your life is worth much more than gold," he said. "I'm just a little concerned that this jilted lover isn't too happy about our coming together like this."

"Ah well," I stated. "Too bad. What's he going to do about it."

"Or she," he said. "I saw the way Colleen was looking at you."

"Yeah, whatever," I said, brushing him off. "I don't know of anyone male or female who'd pay you that much to rescue me."

"All's well, ends well," he said casually.

I felt uneasy. "I'm not sure we can be safe in that assurance," I told him. "Fifty thousand dollars. Is that even ethical?"

"Probably not," he said. "But I completed the job, so payment for a service rendered, right?"

"Right," I replied, suddenly feeling ill at ease.

"So, unless the messages take on a scarier more threatening tone, we just leave well enough alone, right? Keep on livin' and keep on lovin'?" he suggested.

"I guess so," I replied. "Though I think we should be doing something to keep ahead of the game. I think I'd feel better about leaving well enough alone if I knew we could protect ourselves. I know where you keep your gun..."

"No gun is gonna save us from the wrath of a jilted lover," he said jokingly.

"Ha ha, that isn't funny," I said. "If he or she is coming at you with a gun, and you don't have a gun, that could be a problem."

"True. But if he or she's got a knife and you've got a gun..."

"Proportion," he said.

"Fifty grand is no small change," I reminded him. "Whoever it is, they mean business."

"Yeah, well, whoever they are, you're mine now, and all's fair in love and war," he said confidently.

"Hm...I'm yours now, so you own me?" I asked, not liking his possessive tone.

"Not per se, but possession is nine tenths of the law, you

dig?"

"You're a trip Daniel," I said, breaking into a grin. It was impossible to not laugh with him around. Besides, we had to make light of a very strange situation.

4

BEAUTY AND PERFECTION

S hania and I met for lunch the next day, at the café opposite the courthouse. It was easier for her to come to me, and leave the busyness and oftentimes drama of her beauty salon behind.

Shania was beautiful and she knew it. Her hair was up in a ponytail, and she had on hot pink lipstick and matching nails which drew attention to her impeccably smooth golden brown skin. She wore an orange, black and white striped cady dress, one she'd presumably slipped on moments before she left work. She wouldn't be caught dead in her work uniform outside of the salon, despite the fact that it was very on trend.

"So, when am I going to meet him?" she asked, as soon as we sat down.

"Daniel?"

"Who else girl – I know he's the reason you ain't got no time to hang with me these days. How about I come by tonight, just drop in and say hello?" she proposed.

"Should be fine," I told her. "Daniel doesn't like surprises though."

"For real?"

"For real. He's a homebody, likes routine and advance notice. Should be fine though," I told her.

"Better be fine," she stated. Kissing her teeth, she said, "I'm pretty hurt you didn't tell me about Duayne. You could've told me something."

I sighed in response. "I could have, but I didn't. I didn't feel like I could at the time..."

She reached across the table and squeezed my hand. "I should've known something was up. I'm sorry I wasn't there for you."

Tears that I thought were not there anymore, fell.

"No tears, mama, no tears. He isn't worth it," she stated.

"I know that now," I acknowledged, quickly wiping away my tears.

"Better days ahead," she said, looking absently into the distance. "I think I'll have me a sweet tea. You?"

"Same."

She signaled at the waiter to come over, and ordered two sweet teas for us.

"Mr. Daly," she stated. "How is he?"

"Jude?"

"Yeah, Jude. How is he?"

"Good," I told her. "Busy."

"Tell him I still get weak in the knees when I think of him."

I smiled in response. She and Jude had nearly hit it off, but she was too much for him. He couldn't handle her energy, her fire, her headstrongness. A certain man would handle all that she was and love her all the more for it, one day. That one day was just not here yet.

"Tell me about your knight in shining armor. Daniel."

"He's unlike anyone I've ever met before," I told her. "He's very open, very emotional, very real. He wears his heart on his sleeve like it's the thing to do... I don't know how I got so lucky."

"Guess you were meant to be then, yeah?"

"Guess so."

"He still doing his P.I. work?" she asked.

"Yeah..."

"I'm gonna need some background checks done on a few people, you think he can help?"

I laughed heartily. "I'm sure you can have those checks done elsewhere?"

"I could, but doing this'll give me a chance to get to know him better, and'll give me a chance to do some investigatin' of my own. On him."

"He'll be on to you from the word go," I warned her.

"No harm in tryin'. Besides, we want to make sure you avoid a repeat of Duayne."

"No chance of that happening," I assured her, coming to Daniel's defense. "You'll see what I mean when you meet him. He's different. Different as in good."

"Alright, girl, if you say so," she said. "Now, what's this savin' it for marriage shit I hear he's on. Setting yourselves up for failure if you ask me," she said. "Unless you're planning on marrying soon?" she asked, smiling wildly.

"You're too much, Shania. We're just getting to know each other for now..."

"Yep, and living together, playing house while doing it."

"We're figuring things out as we go along...."

"I'm happy for you," she said. "I'm happy because you're happy," she announced.

"Thank you. Now enough about me. What've *you* been up

to?" I asked.

"Been busy with the salon, then there's some excitement to be had after hours. You won't believe it..." she said, quickly grabbing her phone and flipping through some photos.

I was intrigued. "Why, what's going on?"

"Well, there are some new kids on the block, or should I say, new men on the block. Hot, hot, hot! There's about seven of them. They hang out at Bojangles mostly on Fridays. Drinks always on the house, amazing dancers, and the lot of them are single except one I think - Johnny. They're all just after a good time."

I couldn't hide my surprise.

"One's a doctor, two others are lawyers, don't know what the others are or do, but they sho' look good," she announced, winking at the bartender who brought our sweet teas over.

"Sounds suspect if you ask me."

"Interesting is what it is, girl, interesting," she said, showing me a photo she'd taken presumably on one of those nights. In the photo Michone, Gabriella and Angelique struck a pose for the camera. In the background were three of those new men on the block she'd referred to – men I didn't recognize.

"So, this is what you've been up to while I've been gone?" I questioned.

"That and then some," she replied, reaching into her handbag and pulling out a yellow flyer. "You need to come along. For the fitness, of course."

Of course. I smiled in response.

The flyer advertised Aikido, Hapkido, Taekwondo and Fencing on alternate days of the week.

"I signed up to do Taekwondo," she stated. "Tryin' to get

some of the other girls to come along, but it's a struggle. So far only Francesca comes along. I'm sure if the others knew four of those new men on the block were running the classes, they'd be here in a hurry."

I handed her back the flyer. Martial arts wasn't something I'd ever been interested in. It was amazing to watch, but I'd never considered doing it.

"You should come along," she suggested. "Might help give you that extra strength and confidence you need to recover from what you went through."

I pondered her suggestion for a moment.

"What do you have to lose?" she asked. "Don't you wish you could've taken charge over Duayne, defended yourself and showed him what's what?"

"To a point, yes," I replied. In the end, I'd felt powerless with him, and I'd lost my sense of belonging to myself. I'd lost me. To a point. Taking charge over Duayne and showing him what's what could've landed me in a worse situation than I'd been in. He didn't like being challenged.

"I'll pick you up at 6 then, drop you home when we're done," she promised. "It'll be good for you."

It would be, I thought. "Okay," I replied.

The lady at the table across from us laughed loudly at her lover's joke. I briefly glanced in their direction, wondering what had been so funny to make her laugh so loudly and unabashed. Her lover turned to meet my gaze, staring back fiercely at first, seconds before he flashed me a smile and a wave. Arturo. I recognized him from the local arts and recreation center. He ran a local writer's group.

"So, these men. They've just landed on the scene from like nowhere. Every Friday night, it's been free drinks on them, last Friday, it was free dinner, drinks and a show."

"Names?" I asked.

"Okay... I wrote this down," she said, scrolling through her phone to get to her notepad. "Okay, there's Scott, Darius, Elias, Ephraim, Jonathan, Patricio...then there's Craig."

"Craig?" I asked, wondering whether there was any relation to the Craig running Daniel's firm.

"Yep. Craig. He's a lawyer, along with Johnny - Jonathan," she confirmed. "Then there's a few others that hang with, but the guys I mentioned, they're usually always hangin' out together."

"Interesting," I noted, wondering whether Daniel had any knowledge of this, and whether this was the same Craig he'd talked about briefly.

"It's more than just *interesting* girl. Why'd you have to be so boring!"

I laughed in response. "Boring? I'm anything but boring. You should see what my morning was like, the cases I had to deal with."

"I'm not talkin' 'bout you not doing boring things. I'm talkin' 'bout you bein' borin'," she clarified.

I put my glass down with force. "Put it this way, if you saw me and Mr. Brennan earlier, I don't know if you'd say I was boring."

She raised a brow in response then smiled wickedly. "I bet you'd get up to all sorts of mischief with your new man. That doesn't make you any less boring."

"Come on now!"

"Show me you ain't by comin' to the session at the recreational centre tonight," she challenged.

"I'll be there," I said without hesitation, despite my earlier apprehension.

"Good. So, we head back?" she asked.

"Yep, let's do this," I said, enthused with an unexpected surge of energy. She had that effect.

Shania picked me up at 6 pm as she'd promised. Daniel and I had just had dinner when she rocked up at ours.

Though I'd shown her photos of Daniel previously, she seemed mesmerized to see him in person.

"We finally meet," she announced, stretching her hand out to greet him. "A pleasure to meet you," she stated. "I see why she's so taken by you," she added, looking him up and down.

He shook her hand but shrugged off the compliment. "I on the other hand don't see what she sees in me," he stated.

"Well, you look good together. Plus she's happy, and that's what counts for me," she said.

"We're on the same page there," he stated.

"Ready to go?" I asked, wanting to keep it all brief. Daniel was in the habit of asking leading questions, and I was sure Shania's responses would have had him asking a whole load of other questions.

"Yes indeed," Shania responded, looking around. "Got five minutes though. For a tour perhaps?"

I rolled my eyes in response. There *was* going to be plenty of time to show her around. Some other time.

"I insist," she stated. Daniel gave me a quick glance and a half smile as though to ask, *Is she for real?* before volunteering to show her around.

They walked away in animated conversation. Shania loved

it all. The color scheme, the artwork, the furniture, the attention.

I tugged on the waistband of my sweatpants as I stood there alone. *Too tight.* I hardly felt comfortable with my body any more. Duayne had seen to it that I didn't. I ran my hand along the hem of my sports bra. *Too much.* Though I had a sports shirt on top of it, it felt as though I was letting it all hang out. *Too revealing.* I sighed. The thought of changing yet again was an unwelcome endeavour. I didn't have very much different to change into.

"Beauty," Daniel stated, slicing into my thoughts. "Don't overexert yourself tonight, ease yourself into whatever it is you choose. It'll be good for you," he said.

"I hope so," I told him.

"Choose Hapkido and you've got yourself a live-in sparring partner."

I couldn't hide my surprise. "Really?"

"Yes, really," he replied, leaning in to give me a kiss on the cheek. "There's still a lot you don't know about me."

Shania interrupted. "So you two are saving it all for marriage?"

Daniel turned and looked at me, as though he were shocked Shania and I had talked about something so intimate. Before either of us got the chance to reply, Shania stated, "It won't last. Either you'll give in, or marriage will happen. Like any day now. Mark my words y'all."

I rolled my eyes again and Daniel laughed. "You know Shania, you're alright," he said. "She's alright by me!" he exclaimed, turning to me, grinning from ear to ear.

Two of my favorite people got along, and that felt good. I was going to marry him some day. I knew that much. No one made me feel the way he did. No one ever could.

At the recreational center, Shania gravitated towards Taekwondo, while I hesitated. I suddenly felt like retreating, despite having looked forward to the evening. Johnny, the fencing instructor sensed my hesitation. "How about fencing?" he asked. In complete fencing attire, his demeanour commanded respect and revere. He stood several feet tall, had piercing blue eyes, auburn brown hair and a sharp but kind face. He didn't wait for me to respond. Instead, he motioned for me to follow him. I did. Moments later, vest on, helmet on and French foil in hand, fencing became the clear choice.

Class ended too quickly. As I changed out of my gear, I silently resolved to get my own – I felt drawn to fencing, and knew it would be the beginning of a lifelong love of the sport.

Commotion jolted me out of my thoughts as I tried to locate Shania.

"You could've fuckin' told me you'd be hangin' out here, you don't do Tuesdays," a woman yelled.

"Calm down," Johnny argued. "I'm here to let off steam. I don't need you policing me."

A few of the class stopped what they were doing to listen in on the argument.

"This isn't the time or the place," Johnny told her.

She carried on. "Don't expect me to be waitin' up on you or prepping you dinner if you can't even tell me what time you're getting back."

"It's not as if you cook for me anyway," he replied.

She cast him a dirty look then walked off and out of the studio door in a huff.

Johnny stood there, forlorn but for a moment, before shaking it off and announcing to the class, "Right. Show's over, class is over, I'll be seeing you all next week, unless you're coming in on Friday too."

In the distance, Shania was speaking with someone so I stayed behind to talk to Johnny about the possibility of continuing on with fencing beyond tonight.

"Sorry you had to witness that," he mentioned, embarrassed about his other half's behavior. I barely flinched. I wasn't a stranger to that sort of behavior, it was reminiscent of Duayne's behavior.

"You shouldn't let her get away with talkin' to you like that," I offered.

Johnny stood there for a mediative moment before replying, "After everything I've put her through I can take a little anger. I can take a little frustration."

"Sounded like it was more than just a little anger and frustration."

He shrugged in response. "You shouldn't let her talk to you like that," I repeated.

He paused for a moment before responding, "Look, I've known Michaela for a long time, she's put up with me and I'm just grateful she's in my life."

"Sounds like you love her deeply and she barely tolerates you," I said.

Johnny didn't deny this. He simply agreed and nodded his head in response.

"Her tolerating me – it's a kind of love," he said.

I shook my head in dissent, wishing he knew he deserved better. The love he thought he had was no kind of love worth having. *If you say so*, I thought, knowing it was not love pure

BEAUTY AND PERFECTION

and unadulterated, it was a twisted perception of love. No one deserved to be treated like that. I thought of Maya Angelou's *Some Kind of Love, Some Say* and knew how hard it was to see the situation for what it was, when you were in it. How hard it was to discern between love and hate. Until it was too late, that is.

Changing topic he asked, "So, see you next Tuesday? Really good to see you givin' it a go and getting' the confidence up to learn something new. Good parry of six and four. Great lunge."

"Thanks," I replied, chuffed to hear I wasn't completely hopeless at the first try.

He nodded in reply, wiping a bead of sweat from his forehead with the back of his hand. His hair, a rich auburn brown, was all spiked up in places and slick in others courtesy of a generous amount of hair gel.

"Next week we'll do some more footwork and we'll work on your parry of eight," he promised. "Alright?"

"Alright," I replied. Curious, I asked, "What part of England are you from?"

"Surrey," he replied. "Guildford."

I didn't even try to hide my surprise. "Guildford? I know that town pretty well. I went to uni there."

"Really!" he exclaimed. "Guildford Uni? What major and what year?"

"L.L.B. Class of '02."

"L.L.B. Class of '01," he said. "What are the odds!!!"

"What are the odds indeed!" I concurred, smiling wildly. "I don't remember seeing you on campus though," I recalled.

"I don't recall seeing you either," he mentioned.

"Probably because you weren't actually on campus?"

73

"Ha ha, funny that," he said. "I don't know how any of us got through uni," he laughed. "Some pretty wild nights there."

"Work hard, play even harder," we said and laughed in unison.

"Wasn't it your year that was implicated in burning down the medical research labs?" I asked.

"What was that?" he asked, feigning innocence.

"Your year. You lot..."

He laughed in response. "As far as I'm aware...," he started.

"What a dodge!"

"What an *artful* dodge, you mean," he corrected.

We laughed together a little too loudly, causing Shania to turn sharply in our direction.

Calming down, he mentioned, "Guildford's home for me. Well, it was, before I came here."

"What brought you here?"

He hesitated for a moment before replying. "Work."

"I see," I replied. "Shania mentioned you're working locally now?"

"That I am," he stated. "I worked in crime before coming here. Just passed the Texan Bar Exam, so I'm hoping to get started on my own here. That's if they'll let me."

"If they'll let you?" I asked.

The look on his face showed he'd said too much. "That's another story for another day," he stated, conveniently drawing our conversation to a close. "Great to meet you."

"And you," I replied. "We should all get together some-time," I suggested, thinking Daniel might be able to throw some work his way. "Daniel, my other half has a firm specializing in crime, he might be keen on getting you to do a bit of work for him."

He smiled in response. "With your persuasion of course," he joked.

"I'll let your background speak for you. Though, Class of '01 Guildford, that speaks volumes."

"Yeah right," he laughed. "I did graduate with Honors though, if that means anything."

"It means everything. I'll talk to Daniel," I told him. "If it's a character and fitness issue, I can help with submissions."

He fell silent for a moment, before stating, "Alright, sounds like a plan. I'm here 3 nights a week, alternate evenings from 6 pm onwards. You know where to find me."

"Great," I replied. "See you next week," I told him, excited, and eager to get back home to Daniel. The possibility of helping someone out always thrilled me.

"See you then!" he said, raising his fist in the rhythmic left and right wrist swoosh that was recognizable only to Guildford graduates. It had been many years since I'd done it, but I did it back, laughing in the process. "Guildford rocks," he announced, throwing me a salute as I headed off, light-spirited. Shania was waiting for me.

Daniel was keen to hear about my night fencing. I filled him in on all the new moves I'd learnt. That aside, I mentioned Johnny in the context of his being a lawyer, and that he'd recently passed the Texan Bar, but needed to get over the hurdle of getting his license.

"Seems like he's having issues getting his license here."

"What kind of issues is he having?" Daniel asked.

"I didn't ask outright, but it's likely a character and fitness issue."

"Oh, okay," he said, pensively. "You'd vouch for him, on the basis of having met him only once?"

"He went to Guildford..."

Daniel smiled for a moment before stating, "Apart from that."

"Well, if he's got his papers from the UK, he's still licensed as a solicitor there, and he's having issues here, yes, I'd vouch for him. I've been wrong about people – Duayne for one, but otherwise I'm a pretty good judge of character. Besides, if we can help, we *should* help."

"Fair enough," he stated. "I'm a good judge of character too, by the way," he added.

"I don't doubt that," I replied, gently and affectionately touching his lightly stubbled chin.

"I'm being serious," he added. "From the instant I meet someone, I have this uncanny gift of being able to discern whether they mean harm or good. As you can see, I don't have very many friends, but of course I've got you."

I nodded in response. "Lucky me," I said.

"I'm the lucky one," he insisted, leaning in to plant a kiss on my lips.

"So, coming back to Johnny, you think we can help?" I asked.

"Perhaps," he said. "If he's got a current practicing certificate from the UK it might just be an issue of explaining the matter to the board here. That and then some."

"Meaning?"

"It's likely he'll be waiting a while before he's given permission to practice in this here State."

"Can he work with Craig, at your firm, even in paralegal capacity, until then?"

76

Daniel hesitated for a moment before responding, "I don't see why not."

"Awesome." Thrilled, I hugged him. I couldn't describe the passion and love I felt for this man, and the endless nature of his love which extended to the people I loved and cared for. I saw myself being with him forever.

"Baby," he said passionately, interrupting me mid thought. "I've set the bath for you, got a glass of red ready for you. We could watch a movie after dinner, and call it a night?"

I smiled in response. *Any excuse to hold me in his arms*, I thought. We slept in separate rooms, so watching a movie and falling asleep in each other's arms was a form of intimacy we'd both come to love and crave. We'd become inseparable. He for I and I for him.

The days of that week came and went, and before long the weekend had arrived. I woke up Saturday morning to a dozen primroses on the dressing table. Adorned in pink ribbon and a long vase, the arrangement was breathtaking. A handwritten note on the dresser stated:

Temwani,

Thank you for giving me something to look forward
to each morning I rise. I won't go back to living without you.
Love,
 Daniel.

P.s. Primroses = I can't live without you
Love. I felt my heart fill with joy. Daniel had a habit of

77

waking up at 3 am and staying awake. He'd either be up reading, or he'd be up watching something on the television. He must've brought the flowers to me in the early hours of the morning. I did not hear him come in when he did.

I took my time in getting out of bed that morning. It was a clear morning, the skies were an auburn red which would soon blend to blue. A red breasted robin sang just beneath the window and I smiled, reflecting on how beautiful life was. I hadn't thought much about Duayne and what went down that night, and I knew I would have to at some stage, but for now, my focus was on getting back to me and to my new life with Daniel.

A warm extended shower first thing in the morning was very alluring. I looked forward to trying the vanilla straw-berry scented shower gel Daniel had picked up for me the day before. No sooner than I had gotten into the shower than Daniel rapped on the frosted glass shower door.

"I'm heading out for a jog, I'll be back in a few," he said.

"Okay," I responded, peering around the corner to meet his face. Instead, I saw the back of him heading out.

I was in the shower for a little while longer before I decided to come out. Grabbing the towel off the rack, I dried myself partially, before deciding to moisturize in the bedroom. Cracking open the cocoa butter lotion, the smell was heavenly to me. In privacy, I dropped my towel and worked the lotion into my skin. Brusque movement to my left startled me, and I turned to see Daniel standing there in front of me, mouth agape. I'd mistakenly thought he'd already gone on his jog.

I quickly grabbed my towel off the floor and hurriedly wrapped myself in it.

"I thought you were out?" I managed.

"I forgot...," he started. "I been fixin to...I...," then, "Sorry, I didn't mean to..." he said, before finally uttering, "You had me looking at perfection."

"Good save," I told him, embarrassed he'd just seen me naked. "Can you leave now?" I asked coolly.

He smiled nervously before replying "Of course, my love."

With him gone, I hurriedly dressed up then headed down to eat something. Once done, I busied myself around my new home, dusting and wiping down surfaces before I sat down to drink some tea and read the paper. Daniel returned an hour after he'd left. He returned sweaty, his face flushed. I offered him a glass of iced water then continued reading through the paper that lay on the bench.

"Thank you," he said, breathless from the jog.

"You're very welcome," I said, smiling a little too widely, hoping the incident earlier would be forgotten. This was not the case.

"I'm sorry about runnin' in on you earlier," he apologized before awkward silence ensued.

"You're not really sorry," I said in response, lifting my eyes from the paper I was pretending to be so into reading.

"No, I guess not," he confessed. "Truth is, your body's bangin', and you were a sight to behold."

"Thanks for the compliment, though we had an agreement, right?"

"Am I not allowed to admire?" he asked.

"From a distance, yes, and while I'm fully clothed, yes," I told him.

"Well, I'm hoping one day I'll get to enjoy you," he said confidently. "And I ain't talkin' about that happenin' outside of marriage."

Bold. I smiled in response. "I think you need to take a cold shower now," I suggested.

"You got that right," he said, winking at me as he headed off for one.

Daniel looked handsome in a plain white polo shirt, denim blue jeans and brown chinos over the usual cowboy boots. My heart skipped a beat when he flashed me a beautiful smile.

"How about we drive into town? I'll show you some of the places I hang out at, get us some kolaches from the Czech bakery..."

I giggled slightly.

"What's so funny?" he asked.

"Food? More food? I can't get over how you're always hungry."

"Well, maybe I need a good woman to care and cook for me more often," he replied.

"I hear you," I replied. "Can't go past those kolaches though."

"So, it's a date?"

"Date it is," I said. Bumping into Duayne was the furthest from my mind.

"No hesitation?" he asked.

"No," I replied.

"Ready to come out as my girl?" he asked, slipping a hand around my waist, and staring me up and down as though he had a new appreciation for my body.

"Been ready for time," I replied.

"For time, she says!" he laughed lightheartedly. "Then let's hit the road," he said, his voice deep, imploring and charming. "I been ready to show you off as mine, for time."

I met Jolène, his mother, that afternoon. Apart from her blue eyes, I couldn't see the resemblance between her and Daniel, which I found odd, but dismissed the thought no sooner than it had entered my mind. She was warm and welcoming, much like he was. She offered to do up a spread that evening, and though we hadn't planned on being out the whole day, I knew how much Daniel loved his food, so of course we had to agree to have dinner. I also saw it as an opportunity to learn more about him.

Her grand and expansive southern prairie style home was beautiful. The front porch that ran the length of the whole house, a roof with wide overhanging eaves and an interior that incorporated elements of nature added to the mystique and romantic feel of the place. She lived there alone, and had done so for many years after Daniel had moved out and on to college. As Daniel took me from room to room and showed me through every inch of the house, I wondered how she managed to keep the place spotless.

"Mom's a homebody," he explained. "She enjoys the maintenance and all the little things involved in keeping this home spic and span."

Jolène had left one of the bedrooms in the house untouched. Wallpaper adorned with sailboats and ships, coupled with Daniel's mobile planes, cars and trucks in a display cabinet made the room feel alive, as though he'd left there days, not decades ago.

"This is embarrassing," Daniel said, wanting to immediately close the door. "Mom insists on keeping this room as it is, prefers to remember me as her little boy, though I'm all grown up now as you can tell."

"That and for my future grandkids," Jolène stated, listening in on our conversation. Turning to me, she asked, "You happy to stay the night?"

Shocked at her forwardness I turned to Daniel, who looked equally as shocked. "I'm happy to do whatever Daniel plans to do."

"Great," she answered. "No point headin' back home now when there's a place for y'all to stay. I'll make up the bed in the guest room for you both."

"Ma' we live only 30 minutes away. Besides, we sleep in separate rooms."

"Separate rooms?" she asked.

"Yes, mom. Separate beds, separate rooms."

"Well, I guess that ends tonight, then, yes?"

I laughed in response, and Daniel shot me a stern look.

"Let's not get ahead of ourselves, here Ma'. I know you want grandkids bad, but fixin' to get us to stay here overnight for that purpose is no way, Ma'," he stated.

"Offer still stands!" she replied, waving off what Daniel had said.

"Lord knows you'll make some beautiful babies!"

"Mom!" Daniel exclaimed, chiding her for carrying on after he'd asked her to stop.

There was a lot of laughter and joy amongst us as we spent the remaining few hours before we'd planned to head home, together. Jolène spoke of the time they'd lived in Switzerland, and fondly recalled Daniel's love of the lake, spring and summer in Geneva and his love of open air music festivals. He was 15 when they'd left to return to Texas. I had moved to Switzerland when he had left.

As the evening drew to a close, Jolène busied herself about the kitchen, eventually sending Daniel off to fix a loose hinge in the bathroom. She used the time he was gone to talk to me as we put plates away and looked at storing the leftover food.

"He's absolutely and most positively in love with you, I've never seen him like this," she said. "I hope for his sake, you're as into him as he is into you."

"I'm so in love with him," I told her. "I haven't known him long, but he means the world to me."

"Good," she replied. "He's had his heart broken in the past, and I don't want to see him unhappy like that again."

I nodded my head in response.

"I can see the two of you getting married," she said suddenly.

"Mom!" Daniel exclaimed, entering the kitchen again. "Please stop with the not so subtle hints of where you want our relationship to be headed."

"Oh, baby, you know I only want what's best for you," she stated, embracing him fondly.

"I know," he replied. "I didn't bring her here for you to scare her off though."

"Oh, I don't think she's goin' anywhere anytime soon. Not without you anyway," she replied.

Seeing that she wouldn't let up, Daniel stated, "Speaking of going somewhere, we need to head off soon."

The look of disappointment in Jolène's eyes was evident.

"Why don't you come 'round ours next week? I can cook you dinner this time?" I suggested.

Jolène's eyes lit up instantly. "That sounds like a great idea." After a momentary pause, she asked, "There enough time for you to have some peach cobbler and more sweet tea?"

"Of course there is, Ma'," Daniel replied.

The visit to his mother's over, we parked the car by the pier downtown, and got out for a stroll along the esplanade. The stars were out, peppering the midnight blue sky, while the moon hung low, its reflection shimmering on the water.

Daniel slid his hand around my waist as we walked. "I know right now I want to marry you," he said suddenly. "A year from now, two years from now, heck, 20 years from now, my feeling would still be the same – I want you to be my wife."

It was hard to hide my surprise. Shock even. "Daniel, this is all so sudden..."

"What we have here is real," he said. "So real I feel there is no one else for me. There will be no one else for me."

"I'm honored you'd want me as your wife," I told him. "But aren't we moving just a tad too fast?"

He left my side to jump a pace in front of me. I stopped in my tracks and he took my hand in his. "From the moment I laid eyes on you, I just knew you were the one. Something about you just had me wanting to hold you, protect you and be there for you for all times. So, no, I don't believe we are moving too fast at all."

I was touched.

"I've been wanting to settle down for some time now," he told me. "With the right woman. I never thought I'd find her. Until I met you."

Though I was taken aback by his forwardness, I simply smiled in response. "Daniel, you're pretty full on."

"I'm a firm believer of go hard or go home," he said, leaning forward as though he wanted to let me in on a secret. "This is where I go hard," he said. "Figuratively speaking of course," he added. "Though I'd be lying if I tried to deny the effect you have on me. Thank goodness for my Levi's and button downs."

A mental image came up in my mind. Staring through me as though he could read my mind, he stated, "Get your mind out of the gutter, lady!"

I laughed in jest.

"So, what do you say, we make this official?" he asked.

"Official as in let's tell everyone we're an item?" I asked, glad to finally see him wanting to move forward so quickly.

"Official as in let's not waste time here. Let's get married," he said plainly.

"Daniel..."

I gasped in surprise as he fell to bended knee. "Will you marry me Temwani?"

Speechless, I struggled for words. "Daniel, we hardly know each other," I started.

"We'll get to know each other," he promised. "I'll make you happy. I'll give you the world, and you'll be my world." He reached into his jacket pocket and pulled out a ring.

My heart soared. Rational thinking went out the window as I looked at him on bended knee, ring in hand, deep brown wavy hair windswept, his deep blue eyes staring into me and promising me the world.

Marriage. To this man who was so much in love with me. I gushed at the thought. "Is this about sex?" I asked, barely over a whisper.

He smirked in response. "No, my dear. This is about me

wanting to have you to myself. Me wanting to love you to the exclusivity of all others." Not moments later he added, "Okay. Sex has *something* to do with it, but not *everything* to do with it," he confirmed, raising my hand to his lips for a kiss. "It could be the beginning of something beyond words. You as my wife, me as your husband, some babies – one big happy family..."

"Wait, hold up. Babies?" I asked.

"Yes. Babies," he stated nonchalantly. "I'm sure they'll be as beautiful as you are."

"Daniel...," I started, then stopped midsentence as a jogger passed us by.

"Give it some thought," he said. "Say the word and I'll whisk you away somewhere romantic, somewhere remote, to become my lawfully wedded wife."

I nodded in response, completely over the moon that he'd asked me to marry him, but worried there was an underlying reason driving the rush to get married all of a sudden. I voiced my concerns immediately. "Baby, please tell me you're not rushing into marriage for some reason unbeknown to me? Are you afraid the mystery suitor will stake a claim on me?"

He held my gaze for a moment before candidly stating, "Maybe I am a little afraid of someone else wanting to have you, but I know how I feel, sugarpie. I want to give myself to you wholly and fully, and I also want you for myself. Exclusively. Forever. So, please marry me, will you? Don't leave me hanging here. Will you do me the honour of becoming my wife, please?" he asked. Before I had a chance to respond, he added, "I'll stay here on bended knee until you say yes."

I stood there for a while in silence, taking in the beauty of the moment. I had known long ago our lives would be bound inextricably. That we would end up like this, so soon, shook me and woke me up inside. *He would be mine, and I would be his, forever.*

"However you'll have me Teme, however you'll have me. I'll take as much or as little as you're prepared to give," he stated.

"I hear you Daniel. I'll give you everything. In time."

"Okay, baby, hear me out. How about this, we get married just after I ask your Dad for your hand. You want out, we file for an annulment after 30 days. 30 days for me to prove to you it's all worth it. Invest in 30 days and I'll give you 30 plus years. I can't promise you a lot of things but I can promise you that I'll love you and cherish you 'til the day that I die."

I smiled in response and for a moment was lost in thought. I wanted nothing more than to believe him, but in my mind I replayed the possible scenarios. *Of how this whirlwind romance might end up in tears. Of how promises could be broken.*

Before he got the chance to complain that my response to his unconventional proposal was underwhelming, I replied, "Of course I'll marry you Daniel."

He bolted up in joy, nearly toppling me over. Happiness swept across his face and he leaned forward to kiss me fervently.

Pausing for a moment, he stated, "I'll need to ask your father for your hand. How about we make plans for that sooner rather than later? How about we fly out to Switzerland in a few days?"

"You're something else, Daniel, you waste no time," I observed, partly laughing.

"I'm a man on a mission, sugarpie. I won't rest until you're all mine and only mine."

"About Switzerland, and my family. They don't even know we're an item," I said.

"True," he stated. "No time like the present to let them know, right?"

"I guess so," I replied.

He leant in and kissed me deeply and with growing intensity. I drew back from him the moment his lips on mine got too intense, and my head started to spin. "I can't wait to make you Mrs. Daniel Brennan," he said. "We'll weather every storm together. Heck, we'll be the storm."

I smiled in response, hugging him firmly. "You've made me so happy Daniel. I can't wait to call you my husband."

5

BEST LAID PLANS

We sat on the end of the king-sized bed in the master bedroom, the room I stayed in. I'd been up early that morning browsing through wedding dress designs online, and considering who I wanted at the wedding. Daniel joined me after fixing up breakfast. We'd spent most of the night before chatting about the wedding, but I was now curious about the fact that he'd had his heart broken in the past.

"So, your mom said you had your heart broken in the past?"

He shrugged in response. "I sort of did it to myself, really. I shouldn't have placed my heart in the hands of someone who could care less about me."

"What happened?" I asked, curious.

"She was two timing me from the start. I was there just to fill a void, provide for her material needs and help her get through law school," he stated.

"I thought you didn't date through law school?"

"I didn't. This was a full on, straight up serious relation-ship from the start, the whole two years it lasted," he said. "She met my mom and all..." his voice trailed off. From his reaction, the pain still ran deep, and the wounds were still raw.

"You're with me now," I reminded him, squeezing his hand. He squeezed back. Moments later, he bolted up, strolled over to the chest of drawers, opened a small box and took out a handwritten letter, the paper well-creased and worn. Shutting the dresser door, he walked back over to me, and handed it to me. It was a letter, presumably from his ex. The letter read:

Don't you dare accuse me of using you. You freely offered all you gave, and I had no hesitation in taking. Be grateful you even knew me. Someone like you should be happy you got to get the girl. You're not known for your looks. You're nothing to look at, nothing worth writing home about, you're nothing. I'm glad I kept my options open with Mike. He's everything to me. As for you, I'm going to act as though you don't exist. Goodbye and good riddance. I never loved you, I never will.
Steph.

"What a piece of work!" I exclaimed, handing him back the letter. "This should be in the bin, where it belongs."

He nodded in response before scrunching it up and tossing it into the waste paper basket.

"You're with me now, and you're everything to me," I reminded him.

The sadness in his eyes dissipated, and was replaced with pure joy.

"I hit the jackpot with you," he stated.

"And I with you," I replied.

He smiled and nodded his head in response. "Well, up

until I'd met you, I'd decided that love wasn't for me, but something about you just woke me up inside and cheered me up. The moment I laid eyes on you, the moment I got to thinkin' about you and hoping for a future with you...I got to believing in love again," he said. "Let's get married as soon as we can, so I won't have to be without you."

"You mean, so we don't have to be without each other?"

"Yes," he agreed. "You got it. Let's do this."

"Let's," I replied, melting into his embrace, feeling like the luckiest woman alive.

We were up late that night, plotting a guest list and looking at possible reception venues in the Austin area, before deciding on his church, which we would attend together for the first time on Sunday.

There was so much to plan for in such little time. Apart from family, I knew I wanted Ernesto, Jude, Shania and a few others there, I just didn't know how to break it to them that the man I'd just met and fallen in love with had proposed and we were getting married in a matter of weeks. Daniel seemed pretty laid back about it all. After all, all he had to do was turn up.

Interrupting me in thought he stated, "Our big day just can't come fast enough. I just can't wait." He planted himself on the end of the bed we would come to share after we tied the knot, and stared me down, undressing me with his eyes. I pulled my robe in closer.

"Baby, come on now!" he complained.

"Can't stand the heat..."

"I hear you," he replied. "I can't wait," he said again.

I took pity on him. "Sleep here tonight then?"

"What?" he asked in disbelief.

"How about you sleep here with me, tonight?" I asked. "As long as it's just sleep we'll be having."

"Right," he said, eyeing me suspiciously.

"Isn't this what you wanted?"

"I just want you," he replied.

"So?"

"I'm not sure I trust myself to just lie in bed next to you. Not after I saw you nakid and all," he confessed.

"What makes you think I trust myself with you?"

"What are you up to, sugarpie?" he asked.

"Nothing, just tryin' to keep you happy."

"Me here just talkin' to you is keepin' me happy," he announced. "I won't say no to spendin' the night with you though. I'll just have to dress appropriately, for the occasion."

"Meaning?"

"Jocks, boxers, and PJs."

"You're a trip, Daniel," I laughed. "Wouldn't it be easier if I wore something daggy?"

"Darlin' you could be wearing a trash bag and I'd still be turned on by you."

I smiled, and he winked at me. "I guess we're at an impasse then."

"Hm...well, we could apply for our marriage license, and get married a few days later – 72 hours later, I believe it is?" he proposed.

"I don't think we can pull this all together in such a short time," I told him, not keen on rushing things.

"If it's a matter of your family being here, we can let

everyone know now. Get married overseas if we have to," he suggested. "Or we can just elope now, and have the ceremony once we can get everyone together."

"And the purpose of getting eloped now as opposed to waiting?"

Daniel stood up, walked over to me and knelt by the edge of the bed. "I love you and I respect you, but I want you and crave you. I'm not sure how much longer I'd last playing house with you."

"Marriage is more than just sex Daniel."

"This isn't about just sex. You should know this by now. I'm into you. I want to be a part of everything you do, I want to be everywhere you are. I want to do life with you. Marriage is for life, and I want to spend the rest of my life with you," he said.

"Okay," I replied.

"Okay?" he asked.

"Okay," I repeated.

"We apply for our marriage license then we get married as soon as we can?" he asked.

"Yes," I agreed. "I'm sure your mom would be happy to help."

His eyes narrowed in response. "I love my mom, but once she gets to planning, I'm afraid we may be lookin' at a wedding a few months down the track. I want this to happen sooner rather than later. I want this to be about us, not about anyone else."

"I hear you," I replied.

We went to church that Sunday as planned. A man and woman from the church's welcome committee stood at the door. The man shook Daniel's hand, but cast me a strange look that was anything but welcoming. The woman at the door smiled disingenuously and said, "Welcome."

"Thank you," I replied, and she handed me a Bible. Daniel accepted the church bulletin from the man at the door, slipped his hand around my waist and led me to a pew to the front of the church.

Congregants were singing, so we stood, and sang too. Daniel turned to smile at me from time to time, mirroring the joy I felt in my heart from simply being with him.

Daniel's smile vanished when we sat down and he turned to the Bible verse referred to by the Minister. As he turned to the verse in the Bible, what initially looked like a twine bookmark slipped out and into his lap. As he raised it, the shape it formed was unmistakable. The twine "bookmark" formed the shape of a noose.

I felt my stomach sink, and saw the look of disappointment and anger in Daniel's eyes.

"Let's go," he said, a little over a whisper.

I squeezed his hand in response. I was hurt, but thought he should confront the woman who had given him the Bible.

"Let's go," he said again, louder, this time standing up mid sermon. I got up with him and walked out.

"That was fucked up," he swore, as we walked to the car, hand in hand. "Sorry for my language but I'm at a loss as to what to say...you know, how dare they!"

I felt his anger deeply, but chose to remain calm. Racism was something I'd encountered from time to time, and to a point, I'd come to anticipate it. "Baby, people can and they will dare to speak out against us," I told him, well aware of the many future moments when another such incident would occur.

He shook his head in response. "I can't stand to think that someone would mean you harm simply because of the tone of your skin. I can't bear the thought that I am not able to prevent something like this from ever occurring again."

"Daniel, you're such a protector," I stated. "I love you for this, but there are some things you can't protect me from."

"I hear ya'," he stated, clicking the car doors open then dashing to the passenger side to open the door for me.

"So, getting married here is out," he announced.

"You could confront them…"

"No," he said firmly, as he started the ignition up. "I've been going to that church for time, but not any longer. Getting married here is out."

"The pastor at my church could marry us anywhere. How about we try that instead?" I suggested.

"Okay," he replied solemnly. "I'm so sorry about all this," he added.

"Daniel, don't you dare apologize for someone else's small mindedness."

"Small mindedness? That's putting it mildly," he said.

"Let it go, baby," I suggested. "The last thing you should do is let it get to you."

He nodded in response, though clearly still angry. We drove in silence for a while before he asked, "Did Duayne go to church with you?"

"Yep," I replied quickly. "All for show I'm sure," I told him. I hadn't been back to church since my relationship with Duayne had come to an end. I wasn't keen on bumping into him there. Since then, Sundays had become a day of quiet reflection. I'd reflect on my week and try to discern God's intention for the week ahead.

"I see," he said somberly. Silence ensued again before he perked up. "You know, Craig's a lay pastor, maybe he could help?"

I was a bit surprised. "Is there anything Craig doesn't do?"

Daniel laughed nervously. "Come to think of it, probably not."

"Well, let's hope he doesn't do crime."

It took Daniel a moment to get the joke. "Aw, baby girl, you killed it," he laughed away.

I smiled, happy to have taken his mind off the nasty incident earlier, even if just for a moment.

Plans for our wedding underway, I found the nerve to go back to my apartment. I'd given the landlord notice and planned to move out eventually. The furniture would remain. I would only take items of sentimental value with me, most of which could fit in my suitcase. Daniel jimmied the lock and we got in through the side door since I didn't have keys - they'd been left behind the night Duayne had assaulted me.

I could tell by the way things had been left in the apartment, Duayne had been there after the fact. How long ago I didn't know. I threw a few books that were in the kitchen, into the rucksack I'd brought along with me.

"Better Homes and Garden Cookbook?" Daniel stated, glancing at some of the books in the bag. "I see you've been holding out on me, sugarpie!"

I smiled in response. "Not holding out on you, baby. Everything in its time." I imagined I could survive on only his love and all of him.

Suddenly, I felt my stomach dip. I saw the glass door

shatter before I heard it. Everything else was a blur. In slow motion I saw Daniel fall to the ground, clutching his shoulder. He'd been shot. He reached for his gun and shot back. The assailant returned the shot. Forgetting the danger that I might be in, I ran towards Daniel. *Stay back* he motioned.

I waited, feeling helpless. He tossed his mobile phone to me, and I used it to call the Police. As I dialed, Daniel propped himself up against the wall, leaving behind a red stain. His face turned pale from shock. "Now's as good a time as any to profess your undying love for me," he said, half joking. He was shaking now, and I dashed to his side, despite his warning earlier. He'd been shot in the shoulder.

"Man this hurts," he said, shifting to change from his seated position. Kneeling beside him, I beckoned him to lay down in my arms.

"I'm so sorry Daniel, I shouldn't have let you get involved from the beginning. You should have just left me where I was and walked away, you should've..."

"If I had to do it all over, I would do it all again, babe. No doubt," he said. "Now, don't you give up on me just yet, we've still got a lifetime of lovin' to get through," he stated, shaking as he spoke. I leaned in to embrace him and inadvertently made the pain worse. He moaned, then laughed in response, fitfully.

"Sorry Daniel, I didn't mean to..."

"Now's the moment you profess your eternal love for me, yes?" he joked.

I smiled in between tears. "Daniel you know I love you," I told him, wiping a bead of sweat from his brow.

"I've felt it, and I know that now," he said, trembling. The paramedics seemed to be taking their time in arriving.

The thought crossed my mind to drive him to the General Hospital, but I worried that Duayne was still lingering in the area. In the meanwhile, Daniel fought to keep his eyes open as I talked to him. I stemmed the blood flow with my cardigan, and this seemed to help somewhat. *The bullet's probably still lodged in him*, I thought.

"Baby, stay with me," I begged as he drifted in and out of consciousness.

The Police and the paramedics came at the same time. I rode with Daniel to the General, separating only from him when he went through surgery to remove the bullet from his shoulder.

I called Jolène once he was stabilized. She burst into tears on the phone, grateful that he was okay, and grateful that I was with him. She immediately left home to join us at the hospital.

When the effects of the sedative given during surgery wore off and he'd come to, Daniel smiled and stated, "I say we get married sooner rather than later."

"Daniel..."

"Teme. You. Me."

"Daniel, you know how I feel. What's important right now is you recovering," I reminded him.

"Sugarpie, come on now, I'm sure we can do both?" he urged.

I sighed in response.

He interrupted me mid thought. Placing my hand in his, he stated, "Temwani, I will always love you. It's inevitable that love will change, but I truly believe my love for you will get deeper in time, and will stand the test of time. So will you go on this journey with me? Will you let me love you for the rest of our lives, and can the rest of our lives start today, or at least 72 hours from now?"

"Daniel, let's talk after you get some sleep."

"No sleep for me now. Sleep can wait. One thing I know for sure is if today were my last day on this here earth, I would have wanted to spend it with you, as your husband. Let's get married sooner rather than later," he insisted.

"Okay," I replied, slightly overwhelmed by Daniel's swift planning.

"So, we go to Geneva, I ask your Dad for your hand, then we take it from there," he said. He abruptly sat up in bed, hurting himself in the process, and wincing slightly from the pain. A moment later he was back to his plans. "Let's do it. Book the flights. Apply for our marriage licence. 72 hours. Fly back, get married. Let's do this while we can."

"It's not that simple, Daniel," I replied. "You may not be cleared to fly, having being injured and all, plus the police haven't caught whoever it was that did this to you."

"I'd put all bets on it being Duayne," he said abruptly.

"If that's the case, he's still at large," I warned.

"All the more reason for us to split. Go to Geneva for a while. See your folks, catch up with old friends..."

Jolène burst into the room and dashed to Daniel's side.

"I'm okay, Ma'," he said. "You're just the person I need here to convince this here lady of mine to quit town for a bit."

"Quit town?" she asked, alarmed. "Why would you want to do that!"

"To get married," he stated. "I was thinkin' we could go to Switzerland for a bit, meet her folks, I'd ask her Dad for her hand in marriage, then we'd elope?"

"No. You're havin' a proper wedding, right here in Texas," she insisted.

"Mom. With all due respect, it'll be our weddin' and we can have it anywhere we darn please, yes?"

"I've been waitin' for this for a long time now..." she argued.

"Temwani's been waitin' for this for a long time now too, Ma'. *I've* been waitin' for this for a long time."

I looked at the two of them fighting over logistical details. I was happy to do whatever, so long as my family and closest friends could be in attendance. "How about we do both?" I proposed. "A registry wedding in Switzerland, and one here in Texas?"

Daniel stared back at his mom for a moment then at me. "I can dig that."

"Whatever makes you happy," Jolène stated. "I'll be there."

"Good," I replied, happy the power paradigm had shifted back to Daniel and I.

"Craig's a hard man to pin down," Daniel advised. "He was in London for a bit last week, but should be back now. Maybe we can try reaching him again today?"

"I'll get in touch with him," I offered. I'd sent Johnny a message earlier about needing to hold fort at the office while Daniel was indisposed and Craig missing in action. Johnny was all too happy to oblige. "I gave him one of the spare keys," I mentioned.

Daniel stiffened slightly, then replied, "I trust in the fact that you trust him."

Jolène interrupted, "I sure hope he's not out there to use and abuse."

I rolled my eyes in response. "I'm pretty sure he's not," I replied hotly.

She opened her mouth to protest but Daniel put an end to it. "Make nice, will you?" he requested.

"Okay," she replied, taken aback at her son's resistance to her suggestions.

A bubbly young, brunette haired nurse popped in, and in good time. "Can I do a few checks on you now?" she asked of Daniel.

"Sure," he replied, straightening up slightly in bed.

"I see the ladies of your life are here, keeping you company," she said cheerfully, glancing quickly at the chart on the wall, before grabbing the folder at the end of his bed and making some quick notes before starting her observations.

"On a scale of 1-10, can you rate your pain level? 10 being very painful, 1 being not painful at all?"

"A 6," he replied. "Still a bit of pain in my shoulder. My chest hurts a bit too – it's been a bit hard to breathe."

"Okay," she replied. "I'll give you a top up on your pain meds." Her accent was decidedly and unreservedly English. "Your chest pain...you're asthmatic?"

"Yep," Daniel mentioned, surprising me. I hadn't seen any inhalers around the house at all. "I haven't had the need to take my meds for some time now..."

"You know you need to," she replied. "I'll get the doctor to write you up a new script for your preventer."

Daniel nodded in reply, and my heart heaved, feeling for him and having a sense of his mortality. I couldn't bear the thought of losing him.

"Blood pressure good, temperature okay. Doctor will be in shortly for a further evaluation," she promised.

"How soon can I leave?" Daniel asked anxiously.

"The doctor can have a chat to you about that," she replied evasively. "We do have to monitor you for a while longer." I could tell Daniel would rather be elsewhere. Lying in bed wasn't anything he'd be happy doing, even if it was for the purpose of him resting and recovering. Noting his disappointment, the nurse added, "Your wife's welcome to stay overnight here with you. You're also free to walk around when you wish."

Wife. He didn't correct her, and instead smiled at me intently. His mom, feeling left out, stated, "And I won't be going anywhere either."

The nurse smiled slyly, and winked at me inconspicuously. "Be sure to let the doctor know you'll be well taken care of at home, and he might consider an early discharge," she suggested, motioning her head towards me, to Jolène's dismay. She mothered Daniel too much, and I'm sure she would have wanted him at her's instead. All the same, despite her attitude being over the top at times, we both loved her for it. He needed her in his corner.

Johnny came by the hospital to check in on Daniel. Though he hadn't known either of us very long, he was turning out to be a good friend to us both.

"Hey buddy," he said, pulling up a stool and edging closer to Daniel's hospital bed. "Hi Teme," he said, nodding his head to me in acknowledgement.

"Hi Johnny. Thanks for earlier," I said in reply. I couldn't get in touch with Jude or Shania at the time, so I'd called him in my distress over Daniel getting shot. He'd come over straight away, and waited at my place while the police did a thorough search of the premises, cordoned off sections, and compiled evidence.

"Don't mention it," he replied. Turning to Daniel, he said, "You look like you're ready to take on the world," he joked, nudging him playfully in the ribs.

Daniel laughed in response. "I wish."

"Anything I can get you, mate?" Johnny asked.

"Some Texan style barbeque ribs, some kolashes, and an ice cold beer..."

"No beer while you're on your pain meds," I interjected, in protest.

"I'll see what I can do," Johnny said, adding "Okay, without the beer," when he felt my gaze stare him down.

My phone buzzed in my handbag, and I checked it immediately. An email confirmation had just come through re the background check we'd run on Johnny. Daniel wasn't aware that I'd briefly spoken with Johnny about his past. The background check was complete, and by the looks of it, it said nothing different from what he'd already told me.

"Anything I need to be aware of?" Daniel asked. He was too perceptive.

Johnny and I locked eyes for a moment before I offered, "The background check we ran on Johnny's come through."

Daniel shot me a strange look, wondering why I was mentioning it in front of Johnny.

"Johnny's told me a bit about his past," I explained. "I didn't think him knowing we were doing a check on him would be an issue."

"Okay," Daniel replied. "So, results are in? Do tell."

Johnny took a deep breath before stating, "So, a year ago I went off the deep end, got caught with some Coke and some

Molly or MDMA, at work. A couple of the guys in the firm I worked for were doing with, but I took the fall."

Daniel sighed deeply. "And?"

"They pinned me for supplying and using. I pleaded guilty, and cleaned up my act. At least I tried to. It's been a while since I last used."

"I see," Daniel replied, running his thumb over his chin which was lightly peppered with stubble.

"I don't see this as an issue – that and him working for you," I stated. "His work history is impeccable otherwise..."

"You don't have to explain," Daniel stated. "If you're alright with it, I'm alright with him working for the firm."

"Great," I replied.

"Thanks," Johnny said, slightly taken aback. "Though, I understand if you don't want to go any further with this. I understand your reputation is at stake, and you may not want to be associated with me..."

"Nonsense," Daniel replied, reaching for the TV remote. Ads were on, and it all suddenly seemed very loud. He turned down the volume. "I believe in redemption and starting over. I'm not going to stand in the way of that when it comes to you or anyone else for that matter."

A flash of emotion swept across Johnny's face, and his eyes briefly watered. He caught my gaze and averted eye contact immediately.

"Thanks for that. I'm forever in your debt," he said.

"I'll hold you to that," Daniel said in response, before adding, "Where's that ice cold beer you promised me..."

I raised a brow and kissed my teeth in response.

"Only kidding baby, only kidding," Daniel said. "An ice cold soda – a Dr. Pepper to be precise, would be real nice right about now."

Johnny stood up immediately. "I'll see what I can do mate," he vowed.

From the way Johnny jumped to fulfil Daniel's requests, I could tell from the start that the two of them together would be trouble.

6

KNOTS AND CROSSES

In the end, we took the 72 hour license option and made it official by tying the knot in a small low key ceremony. Just the two of us. Johnny was our witness.

The only word I could use to describe Daniel that morning as he stood before me at the altar was beautiful. His tanned skin shone a light bronze, his hair was trimmed with a few wayward curls loose. He had tears in his eyes when I stood before him, dressed in a white lace gown. "You're absolutely breathtaking," he said. "I can't believe you'll be all mine, forever."

"You're beautiful and our love is beautiful," I told him. "I can't wait for you to be mine as well. I can't wait to be Mrs. Brennan."

The Minister said a blessing over us both. "Take these rings as a symbol of your undying and eternal love for each other. May your love never wane, may it always trust, may it always hope, and may it always believe."

And so we became one. Mr. Daniel Josiah Brennan and I.

"I don't have much disposable cash, but I managed a little something for you," Johnny stated after the ceremony.

"Now, both of you, don't turn around until I tell you to," he requested, dashing off momentarily.

We didn't have to turn around. The hum of the car's motor told me his surprise had something to do with a classic car. The hum came to a halt, and Johnny got out.

"Turn around now," Johnny requested. We turned around to see a freshly polished Shelby Cobra adorned with ribbons.

"Yours until you're back from your honeymoon," he announced, handing Daniel the keys to his Shelby Cobra.

Daniel, clearly touched, hugged him deeply. "Thank you man," he stated.

"Congratulations to you both," Johnny stated, giving me a kiss on either cheek. "Wishing you every happiness, and every success. You deserve it."

Turning to me, Daniel offered, "Give me your hand beautiful girl."

Our first night as a married couple was spent at a small beach cove resort a stone's throw away from Galveston Island. As we made our way up to our floor via the elevator, Daniel could not keep his hands off me. We weren't alone for long. The lift stopped and a woman in the lift commented, "Beautiful dress".

"Beautiful bride", Daniel said in response.

"Beautiful babies," the woman replied.

"Touché," Daniel stated, blushing slightly. "I can't wait to get my hands on you," he whispered in my ear.

The woman stepped out of the lift. Daniel hastily pressed for the doors to close.

Our room was on the 10th floor, at the far end of the corridor. I followed after him, the train of my dress floating lightly behind me. "Slow down will you?" I requested as he dashed through the hall, my hand in his, anxious to get me alone.

"Room 1063," he announced once we got there. Swiping the door open, in a move that took my breath away, he swept me off the floor and into his arms and over the threshold of the door.

"Daniel!" I exclaimed.

"Happily ever after," he stated, grinning from ear to ear. He walked a few steps before putting me down. "I will never stop loving you."

"Nor I you," I said.

"Things will inevitably change, but my love is here to stay," he declared. "I promise you this." After a while, he stated, "A little less conversation?"

I laughed heartily. "You certainly know the right things to say and when to say them, I'll give you that."

"What else will you give me, huh? Huh?" he said jokingly.

"Well if you help me get out of this dress I'll show you."

His hands fumbled at the hem of my dress. Loosening the corset's strings he kissed me fully and deeply. "You were well and truly worth the wait," he whispered.

As we lay in bed, Daniel's phone buzzed on the bedside table. A rude awakening in the midst of quiet. Daniel stirred slightly, eventually yet reluctantly reaching for the phone. Sleepily reading the message, the contents of the message caused him to fully wake up.

"Here we go," he stated, placing the phone back on the bedside table.

"Who is it?" I asked.

"The Jilted Lover strikes again."

"Why, what's he saying now?" I questioned.

Daniel handed me his phone. The message read:

Well, you've certainly outdone yourself this time.

A second message came through moments later:

I suppose congratulations are in order, though, I loved her first. This won't last.

"Did you see this other message?" I asked, handing the phone back to him.

He read it and sighed heavily. "He really needs to step off."

"Well, we *are* together for life now," I reminded him.

"I'm not gonna let this continue, he said adamantly, typing a message back in reply:

What God has put together, let no man tear asunder.

He showed me what he typed before sending it off. Moments later, another message came through:

What makes you think God intended you and her to be together and not her and I? I loved her first.

I saw anger rise in Daniel as he hurriedly dialed the number he'd received the message from. The phone rang several times before reaching a message bank service, in German. Daniel angrily typed back another text message:

I'm her husband now, and she's my wife.

The message in reply was:

She'll always be my first love, and I dare say I'll always be hers.

"Come on now!" Daniel exclaimed in frustration, before asking, "Temwani, are you sure you don't know who this is?"

I closed my eyes and paused for a moment in quiet thought. *You'll always be my first love,* he'd said. I could hear his voice clearly as though it were yesterday. I was reminded of a prospective love lost, and a dream romance that did not eventuate many years ago when I was in Australia. The man in question had adored me, and had worshipped the ground I walked on. I was not ready for him at the time, and it had been a while since I'd thought of him. At the time, I hadn't any interest of remaining in Australia long term after I'd completed my studies, so any relationship that might have eventuated, might not have lasted. At least this was how I felt at the time. Despite the passage of time, thoughts of David pervaded my mind when I was lonely. At those times, I wondered how my life would have been had I taken a chance on him. I hadn't felt lonely for a time, and as such, I hadn't thought of him for a time.

"Seems to me you do know who he is," Daniel concluded, interrupting me in thought. "Am I wrong?"

I didn't want to acknowledge it, but he was right. "There's a guy I knew in Australia many years back who did say I was his first love. No one else has ever said that to me. We never dated, we just – hung out. He tried to convince me to be with him, while I largely avoided falling in love with him," I told Daniel.

Daniel raised a brow and shook his head. "What's his name?"

"David," I replied quickly.

"So...he's Australian?"

I nodded to the affirmative.

"How long ago was this?"

"2004. Twelve years ago."

"Sounds like he was smitten by you," he managed. "I don't blame him, but you're mine now, and he needs to back off."

"Let me..." I started, asking him to give me his mobile phone. I typed out a text:

David. I'm with Daniel now. I'm happy. I've found my happiness with him.

An instant reply came back:

Given half a chance, I know you'd be happier with me.

"Show me?" Daniel insisted. He didn't like what he read. In his ire, he vigorously texted David back:

Stop being such a coward, come out of the shadows and make yourself known.

David's reply came through with equal vigor:

A coward is not anything that I am. Lurking in the shadows is not what I do. I'll make myself known to you in due course. Be careful what you wish for. She might just end up falling in love with me again and out of love with you.

No chance of that. Daniel replied.

David's response was:

All's fair in love and war.

"I'm switching this here phone off," Daniel said, in frustration, quickly turning off the phone, as though he were afraid of what would come next. He placed it on the far end of the bedside table.

"I wish I'd known about your history with him," he stated, suddenly.

"I'm sorry Daniel, I didn't think there was anything to talk about. As I said, we weren't even together. If circumstance had allowed, we might've been an item, but we weren't. I'm with you now, and I promised to love you forever," I reminded him, initiating a deep kiss which took the look of worry out of his eyes. My eyes meeting his, I set his hand on my heart. "I'm all yours," I told him. "No one can hold a candle to you."

He returned my kiss with deep intensity, and we molded into one another, rising and falling like the Texas sun would meet the horizon. I was his, and he was mine, for all time.

"I feel as though I'm about to lose you," Daniel stated as we lay in bed together, sated after our lovemaking.

"I'm not going anywhere, baby."

"This man that loves you so deeply he'd pay me fifty thousand dollars just to ensure your safety – I don't know how comfortable I feel knowing he's aware of our every move. I also don't like the fact that he thinks there's some kind of battle on for your love. The way I see it, he lucked out and that boat sailed a long time ago. You're with me now, and he needs to leave well enough alone. I didn't like his last message one last bit," he admitted.

"I hear you," I replied. "As I said before, I'm not going anywhere."

He turned to lie on his side and ran a hand along my belly, tracing a circle around my navel.

"How long do you want us to wait before we have babies?"

Babies, I thought to myself. "If it wasn't for Jensen, I'd say we could try straight away, but knowing Jensen..."

"Quit prosecutions, come work for my firm," he suggested.

"That's tempting, but I'm going to have to think it over."

Running a hand through his sun kissed hair which now had streaks of auburn running through it, he stated, "I can't get over how this David guy is so into you. After so many years. I don't know how he knew you needed help when you did, but I don't like his attitude one bit."

"Don't worry about it Daniel. Don't let him get to you," I advised.

"Where's Goliath when you need him!" he said absently.

"Daniel!" I exclaimed.

"I know, I know. We all know that David wins over Goliath anyhow. I just wish I could do something to scare him away or put him off you. It seems the closer we become, the more he wants you."

"I'm not worried," I told him. "The David I knew wouldn't hurt a fly."

"Maybe he's changed."

"If he cares anything for me, he'll respect that I'm with you now."

"Oh, I don't doubt that he cares for you. I just don't think he respects me at all," he stated.

"Okay. This is our night. We're married. Let's focus on us," I advised.

"I can dig that," he replied, tracing my lips with his finger, before he planted a kiss on my cheek then reached over for the phone again.

"Couldn't resist, could you?" I noted.

"This ain't fair. It's our wedding night, and he's come to crash the celebration."

"Don't let him ruin this for us," I begged.

He nodded in response, absently, while he scrolled through the phone messages.

A text message came through as he did:

Temwani, I should have grabbed a hold of you with both hands while I had a chance.

Daniel typed back:

BACK OFF.

David replied:

She may be with you now, but I'll take friendship with her any day.

"Friendship my ass," Daniel spoke out loud, clearly annoyed. "I'm sick of this. This has to end."

"Give me the phone," I requested. "I'll ask him to stop."

Daniel reluctantly handed me the phone. I typed:

David, if you care anything for me, please stop tormenting Daniel.

David replied, *I can't help how I feel about you, and I can't help how he'll respond.*

David, I know you're bigger than this, I replied.

Moments passed before David stated:

As I said, I'll take friendship any day, if it means me being a firm part of your life.

"Show me?" Daniel insisted. He read the messages and shook his head in response. "So much for you shutting this down."

I rolled my eyes in response. "I'm trying Daniel. I'm trying."

Another message came through. Daniel still had the phone in his hand.

I'll be seeing you. The message read.

Of course, Daniel couldn't resist responding:

Not if I have anything to say about this.

David replied:

Right. This is getting old. She can be friends with whoever she wishes to be friends with. I'll be seeing you, David replied again, then there was silence. No more messages.

"I'm pouring me a drink," Daniel announced. "This whole ordeal's got me reeling."

"Don't take it personal Daniel."

"It's hard not to," he stated. "He's still completely en-amoured by you, and yet you're saying nothing happened between you two."

"Nothing did, apart from sparks flying from his end," I said.

"I understand how he feels. It's just..." he started. "You're mine now." He grabbed two tumblers off the bench and filled them with ice from the dispenser. "You're mine, and I'm yours, and I'm not planning on letting you go." A bottle of passionfruit flavored Alizé caught his eye. "A bit of Alizé?" he asked.

"I don't see why not?" I said, a little concerned about David's insistence but wanting to get back to enjoying our first night of married bliss.

Daniel joined me back on the bed, and handed me the glass of Alizé. "To us," he toasted, raising his glass to meet mine.

"To us," I echoed. We locked arms, and he drank from my glass and I his. I nearly spilt my drink all over him. He laughed heartily.

"Seems like a little sexy time is in order," he said, taking my glass from me and placing it on the bedside table. "How about we try something different this time? Like, I don't know...something unconventional?"

"You're going to have to show me," I said, laughing lightly. I was happy. For the first time in a long time, I had found happiness and love in the most unexpected of places. Just as he wasn't planning on letting me go, I wasn't planning on letting him go.

7

HEAT ON

Our week away on honeymoon seemed too short. While Daniel busied himself with investigative work, I threw myself back into work at the prosecutor's office. Problem was, I no longer enjoyed working as a prosecutor, and as such, I was feeling the heat on my return to the office. Though Daniel was a formidable lawyer, by virtue of my marriage to him, I became the enemy. With the exception of the occasional company and camaraderie of Jude, Ernesto, Sylvia, Malik and Sarah, I found myself isolated and essentially a *persona non grata*.

The final case I worked with Ernesto solidified the feeling of disquiet and unease that I felt in my role as prosecutor. Ernesto delivered his usual sharp, concise closing argument and the jury convicted the defendant, a senior lawyer, as predicted. Despite his plea of guilty, and no prior history of offending, we secured a conviction of years as opposed to months, in addition to disbarment.

"Well played Counsellor," Ernesto said to me, as the defendant was being led away from the court room's dock.

I nodded in response. "You were brilliant," I told him. "As

per usual. No surprises there."

I didn't feel triumphant. He sensed my sadness and stated, "You know, when you get to the top, you'll find you have fewer friends."

"You would know," I stated, somewhat sarcastically. "You might have few friends, yet you're admired by almost everyone around here and beyond. Meanwhile, I've lucked out in the popularity contest."

He ran a hand through his jet black hair and stated, "Well, you becoming Mrs. Daniel Brennan didn't help the situation," he advised. "Still, you deserve happiness, and if he can give it to you, everyone else can be damned."

I smiled at his remark. "Thank you, Ernesto."

"No need to thank me," he stated. "I know how you feel, but leaving now, is it the right thing to do?"

"I can't see any way I can stay," I said.

"Well, you'll always have a home here," he reminded me. "Might be a chance for you to work in a new area of law, maybe have some babies, and come back refreshed..."

I rolled my eyes at the mention of babies.

"Enjoy your marriage," he said. "I wish I'd enjoyed mine," he mentioned, referring to his previous marriage to Jamila. Jamila had since moved on and married Kevin, an attorney at the Public Defender's office.

"Thank you Ernesto," I said. That afternoon would be my last afternoon at the District Attorney's office.

I browsed through one last file that afternoon. The one Jude had been trying to get me to have a look at for time.

A series of vigilante style crimes were occurring regularly

enough that it wouldn't be hard to conceive that they were linked. The file Jude asked me to look at linked the more recent crimes to offences committed against children and the offenders who committed them. A community centre frequented by newly released offenders had been burnt down to the ground.

I wrote a note advising for a thorough investigation to be carried out, one which would involve revisiting the scene and rechecking the fingerprint samples that were found at the scene, lifted from a silver lighter. The lighter itself was of interest. The letter B was engraved into it, along with a symbol I didn't recognize.

A knock at the door startled me. It was Jude.

"Congrats on the win," he said. "Though you don't seem too happy darl'. What's going on?"

"The usual," I told him. "You know."

"No, I don't know. You haven't confided in me in a long time." Motioning towards the armchairs by the bay window, he directed, "Come, let's sit."

I reluctantly tore away from the file I'd been reading. *He is going to find out sooner or later, you may as well tell him now.*

"Jude..."

"Temwani..."

We spoke at the same time.

"You first," he said.

"Things haven't been the same since I took that leave of absence a few months ago."

"Well, you can expect that. You're our star prosecutor, and when you left without notice, there were big shoes to fill. Everyone else had to work on your files, and let's just say, not everyone can handle the heat," he explained.

I nodded in response.

"I know why you disappeared," he stated. "I found out on my own. I'm sorry I couldn't have been there to help you," he said, resting a hand on my hand and squeezing lightly.

I felt my eyes well up with tears.

"He won't get away with this," Jude promised.

"I'm not filing charges against him."

"*We* can, with the police. *I will pursue this*, on behalf of this office."

"Jude..." I turned away from him, in tears. "I've lost so much already, I don't need to be humiliated further."

"I understand your position, but..."

"Don't," I warned, getting up abruptly.

He stood up with me. "Sorry Teme, I didn't mean to upset you like this. Please sit down," he requested.

I stood there for a moment, wiping tears out of my eyes with the palm of my hand, grateful I was wearing waterproof mascara. My face would be a mess otherwise.

"I'm resigning from my role as prosecutor, today," I told him, sitting back down.

Shock swept across his face. "That's a little rash, isn't it?"

"No, I wouldn't say so," I told him. "I'm tired of having to deal with the judgement, and Jensen, well, she's unrelenting."

"Teme, you're an amazing prosecutor. Don't walk away from this. We need you. *I* need you," he said.

"You're being dramatic, Jude," I replied. "You'll manage just fine without me."

"I'm being serious Temwani. Who am I going to call up in the middle of the night when I'm stuck on the application of a point of law?"

"You'll get by, Jude," I assured him.

"I'll be missing you," he declared. "I am after all, your work husband. This being said, I expressly forbid you from doing anything to break up this here union of ours."

I laughed lightheartedly in response. Jude adored me, and had taken pains to let me know over the years, just how he felt. Still, we were just friends, and would always be just friends.

"Jude, I'll miss you too. I'm only a phone call away though," I reminded him.

"True, but we both know how these things work. The calls will get fewer and fewer in between, until they are no more," he predicted.

"I won't let that happen," I told him.

"I'll hold you to it," he said, leaning back into the armchair. "Ernesto will be cut."

"He knew my plans before I even said anything. He thinks I'll be back in no time."

"Well, I hope he's right," Jude stated. "So, when's your last day?"

"Today."

"Whoa. That's too soon."

"It couldn't be soon enough for me," I told him.

He stroked his chin anxiously. "Surely things can't be that bad?"

"You don't know what it's like, Jude. It feels like I'm public enemy number one around here. Me changing my name to Brennan hasn't helped none."

"Oh, that," Jude replied, his eyes narrowing. "He upset a few people around here as a defense attorney."

"Sounds to me like he was just doing his job. If we don't

have enough evidence to convict, we shouldn't be wasting any time or resources pursuing matters and seeking to prosecute," I said sharply.

"Understood, but it's complicated. You haven't seen the files," he rationalized. "He's suspended for a reason."

I raised a brow in response.

"Anyway."

"Anyway," I replied.

"Are you pregnant?" Jude asked all of a sudden.

I couldn't hide my shock.

"You've got that glow about you, and all this rash decision making's gotta be coming from somewhere else."

I was a few days late with my period, but didn't consider it to be unusual. I'd put the lateness down to stress.

"I've seen you two together. I'd say you'd get pregnant just by looking at each other."

"Jude." I rolled my eyes in response.

"Okay, I'll give it a rest," he promised. "I just think you need to rethink leaving. Maybe just take time off and come back when you're ready to."

"Jensen will just love that," I said sarcastically. "I've had just about all the time off I can take."

"I hear you," Jude said sadly. "I'll miss you terribly if you leave for good though."

I leaned in to hug him, and we held each other for a moment.

"So, if you're not pregnant, let's have a few drinks afterwards?"

I nodded in response. Being pregnant was a possibility not a probability. "Okay."

"Good," he said, somewhat satisfied. "So, you've had a

look at my file?" he asked. "What do you make of it."

"It's a bit of a worry," I stated. "Vigilante justice?"

"Certainly seems that way."

"Have you seen the lighter?" I asked.

"I have."

"Mention was made of a symbol on the Zippo lighter. Anything of note?"

"I didn't get a chance to look at it in detail, Murph was all up in my face about staying out of the evidence room, and looking at the photos instead. The symbol's unclear from the photo, but when I looked at it in the evidence room, it's a 3D hologram image of a sundial."

"A sundial? Strange."

"That's what I thought too. Except this sundial is exactly like the one near London Bridge," he said, taking out his mobile phone to scroll through some photos. "Here. This one."

I agreed with him, and pondered on the significance of it.

"So, perhaps there's some link to London?" he conjectured.

"Hm... but do you think it would've been left there intentionally?"

"No," he said abruptly. "Not intentionally. Whoever it was, they got careless, I think." Closing the file, he stated, "Let's do this. Pregnancy test, drinks and food. In that order."

"You're not letting this go, are you?" I asked, referring to his hunch that I was pregnant.

"You know me, Teme, once I get an idea, I'll run with it and see it through. So chop chop, let's get going."

I sighed in response. I needed to call Daniel and let him know I'd be running late, but first I needed to draft my resignation letter.

Jude was still in my office when I rang Daniel up.

"Howdy," he answered. "What's up?"

"I'll be a little delayed coming home tonight."

"Oh?"

"Just having drinks with a friend," I told him.

"What's the occasion?" he asked.

"Do I need an occasion?" I snapped.

Silence met me on the other end of the line. "Just asking," he said after a pregnant pause.

"I'm handing in my resignation in a few," I told him.

More silence ensued, then, "Is this something we can talk about before you do?"

"No," I told him.

"I think we should talk about this," Daniel insisted.

"Look. I've made up my mind. It's my career, my life."

"Our life, you mean," he interjected.

"Whatever."

Another pause before he replied, "Okay, let me know where you'll be, and when you'll be done, and I'll be there to take you home."

"Thank you baby," I said, almost in tears.

"We'll get through this," he stated. "You and I," he added, for extra emphasis. "See you then, baby. Love you."

"I love you too," I replied, ending the call.

"All good," I said, placing my mobile back on the table and turning to Jude.

"Good," he replied. "So, first stop, the pharmacy or wherever else it is you can pick up a pregnancy test."

"Jude, that's pretty presumptuous of you."

"Not at all," he replied. "I'm just looking out for you. Don't want you drinking while you're pregnant," he explained. "Besides, if you're pregnant now, and you hand in your resignation now, you'll forfeit all that time you've built up to specifically allow for you to take maternity leave."

The thought hadn't crossed my mind, mainly because pregnancy hadn't crossed my mind. Up until Jude had mentioned it.

"It'd look pretty strange if I went to the shops to get something like that on my own."

"Jude, quit it please."

"I'm being serious Teme. No drinks tonight unless you do. I tell you, you are."

I did a quick once over of my office. Everything I had would fit into a small box.

"When do you plan on telling Jensen?"

"I'm emailing her now," I said nonchalantly.

Jude arched forward in his chair and slipped off his glasses. "You can't be serious!"

"I'm dead serious."

"Okay," he said, standing up. "I'll be back in a few. I'll help you pack when I'm back," he offered.

Jude came back with some Boules de Berlin, some flavored mineral water, and three different pregnancy tests.

"Go on then," he urged.

"Jensen first," I replied.

"You're so stubborn, Temwani."

"You're so persistent, Jude.

"You do know how babies are made, don't you?" he asked.

"Of course I do, Jude! What kind of a silly question is that!" I exclaimed.

"Well, you're either trying for a baby or you're not, right?"

"It isn't that simple. If you must know, we use protection all the time but there have been a few accidents if you know what I mean. He's very well endowed. Anyway, neither one of us believes in the morning after pill so..." I explained.

"Right," he replied, getting the picture. "Go on then, find out now. The sooner you know the better off I'd be..."

"Hm... The better off you'd be? How'd you figure that?"

"I find out whether you're definitely staying or whether you're going. Just do the test now, will you?"

"Okay," I replied, clicking the send button on my email to Jensen, then slipping the tests into my handbag and heading for the toilet.

A pale pink line shone on one test, a deep blue line on the other, and the word "*Pregnant*" appeared on the final test. Pregnant was the last thing I'd expected to be, but I quietly felt excited over the fact that I was carrying Daniel's baby. Having said that, I was also shocked. Jude had been right. Shooting off that email to Jensen just then and there might not have been the best thing to do. Daniel was suspended pending finalization of investigations, and it wasn't clear how well his private investigations business was doing. The fifty thousand dollars he'd received from saving me was slowly running out. Leaving work at that time may not have been the right thing to do. This said, I wasn't certain I could last a few more months, let alone weeks and days in the District Attorney's office. Me being pregnant would not

125

change my feeling. I had to leave.

The look on my face would have said it all. "I knew it!" Jude said, pumping a fist in the air, before offering an over enthusiastic congratulations. "So, you get to stay, right?"

I shook my head in response. "I've already sent through my resignation letter. I'm leaving."

He swore under his breath. "Come on Teme!"

"Jude, I planned to leave anyhow. Nothing and no one can convince me to stay at this stage."

"Shame I couldn't convince you to stay," he replied. "On my own, I'll be like Starsky without Hutch."

I giggled in reply. "Don't be so dramatic Jude. You'll be fine without me here."

"Clyde without Bonney."

"Jude."

"Mulder without Scully," he said.

"Jude!"

He smiled in earnest, and spoke with a tinge of sadness. "You get the picture, right? I'll be lost without you here."

"Jude, you'll manage fine without me here."

"So the divorce is final," he stated. My heart sunk at the mention of the word divorce.

"What are you talking about?" I asked.

"There's no turning back now, our divorce is final right?"

"Jude, what are you on about?" I asked, organizing the files on my desk.

"Our divorce. I *have* been your work husband for five years now, and I'm sad this will be ending in divorce."

"Jude... this isn't the end of the world as we know it. I'm leaving work, yes, I'm not leaving you."

My phone rang. *Jensen.* I didn't pick up.

"She must be ropeable," Jude conjectured.

Not long after, a knock came on my door. Charlotte, a new intern who'd been working closely with Jensen, stood there, with a message from Jensen Almighty.

"Jensen has asked that you make your office available by the end of the week."

Jude didn't hide his displeasure. "Bloody 'ell."

"Tell her the office will be available tomorrow," I retorted.

Jude gasped out loud. "For goodness sakes Teme."

"Everything I need to take with me will fit into a small box," I told him. "In fact, tell her I'll give the keys back to security before I leave today."

Charlotte stood there for a while longer than she needed to as though to say, *Don't shoot the messenger.* Nervously wrapping her blond hair around a finger before tucking it behind her ear, she stated, "Okay. I tell her." *A day with Jensen was all it took*, I thought to myself. She looked worn out and worn down.

"How about you join us for drinks?" Jude proposed, breaking the ice.

"I'm not sure...I..." she commenced.

"Go on, you know you want to," Jude said, giving her a wink.

"Okay," she said, smiling prettily, for Jude's benefit I was sure. "I'll just tell Jensen..."

"No hard feelings," I told her. "See you in a bit."

When she was gone, I turned to Jude. "Forget drinks. Let's go dancing!"

He threw his head back in laughter. "You're something else Teme and I love you for it."

My office was packed up in no time, and by the end of the evening, Jude had self-appointed himself Godfather of the child I was carrying.

Daniel seemed to be in a bit of a huff when he picked me up that evening. He wasn't very good at hiding his displeasure.

"You leaving the D.A.'s office, that's a little sudden," he stated. "We could've talked about this beforehand."

"I'm done talking about this."

We drove in silence.

"How was your day?" I asked.

"Nothing to report," he answered abruptly.

"Don't give me attitude, please," I told him.

"Pot calling a kettle black, yes?"

"What's your problem, Daniel?"

"You wouldn't understand," he replied.

"Try me."

"Your *friends* at the D.A.'s office are unrelenting. They're out for blood," he explained.

"So, you fight it. You know, you still haven't told me about what happened in the first place."

"I thought your friends would have enlightened you by now," he replied, somewhat angrily.

I lost it. "My friends have been nothing but supportive of you. I'd appreciate it if you'd talk about them with a little more respect than that."

"Right," Daniel replied, sharply.

"Look. I've had a busy day – a difficult day, and I don't need you adding to it."

"Likewise," he replied.

"I don't need this," I told him.

"Temwani, let's not fight," he requested.

I was tired and annoyed. The moment he pulled into the driveway, I wretched the car door open and got out of the car, shocking him.

"Come on now," he stated, following me through the front door. "What's the problem anyway. Time of the month?"

I kissed my teeth in response as I threw my coat over the coat rack. "Really?"

"Sorry babe. Slip of the tongue," he said apologetically. "I didn't mean to..."

"Are you kidding me?" I questioned in disbelief. "You know what Daniel? Take your stuff and go. You're no better than the men I've been with in the past." I regretted those words the moment I'd said them.

A flash of pain swept across his face as he registered what I'd just said. "Alright," he said. "I'll go."

"No. *I'll* leave." Without further thought, I spun around on my heels, grabbed my handbag and decided to spend a night or two at the local hotel. I would be back, just not that night.

"Baby, don't go," he begged.

"I'm out," I told him, slipping past him and down the corridor.

He stood there stunned, as I walked out the door. I speed dialled a taxi which arrived not long after. I planned to stay away from home for a few days and to work at depending on myself again. I was carrying his baby, but felt the need to do things alone. For the moment at least.

8

JUSTICE SERVED

I checked into a hotel not far from home that night. Exhausted, I slept immediately my head touched the pillow. The next morning, I woke to a series of messages from Daniel. In my state of exhaustion, I hadn't heard them come through the night before. I checked in with Facebook, and instantly a chat commenced. I should have disabled the chat function as I wasn't prepared to talk to Daniel just yet.

How are you? You're hard to come by, he said.

Been busy. I'm fine, thanks for asking. I replied.

We're still married you know, he said.

Tell me something I don't know, I challenged.

Come home, he insisted. *Can we take this offline? Can I call you?*

I don't need your drama, I replied.

Never said anything about drama, he said.

You are drama, I said.

Please, he begged, after a slight pause.

Okay, see you at home, tonight, I replied.

Okay. See you then, he replied. *I love you.*

I love you too, I wanted to type back, but I didn't. Being stubborn got the better of me, and I knew my not replying in kind would cut him. I loved him dearly, but I hated his short temperedness, directed at me.

In my heart, I knew we'd be back together in no time. I'd break the news that I was expecting, and we'd straighten things out, get back to where we both belonged.

I showered quickly and decided to check out of the hotel by midday. I still had clothes at my apartment which I could quickly get. I called Jude, and he came up to meet me at the hotel in a hurry.

"You could've stayed at mine," he stated. "Were things that bad last night?"

"In retrospect, no," I replied. "Daniel's a bit of a hothead, and I just needed a moment alone to collect myself," I told him.

"Didn't you know Mr. Brennan was a bit of a hothead?"

"No," I told him. "I guess you'd know all about it, given you guys initiated further proceedings against him. He was pretty annoyed last night, mentioned something about you all being out for blood."

"*You all* used to be you as well, yes? You used to be part of the same team?"

"Used to be is the operative phrase," I reminded him.

"Okay," Jude acknowledged. "If it'll make you happy, I'll wash my hands clean of his matter, though in doing so, I can't guarantee Jensen won't get involved," he said. "In fact, I can almost guarantee that she will get involved now, since she's pretty peeved you've left."

"She won't win," I replied. "Daniel hasn't said much at all about what happened, but the truth will prevail. You know

I'm right."

Jude nodded, wholeheartedly agreeing with me.

"Truth doesn't pick sides," I added.

"True that," he replied, walking around the hotel room as though he would notice anything of note. "On another note, apart from the argument you two had last night, you've been happy?"

"Very," I told him. "You know we haven't spent a night apart since we met.

"Awe, that's sweet," he said sarcastically. "I'm sure he was missing you," he assumed. "So, where to now?" he asked.

"My apartment," I requested. I hadn't been there since Daniel had been shot.

"I thought you'd given back your keys and all?" he asked, surprised.

"I'd planned to, but Daniel got shot and all..."

"Sure," he replied. "Ernesto's got carriage of that matter," he advised. "Seems like something Duayne would do."

I nodded in agreement.

"Anyhow, the sooner you're out of there, the better."

"Yep," I agreed, he was completely right about that.

We got there in no time. The apartment was no longer cordoned off and marked. Inside, it seemed cold, empty and soul-less. Everything was as we'd left it last.

"How about we organize a removalist today, get everything out?"

"Okay." I liked his thinking. For as long as I'd known him, Jude made things happen. Quickly. He didn't waste any time.

"I'll call up some guys now, everything you own here will be out by this afternoon," he promised. "Time to move on," he added, before pulling me in for a hug. "Duayne will be sorry he hurt you. Anyone who messes with you, messes with me. Mr. Brennan included," he said, surprisingly. As we walked out of the apartment and back to his car, he asked bluntly, "I gather you're going to work for him now?"

"I've considered it," I replied.

He nodded again before stating, "Just don't forget I'm not the enemy. Neither is Ernesto. No matter where you are, you can call on us, and you can always come back," he assured me.

"Thank you Jude."

"Jensen's not going to be D.A. for long," he predicted.

"Oh?"

"You didn't hear it from me," he stated, going before me, opening the passenger door of his Saab and sliding my duffle bag with clothes onto the back seat. "Ernesto wants you back on board when she's gone," he announced.

"Interesting," was all I could say.

"Once a prosecutor, always a prosecutor." Jude said with finality.

Jude dropped me off at home, and I quickly jumped into my car without going inside the house. Daniel didn't appear to be home, but just in case he was, I wanted to avoid talking to him until that evening.

With Jude having to return back to work, I called on Shania to accompany me to the doctor's to confirm my pregnancy via ultrasound. She left the beauty shop in a hurry, agreeing to meet me there.

The quick trip to the doctor revealed that I was indeed pregnant – 6 weeks along, and not with just one, but with two babies. Shania burst into excited chatter. "Omg, Omg, Omg!!!" she started. "I knew you would get pregnant just by looking at each other! Twins, wow, you must've been doin' a lot of looking!"

The technician and I burst into laughter. "Any twins in the family?" he asked, mid chuckle.

"My husband's an only child, and from my side, no twins."

"Interesting," he said, wiping the gel off the Doppler, and writing a few notes down. "Please book in to see an obstetrician and look at managing the pregnancy that way." I rolled my shirt down over my belly, elated at the fact that Daniel and I were going to be parents.

I drove to Daniel's firm afterwards, in hopes I could catch up with Craig. I caught him on his way out, he met me at the door.

"How are we?" he asked, reaching out to shake my hand. I shook his hand, immediately noticing the strength behind him. "Sorry, busy afternoon and I'm on my way out now," he said, casting a contemplative glance my way before looking at his wristwatch. "It's 5.30 pm now. How about we discuss this over dinner?" he offered.

"Sure." *If I can stomach it*, I thought.

"There's a brilliant Japanese restaurant just down the road...," he started then stopped suddenly. "You expecting? When are you due?" he asked.

Craig caught me unawares with his abruptness and awareness. "Not a lot gets past me," he said, smiling. "I can see it in your face. You've got a secret." He noted. "Or two. But don't we all."

"Only a few weeks now," I responded, despite hoping I could keep it a secret for much longer.

"Congrats to you and yours," he said heartily. "So, no Sushi tonight, but there is Teppanyaki," he said.

I felt a tinge of sadness. I'd wanted to share the news with Daniel first, but after the way we left things last night, he wouldn't be the first to know.

"Let's do this," Craig said, interrupting my thoughts.

"Try some ginger and lemon tea," he suggested. "The nausea should ease up in a few weeks, by the end of your first trimester."

I stopped, for a moment. "Is it that obvious I'm pregnant?"

"Not obvious, no," he confirmed. "Though not a lot gets past me," he stated as a matter of factly. "Your secret's safe with me."

"Who says I'm keeping secrets?"

"Not a lot gets past me," he repeated.

Changing topic he asked, "Tell me about the moment you decided you no longer wanted to be a prosecutor."

I did. I had been so proud of being a prosecutor until that day. I never would forget the day the former attorney was being led from the docks to spend five years in prison for misappropriating a client's funds whilst he was in the throes of depression. Since that day, my work as a prosecutor had a lacklustre tinge. It was no longer us against them. I started to feel as though there was no humanity in the work I did as a prosecutor. No middle ground.

"You'd make a brilliant defence lawyer," he declared. "Are you prepared to have your former colleagues see you as the enemy? Are you prepared to lose your good standing with the bench? You won't be one of their favourite prosecutors anymore. You'll likely be a thorn in the side of a lot of people."

"I'm prepared. It's either all in or all out, and I'm all in."

"Great," Craig stated, adjusting his glasses. Steely blue eyes gazed into me and I looked away.

"There isn't much point in avoiding Daniel," he advised. "He loves you deeply."

I shrugged in response. "He needs to cool off," I stated.

"He's only human," Craig reminded me, talking a large swig of water from his tumbler. "He's bound to make mistakes."

I placed a hand on my belly, thinking of the fact that I hadn't even told Daniel that I was expecting.

"I won't say a thing, but please don't delay in telling him," he urged. "Life is short, time is fleeting." Craig had a way of putting things that encouraged one to be spurred into action. "So, tomorrow, 9 am?" he suggested as a start time. "Daniel's been a silent partner after the board's determination, and I make *most* of the decisions around here, if not all of them."

Interesting. "I'll be in a little after 9 am, I told him. "If that's okay. I'll be at the doctor's."

"Not a problem at all," he said. "As I mentioned, things are pretty relaxed around work, though communication is key." Settling the bill, I noticed a concerned look on his face. "I think I need to go back to the office, I left a critical file there. Got distracted I guess."

"Oh okay."

"Yes, you're quite the distraction," he joked.

I smiled in response, not knowing how to take him or where to place him.

"I can show you around while we're at it, just in case I'm not in first thing, though Johnny knows the deal, and can show you the ropes," he said.

I hoped I would fit into work as a defense attorney, and felt relieved and optimistic that I'd be working with Craig, and

Johnny.

Time was getting on, but I knew Daniel would be at home when I got back. I agreed to go back to the office with Craig.

Johnny wasn't around when I'd stopped by earlier on, which had me wondering at the time, whether he was with Daniel. He was there when Craig and I went back though, perusing a few files. Boxes of files filled one room. "Discovery," he noted. "How are you Teme?" he asked. I could hear concern in his voice.

"She'll be working with us from tomorrow onwards," Craig announced.

"Right!" Johnny exclaimed, somewhat excited at the prospect. "Well, we could certainly use the help. "I gather you left prosecutions for good?"

Craig answered for me. "Counsellor doesn't plan to return to working for that office any time soon."

"Good o'," Johnny stated, wanting to say more but Craig cut him off.

"You had dinner?" Craig asked.

"I had something earlier, with Daniel," he said, casting a glance my way.

"Good then. I'll be here for a little longer, use the time to get through what you can then we'll call it a day," he proposed, turning on the TV.

"Alright then," Johnny replied.

"A community housing project which served as a home for convicted sex offenders has been burnt down to the ground," the news presenter announced.

"All's well ends well," Craig stated.

I raised a brow in response.

"While no one was injured, the patron of the centre says it was a low blow, devastating a community that is already devastated," the presenter continued.

"They have nowhere else to go!" a patron of the community centre stated.

Craig abruptly flipped channel. "Shouldn't have been committing offences against children in the first place!" he remarked.

"You alright there Craig?" I asked, wondering at his sudden outburst.

"Yeah," he replied. "Tell me you agree with me - they deserved what they got right?"

"I can't say that," I replied. "Burning down the place where they were living isn't right."

"I'm sure the neighbours would agree with me," he said smugly.

"Taking matters into one's own hands isn't justice," I argued.

He smirked in response. "Oh but it *can be* justice," he said slyly. "What those men have done - they don't deserve to breathe."

"That's a bit extreme Craig. There *is* such a thing as redemption, right?"

"Redemption, my eye. No one there was planning on redeeming themselves anytime soon," he said.

I rolled my eyes in response. "Not all human beings are bad news. Including convicted offenders."

"Whose side are you on anyway?" he questioned.

"I'm on the right side of the law..."

"Hey guys," Johnny interrupted. "Lovers tiff?" he asked.

"Ha ha very funny," I said. Craig scowled at him.

"It was so funny you forgot to laugh, ey?" he joked, jabbing me gently in the side. It was impossible to be serious where Johnny was concerned.

Craig eyed him suspiciously before stating, "The right side of the law is the side that ensures justice is served all the time, every time. No exceptions."

"No need to be so self-righteous mate," Johnny said, to Craig's ire.

"Yes, I'll take that with a pinch of salt, given it's coming from a two time convicted drug offender."

A flicker of shame flashed in Johnny's eyes, and he cast me a quick look, seemingly embarrassed. "That wasn't necessary, Craig. I'm doing my best. Addiction is addiction."

"So said the convicted sex offender," Craig snarled. "Get your act together, mate," he added, walking off, without giving Johnny a chance to respond.

"That was a low blow," I remarked, Johnny standing there stunned.

"Yeah, well he's gotten pretty good at hitting below the belt," he replied.

"Don't worry about it," I assured him. "I don't think any less of you."

"I find that hard to believe," he said. "But that's not material," he added, changing topic.

"What is material is the fact that the District Attorney's office is wanting to keep the suspension on Daniel's licence for now or have him disbarred."

My heart sunk. "What?"

"Well, he's been accused of misleading the court, and failing to obey a court order. He's also been accused of violating rules on ethics. An ethics investigation is underway," Johnny

139

informed me.

"He hasn't talked to me about any of that," I advised.

"Well, he needs to. Burying his head in the sand isn't going to make this all go away."

"I'll talk to him," I vowed, immediately getting my phone out to call him.

"You need to go see him. You need to go home. He's lost without you," Johnny stated. "Anyhow, let me know how you get on," he said. "Craig doesn't seem concerned."

"I figured that," I added, noting it odd that Craig wasn't concerned at all about Daniel, given he was a partner.

"Hey, Johnny, before I go, just a quick question for you?"

"Shoot," he said, giving me his undivided attention.

"This is off topic but, do you know anything about a fellow named David? David Davenport? He's Aussie."

My question left him looking and feeling hot under the collar. *He knew something.* "David?" he asked. Johnny was an open book to me, which made it hard for him to lie or withhold things from me without me picking up on it.

"Yes, David," I replied.

"Well, I know him as Davey D."

"Okay?" I said, half asking and curious to know more. "How do you know him?"

"We grew up together," he stated. "Orphan home for boys, in Tassie - Tasmania."

"Interesting," was all I could say. Daniel would be even more interested to know that.

"Why do you ask?"

"Daniel's been receiving messages from him for quite some time now. Daniel didn't know this at the time, but David engaged him to rescue me when I was in a tight spot because of Duayne. How he knew to rescue me then, I don't know. Anyhow, I realised only recently that this guy that's been quite literally harassing Daniel over him hooking up with me is David Davenport. Last message was a bit off. Seems like he'll be heading here soon."

"Right," Johnny stated, intrigued. "And you know him how?"

"We met in Aus many years ago."

"Old flame?" Johnny enquired.

"Not quite," I replied.

He smiled in response. "I wonder whether you're "Miss Wonderful?" If you are, he's talked about you over the years."

"Oh?"

"Yep. At one stage he had some grand plan to win you over. Then military service happened and we lost touch for a bit. For a number of years."

"Military service?"

"Yep."

"I never pictured him to be the kind that would join the army?"

"He really wanted med school to happen for him, so that was part of the deal," he explained. I silently wondered what David's next move would be.

It took a while for Daniel to open the door. His face was gaunt and pale. Curtains were drawn despite it being early afternoon. He flicked on another light. Files and papers cluttered the dining room table, despite being in an orderly pile. The house was otherwise meticulously clean.

"We need to talk," I said. "I don't like the way we left

things last night."

"I don't either," he replied. "We need to talk to each other."

"You didn't even fight for me Daniel."

"Look. I was hurt. You said in no uncertain terms that you didn't want me there. You left. You didn't give me much choice. I'm here now, Teme. I've always been here. I always will be here, that's if you still want me," he said. "That's if you still need me." After a slight pause, he added, "I command you to come home now."

"You command me?" I questioned, in disbelief.

"Look, I just need you to come home."

"I'll come back when I'm ready to, and when I feel you've lost your attitude," I insisted.

"Okay," he said, flatly.

A pause ensued, before he stated, "You're really hurting me, Teme."

"You don't think I'm hurting too?" I asked.

"Look, deep down I knew I'd never be enough for you. So if you've said all you want to say, please leave. I'm hurting over you. You've clearly decided I'm not worth being with, and that what I've got to offer you is not worth having."

"Daniel..."

"You're not even wearing my ring," he noted.

"Daniel..."

He cut me off again. "We done been through so much together to just throw it all away. But if you want to leave, just leave," he said, gesturing towards the door.

"Daniel, I'm not leaving," I replied abruptly. "I'm not going to let you get away with pushing me away." He seemed surprised at the tone of my voice. "For goodness sakes Daniel,

I'm not wearing your ring because I've got terrible oedema, and your ring just doesn't fit anymore. As I said, I'm not going to let you get away with pushing me away. Me and the babies are the only family you've got, and we're not going anywhere fast."

The look of shock on his face was priceless.

"Oedema... what? Did you just...wait. No, seriously? A baby. Babies?"

I nodded in response. "Six weeks, but it's pretty clear we're expecting two."

No sooner than I thought he would faint, the palor in his face faded, and his face lit up with joy. He swarmed me, placed a hand on my belly. "For real?" Happy tears fell from his eyes. "I can't believe I'm going to be a father. I mean I *am* a father. I can't believe..." he took a step back in pause. "I truly hope I can be the father they need, and be the husband you need. With the mess I've made of everything else, I just want this to succeed." He cupped my face in his hands, leaning in for a passionate kiss. "I love you so much babe."

"I love you too, Daniel," I replied, glad to be back where I belonged.

Over his shoulder, I noticed the pile of papers on the table. News stories about the series of events unfolding in town. "*The Brotherhood*" was written in bold on all papers. The group that Ernesto had mentioned to me, loosely, in conversation.

"Research?" I asked.

"Sorry?"

I motioned towards the papers on the table.

"Oh, that," he said. "The Brotherhood."

"Any leads?"

He shook his head to the negative. "No, but one thing's clear. The Brotherhood have noble intentions. Getting to people who have done wrong and deserve to be punished is great. Exacting revenge on them isn't." He grabbed his leather bound Bible off the side table. "Look here, according to Romans 12:19 - *Beloved, never avenge yourselves, but leave it to the wrath of God, for it is written, Vengeance is mine, I will repay, says the Lord.* They need to be stopped," Daniel determined. "So, I've been doing a bit of investigating into them. How much do you know about them?" he asked.

"Enough to know that you need to leave well enough alone," I replied.

"Does Ernesto have something to do with it?" he asked.

I shook my head, shocked. "Why would you even suggest that?"

"Well, he's the one who referred you to them. He's also got an unforgiving attitude when it comes to crime. The thought of a vigilante group operating under his nose without repercussion seems feasible, yes?"

I pondered for a moment before agreeing with him.

"I've asked Craig whether he's seen or heard anything and he seems to not know anything at all," he told me.

"Or so he's saying. If he did, he probably wouldn't tell you," I suggested.

"What's that supposed to mean?"

"This is Craig we're talking about," I reasoned.

"What you're sayin' doesn't make much sense to me. Please elaborate, baby," he urged.

"Okay. Have you noticed Craig's sense of righteous indignation? I was surprised at what I witnessed earlier on, and how self-righteous he appeared. Have you ever noticed him get happy when he learns that someone has been locked up? Have you witnessed a tirade about *"Crims getting away with bloody murder all the time?"* He feels strongly about justice and the administration of it."

"I can't say I have baby," he stated. "I haven't worked closely with him since the suspension. Prior to that I didn't notice anything unusual."

"Before I left the office, I asked him about his long suffering anger and attitude to crime, and he claims that his anger is justified as he's angry at what angers God Himself. His exact words," I emphasised. "I've told him that it isn't up to us to exact revenge or to ask for revenge to be exacted on anyone - vengeance is to be left to God."

"And what did he say to that?" Daniel asked, intrigued, putting his mug of hot chocolate down.

"He shrugged it off, but not before he lectured me about a twisted version of restorative justice."

"As in?"

"He says vigilante action should be justified where the system fails to come up with an appropriate means of restoring justice to the victim," I said.

Daniel raised an eyebrow. "What else has he been saying?" he asked, leaning in as though I were letting him in on a secret.

"He hasn't said anything specific on this, but I have a feeling he's a part of The Brotherhood."

"Hm." Daniel shifted uneasily in his seat. "I wish I'd known all of this before I'd asked him to become a partner in my firm."

"Surely you had some idea? You at least knew how strongly he aligned more with the role of prosecutor as opposed to that of defence attorney?"

"No," Daniel replied, lightly tapping the table with his index finger. "I didn't know that. Though I *have* had feedback from former clients on how they felt he wasn't following their instructions. Mind you, these were clients who ultimately lost their cases."

"Sounds a bit suspect to me," I said. "What if he's throwing the cases?"

"I surely hope he's not!" Daniel replied a little too quickly. "It'll be outrageous if he was!"

"Well, as far as I'm aware, there's no proof that he's not," I said.

"Right," Daniel said before switching topic altogether. "I'm in the mood for love, can we worry about this some other time?" he asked, tenderly embracing me and planting a kiss on my naked shoulder. "I missed you like crazy last night," he confessed.

"I missed you too, cowboy," I replied, melting as his strong arms held me firm, not wanting to let go.

The next day, at the office, Johnny was noticeably on edge. The McInnon file," I repeated. His hands trembled as he searched through the seemingly insurmountable pile of files on his desk.

"You okay?" I asked.

"No, but I'll get there," he told me.

"I'm asking again, are you okay?"

He flipped the computer on and showed me the email from Craig:

*We don't need someone with your blue sky thinking in our firm.
I regret to inform you that there is no longer a position available
for you at MacCauley and Brennan Lawyers.*

"I don't know what I'm going to do now," Johnny said. "Michaela's not going to be very happy at all."

"Michaela's going to have to deal. You're not out of a job. Craig can't make a unilateral decision to fire you. He also can't fire you without grounds," I assured him.

"Well, he insists he has grounds, and he says he's within his power to do so. I took longer than expected on the merger file. So many things going on with Michaela...I probably do just need to walk away from this, he never wanted me here in the first place."

For a moment, I saw red. *How dare Craig.* "Don't worry. Daniel will have a say in this as well, and I'm sure Daniel will say you'll stay."

Johnny turned away from me and I caught a sense of fear in him as he wiped a bead of sweat off his brow. *Something else was eating him up inside.*

"I'm not going to push you to tell me what's bothering you, but I hope you know you can tell me anything. No judgement."

He nodded his head in response. "Thanks for your support."

"You're welcome. So, you know you can tell me anything?" I repeated.

"I do, but you'll find out soon enough," he replied.

I didn't like the sound of that. "Please tell me, Johnny?"

"Not here," he stated. The front door slammed and I heard footsteps approaching. *Craig.*

147

"You still here?" he exploded at Johnny, not realizing I was there. "Oh, hi Temwani," he said awkwardly.

"Daniel's not going to be happy with your decision to let Johnny go, I'm sure," I predicted.

"Well, I do have controlling interest in the firm now, so what I say goes, unfortunately for him," he stated.

Controlling interest? I was shocked. "Controlling interest? That's news to me," I replied.

"His pending disbarment made it possible," Craig stated, haughtily.

Johnny quickly got up to go. "I'll be seeing you Temwani," he said. To Craig, he stated, "I'll be out of here before you know I'm gone." He left without giving either of us a chance to respond.

Turning to me, Craig announced, "I've got your best interests at heart, Temwani. Don't think for a moment that I don't."

"Could've fooled me," I told him. "Daniel may not be here, but he's got as much right to make decisions around here as you do."

"Had is the operative word. *Had*," Craig corrected. Switching topic, he asked, "You hungry? How about I take you out for lunch?"

"No," I quickly replied. "You want me to work here with you, you need to start respecting my perspective, and you need to start respecting my husband."

"Look. Daniel needs to act less from the heart and more from the head. I'm merely doing him a favour in letting Johnny go."

"I don't think he'll agree," I replied.

"You'll see," he said, cryptically. Impatient, he asked

again, "How about I take you out for lunch?"

I could see there was no getting out of that invitation so I said yes. As I gathered my belongings to go, I grew ever curious about what had gotten Johnny spooked.

I caught up with Johnny sooner than I thought I would. He turned up at our place that evening.

I immediately implored him to tell me what he'd been meaning to say previously.

"Please keep this to yourself," he begged. "Not even Daniel can know about this."

As much as I didn't like the idea of keeping secrets from Daniel, I agreed.

"I'm a member of this group called the Brotherhood. We're a vigilante justice group," he stated with bated breath.

"Okay..." *The Brotherhood.* The infamous Brotherhood.

"Anyhow, Craig... well, I got careless and I sort of let the boys down," Johnny confessed.

"How so?" I asked.

"All you need to know is I let them down, and now Craig wants me out," Johnny admitted.

"That's not telling me anything," I replied.

"Well it's more than I should have told you in the first place," he stated.

"Tell me one more thing," I requested.

"Hm...I don't know, I've told you too much already."

"No matter. Tell me, did the Brotherhood have anything to do with that property that was set alight a few weeks ago?"

Johnny hesitated before replying. "Yes."

"The D.A.'s office is hot on their trail," I advised, recalling the last conversation I'd had with Jude.

"I figured that," Johnny said. "Craig's figured that too, and thinks I'm too much of a liability so I'm out."

"Well, there's always a silver lining. If the Brotherhood's going down, you won't be going down with them," I told him. "No need to think of an exit plan, you're already out."

Johnny laughed nervously. "I'd like to believe that, but knowing Craig, he'll probably get the blame shifted to me somehow. I am as he put it, *the weakest link.*"

I could tell Johnny wanted to say more, but the clanging of keys at the front door alerted us both to the fact that Daniel had come back home. As much as I was burning to confide in Daniel, a promise was a promise, and I was not going to say anything to him.

"What's going on here?" Daniel asked immediately.

"Craig's let Johnny go," I quickly answered, in an effort to prevent Daniel from getting more suspicious than he already was. "Apparently he's got controlling interest in the firm now," I advised. "He says your pending disbarment made it possible."

Daniel threw the keys down on the bench then ran a hand through his wavy brown hair. "There will be no disbarment," he announced. "Justice will be served," he said. I hoped for his sake that it would be. Sighing, he added, "The man's out of line. I should've known having him on board would come back to bite me in the behind," he said regretfully. Turning to Johnny, he stated, "About the job, we'll sort something out. Don't you worry. I've got a few things you could help me with in the interim."

9

DEUCES

My phone buzzed in the middle of the night. A message had just come through.

Daniel still had his hand around my waist as I lay in bed next to him. I gently nudged him and he strengthened his embrace around me. We were both back where we belonged.

I reached over to my phone on the dresser and lightly tapped the screen. *Shania.* She'd sent me a text message with a photo attached.

The text read:

Seems like someone was out last night having a good time without you.

Though the lighting in the photo was bad, I would know his face anywhere. *Daniel.*

I sat up in bed and examined the photo in greater detail. Daniel startled at my sudden movement. "You alright?" he asked sleepily.

I looked at the photo again. A bevy of women surrounded him and he was all smiles, drink in hand.

"Where were you last night?" I asked.

"Home," he replied.

"The whole night?"

Groggily sitting up, he asked, "What's this about, babe?"

"Just answer my question, Daniel."

"Yes, I was at home. The whole night."

Being with Duayne had meant trying to discern lies from truth and truth from lies. All the time. I wasn't prepared to play such games again. Photos didn't lie, and Daniel was probably not telling the truth.

"Daniel, I don't have a problem with you going out and hanging out with friends. But you've married me. We've got babies on the way. You telling me you were at home when you were not, is just not on. You being seen out on the town, in a swarm of women, isn't on."

He flipped the night light on. "I don't know what you're referring to."

I showed him the photo Shania had sent through. He looked at the photo through sleepy eyes.

"That isn't me," he said point blankly, handing the phone back to me.

"It sure looks like you," I argued.

"Look. I was where I said I was last night. It sure looks a lot like me but it isn't me."

I sighed and rolled my eyes in response.

"Funny thing is when I was out last night grabbing a bite to eat, a lady outright cussed me out in public. I couldn't understand what she was referring to, but she was dead set on the fact that I had done her wrong somehow."

"Seems to be a recurring theme," I muttered.

"Stop right there. Have I ever given you reason to doubt me? Have I not been true to my word?" he asked. "There's got to be some explanation for this."

My mind flashed back to the ultrasound and how the technician had insisted that twins run in the family. *No twins on my side of the family,* I'd said. Daniel was an only child, as far as he knew. *Did he have a twin?*

"Is it possible that you have a twin?" I asked.

He laughed nervously. "I think I'd know if I did," he said. "I spent most of my childhood wishing I had a brother. I think I'd know if I did."

"What if you did somehow?"

"It's a stretch, but looking at that photo, I'd be willing to consider the possibility," he admitted. "Okay, ask Shania where she supposedly saw *me* last night," he suggested.

Shania's text message in reply read:

Le Jazz. Sandra took the photo, she too saw him here last night. I've asked around tonight, and he's here every night apparently.

Daniel wasn't out clubbing every night. I knew that much for sure.

Well, he's here in bed with me. I replied. I couldn't resist.

He might be there with you now, but I know what I saw, she replied.

Why didn't you say anything earlier? I asked.

I didn't want to kill your joy, she reasoned. *But I thought about it and you don't need to be dealin' with some bullshit like this when you're pregnant,* she said. *Don't be fooled,* she added.

Goodnight Shania, I replied. *I'll call you tomorrow.*

I placed the phone back on the dressing table.

"I love you babe," Daniel stated, notably concerned. "I wouldn't lie to you, I wouldn't waste my time canoodling with other women when you're more than enough for me. You're everything to me. I thought you knew that," he said,

153

wrapping his arms around me.

The slight panic in his voice moved me. I was just as curious as he was to find out who this person was. "I love you too baby, and I believe you. Let's find out who this guy is, and take it from there."

"I agree," he said, yawning as he spoke. "Get some rest sugarpie," he advised, lying back down again, hand firmly on my belly. "Let's talk more in the morning."

I nodded my head in agreement, flipping the light above us off before inching towards him and falling asleep in his arms.

The following night, we headed to Le Jazz, the club where Shania had allegedly seen Daniel last. Being Friday night, the likelihood of his supposed twin being there was great. I wore a black lace dress, one which fit snugly and flaunted the developing pregnancy well, and paired it with my red ballet flats. Daniel wore blue jeans and a crisp white shirt.

His lookalike sat at the bar, excitedly talking to the female bartender. Smiles abound, her face was flushed from laughing at whatever he had said to her. Trying not to appear too obvious, I snuck into the corner of the bar closest to him and waited for a moment. I wasn't showing enough to raise eyebrows at the fact that I was pregnant and at a bar. I didn't have to wait for long to be served. Almost immediately, the man ahead of me in the queue motioned for me to go ahead of him. I thanked him. At that moment Daniel's lookalike turned, as though acutely aware of my presence. "Can I get you something?" he asked smoothly.

"A sparkling lemon water," I requested. Upfront, the resemblance to Daniel was uncanny.

"Call me Dave," he said assertively, offering his hand. Finding out more about him was going to be easier than we thought. "A sparkling lemon water," he repeated to the bartender who he'd been talking to before. She smiled then gave me a hostile and brief once over before tending to his request.

"We've met before," he stated as a matter of factly, face to face with me.

"You're mistaking me for someone else," I said, certain I would have remembered him had we met before.

"Cadburys chocolate, raisin, no nut," he offered. "Your favourite?"

"Nice trick," I mentioned. "You could have found that out in a myriad of ways."

"Really?" he questioned. "How about this. Peach ice tea and premade carbonara?"

I stared at him blankly. Those *were* some of my favourites.

"Now...do you recall the summer of '04 when you spent time in Australia on exchange?" he asked. "On the Gold Coast?" he asked. "Do you remember the little corner shop in Mermaid Waters?"

"Yes, I do..."

"And the car you drove that day - you couldn't work out the gearshift, I came out to help you figure it out - you had to lift the knob then pull back for reverse?" he asked, taking me for a stroll down memory lane.

"I don't get how you know all this?"

"Remember how I tried to chat you up every time you came into the shop?" he recalled.

"I..." A brief memory entered my mind and I recalled a nervous, anxious guy who'd tried to talk to me, but I'd

155

ignored him. *David.*

"Remember Broadbeach and the Blues Fest?" he asked, hoping he'd jolt my memory. "Dave. David Davenport," he offered again, winking this time and flashing a perfect set of teeth and dimples. My heart fluttered as I remembered his smile and those dimples. He had a moustache back then. When we'd first met, I had my hair in two ponytail plaits, and wore an old shirt and ripped jeans. I was in the middle of an exam cramming session, and couldn't be bothered to put on anything fancy to leave the house. I had planned a quick trip in and out of the local grocer, for snacks to keep me fueled while I studied. When I reached the till, David stopped service momentarily to randomly tell me how beautiful I was. I remember thinking how inappropriate he was, then thinking that he didn't know what he was talking about. *David.* The man who'd ordered the job that fateful night, and had gotten Daniel to rescue me.

"I thought you were beautiful then. I think you're even more beautiful now," he said bluntly.

"Flattery will get you nowhere," I promised. "It didn't get you anywhere then, it won't get you anywhere now," I said.

"So you say," he said, half smiling. "But you did go for my brother, who is biologically a carbon copy of me," he noted. "What kind of game you runnin' girl?" He joked.

Brother. No wonder the similarity was uncanny. But Daniel had no other siblings as far as he knew. Regardless of that, it was clear they were related, they were twins.

"So, you're here to challenge the status quo?" I asked.

"No, I'm here to show you what I'm made of," he replied. "I'm here to tell you what I should have told you all those years ago. I'm absolutely taken by you, and I want us to pick up where we left off. I've carried the memory of you in my heart, mind and soul all these years. It's high time I got back where I belong."

"Which is nowhere," I replied, bursting his bubble.

"Hm...," he said pensively. "Funny, I recall things differently."

"How so?"

"We met, we had a good time, I tried to get with you, you kept blowing me off, til that one night at Tom's place, I thought you were willing to give being with me a go, but that led nowhere in the end..."

"Yeah, well, what good did that do – you disappeared a week later, and I never heard from you again. I tried calling you..."

He shook his head in response. "And I tried calling you. I had to leave when I did, and couldn't say goodbye."

"You know, you said you called, yet I got no messages from you."

"I left messages, you probably just didn't get them," he said.

"Or you never called."

"Of course I called," he said, frowning in response. "We had bricks for phones back then. The likelihood of messages not coming through was high if I recall correctly."

I tried not to laugh but I did.

"Look darling, I've wanted to go back in time and meet you again, see how our lives would have turned out had we kept at it...," he said. "I came back, and you were gone," he said. "A friend of yours told me you'd gone back to Switzerland. I tried making contact with you through Friendster, couldn't get to you for many years. Then I hear you're in Texas, and you've fallen in love with someone new."

I listened intently, reflecting on the fervour with which he told me his side of the story. Looking at him now, the resemblance to Daniel was clear. They were identical twins, and looked like mirror images of each other, save for the scar on David's face that ran from beneath his nose to the top of his lip. Impulsively, I raised my hand to touch the scar.

"Cleft palate," he said abruptly when my hand met his face. He kissed my fingers and I quickly pulled my hand away.

"I didn't know you had such a scar – you were *heavily* moustachioued back then," I recalled.

"Indeed I was," he said, laughing fitfully. "Remember how you'd told me you'd consider dating me if I lost the moustache?"

I nodded in response.

"Well, here I am, *sans moustache*," he said, opening his arms wide in gesture to pull me in for a hug.

"You know I'm married, don't you?" I asked.

"Does it look like I care?" he asked, leaning in further to talk to me. I could smell his aftershave. *Burberry for Men*. The scent took me back to a moment with him several years ago, the last time I saw him, the one time I'd agreed to go on a date with him. A lot had changed since then, but the passage of time had made David more becoming. More beautiful, more desirable. Casting the thought aside, I turned my mind to Daniel who sat at the bar not far from us. I didn't know how to break the fact that I'd almost had a thing with his brother many years ago.

"Should I tell him, or will you?" David asked, reading my mind.

"There's nothing to tell," I stated.

158

"Oh yes there is," David challenged. "Given half a chance, we could've been together."

"I hear you, David, but that didn't happen. Instead, Daniel and I happened."

"You and Daniel wouldn't have happened if it wasn't for me," he stated.

"You know, Daniel's been there for me in more ways than one. He's been looking for me all his life, and it feels like I've been looking for him all my life." I said.

David leaned in closer. "Therein lies the problem darling. You *feel like* you've been looking for him all your life. Could it be that you feel you missed an opportunity with me and you've really been looking for me? I mean, what are the odds that you'd fall head over heels in love with my twin brother when it's me you saw first? Your heart wasn't receptive to me then, could it be that your heart is receptive to me now? Could it be that..."

"Don't go there David," I said. "If we were meant to be we were meant to be."

"You and him? Or you and I."

"I think you know exactly what I'm saying. Stop tripping'," I warned.

He shook his head, half smiling again. "Alright, I hear you, darling. What you're tryin' to say is that I never had a chance. Not then, not now. If that's the case, I'll keep my fantasies, up here," he said motioning to his head, "...and in here..." he said, tapping his heart, "...and you'll live your reality with him...," he said with finality, his fingers gracing my fingers, briefly lingering on the imprint that was left on my ring finger from the wedding band I wasn't wearing. "Just so you know, as long as I'm alive, I won't give up hope

159

on you loving me one day and living a new reality with me in it." I quickly pulled my hand away from his. Daniel was watching, and I did not want to give him the wrong idea. "In the meantime, you'll have to get used to me being around, I'm family now," he said, winking.

The music at the bar seemed to have suddenly gotten louder. There was no denying that David was an incurable flirt and would continue to be persistent in getting his advances across.

"I'm married to your brother. Act like you care," I stated over the music. He didn't seem to care.

"Fair game if you ask me," he said jovially, flashing me a cheeky smile. "I don't see a ring on your finger," he noted. It was quite obvious how much he enjoyed challenging the status quo. Or was it an attempt to disarm me and get me to drop my defences? I didn't have to wonder much longer. Daniel stepped in.

"I see we have the same taste in women," Daniel stated as a matter of factly.

David smiled, getting up from his stool and giving him the once over. "That and then some," he said. He didn't appear surprised to see Daniel. He'd been expecting him.

"I'm David, your brother. Literally separated at birth," he stated.

Daniel acted cool, but I knew inside he was trembling. "Okay. Alright, I can see the resemblance. How long have you known? Like I never even knew you existed. Until now."

"For as long as I can remember," David replied.

"I don't know whether to hug you or to punch you," Daniel stated. "The last few weeks have been rough, though I take responsibility for my part in the mess I made. Your being here only added fuel to the flame, though."

"I'd take a hug any day over a neat right hook, mate." David stated, his Aussie accent a clear and smooth drawl.

"A neat left hook," Daniel corrected. I couldn't tell whether he was pleased or pissed, though I noted he was a little out of character, and a little less confident than usual.

"Ah, you're a leftie. One thing we don't have in common," David said.

Daniel looked puzzled. "Leftie as in left-handed," David clarified, his Aussie accent quite apparent.

"Right," Daniel interjected. "If you were anything like me you'd want the left hook and not the hug."

They stood there face to face. Near spitting images of each other save for a few differences. David was a leaner, romantic looking version of Daniel. His hair was wavy and untamed, more of a sun-kissed copper brown hue than Daniel's warm chestnut brown hue. Oddly their laugh was the same. As was their smile, dimples and all. Daniel didn't laugh or smile as much as David did, whereas the laugh lines on David's face were evident. Other differences were much more subtle, and I would come to know them in the weeks that followed.

"Mate, I never pictured I'd be a dead ringer for you. It was fun while it lasted," David confessed.

Daniel and I looked at him blankly. "Dead ringer – looka-like," David explained. "Looks like I'm going to have to school you on a bit of Aussie lingo, mate."

They pumped fists.

I suggested dinner. David quickly agreed. Daniel took convincing this time, which was unusual, where food was involved. "I have to eat. The babies have to eat," I told him.

"Yes, of course," he said almost mechanically. The fact

that he was clearly shocked at David's sudden insertion into our lives was slowly becoming apparent. "Babies," he said proudly. I'm going to be a father!"

"And I'm going to be an uncle. Congrats," David said wholeheartedly, giving him a huge pat on the back.

The look on Daniel's face said it all. Beneath the joy of meeting his brother again after years of separation lay a myriad of questions and a clear undercurrent of doubt and apprehension. I imagined that he wondered why David had stayed away for so long, and why he had come to find him now. I imagined that he wondered why David had suddenly staked a claim on me after all these years.

They were deep in discussion when I stepped away from them to go to the Ladies.

"You staying somewhere local tonight?" I asked of David on my return.

"Yep, a motel off Interstate 35 has been my home for the past few weeks," he replied.

"Surely you can't continue staying there," I stated, concerned, looking at Daniel for consensus. He avoided my gaze.

"I'll be fine. I'm a bit of a rolling stone," David explained.

"He can stay with us, can't he, Daniel?" I asked, nudging him on the shoulder and commanding his attention. The expression on his face showed he was not very enthusiastic about that idea.

"Sure, he can," he said reluctantly. "For now."

"Hey guys, I'll introduce you to a few of my mates in a bit? We've got a private booth in the back. You alright to hang for a while before taking off for the night?" David asked.

Daniel cast a glance at his wrist watch. "It's getting late, it's going on 9 o'clock now..." he started.

"Way too early to be getting back," I said, much to Daniel's dismay. "Let's hang for a while," I insisted.

David winked at me in response. "I'll be back in a moment. Wait here."

Turning to me, Daniel asked, "So, you know him for sure?"

My stomach sank. "Yes. I do. Met him in Australia."

"You had a thing?" Daniel asked point blankly.

"Yes, and no. Close but nothing eventuated."

"I see," he said in response, deflated. He ran a hand across his forehead, something he did when he was anxious.

David was back in moments, as he'd promised. "The kitchen's closing in 10. I took the liberty of ordering a few meals we can share," he announced. "Come, our table awaits."

David introduced us to a few of his friends that night, Jeremiah being one. At least 6 foot, he towered over me, and came across as being very peaceful in spirit. His eyes, a startling grey blue, were in stark contrast to his sable skin. Daniel and I settled in to a booth, and he joined us while David went to the bar for some more drinks.

"You alrie mon? You look like you gonna crack," Jeremiah noted, giving Daniel a friendly pat on the shoulder.

"That's one way of putting it," Daniel said in response.

"Lighten up man, things are never as bad as they seem," Jeremiah advised.

"Right. I'm not sure they can get much worse," Daniel said. I could tell he was cut at the fact that David and I had known each other in the past.

"This beautiful woman is your wife?" Jeremiah asked.

Daniel nodded in response. "Never underestimate the power of hello. You made it past hello. You convinced her you're worth it. Now's the time to focus on today so you never have to say goodbye tomorrow."

"I hear you," Daniel replied.

"Beautiful lady," Jeremiah said, addressing me. He flashed a perfect set of teeth when he smiled. "You love him, yes?"

"I most certainly do," I replied.

"Love is the greatest of all things. And marriage. A union of two souls. What God has joined together, no man will be able to separate," Jeremiah said. Quoting scripture, Jeremiah was speaking the language Daniel understood. I saw Daniel noticeably loosen up.

"I hear you. Thanks for that. You're alright man," Daniel said. "Come here often?" he asked, trying to place him.

"No mon'," Jeremiah replied quickly. "Just came here to hang loose after work. Dave managed to rope me into coming tonight."

"I see," Daniel replied. "What do you for a livin'?"

"I'm a surgeon – Maxillofacial," he replied. "David's our visiting Maxillofacial surgeon," he explained.

"Hm..." Daniel said, pensively. "Visiting?" he asked.

"Yep, just on secondment from his practice in Australia," he said. "He's somewhat of a pioneer in the field, we're lucky to have him on board, training our younger fellows in cleft palate surgery."

"I see," Daniel stated, somewhat taken aback. Jeremiah could sense that discussing David was a sensitive subject, so he changed topic, choosing to discuss me instead.

"So, how did you meet?" he asked.

Daniel and I looked at each other, then both spoke at the

same time.

Jeremiah laughed. "You two are so in sync with each other."

I smiled in response, but noticed Daniel was not as jolly. I squeezed his hand under the table. He squeezed my hand back, and I noticed the look in his eyes was forlorn.

"What's wrong?" I asked, above a whisper.

"Nothing," he said.

"Daniel, don't tell me it's nothing."

"I'll tell you later," he said.

"Guys, do you need a moment alone?" Jeremiah asked.

"No," Daniel and I said in unison.

"Great," Jeremiah stated. "You still haven't told me how you met, I'm keen to know."

I squeezed Daniel's hand under the table again and replied on his behalf, "A series of unfortunate events brought us together, and the rest is history."

"Well, sounds like it was luck that brought you together, but that doesn't explain much, why not tell me how you met?" Jeremiah questioned. "Dave was saying you were both lawyers? I guess keeping secrets, that's to be expected?"

Daniel said nothing but frowned in response. David came back before we had a chance to answer Jeremiah's many questions. He slipped a virgin colada my way, and gave a beer to Jeremiah and Daniel. David had a flavored mineral water.

"Thanks mate," Jeremiah said in response. Daniel thanked David under his breath and took a quick swig of his beer. Sitting next to him, I could feel the nervous energy and trepidation. *He should be happy he's met his twin brother, happy he has a brother at all, let alone a twin*, I thought, but saw his feelings were mixed.

"I've been trying to get them to tell me how they met," Jeremiah started. "Don't they make a sensational couple?"

David smiled in response. "Guess you could say fate had something to do with it." Staring straight into Daniel's eyes, he stated, "Some guys have all the luck."

Daniel averted eye contact and quickly turned to me. "We make tracks?"

"In a bit," I told him, keen to find out more about David. "We haven't even eaten yet."

Daniel sighed heavily in response. If he could leave then, he would have, I was sure. His behavior was unexpected to say the least.

Daniel hardly ate. Midway through our meal, he asked me to venture away with him. He wanted to talk to me privately. Outside, by the stairwell leading out of the club, Daniel and I argued over the decision to allow David to stay with us. I argued that it would be a perfect opportunity for him to get to know his brother. Daniel argued that it would be a perfect opportunity for his brother to court me.

"Babe, you saw him. He's a bigger, better version of me, he's got the walk to match the talk. He's a surgeon. He's madly in love with you, he paid me fifty thousand dollars to keep you safe that night... I feel like we're just getting to be happy here and he's here to shake things up. I'm terrified of losing you," he confessed, clearly feeling threatened.

"I have free will, you know," I told him. "Things won't happen unless I want them to happen," I said. "Don't forget I'm married to you."

"When has that ever been an obstacle to any man on a

mission to get the girl of his dreams!" Daniel argued. "He's clearly still in love with you, and though he says he's happy for us, I know he'll stop at nothing to get you interested in him."

"You don't know that!"

"I do," Daniel replied.

"Oh, so he's told you that?"

"No, he doesn't have to tell me anything. I'm a man, I know what he's thinking."

"He isn't just any man – he's your brother," I reminded him.

"Yeah, and?"

"He respects you? I'm sure he wouldn't try to break us up."

He leaned back onto the staircase. "You wanna bet? He might be my brother, but he doesn't respect me at all," he claimed. "Don't you remember the messages he sent after I rescued you? He's come here to stake a claim on you. The fact that we're brothers is irrelevant."

I realized then that arguing with him would get me nowhere, and that the issue was not just about David being into me, it also had to do with Daniel's identity. Up until this moment, he'd believed he was an only child. Now, he had a twin brother who knew more about his family background than he did. He'd virtually gone through most of his adult life believing certain things about himself, but now that his brother was here, he had to consider the fact that things were radically different from what he'd believed them to be.

Sudden movement behind the staircase startled us both. A man appeared from the darkness.

"Nearly scared me to death, man," Daniel said.

"Sorry, didn't mean to," the man said. Stepping into the

light, I noticed dirty blond locks that were extremely matted, a shirred black shirt that was ripped in places, and trousers without shoes. The man smelt of soot and stale cigarettes. I pressed into Daniel, and he held me tenderly. Instead of veering to go, Daniel stood there.

"Man, can I trouble you for a dollar?" the man asked.

"Sure," Daniel replied, checking his pockets for some loose change. He took the coins that were in his pocket and placed them into the man's hand.

"Thank you, man."

Daniel then reached into his back pocket for his wallet, opened it, and took out a few bills. Briefly checking what he had, he rolled the bills up and placed them in the man's hand. "Get yourself somewhere decent to sleep tonight. Get yourself more than just something to eat," he said.

The man briefly counted the bills aloud, but under a whisper. "Bless you man, bless you. God bless you. Thank you so much. Thank you, you don't know what this means to me," he said visibly shaken and overwhelmed at Daniel's kindness.

"Don't mention it," Daniel said, slipping his hand back around my waist. "You take care man," he said, and we walked a short distance from the stairs. "We head back in?" he asked.

"Yes," I replied. Before we walked back up the stairs, I stated, "You need to know that David being here doesn't change the way I feel about you."

"I should hope not," he said, his voice deep with concern.

"Daniel, I'm with you. He just can't sweep me away from you."

"A man in love can be very persuasive," he argued. "Trust

me, I know. I was able to convince you that I was worth your time."

"Daniel, give yourself, your entire being, your essence, some credit. I fell for you too. Deeply. You didn't have to work that hard to convince me," I told him.

"I hear you, but I need you to hear me. A man who'll pay fifty grand to have you rescued is willing to do a whole lot more to make you his."

"And I'm a woman in love, with no one else but you," I assured him. "I know what I want, and what I want is to be with you." For a moment, he seemed convinced. He pulled me in and kissed me deeply, in earnest.

"I wish we could just split, and lose this crowd," he said, gently rubbing some stray lipstick off my mouth. "Go home, do something naughty."

"Me too, but just not tonight," I told him, smiling as I wiped off the lipstick that had transferred to his gorgeous lips. "Your brother's staying with us, remember?"

"I hope I'm not going to regret having him live with us, even if it is just for a time."

"Think positive baby. Look at it as a chance to find out more about him, and indirectly, more about you."

"Okay," he agreed, reluctantly.

"And we can still do the naughty," I told him. "Just have to start closing our bedroom door and you're going to have to work at being a little less vocal."

"Sounds like an alright plan," he said, loosening up a bit. "Well, I'm looking forward to consuming you and having you to myself," he stated, giving me a playful squeeze on the behind as we walked up the stairs.

Inevitably, our plans got delayed. When we got home, I freshened up then rushed around, fixing up the guest room for our visitor. David. A past prospective love, he was now my brother in law.

"A Scotch?" Daniel offered, pouring himself one.

David declined. "I don't drink," he said. I'd noticed he didn't when we were out but had assumed it was because he'd offered to be the designated driver.

"What can I get you then. A Coke?"

"Naw man, just some water."

"Any reason why you don't drink?" Daniel asked suspiciously.

"I'm not a fan of dulling my senses," David replied. "I fancy myself a bit of a hedonist."

Daniel raised a brow and took a deep swig of his drink.

"Plus there's the fact that I never know when I'll be called out to deal with an emergency procedure at work," he explained.

"I see," Daniel replied, unconvinced.

"Just some water for me," he confirmed. "I *am* a little peckish though. I know it's after midnight now, but can I fix us all up something to eat?" David asked.

"Go for it," Daniel said.

"I'll show you the kitchen and I'll show you around the rest of the house," I stated. "I'll get you that water."

"Great," David said. "Anything you can't eat, big brother?" he asked, turning to Daniel.

I saw Daniel flinch, as though slightly taken aback at the mention of the word brother. He shook his head in response, and replied, "No, anything in that kitchen – *my* kitchen, I can eat. As I said before, go for it," he suggested, pouring himself another Scotch.

"Will do," David said, somewhat curtly. He seemed somewhat relieved to leave Daniel's presence.

I could tell that having David in our house would take some getting used to.

"So, this is where you live," David said, as a matter of factly as I showed him through the house. "Are you happy, Temwani?" he asked all of a sudden, stopping in his tracks and startling me with such a direct question.

"Of course I'm happy, David." I answered quickly.

"Of course you are," he said in response. "How far along are you?" he asked of my pregnancy.

"A few weeks shy of three months now," I told him.

"Pregnancy suits you," he said quickly. "You're even more beautiful than I recalled."

I sighed in response. "Thank you David. But you're not allowed to flirt with me."

"Oh. I'm not allowed to pay you a compliment?"

"You know exactly what I mean," I told him.

"Yeah, I understand. My brother Daniel won't be too happy," he acknowledged, sourly.

"That's part of it," I said, leading him to the patio. "So, this is it – our house. Your room is just off the living room area, where Daniel is..."

"Ah yes, I'm not prepared to waken a sleeping dragon at the moment," he said, referring to Daniel. I giggled in response.

"I see I can still make you laugh," he said, squeezing my arm affectionately.

"Yes, I'd forgotten how much fun you were. You were the life of the party."

"That may be the case, but I wasn't enough for you at the time," he said somberly.

"David, things were complicated back then. I wasn't looking for love."

"You weren't even open to it," he corrected.

"That's not entirely true," I reminded him.

"Oh?" He was facing me directly now, his deep blue eyes staring into me, beholding me whole.

"Never mind," I told him, not wanting to again explain how I'd desperately tried to get in contact with him through friends, weeks after he'd left.

"You know, I'm not sure if me staying here is the right thing to do," he said. "Daniel wasn't exactly thrilled to finally meet me. He isn't exactly thrilled to have me here tonight."

"No, but he'll come around," I hoped.

"I'm not sure about that..."

"Sooner or later he'll have to, you're family," I reminded him.

"We'll see," he said hesitantly. "Let me fix us up something to eat," he said, changing topic.

The David that busied himself in the kitchen was a different David from the one I'd known all those years ago. The David I knew back then was awkward, hesitant and impressionable. He was also outgoing to a fault, with a false sense of bravado, to avoid drawing attention to his insecurity and unease as he grew from a boy into a man. This David was confident, full of purpose and radiant, in body, mind and spirit. He spoke of Australia with deep fondness, and laughed with reckless abandon when he recounted the memory of friends since gone, and scandalous house parties.

He was in the middle of recanting the story of how a major fight had almost broken out over a missing Bacardi Breezer when Daniel stepped in.

"Howdy, howdy," he said. "Am I interrupting something special here?"

"No, no, not at all," I said. "David was just reminding me of the fun we had back when I was at uni in Oz."

"I see," Daniel said, eyeing his brother suspiciously. "Any chance I could get something to eat?"

Always hungry, I thought.

"Of course you can," David said. "I'll plate it up now. Take a seat Temwani," he suggested.

He plated up Eggs Benedict – poached eggs, hollandaise sauce on toasted ciabatta bread.

"This is amazing David!" I exclaimed.

"It's not bad," Daniel said flatly. I kicked him under the table and he frowned in response. "It's pretty good," he said quickly.

"Thanks guys," David said in reply. "Thanks for letting me stay with you while I'm in town. Hospital food and room service gets old after a time - there's nothing like a home cooked meal."

"Amen to that," Daniel said, winking at me.

I smiled back at him, but noticed the wistful look on David's face.

"Where'd you learn how to cook so well?" I asked.

"I've been alone for a long time," he said. "Time on your own gives one enough time to do any number of things."

"Yeah, and I bet ain't none of them are pretty," Daniel said sharply.

I rolled my eyes in response. The rising animosity from Daniel's end was stifling.

"Thank you for the meal, David. Tea or coffee?" I offered, getting up.

"I'll have some tea," David said, gathering up the plates.

"I'll do that," I insisted, taking the plates from him and urging him to sit down. "Thanks for that, but you're the guest here."

It was easy to tell them apart. David had a strong Aussie accent and rich auburn brown hair. Daniel had a distinctively southern accent and chestnut brown hair. David was chatty and energetic, Daniel, somber and reserved. For now at least.

Exhausted after doing the dishes, I went to bed alone, leaving the two to catch up. I woke not long after to raised voices. They were arguing. The clock on the bedroom wall read 5 am. Daniel hadn't been to bed yet. Craving grapes, I made my way to the kitchen where they were still both seated.

"You're suggesting she'll eventually leave me for you?" Daniel questioned.

"You might be married to her now, but I loved her first," David insisted. "I still love her now."

"Keep this up and I'll run you out of town," Daniel threatened. "She's my wife now, and she isn't your anything and that's how this will be from here on out."

"You need to cool down. I'll try talkin' to you when you're sober," David said, getting up to walk away. He startled slightly when he saw me standing at the kitchen door. "Sorry we woke you," he said, walking off.

"Having him here was a mistake," Daniel said moments after we heard David shutting the bedroom door of the guest room.

"You need to be reasonable," I told him. "I understand you feel threatened by him, but you getting all riled up over everything isn't the way to be. He *is* your brother after all."

"Babe, I just can't stand this. Everything I've believed about my family, my upbringing, according to him, is a lie. About the only thing that isn't is what we have. Or is it all subject to change too, now that he's here?" he questioned.

"Of course not, Daniel. What we have is for life," I reminded him. "I think you're thinking too much, right now. Get some rest."

"I wish I could, but I can't," he said. "Amongst other things, my mom's been lying to me about a lot of things all this time."

"Such as?" I asked, curious.

"Call me stupid but I didn't know I was adopted."

"Daniel..."

"And I guess I fell out of the stupid tree and got hit by every branch on the way down, as I was stupid enough to think that running away with you that night, and making you mine, would mean I'd get to keep you forever."

"Daniel, I think you're taking this too far. Nothing and no one will keep me from you."

Unconvinced, he stated, "I hope you remember you said that, one day."

"Daniel..."

"His being here means war. *C'est la guerre.* He's come back to stake a claim on you."

"You're being very dramatic right now. Besides, you can't stake a claim on someone who has no wish to be possessed," I said.

"Well, that's what Jesse thought about Lestat in the *Vam-*

pire Chronicles. And we both know how that ended up."

What the? "I think you've had way too much to drink, your thoughts are getting away with you, and you desperately need to get some sleep."

"Trust me, sleep is the last thing I need," he argued.

"Trust me, sleep is the very thing that you need, *Lestat.* Dawn is rising," I told him, grabbing him by the hand and forcibly directing him towards the bedroom.

There was no sleep to be had by Daniel. He insisted we sit outside on the porch and talk it out. It was all about David, and he wouldn't give it a rest. "Aren't you curious to know why he's here all of a sudden? Don't you think he's here for something else?"

"Other than for me, you mean?"

Not amused, he waved off my response, stood up to go, deciding to head inside for a while.

I sat on the porch for a while longer and David joined me, a glass of freshly pressed orange juice in hand.

"For you," he said, offering it to me immediately.

"Thank you," I told him.

We sat in silence for a while before I asked, "So, David, what do you believe in?"

"What do you mean?"

"What's your M.O. – your *modus operandi?*"

"You're gonna have to talk to me in plain speak," he laughed. "I don't speak lawyer-speak."

"Right," I laughed, taking a sip of my juice. "Simple question. What gets you out of bed in the morning these days – what do you believe in?"

He paused for a moment before stating, "That's easy. I

believe in love everlasting, I believe in love in action. I believe in showing more than telling. I believe that actions speak louder than words, and I live my life doing to others – helping others how I can."

"That's noble," I said.

"I believe my love for you is real, and I believe one day we'll be together," he said without flinching.

David's phone rang in that instant, causing him to jump. He answered immediately he saw the caller display. "Right. Right," he said, listening intently. "I was just..." then nodding his head, he stated, "Alright. I've got it, Craig. Don't need to be so dramatic," he said, hanging up without saying goodbye.

Craig, I thought. "That sounded pretty intense," I said. "Craig?" I asked, wondering whether there was any correlation to Craig MacCauley, Daniel's partner in the law firm.

"Craig – we're practically family, we go way back," he said.

Daniel appeared in the doorway, likely after listening in around the corner. "Not Craig MacCauley I hope?" he asked.

"MacCauley, that's the one," David said casually.

The color drained from Daniel's face. "Man, how far do the lies go!" he exclaimed. "You mean to tell me he knew I had a brother all along yet he said nothing to me?"

"Look, that's a matter for you and Craig," David said abruptly. "He has his reasons."

"Seems to me y'all are in the business of lying, scheming and justifying your actions in the name of power and love."

David raised an eyebrow in response and said nothing. Daniel gave me the once over before heading off.

Daniel wasn't home for dinner that night. We found him

out drinking, at a waterhole about 30 minutes away from where we lived.

"You shouldn't be out here this late," he muttered under his breath, at me. "Neither one of you should be here."

Without hesitation, David stated, "Well, guess what. We are." After a brief moment, he added, "You shouldn't be out here yourself."

"I'm not even American. I'm Australian, man," he stated.

"That's not even something to get upset over mate," David rationalised.

"That's easy for you to say. You've always known who you are. I'm finding out that the things I thought I knew I don't know at all. I don't even know who I am anymore," Daniel claimed.

David shook his head in response. "You've always been my brother, always will be my brother," he said, in an attempt to make Daniel feel better. It backfired.

"You mean, I'll always be a lacklustre version of you?"

"Naw man. Stop putting words into my mouth," David said sharply.

"Whatever," Daniel replied abruptly.

"Come home baby," I urged, trying to convince him to leave his drinking at the bar.

"Not just yet sugarpie. Not just yet," Daniel replied.

In annoyance I snapped at him. "You can't be out here drinking away..."

"What choice do I have. He's staying with us," he replied, motioning over at David as though he were some sort of a disease.

"Build a bridge," David stated.

"Why in the heck would I want do that?" Daniel queried.

"Build a bridge and get over yourself, mate." David stated.

I could see Daniel was trying his level best to keep his cool. It wasn't working. He signaled at the bartender to get another drink. David asked the bartender to ignore his request.

"He's had enough," he said.

"How dare you!" Daniel interjected, fire in his eyes.

"You've had enough mate," David repeated.

"I'm a grown man, I'll do what I want, when I want," Daniel announced.

"If you're a grown man, start acting like one," David advised. "You can't have your woman out here all worried about you. Time to go."

Daniel shot a glance at me then looked away when my eyes met his. David was speaking truth, and I wasn't sure he could handle it. "I'm sure she understands," he stated, turning back to David. "It's not every day that your world comes crashing down on you."

"I know it's hard baby, but drinking yourself into a stupor isn't going to change things at all," I said, and I leaned into him, nearly toppling him over his bar stool. He braced me and laughed drunkenly.

David tugged on his arm. "Time to go, mate."

Daniel resisted. I could tell it wasn't going to end nicely.

David's deep blue eyes met mine and he stated, "Can I talk to you outside?"

"Sure," I replied. Daniel raised a brow and kissed me on the temple before I walked away from him.

Outside, a light rain had started to fall.

"I'm not sure he's going to cooperate and come back with us now," he told me, hands in his pockets. The night air blew some of his hair across his face and he turned opposite to the wind, shoulder length locks falling back in place.

"I don't think so either," I replied. "He's pretty cut that his mom's not his mom, and that he's been lied to all this time. He's probably even more cut to know that we knew each other before he and I met."

"Fair enough," David replied. "Being upset is one thing. Carrying on is quite another."

"I hear you," I replied. "Maybe if food's involved he would come quick."

"You reckon?" he asked, half laughing. "He does love his food."

I laughed lightly with him. "It's worth a try."

Back in the bar, I tried to convince Daniel to leave. Despite the enticement of a warm meal, he refused to budge. Apparently, he'd had a meal beforehand.

Contrary to our wishes, in our momentary absence, the bartender had decided to leave the bottle with him. *Couldn't he see how drunk Daniel was?*

David took the bottle away from him. "This ends now," he announced. Handing me the car keys, he said, "Please drive yourself home. Get some rest. I'll walk him home."

Outside it was likely still raining. "You shouldn't be walking in the rain," I stated.

"It'll be fine. I'll walk the drunk out of him then cab it the rest of the way if we have to. That's if he's not chucking up everywhere by then. Go home. He'll be alright," he assured me.

"David..."

He interrupted, "Don't worry your pretty little head about this. I got this. See you in a bit."

"Okay," I said, grateful he was there with Daniel. As

I walked away and headed for the car park, I heard them arguing. *At least Daniel was in safe hands.*

"Daniel?" I called out, the next morning. Silence met me. I could hear his voice in the bedroom, he was probably on the phone. I made my way over to the bedroom, cracked open the door to see him kneeling at the end of the bed, head in his hands. "Lord, it's so hard for me to stay strong when my world's falling apart right before my eyes. Please give me the strength I need to make the right decisions, the faith I need to..."

The door creaked and he startled, realizing he was not alone. He acknowledged my presence with a nod, before closing his eyes again and stating "...in your name I pray, Amen."

"How are you?" he asked, getting to his feet. "Where were you?" he asked, before I'd had a chance to answer the first question.

"I'm fine," I replied. "I left a message on your phone telling you where I'd be. I was out with David." He sidestepped me and shook his head in response. "You were pretty off your head earlier," I rationalized. "I didn't think you'd mind."

He shook his head further before replying, "I don't mind you going out. I do mind what you do with my brother."

His tone surprised me.

"From now on, where David's involved, please tell me what you plan to do and when, and I'll let you know if I mind or not," he said abruptly, before planting a quick kiss on my forehead and walking away.

I couldn't be bothered to take issue with him on the topic

yet again. I understood the animosity towards David, but wondered when he would come to terms with the fact that I was his, I loved him, I was married to him, and was carrying his children, and that such a bond would not and could not dissipate overnight.

I avoided him for a good hour, busying myself around the house before showering and freshening up.

"Where's David?" he asked, as soon as I joined him in the living room, on the sofa.

"He's doing a shift at the hospital. Not sure when he'll be back."

He nodded his head in response and reached for my hand. "I'm sorry about earlier. I'm sorry about yesterday and the day before. I'm just all tore up inside about everything. My life, my identity, my career – the only thing that's right is you and the babies, and I feel I could lose you too. I'm at a loss as to how to be right now."

I slipped my arm around him and pulled him into me. "Don't be sorry for being. I can't imagine how you feel. I'm here for you. Just tell me how I can best be there for you."

"I don't know...it's all... I mean, Jolène isn't my mom. I wasn't born in America, I was born in Australia. I didn't know I had a twin brother 'til the day before yesterday. I don't know a thing about where I'm from apart from what he tells me. Then there's my career. The likelihood of me losing my license for good is great. Everything I've worked for is goin' up in smoke right before my eyes."

"Baby, you've got me. You've got us," I said, placing his hand on my belly.

"I hear you sugarpie," he acknowledged, still uncertain. "I wouldn't have you though, if it wasn't for David, and if

David had his way, *he'd* have you. I feel he'll stop at nothing to make you his."

"I'm not sure he'd do that to you."

"Wanna bet?" he challenged. "He's told me in no uncertain words that he's going to be waiting in the wings for me to stuff up then he'll make his move," he said. "He's already making moves."

I knew David. In the few days we'd spent time together, I could tell he was persistent. His whole reason for being here was persistence. The fact that he'd looked for me all these years showed persistence. Surely me being with Daniel, being married to him would encourage him to stop pursuing me.

"I'll talk to him," I offered.

"You'll do no such thing. The mere fact that you're concerned about me will give him an opening. As far as he's aware, I'm doing fine, okay? No discussing my concerns. Please. For my sake, let things be. Last thing I need is for him to kick me when I'm down."

"I'm sure he wouldn't do that to you Daniel. He's told me he's always longed for a brother, and that he'd do anything for you."

He laughed suddenly. "Trust me, he won't."

"How'd you figure that?"

"He says he'd do anything for me, but I'm sure if I told him to leave you be and leave town, he wouldn't."

"Why would you want him to do that anyway? He's just gotten here. Don't you want to have family around, now that you've found out that you're not who you thought you were?" I asked.

"You don't get it," he said sharply. "We might be related

by blood, but that doesn't make him any less of a stranger to me, nor dare I say an enemy."

"Daniel, you're being overly dramatic."

"Easy for you to say. You're not in my shoes," he stated, getting up abruptly.

"If God's allowed this to happen He'll use it for good. *Romans 8:28.*" I quoted back the verse he once quoted to me, many weeks ago, when I was trying to make sense of what Duayne had done to me.

"That was different babe," Daniel argued.

"No matter, baby. It'll all come together for good."

"I wish I could say I believe that. In this moment, I don't," he said, leaning against the wall before falling to his feet. "What have I done to deserve any of this," he lamented. "I've tried to do everything right by everyone most of my life, if not all my life. I haven't done anything to deserve this..."

"Baby, it'll all work out, just can't see it now," I told him.

He sighed in response, remaining in a kneeling position on the floor. I joined him and beckoned him to take my hand.

"Baby, I'm your family. These babies and I, we're your family," I told him. "I'll always be your family."

He stared deeply into me, as though to ascertain whether there was a remote possibility this wouldn't be the case one day. He wanted to say something but he didn't. Instead, he nodded his head in tacit agreement.

"My family is your family. You don't have to feel alone."

He leaned in to hug me, but his sheer force toppled me over. In a swift move he braced me so I fell into his arms.

"Sorry babe. You okay?"

"I'm fine," I laughed, resting my head on his shoulder. I made a mental note not to lie on my back for long.

"I could stay here with you, forever," he vowed.

"Realistically, you couldn't," I challenged. "You're always getting up, walking away, you just can't stay still."

"Okay, you got me," he replied. "But I can move," he said, rolling over so he was almost on top of me. Tracing an invisible line from my lips to the crest of my cleavage, he stated "I can think of nothing better than for us to make the most of this time alone. Without interference, house to ourselves."

I smiled at the thought.

Flipping me over so I was on top of him, he stated, "I'm in the mood for love. How does that sound to you?" he asked, kissing me deeply, only allowing me to reply with a moan between kisses. His touch was exhilarating, fulfilling and wholesome. "While we've still got the place to ourselves, let's. I'm in the mood to love you down."

"I'd love to love you," I whispered, trembling in anticipation of his touch.

We were up watching an obscure B grade movie on TV, sharing a tub of vanilla flavoured Blue Bell ice cream when David came back from work. I'd given him a spare key so he could come and go as he pleased.

"Hey," he greeted Daniel and I as he walked through the door. Daniel managed a nod in acknowledgment but said nothing while his mouth was full of ice cream.

"Hi David," I replied.

"How's things?" David asked, slipping off his shoes. He'd changed out of scrubs at the hospital, and looked refreshed, despite having worked a 12 hour shift.

"Good," Daniel stated, his tone decidedly friendlier.

"Excellent," David replied.

"Can I fix you up something to eat?" I asked. "Or get you some ice cream?"

"No ice cream unless you have some of the non dairy variety?"

"It wouldn't be ice cream then, now would it?" Daniel stated.

"I guess not," David replied. I looked at him, puzzled. "I'm allergic to dairy," he advised.

"Oh," I replied, having my last spoonful. "How allergic are you?"

"Very," he replied. "As allergic as I am to shellfish and peanuts."

"Sorry to hear that," I replied. "Can I make up something for you to eat?"

"Naw, I'll be fine. Had something before leaving work," he said.

"Anything else you can't have?" Daniel asked, in a somewhat uncaring tone.

"I'm a vegan," he replied.

"What are you doing not eating meat, brother?"

"I haven't eaten meat in years, it's a choice."

"Not even fish or...egg?"

"Nope," David responded, slightly irritated. I recalled that he'd prepared a meal for me the other day but had not eaten.

"Man, I guess we have less in common than I first thought," Daniel stated.

Whatever that's supposed to mean, I thought.

"I see you're doing better," David stated, referring to the previous night's drinking episode.

Daniel raised a brow at him. "I was doing fine last night."

"If you say so," David replied. Turning to me he stated, "I'll be taking a bit of a kip now, see you later on."

I nodded in response.

"A what?" Daniel asked as David walked away.

"A kip. A nap." I explained.

Daniel shook his head. "I'm supposed to be Aussie, yet I can't even speak that language."

I laughed in response. "It's not a whole different language Daniel. It's slang."

"It may as well be another language," he said, brooding over something else.

Silence ensued as we continued watching the movie. Suddenly hitting the pause button, Daniel stated, "I don't want you to even entertain the notion of Jolène being a part of our babies' lives. As far as I'm concerned, she lost that privilege the moment she decided to lie to me about everything."

"That's a bit harsh," I replied. "I know you're hurting but..."

"If you know I'm hurting, you'll understand that she can't be a part of my life anymore."

"Daniel, she raised you."

"Teme, she lied to me. She's been lying to me. She's still lying to me. She's telling me she has no idea who my father is, and I have the feeling she knows very well who he is," he suggested.

As a mother to be, I couldn't imagine myself ever lying to my children to the extent that Jolène had lied to Daniel. "Maybe she's protecting you?" I offered.

"More like she's protecting him," he replied, getting up. "She won't even tell me why she only took me, why she didn't take David as well."

"Sounds pretty suspect," I replied.

"Yeah, well, she's a *persona non grata* as far as I'm concerned, and I don't want you associating with her under any circumstances whatsoever."

I knew he was angry, but I hoped that his anger towards Jolène would dissipate in time. She did raise him. Credit where credit was due, she had raised him well.

"Baby, you're angry, and in your being angry, you might be making decisions that you'll regret," I warned.

"No, I'm not going to change my mind about this. She doesn't deserve to be a part of my life anymore," he said, sternly. "Where do the lies end and where does the truth begin? My Texan birth certificate is no doubt a forgery. She's not my kin," he said, walking away. "I'll be back," he promised, getting up abruptly.

Moments later, I heard him pounding on David's bedroom door, so I rushed up after him. "What are you doing!" I exclaimed. "He's just told us he's getting some rest. Whatever it is, it can wait, yeah?"

"Stuff takin' a *kip*," Daniel replied. "I need answers, and I need them now."

I rolled my eyes in response. "Let it rest for now, will ya'?"

Daniel turned the door knob on the outside at the same time as David turned it from the inside and pulled the door inwards. "You should listen to her," he stated in annoyance. "Whatever it is, it can wait."

"No," Daniel replied. "I've had a lifetime of waiting to hear the truth. This ends now."

David sighed heavily, red-eyed and clearly exhausted from the night before and his shift at the hospital which had ended not long ago. "Mate. Whatever it is, it can wait. I'm knackered – what with my shift today at the General, and babysittin' you last night..."

Daniel ignored his comment and pushed through into the bedroom. "You can sleep later. I need answers now."

"Daniel!" I exclaimed, as David stood aside and Daniel pushed his way into the room. He cast me a dirty look before starting off on a tirade.

"How dare you ask me to wait longer for something you have known for most of your life? I need to know who I am and where I come from. You can't choose on whim when you'll tell me what. The lies end now, and the truth begins from here on out."

"Okay, I'm really needing to get some sleep here, so if you don't leave me alone right now, I'll job you," David threatened.

Daniel paused and shook his head in response. "Speak English mate."

David turned to me in annoyance. "Will you please tell him to leave me be? I'm completely shattered - I need to sleep."

"Daniel, let him rest," I requested.

Daniel paused for a moment, his anger somewhat dissipated. "Alright. Before I leave you be, answer one question for me please."

"Shoot," David said.

"Why did Jolène take me and leave you?" he asked.

"Why don't you ask her?" David snapped.

"So, you know the answer to my question, you're just refusing to answer, right?"

"It's nothing like that mate," David replied.

"What is it like then?"

"It's like this. You want to know why Jolène did what she

did to us, you ask her," David said firmly. "Now if you'll excuse me, I need to get some sleep."

"Okay," Daniel stated, not satisfied with his response. "One more question. What do you know about our father?"

"As much as you do. Nothing," David quickly replied.

Daniel didn't believe him. "Oh, I'm pretty sure you know more about him than I do."

I could tell David's patience was wearing thin.

"Daniel, there's still tomorrow," I reminded him.

He scoffed at the suggestion. "Tomorrow? I needed to know this like yesterday." Turning to David, he added, "If you can't help me, I'll find out on my own."

"Fine," David replied, flopping on to the bed, closing his eyes. "Now, will you let me sleep?"

"For now," Daniel replied, heading out the door.

10

BROKEN

T he smell of freshly brewed coffee and pancakes wafted through to me as I lay in bed.

I heard his song. His tender voice amidst clanging of dishes in the kitchen. My heart soared at the beauty of his song. I tiptoed down the stairs, and stood by the door, not wanting him to break from singing. "Hallelujah, hallelujah..." He turned to face me, suddenly aware that I was there. Motioning for me to sit, he continued singing.

"You sing?"

"Not professionally, no. It's just something I enjoy doing. Makes me feel alive."

"Made me feel alive," I replied.

He flashed me a smile, then gestured for me to sit down.

"I've overstayed my welcome here," he stated. "It was silly of me to think I could come here and make things work with him. He's family, but he clearly does not want me around."

"He doesn't own Texas, you shouldn't have to leave on his account."

"I shouldn't have to, yes. But this is bigger than me. There's your happiness I need to consider too. Right now

I'm just being a thorn in your side."

"More like a thorn in his side," I corrected him. "You've been nothing but good to me."

"Glad you think so," he said, somewhat relieved at my statement. "I try. Can't do anything less."

"So, you'll stick around a while longer? You've only just got here," I added.

"I've been around longer than you think," he replied.

"Stalker!" I joked.

He poked me in response. "Okay, I'll stick around for a while longer. Only for you," he stated, as Daniel walked in.

"Howdy," Daniel said, curtly. "Only for you, what?" he asked.

"Never mind," David replied.

"I thought I asked you to step off and lay off making moves on my woman?" Daniel questioned.

"He's not making moves on me, Daniel," I replied.

"Coulda fooled me," he stated.

Daniel flaunted a notebook at David. "Thought you might be missing this here little black book of yours," he taunted.

"Give that back to me," David commanded. "You shouldn't be going through my stuff."

"I'll do whatever I please, in my house. My rules here," Daniel postured.

"Don't worry mate, I'll be out of here in no time," David said in response. "Give it back to me," he repeated, motioning towards the notebook.

"Nice drawings, nice poems..." Daniel said, flipping through the book. "But sorry to break it to you - she'll never be yours," he promised.

"Give that back to me," David insisted.

Putting it on the table, Daniel said, "Here." David quickly grabbed it.

"She'll never be yours," he stated again.

"Never say never," David replied.

"Whatever."

Intervening, I stated, "Will you two just chill? Can't you just get along? You're brothers for goodness sakes."

"I'm heading out for a bit," David stated. "For a few days actually."

"Leaving so soon?" Daniel asked sarcastically.

"I'll be back Sunday," he mentioned. "Give you two a bit of privacy."

"Don't be silly David, you're not in the way," I assured him.

"Teme, if the man wants to leave, let him leave," Daniel suggested.

David winked at me. "Told you I'd overstayed my welcome."

"Daniel, be reasonable," I begged.

Daniel wasn't listening. "You were on your way out?" he queried, motioning towards the door.

"Uh hm," David replied, winking at me once again, despite knowing it would infuriate Daniel. "You know where to find me if you do need me." Though he was smiling, the hurt in his eyes was quite apparent. There was nothing else left to say. Turning to Daniel, he promised, "I'll stop pursuing her. The moment that you start treating her with more respect than you have been, I'll respect your wishes, I'll stop pursuing her, and I'll leave her alone."

Daniel was livid. "Are you cruisin' for a bruisin'?" he questioned, clenching his left fist and standing akimbo.

"First last night with you walking around half nakid, then this morning with you swooning over her and trying to woo her with your singing and cooking, then that notebook of yours and now this. You don't know the first thing about respect, David," he argued. "You can't respect the fact that she's mine, you can't respect the fact that this is my territory and I will tell you how this will go down."

"Oh man, you are so full of it," David replied, half laughing. "Me walking from the shower to the room with a towel around my waist is me walkin' around half naked? Me singing while I prepare breakfast for us all is me wooing her? Me using my journal to reflect on my life, and my comic strips... this isn't a big conspiracy to snatch her away from you, you know. She's not an object to behold. She should be free to be wherever she wants to be, and with whoever she wishes to be. You can't control every aspect of her life, including the friendships she makes."

"Friendships? Are you kidding? Friendship is not what you're after, she'll give you an inch, you'll take a mile," Daniel assumed.

"You got it wrong. Friendship *is* what I'm after," David replied. "It's the only thing she will give me – she has eyes for you only. Pity you can't see that."

"I wasn't born yesterday, *mate*," he said, putting on an Australian accent. "I see the way you look at her. I read what you wrote about in that there book of yours. Nothing good will come of you being in her life. Matter of fact, nothing good will come from you being in mine – it's inextricably linked to hers."

"You done yet bro? You done using big words, throwing your weight around? Nothing good will come out of you being a control freak," David replied somewhat patronizingly. "You want me gone, say the word, no need to be nasty about it." Turning to go, he stated "For what it's worth, I've loved her longer than you have."

Daniel had been trying his level best to keep calm, but David's last comment threw him over the edge. "You know what? Fuck you, man. You're not welcome here any longer."

"I wasn't planning on staying here much longer," David stated. "And it's not as though you welcomed me here with open arms in the first place. But yeah, thanks for telling me what I already know."

"Daniel!" I exclaimed, annoyed that once again he was letting his insecurities dictate the way things would play out. "I have a say in this too. This is our house. David, you're welcome to stay for as long as you need to."

"Thanks Teme, but I know better than to stay where I'm not wanted. I'll respect your husband's wishes and be gone," he assured me. "I'm out for now," he said, checking his pocket for keys and wallet before casting me a furtive glance which Daniel did not catch, and sauntering out the door.

I followed after him. "David..."

"I'll see you around," he replied. "I've got your number."

"Where are you going?"

"Need to find me somewhere to crash the night, and then I'll be heading downtown."

"Downtown?"

"Yep," he said absently before singing the Petula Clarke song, *Downtown*.

Daniel was right behind us. "Will you just git now?" he said to David who winced as though he were in pain, then frowned in response.

"No need to get nasty," he replied, before saluting me and walking off to his truck that was parked down the road.

In that moment, I hated Daniel.

I played matchmaker for David in an effort to get him to lose interest in me. A few days went by, and I didn't hear from him. I assumed it was because he was otherwise engaged. I was partly disappointed, partly happy that he had finally moved on.

Then I heard from Shania. He was in love with someone else apparently.

"How do you know that?" I asked, surprised.

"He told me," she said.

I was livid. Livid that I had introduced my friend to him only for it to go nowhere. Livid that he was probably up to his antics of being with more than one woman at a time, and didn't have the decency to let Shania know that he was not interested.

I called David up and we agreed to meet for coffee that morning.

The café within the courthouse was relatively empty for the time of day. Callover, I thought.

My matter wasn't on until later on that morning.

David was already there when I walked in. He wore a navy blue polo shirt, khaki trousers and chinos. He greeted me with a kiss on the cheek. "Been a while," he said. "Missed you. Was your phone broke?"

I was livid. I tried not to let it show, but he noticed straight away.

"Say it," he urged. "You've got something to say, say it."

"Shania."

A look of surprise shot across his face, before he smiled nervously. "What about her?" he asked.

"You're unbelievable," I replied.

"You should know better than anyone else that I'm good for one thing, apparently."

"And what's that?" I replied, trying hard not to let my anger loose.

"Picking them up and laying them down," he said, curtly. "Look, are we going to actually have coffee or did you bring me here to tell me off?"

I rolled my eyes at him. He gave me a slight smile, undeterred. The waitress walked by, and he flagged her with a wink. She turned back and came to our table right away. "Just a strong black for me, and a white hot chocolate for the lady."

I waited for the waitress to leave before I ripped into him. "You know, you can't just go around making assumptions about me. You can't presume to know what I want before I want it."

He smiled, clearly amused. "You did want a white hot chocolate, didn't you?"

I rolled my eyes at him. "Yes, I did. You also can't just go around *"picking them up and laying them down"* as you put it. Shania is not just an object of your desire. She deserves better."

"I know she does. That's why I told her I was not long-term relationship material," he replied in his defense.

"That isn't what I heard."

"Well, what *did* you hear?" he asked.

"She says you told her you were in love with someone else."

"Hm. Look, I'm sorry I hurt your friend," he said, and in

that moment, he seemed sincere. "I can't be something I'm not, and I can't give her what she's after."

"I thought you were better than that David. You could have at least given me the heads up - were you lying when you said that you were wanting to settle down? I was trying to help out, trying to introduce you to someone special."

"No, I wasn't lying," he replied.

"Then why..."

"As I told Shania, I'm in love with someone else. What I didn't tell her, was that it looks like the lady I'm in love with will never be mine," he said, in a somewhat somber tone. "You."

My heart sunk. "David..."

"I know," he said. "It's a lost cause," he acknowledged. "But I do love you with a passion. I've loved you ever since I laid eyes on you."

The coffee and hot chocolate arrived.

"Daniel is the better man. He always will be," he said, morosely. "If we were to ever be, I would probably only sabotage things eventually. I would end up hurting you," he predicted.

"David, the experiences you had growing up have made you who you are but they do not and should not define you."

He laughed, awkwardly. "You wanna bet?"

I sighed in response. An awkward silence ensued.

"Just let me love you, Teme. Just let me love you from a distance," he urged. "In fact, I don't need your permission. This is what I'll do," he confirmed.

"David, you know I'm committed to Daniel."

"I know," he said. "And I'm glad you are," he stated, stirring two teaspoons of sugar into his coffee, and one into my chocolate. "I want you to be happy. I want you to be with someone who will cherish you with his all. I'm not perfect. He's as close to perfect as they come. My brother is that man."

We were breaking ground, I thought.

"But just in case he isn't, I'll always be there, waiting in the wings to swoop in," he promised, making a wing sign with his hands.

I laughed in response. "You're too much David."

He smiled a beautiful smile that made my heart flutter unexpectedly. "So, can we shake on this?" he asked. "I promise to love you from a distance, and you promise to stop hooking me up with other women?"

"I promise." I offered my hand for a shake. I should have known better. His touch was electric. Instead of a shake, he brought my hand to his lips for a kiss.

I quickly pulled my hand back. Not quickly enough. Daniel stood there at the door of the café, likely there for a coffee and to prep before going into court. He'd been called in as an expert witness in a kidnapping trial.

"Sugar," David said under his breath. "Looks like I have some explaining to do."

Daniel stood there at a distance, turning away as though he hadn't seen us when he had.

"I'll talk to him," David promised, getting up to meet Daniel at the door.

Daniel faced David, suit coat over his left arm, briefs in the other hand.

Daniel talked, while David listened and nodded in response. David wasn't smiling when he walked back to the table. His face was flushed and he seemed somewhat flustered. "I'm heading off now," he said abruptly. "Take care of yourself," he said, avoiding eye contact and making a bi-line for the door. He left his phone on the table. Before I could call out after him, he was gone.

Daniel ordered a coffee to go, and motioned for me to join him at a different table closer to the front.

His tone was cool, aloof. "You really need to stop seeing him."

"He's your brother, he's a friend."

"I'm demanding that you stop seeing him," Daniel insisted.

"Don't be ridiculous Daniel."

"You've been warned," Daniel stated.

"Whatever that's supposed to mean," I replied.

"I'm not going to be nice about this anymore," he replied. "I've gotten to the stage where I've had enough, and if neither of you will hear me out and allay my concerns, I'm making certain things known, and I won't be apologizing for anything I do next to protect you."

I wanted to argue with him, but chose not to. It was a battle I wouldn't win.

Jude stopped by our house that evening. Daniel wasn't happy to see him.

"I'm not here to start anything," Jude stated.

"Why are you here then?" Daniel questioned. "Hasn't your office done enough already?"

"I'm not here on behalf of my boss. I'm here as a friend."

"Some friend you turned out to be!" Daniel said snidely.

"Daniel!" I interjected. "Jude isn't the enemy, he's on our

side."

"I've got no proof of that," Daniel said cooly.

"Believe what you will Mr Brennan," Jude said courtly. "I know where I stand, Temwani knows where I stand, and that to me is everything."

Daniel looked from Jude to me then from me to Jude again. "I can't just trust anyone these days," Daniel stated. "I trusted Craig and look where that got me."

After a brief pause, Jude spoke. "I'll help clear your name," he offered.

Daniel laughed slightly in response. "I'm sure that'll come at a price."

"There's always a price to pay," Jude replied. "You're going to need to name yours one day."

"Yeah, whatever," Daniel replied.

"This disbarment is going to happen. Nothing you can do to stop it," Jude warned. "Nothing personal. You're just in the way."

"Yes. Some friend you turned out to be," Daniel said.

"As I said, nothing personal. Don't shoot the messenger," Jude stated, before turning to go. I wanted to ask after him regarding Daniel's disbarment, but knew he would remain tight-lipped about it all.

I made myself scarce through the day, so as to avoid seeing Daniel and dealing with his crabby mood and animosity towards David. As a result, he got into the habit of of ringing me at work, constantly. I chose to respond to some of his messages, not all, which infuriated him further. After a series of days when I did not return his calls during business hours, he decided to turn up at the office.

Craig was seated across the desk from me - we were reviewing a brief prior to his late morning court appearance. The clock had just struck 9 am.

Daniel came in not long after. He wore a black leather jacket, Pearl Jam t-shirt, stonewashed black jeans and brown loafers. Clearly he'd taken the day off from work. He helped himself to the seat at the table to the right of me.

"Can I talk to you?" he asked of me.

"She's in the middle of something," Craig insisted. He'd grown to dislike Daniel with a passion, dismayed by his treatment of David.

"Can I talk to my woman alone," Daniel asked, his voice slightly raised.

"Like I said, she's in the middle of something," Craig repeated.

"I can speak for myself," I said. "Whatever you have to say Daniel, say it now."

"I demand to speak with you on your own," he said, pulling the chair in front of him out, and sitting down.

"Don't come in here making demands," Craig warned. "Don't come here into my offices making demands like that."

Daniel slammed his fist on the table. "Your offices? It is still my name on that door!"

"Might be your name on the door, but your wife is a partner in this firm now, not you. Therefore, it's her name on the door. This hasn't been your place of business for a while now," Craig replied. "You need to handle your other business. Away from here."

"You need to stay the heck out of my business," Daniel retorted.

"I'll stay out of your business when you start acting right," Craig replied, adding fuel to the flame. "She doesn't need your drama," Craig said firmly.

Daniel then did the thing he was so good at doing lately – he abruptly got up and walked away, slamming the door on his way out.

Craig turned to me with a puzzled expression on his face. "Is this guy for real?"

I sighed in response. "If he doesn't like the sound of it, he's out."

"Seems to me he can't handle the truth," Craig said. "Or much of anything else."

"He's pretty sensitive," I explained, knowing him all too well.

"Stubborn as, if you ask me," Craig commented before switching topic altogether. "Right, now the Petersen file. 10 am tomorrow, conference call. You got this?"

"I sure do," I told him, admiring how he was able to quickly get back to business and not let the drama affect him.

"I meant what I said," he started. "About Daniel acting right. He needs to get right with you, or he'll continue to be a *persona non grata* around these parts."

"I hear you," I replied.

"He needs to cool off and act right," Craig reiterated.

"That's up to him," I mentioned.

"Yep. Just be sure to remember that. Don't let him make it about you," he said. "Now back to working on those closing arguments."

We bumped into Daniel again at the neighbourhood diner.

Craig had proposed we get together over dinner with David and Jeremiah to discuss a charity do the hospital was planning on hosting.

I had barely sat down when Daniel turned up, demanding that I leave with him.

"She's staying," David said, speaking on my behalf, "She just got here. Give her a chance to get something to eat, to kick back with some mates..."

"Not on my watch," Daniel stated, standing akimbo.

"Whoa," Johnny remarked. "Cock block in full effect!"

I tried not to laugh out loud but it was hopeless. Impossible where Johnny was involved. Daniel caught the tail end of my laugh and cast me a dirty look.

"Tell me about it," David said, getting up to go. "Ain't nothing wrong with a little friendly get together," he stated. "Obviously any sort of get together is out of the question, as far as you're concerned," he added.

"Great, so you know how I feel," Daniel said, eyeballing me before turning to go.

"Hold up, Daniel," Johnny urged. "You need to let loose man. Stop taking it all too seriously."

"Easy for you to say, you haven't got anything to lose," Daniel said.

"We've all got something to lose, mate. I'm no exception," Johnny said. "Come with me out back," he requested.

"Now why on God's green earth would I wanna do that!" Daniel exclaimed, eyeing him suspiciously.

"Just come with me out back now, will you?" Johnny requested.

Daniel stayed put, assessing the situation.

"Alright," Johnny stated, reaching into his suit pocket for

his keys. "Here," he said, placing the keys in Daniel's hand. "The keys to my '76 Shelby Cobra," he declared. "Let loose. Take her for a spin. I'll ride shotgun."

Clearly tempted, Daniel fiddled with the keys in his fingers. Looking over at David, Craig, Shania and myself, he asked, "And leave you all here? No thanks."

"Give it a rest will you?" Johnny demanded. "The best way to lose someone is to hold on to them too tightly."

"Ain't that the truth," Craig stated, as Daniel still stood there, unconvinced.

David stood up to speak with Daniel. "Look, it's a public place. We'll be here when you get back," he promised. "I give you my word."

For a moment, Daniel stood there, torn. Eventually, Johnny's proposition won him over. "A spin in the Shelby Cobra it is then," Johnny announced. "See you all in a bit," he said to us all, winking at me as he walked away.

11

THREATS AND PROMISES

"Did you know his brother was loaded?" Shania asked as we sat chatting over a cup of coffee and iced chocolate across the road from her beauty salon. I gave her a dirty look. "Shania, what are you on about?"

"Okay, well, I guess I shouldn't be surprised. He *is* a doctor *and* a dentist after all. Therefore, he *is* loaded."

"I'm sure he manages alright," I replied casually. David lived modestly and wasn't one to flaunt what he had.

"Don't know why he walks around acting like he ain't got nothing, when he's got enough to put down for his own place," she stated, puzzled. "Guess he doesn't want to draw attention to himself?"

"Don't know, maybe," I replied, distracted by the text message I'd just received from Daniel.

Where are you? he asked.

Out. I replied.

"I hear he's looking for a place to live now?" Shania asked.

"Well, you know more than I do," I replied.

Out where? Daniel texted.

Out. I replied again. I could tell he was getting impatient.

"Tell him to come by my place sometime," Shania stated. "Or better yet, how about we do a double date night at mine?"

"Not sure Daniel will be interested - he seems to want to cut David out of his life completely," I replied.

Am I going to have to physically come and find you in order for me to know where you are? Daniel texted.

"What's up girl? Obviously someone's blowing up your cell and it's putting you on edge," Shania noticed.

"Daniel," I stated, showing her the text messages he'd sent.

She giggled, throwing her head back in laughter. "Girl! What's up with that!"

"Your guess is as good as mine," I replied. "He's been carrying on like this since his brother turned up."

"Understandably," she stated. "The King's afraid of losing his crown," she said, half laughing. "Are you going to tell him where you are?"

"Why should I? There'll be more questions when I do. It won't stop there," I said, from experience.

"You need to put him in check," she suggested. "Don't let it get outta hand," she stated. "Not wanting another Duayne in your life now are you?"

"That's different," I argued.

"Really? The way I see it, his behavior is on that continuum of controlling behaviour," she reminded me.

"I suppose," I stated. "He's just a little insecure, now his brother's around."

"Not surprisingly," Shania asserted. "David's giving him a run for his money – you being the figurative green."

"You're shocking, Shania." Another text came through. *Why do you have to be so difficult?* Daniel asked.

I couldn't resist replying, *Why do you have to be so insecure?*

A further text came through. *Early dinner?* This text was from David.

"What's he saying now!" Shania queried. I showed her Daniel's text and my reply. She laughed heartily in response. "You're not helping things, Teme."

"Daniel needs to learn to trust me more," I replied. To David's message, I texted back, *I'm with Shania at the moment. Can she come with?*

Sure, he replied. *The Bayou on 23rd Street, 20 mins?*

K, see you there I replied.

When we arrived, David was out front, sitting at one of the outdoor tables. He stood up quickly when we approached, and greeted Shania with a kiss on the cheek, and I with an embrace and kiss on either cheek.

"So, you girls up for an early dinner?" he asked, cheerily.

"I'm famished," Shania stated. I nodded to the affirmative.

"Good. Best vegan Texan grill I've ever had is here," he noted.

"I see," I said. The Texan sun shone on his wavy locks giving his hair a golden brown hue. His perfect lips and mouth formed a wide, dimpled and welcoming smile. "Good to see you," he said softly. The baby blue cotton shirt he wore brought out his deep blue eyes which glistened ever so slightly as he smiled at me.

"Would you rather we sit inside or outside?" he asked.

"Either is fine," I said.

"Inside it is then," he replied. The brown khaki pants he wore hugged his body tightly enough. David's body was Daniel's body, enhanced. I tried not to stare.

He noticed me staring and winked knowingly. I quickly

diverted my eyes away from him.

"I hear you're homeless?" Shania chimed in.

He laughed unexpectedly. "Is that what you're being told?"

"Yep, though you don't have to be. My door is always open," she stated, openly flirting with him.

He raised a brow in response, before saying coyly, "I'm a bit of a rolling stone, so I won't be needing a home. For now, anyway."

"Plans to move on?" Shania asked.

"That's for me to know and you all to find out," he replied. Changing topic, he asked, "What can I get you two to drink?"

"A sweet tea for her and a long island ice-tea for me," Shania interjected.

"Okay," David said cooly. Shania was playing a game she thought she could win, while I was annoyed at Daniel's possessiveness.

"I'll be back," Shania stated. "Just a quick trip to the Ladies to powder my nose," she said, winking at David as she got up to go.

David humoured her and gave her back a wink. *Shameless flirts.*

The moment she was gone, he turned to me. "We didn't get to talk properly at the diner. Firstly, I want to apologise for walking out the way I did that other day at the café. Daniel said some pretty hurtful things, and I just thought a bit of space would do us all some good."

"Okay," I replied. "You did leave in a bit of a rush, and when you came by later to get your phone you didn't even say hello."

"Daniel didn't let me. I had no choice."

"Oh," I said. "There I was thinking you were avoiding me."

"That's partly true. But you know me. I'd be around you all the time if I could," he confessed.

Hi statement made me flushed in the cheek.

He smiled at the effect. My brown skin was fair, and I must've been visibly blushing.

After a brief pause he stated, "I have a confession to make. I haven't been completely honest with you. I came here to locate and connect with my brother, but I also came here to connect with you."

"Okay, that's no secret David. Is there anything else you've been holding off on telling me?" I asked. "It sounds like there's more."

He nodded to the affirmative, looking somewhat ashamed. "I've been monitoring you from a distance," he stated, trying to avert my gaze.

I nearly chocked on my drink. "Excuse me?"

"I work for an Australian intelligence group, and I've been monitoring you from a distance. Not because you're a person of interest, but because I felt the need to look out for you and protect you," he said.

"Okay, did I hear you correctly when you said you've been *spying* on me?"

He nodded sheepishly to the affirmative. "I wouldn't call it spying, that's too strong of a word to describe what I've been doing," he said.

Shania returned, but he held my gaze for a while longer than he should have. "I had no choice but to do it at the time," he said. "I'm sorry."

"There's always a choice," I replied. "Hope you enjoyed the view," I stated sarcastically.

"Come on now, it wasn't like that," he said quickly.

"What wasn't like what? What was it like, then?" Shania asked, curious. "Fill me in on what I missed out on!"

David, whose gaze had not left me since we started talking gave me an apologetic look before turning to Shania. "Nothing for you to be concerned about," he stated. "So, are we ordering now?" he asked, changing topic, his manicured hands gracing the laminated restaurant menu.

"I've suddenly lost my appetite," I said, livid at his confession. I knew he had sought me out but I didn't know the extent to which he had been prepared to go to locate me.

"Don't be like that Teme," he urged.

Impatient, I asked under my breath, "How long? For how long was I under surveillance?"

"Can't we talk about this later?" he asked, motioning towards Shania.

"You started this."

Shania raised a brow and browsed her mobile.

"I'd rather talk about it later," he said loudly, grimacing slightly.

"Fine," I retorted.

"Whatever it is you need to say, don't mind me!" Shania announced, taking a big swig of the drink she'd just received. An even bigger swig followed.

"You planning on going easy on your drink?" David asked bluntly.

"I won't be going easy on my drink," she replied. "Though I can go easy in another way," she stated, batting her eyelashes at him.

He laughed at her forwardness. "I appreciate your candour Shania. Honesty can be hard to come by these days," he said, as though in a slight dig to me.

"Yep," I replied. "Honesty is a loaded word. Some people are only honest when it suits their purposes."

He shifted uncomfortably in his seat. I could tell that my words had hit a nerve. Avoiding eye contact with me, he turned his attention to Shania. She was all too happy to oblige.

"I've got a bone to pick with you Shania," he started.

"Oh, *do you now?*" she questioned, giving him a sly look, and raising an eyebrow.

"You can stop spreading those insidious rumours about me being a man about town," he requested, a little under a whisper.

"I don't know what you're talking about," she replied.

"Oh, *don't you now,*" he stated sounding slightly peeved.

"It's not a rumour if it's true, is it?" she challenged.

"And you would know all about the truth, right?" he asked, staring her dead in the eye.

Shania kissed her teeth and dropped her glare.

David smirked in response. Not long after, a tall, handsome, dark haired and well-coifed waiter breezed past our table. David raised a hand, signaling for him to return. Tray in hand, he spun around on cue. "Whatever she's having next," David requested, motioning towards Shania who was trying her level best to pretend she wasn't into David. "Make it two," he said. Casually glancing over at me, he added, "And a mineral water for the lady. With a slice of lemon. Hold the ice."

I rolled my eyes in response. "You can't begin to presume you know what I want, David," I protested.

"I'm sure I wasn't wrong," he replied, with a wink. He wasn't wrong. He knew me so well it was scary. The waiter smiled in response to our little tiff and breezed off.

"Too confident for your own good," Shania interjected. "Man about town," she added.

David clenched his jaw in annoyance. "Yeah whatever," he retorted. I could see she was starting to annoy him quite a bit. Turning to me again, he asked, "Are you going to forgive me? Or am I in the doghouse for now?"

While I couldn't get over what he had done, on some level I felt reassured that he had been there, watching, surveilling. Had he not been watching, the situation with Duayne may well have ended up differently.

"I suppose I ought to be thanking you for doing what you did as it saved me. Things didn't turn out exactly as you'd hoped though," I stated.

"No, they didn't," he replied. "Early days yet," he stated. "There's still a chance."

Shania's phone rang and she stood up and walked away to take the call.

With Shania gone, David used the chance to chat me up.

"So, now I'm forgiven, Temwani, I've got something to give you," he said deeply. He handed me a gift wrapped in pink paper and fushia pink ribbons.

"What's this?" I asked.

"Open it," he insisted.

I unwrapped the paper. A bottle of perfume. *Laura Biogotti, Venetia.* "Oh my gosh!" I exclaimed. "Where did you manage to find this?"

"I have my sources," he said, looking very pleased with himself. "Better not let your old man know who you got it from though," he joked. On a more serious note he stated, "I can't even look him in the eye anymore. I'm afraid that if I do, he'll see all the love I still have inside of me, for you."

"Oh, he sees it alright. What he doesn't see he feels," I told him, sighing in response. David's continued declarations of love were wearing me down slowly. I needed to watch my step with him. Too close, and I felt I might slip up and into his arms.

"Am I truly forgiven?" he asked, interrupting me in thought.

"Forgiven for what?" I replied. "It's already forgotten."

A sign of relief swept across his face. Though I forgave him, all was not already forgotten, but I let him believe so. I quickly slipped the gift into my handbag as Shania made her way back to us. Before she sat down, David caught my eyes, winked again and smiled. I felt my heart flutter, and wished he didn't have it in him to make my heart and my entire being, melt.

Daniel greeted me warmly when I got home, which I found suspect considering the text exchange we'd had earlier.

"You smell different," he noted. "I love that fragrance on you. What is it?" he asked.

"It's something I used to wear many years ago. Venetia, by Laura Biogotti. It went out of production, but I managed to get me one today."

"Oh. From where?" he asked suspiciously.

I averted my eyes from him, knowing he wouldn't like the answer. "David managed to get it for me, as a gift."

He kissed his teeth in response, changing from being warm and kind to cold and furious. "Do I need to lay down the law here when it comes to him?" he asked, angrily.

"Don't be ridiculous Daniel," I replied.

"Oh, so I'm being ridiculous now, am I?"

"I didn't say you were ridiculous, I meant that you coming up with rules to govern my interaction with him would be ridiculous."

"Do you want him? Do you want to be with him?" he questioned.

"No Daniel, I want to be with you," I said firmly, but couldn't deny the chemistry I felt when I was with David.

"Okay, you want to be with me, you're going to have to quit hanging with him," he ordered.

"Daniel, he's your brother. Of course he's going to be hanging out with us," I replied.

"Hanging out with *you*, I said," Daniel clarified. "I don't want to see or even hear that you've been socialising with him on your own. You wanna hang with him, guess what, I'm hanging with you too," he said point blankly. "I expressly forbid you from being with him anywhere, anytime, anyhow and whatever which way, alone."

I could feel anger surging in me. "I don't like the things you're saying and I don't like the way you're treating me right now. You don't own me."

"Sugarpie, the fact is you're mine and I've got every right to insist on you behaving a certain way. I've got every right to insist on you not doing things to jeopardise our relationship," he stated.

"The only one jeopardising our relationship right now is you, with your insecurity and your need for control," I replied. "He's your brother for goodness sakes..."

"He's also a man in love with you, who won't stop at anything to get you," he speculated. "And no, I'm not insecure," he added. "What you're doing to me would be enough to drive any man in love around the bend."

"You're kidding, right?" I conjectured. "What *I'm* doing to you?" I asked, getting heated. The twins kicked wildly in my belly. "This is all you," I said. "Is this how it's going to be from now on? You trying to control me, you trying to dictate how I should live my life? You can't keep me sheltered Daniel. I'm yours to behold, I'm not yours to own."

"Settle down, babe," he urged. "Let's not argue."

"Let's not argue? You expect me to take what you're giving and just accept this as is?"

"I expect you to take me for what I am," he stated. "There's no denying I'm a jealous guy, who wants you for myself."

I rolled my eyes in response. "So you *are* insecure. Daniel, this is stifling. I can hardly breathe when you behave like this..."

"I know how to make you breathless," he stated, approaching me, intent in his eyes.

I resolved to decline his advances and cut him short. "You don't own me, you can't tell me who I can and cannot befriend," I stated.

"Well, I can certainly try," he said, kissing me on the nape of my neck. "Lover, wifey, friend, last time I checked I was still yours and you were still mine."

I pulled back from him, determined not to give in. He appeared surprised, for a moment, but continued to pursue me. Though his touch was tantalizing, I needed to make my point clear. "Daniel, no."

He ignored me. "I'll pretend I didn't hear you saying that. It's been weeks since you put out, and you're not going to turn me down now. I know you want this," he said somewhat angrily, gruffly unbuttoning my blouse.

"Daniel, stop," I insisted. "I don't want this. Not like this. Not with you so angry at me. Not with you thinking you own me."

He scowled in response and finally stopped pressuring me to make love to him. "Damn him," he said loudly enough for one of the babies to kick, and for that kick to be visible on the outside.

"Whoa," he said, suddenly remorseful for his attitude. Forgetting his anger, he placed a hand on my belly and tapped lightly. The twins kicked in response, and he smiled briefly. "Can't wait to meet our babies. Hope we can stop with this fighting."

"You and me both," I stated.

Taking my hands in his, he stated, "I love you so much Temwani. I wish things didn't have to be so complicated. Things were fine before he stepped on to the scene..."

"Can't blame him for all our issues. We had issues before he even turned up," I reminded him.

"I know, I know," he acknowledged. "I guess I have to find a way of learning to let go. I should really trust that you wouldn't do anything to hurt us, and that what we have here is real," he stated.

"You should know I wouldn't do anything to hurt you," I replied.

"I just...I don't believe you when you say you're not falling for him," he said. "I feel he's slowly convincing you that being with him is the way to go."

"You give him too little credit. He wants me to be happy. With you."

"Yeah, right," he responded, sarcastically.

"You know, we ought to thank him," I stated.

"And why's that?" he asked, haughtily, as though the thought of thanking David for anything was preposterous.

"We wouldn't be together if it weren't for him," I stated.

"What do mean by that?" Daniel asked, intrigued.

"He's had me under surveillance for some time, partly because he wanted to find me after all these years, partly because he had to. Anyhow, he was the one who prompted that message to you, that led you to find me that night. He's been watching me for time."

I watched the look on his face turn from intrigued to furious. "What do you mean he had to. The fuck?"

"Do you have to swear?" I asked, slightly peeved. "He told me today, and he apologized."

Shaking his head, he stated, "I knew he was into you, I just didn't know how much. He's practically obsessed." He stood up and paced the floor for a while. Back and forth, back and forth. He sat back on the sofa next to me, and ran his hands through his dark brown hair.

"Seems I'm going to have to lay down the law when it comes to you and him," he stated.

"There's no me and him, Daniel," I said. He wasn't listening.

"I'll believe it when I see it," he stated. "This goes back to what I was saying before. He'll stop at nothing to get with you. I just wish you weren't so into him so you could see what I can see."

"Daniel, I'm done with you accusing me of things I do not feel."

"It's not an accusation if it's true," he corrected. "I know you well," he added.

I sighed in response. "There isn't anything I can say to convince you otherwise then," I concluded.

"No, there isn't," he stated.

"Fine then."

"Fine," he replied storming off in a huff. I didn't have to wonder where he was headed. It likely had something to do with David.

Daniel was gone for several hours before he returned. I was in bed by the time he got back. When I heard him walk into the bedroom, I closed my eyes, and pretended to be asleep. He planted a kiss on my cheek, and as I lay in bed, eyes closed, I heard him strip off his clothes and get into the shower. I reached for my mobile phone but noticed it was not on the dresser. *Daniel!* I heard the droplets of water fall in the shower, and imagined him standing there in the bathroom, scrolling through the messages on my phone. Resisting the urge to surprise him, I lay there in bed, for what seemed like an eternity. *Not a very good detective*, I thought. *How obvious.* My word clearly meant nothing to him.

After a good ten minutes, I heard the shower door finally close. *He's actually taking a shower now*, I thought. *Time to get a new phone.*

Shower done, he slipped into bed, completely naked. Spooning up against me, I felt him beckoning me for some action. Though still peeved at him, I obliged, wanting to get it over with, and wanting to be at peace with him. Obliging would put me at peace with him. It didn't take him long to get satisfied. I lay there next to him, waiting for sleep to hit. Moments later, when his hand around my waist felt heavy with sleep, I slipped out of bed, phone in hand.

I sent a text message to David. *You okay?*

He replied instantaneously. *I'm fine. You shouldn't be texting me.*

I'll do as I please, thank you very much, I replied.

A slight pause ensued before he wrote back. *I meant, whatever you do, do not contact me, not now, anyway. I've just been served with a restraining order.*

I felt pure rage rise within me and stared at him sleeping peacefully next to me. *Who did he think he was?*

I'll be seeing you, David replied. *Get some rest.*

I worked from home the next few days, stayed up late and slept through the mornings. Overnight, Daniel and I became strangers living under the same roof. He'd return from work, exhausted, and would fall asleep on the sofa. I had no energy to pursue him or request anything be different. If I had to be honest with myself, I enjoyed the break from his drama. When we weren't talking, we were not arguing. When we weren't arguing, we were at peace with each other. I found solace in that in itself, yet felt a deep loneliness inside.

David checked in with me daily, and though I knew Daniel was reading every message, I wrote back. The texts were short and simple, centering around the weather and work. There was so much to say, but I was not willing to rock the boat. Not just yet anyway.

The second week into my hiatus, I woke up earlier in the morning – the moment I heard Daniel leave for work. He'd arranged for the installation of a security fence, one which would ensure that any visitor would need to use the intercom to enter, or use a code. I decided to go for a walk, as it had been several days since I had been outside.

On my return from the walk, I checked the mailbox that was now on the other side of the fence.

A small unstamped parcel addressed to me was within. It hadn't gone through the postal system, it had been dropped off sometime between last night and this morning. I instantly recognized David's handwriting. I opened the parcel to find a book. James Baldwin's *If Beale Street Could Talk*. A note within the book read:

"*I picked this up at the market last week, and of course I thought of you.*
D. x

A further note within the inside jacket of the book read:

Don't ever feel alone in this world.
I'm in your world.
You are my world.
D. x

I felt my heart melt at the thought that he believed I was his world, but my conscience told me otherwise. *Snap out of it. Daniel will be ropeable if he were to find out you were still allowing David to woo you.*

I walked back up the driveway heavyhearted. I felt imprisoned in my life with Daniel. Living behind gates that were meant to keep one person out made me feel even more so. I struggled to come to terms with the fact that I'd escaped a controlling and abusive relationship with Duayne, only to end up in a controlling relationship with Daniel. Maybe David was right, Daniel didn't deserve me.

I felt conflicted. Things had to change between Daniel and I, and it would need to happen before the twins arrived. I worried alone that afternoon when the twins wrere quiet and moved very little. The stress wasn't helping, I could tell. The rest of the morning, I battled belly cramps and back pain. Telling myself that it was just as a result of not drinking enough water, I heated up some hot milk and sat on the sofa for the rest of the day, checking my messages on my phone from time to time. I requested the day off from work, and Craig sent through a text message asking me to take it easy.

Not having much of an appetite, I skipped lunch and slept through the afternoon til early evening. That night, I woke up to even more painful excrutiating back pain, belly cramps and a pool of blood on the sheets.

I reached over for Daniel but he was not there. Probably still at work, as had become the norm these days. The pain was excrutiating. I called David. His phone rang out, then was picked up. A chirpy female voice answered the phone. "Sharlene on Doctor Davenport's phone, can I take a message?"

I paused, contemplating before I responded. "I need his help."

I could hear David in the background, a little over a mumble. "Okay," Sharlene stated. I wondered who she was and where they were. "He's in surgery at the moment, he says he'll call you back in a few."

I called Daniel again. His phone rang out. I left a message and decided to call the paramedics. I jumped into the shower to clean off the blood, but it trickled continuously. For a moment I sat there on the shower floor, crying, hoping the babies would be okay. I prayed.

It seemed like an eternity before the paramedics arrived.

"Blood loss?" the female paramedic asked, slipping a pulsometer onto my finger, and a blood pressure cuff on my left arm. I nodded in reply. "How much?" she asked. I didn't know. "Did you put on a sanitary pad to catch the flow?" she asked. I nodded in reply. Initially I had. "How many pads did you go through? How many weeks are you?"

"Two pads. I'm 28 weeks," I replied.

My phone rang but it was on the kitchen benchtop. Jake, the male paramedic, handed it over to me.

"I'm on speaker," David stated. "In the middle of surgery. I'm a little worried about you, you calling me at this time is unusual. Is everything okay?" he asked.

In between tears, I said, "I've lost a bit of blood...I'm on my way to the ER."

"The General or the Presby?" he asked.

"The Presbyterian."

"Okay," he started. "I'm at the Presby. I'll find you when you come in," he promised, bringing the call to a close.

Triage over, I lay in bed, closed my eyes and cried. Feeling alone, I remembered David's note. *"Don't ever feel lonely, I am in your world..."*

A tender hand brushed my cheek and wiped away my tears. I opened my eyes to see David sitting by my bed, in medical scrubs. Though his sea blue eyes were filled with worry, he smiled and said hello. Taking my hands in his, he stated, "I'm glad you and the babies are okay."

I felt warmth rise in my chest as he stared at me deeply. Tears threatened to fall, and I could not hold back. "Don't cry," he beckoned. "Don't cry. I'm here for you."

In my sadness I thought about the restraining order. "What about the order?"

"What about it," he asked, unmoved. "There *is* such a thing as lawful excuse isn't there?"

"I guess..."

"Where is he anyway. He should be here with you. He should have been there with you."

"To be honest, I have no idea where he is," I replied. "He's not picking up his phone, I've tried him several times..."

"Right," David replied, sounding peeved. "Let's hope he'll be here soon enough." Changing topic he stated, "You're in good hands here." Leaning forward as though he were letting me in on a secret, he advised, "I've asked a friend to look in on you. Sharlene. She was the scrub nurse in theatre," he explained.

"I figured that," I lied, recalling the slight pang of jealousy I'd felt when she'd answered the phone initially.

"I'm clocking off in a few but I've asked her to come and check in on you from time to time."

"That's sweet of you," I replied. "I'll be fine though."

"I know you *will be* fine. But no need to be all stoic and all right now. It's okay for you to admit you need support. It's okay for you to admit you *need me*," he said as a matter of factly.

"David..."

"Yes, I'm incorrigible," he stated, laughing heartily. I laughed along with him, forgetting my sadness.

"Seriously, where *is* Daniel," he asked, as puzzled as I was about Daniel's whereabouts.

I grabbed my phone off the side table and rang Daniel again. No answer. I didn't bother to leave a message this time.

David stood up and removed his phone from the pocket of his light blue scrubs. "I'll give it a go," he suggested. I could hear Daniel's phone ring several times before the answering machine beep. In a deep throaty Aussie accent, David said into the phone, "This is David. Your wife's in hospital. Where the bloody hell are you?" he asked. Hanging up, he stated, "That'll get him here in no time."

I sighed in response, grateful he was there with me, but wondering where Daniel was.

"I'll stay here with you 'til he comes in," he promised, plunking himself into the seat next to me.

"I've never seen you in scrubs," I noted.

"I've never seen you in a hospital gown," he replied.

"Touché."

He smiled in response.

"What are you doing on the maternity ward?" I asked.

"Repairing a cleft palate on a set of twins," he stated quickly. His phone buzzed wildly and he picked it up. "Yep.... Okay. Look mate, I don't care how you get here. Get here," he commanded. "The Presby," he stated. "Room 218." Hanging up, he turned to me, "He's on his way."

"Okay," I replied. "Where is he?"

Tight lipped, he replied, "He'll be here."

I could tell by the look on his face, he wasn't pleased.

"David, where is he?" I asked again.

"He's been out and about...drinking," he replied. "Says he'll have to take a cab to get here." Noting the concern in my eyes, he replied, "If they discharge you tonight, I'll take

225

you home."

I felt sadness and anger at Daniel's behaviour. Not only had he not come home, but he had failed to get in touch with me, failed to return my calls, and failed to be there when I needed him the most.

"Teme," David called out. "Try not to worry. I'm here for you."

My door was partly ajar and through that opening, I heard commotion in the form of a raised voice then some deep and pronounced male giggling. Moments later, the platinum blond blur that was Johnny burst into my room.

David sat up in his chair, startled.

"Teme." Johnny started. "These are for you," he announced, pulling out a bouquet of yellow roses from behind his back. With a slight swagger, he made his way over to me, to David's fury.

"Easy mate, hold up," David challenged, standing up in an attempt to block his passage. "Where's Daniel?," he asked.

"On his way," Johnny replied, swiftly darting past David to get to me. His energy was contagious. "Sorry to see you're up in here. Hope all goes well. Didn't mean to keep your man away from you tonight, had one drink, one thing led to another, and..." he stopped short, as though not wanting to incriminate himself. "The short and tall of it is he's here now."

Though angry at Daniel for not being there, I smiled in response to Johnny's apology and accepted his flowers. *Johnny is bad news*, I recalled David saying to me one afternoon, when we bumped into him at the Lakeside Café. *He might be bad news but his positive energy and zest for life is always welcome,*

226

I thought.

Johnny plonked himself down in the seat next to my bed with reckless abandon. David looked at him suspiciously. "You're not planning to stay, are you?" he asked.

"Just hanging around for Daniel, he won't be able to drive himself back home." Johnny admitted.

"You got here by taxi, didn't you?" David asked skeptically.

"I drove here," Johnny stated, chuckling slightly. "What's with the interrogation Doc?"

"You're off your head mate," David said sternly. "You're in no condition to drive!"

"Somebody stop me!" Johnny said mockingly in his best Jim Carey voice. Carelessly, he nearly toppled over the glass of water on the tray next to me. Seeing ahead, I sturdied the tray. "Taxi!" he exclaimed, giggling over the fact that he'd nearly spilt my water. It was belly laughs for me.

A furious David stated, "Right. I think it's time you left. Temwani doesn't need this drama."

"I'm not going anywhere, *matey*," Johnny announced in a comical Aussie accent. "As I said, I'm waiting for Daniel to catch up so I can give him a ride home. But if you insist, I'll be taking a taxi. Taxi!" he exclaimed again.

"Alright," David said, clenching his jaw. "Settle down then," he ordered, moving to stand by the right side of my bed in a protective stance.

Johnny ignored him and made small talk with me. "You know, I've got a good name for your little boy," he stated. We'd recently found out we were expecting one of each - a baby boy and a baby girl.

"You do?"

"Yep, you better name him after yours truly," he joked.

"I'd be *completely* honoured if you did."

I laughed gregariously in response. "You are pretty full of yourself Johnny, aren't you?"

"Not full of myself, no. Full of surprises, yes," he replied.

"Well, you're a surprise we'd rather not have at the moment," David interjected, eyeballing Johnny.

"Whatever mate," Johnny replied. "Can't stand the heat, get out of the fucking kitchen..."

"Settle down," David insisted. "She needs to take it easy, and you're not helping," he urged.

"You need to take it easy," Johnny replied in jest. "Need to get that big old stick out of your ass."

David frowned in response, deciding to ignore him for now. He absently scrolled through his phone, pretending to be otherwise engaged.

Not for much longer. Daniel rushed into the room moments later. "I came as quickly as I could," he said, adjusting his tie. "How are you – how are the babies?"

"We're all fine," I said tearfully.

"What happened?" he questioned. The smell of booze on his breath was quite apparent. My heart sunk at the fact that he had been out drinking again when he was supposedly at work.

I explained.

He wasn't listening. A furtive glance in David's direction, interrupting me mid speech, Daniel stated, "He shouldn't be here."

Okay, I'm here in hospital, and all you can comment on is the fact that David's here with me? "Really?" I asked.

"Yes, *really*. He shouldn't be here. We had an agreement," Daniel stated.

David interjected, "I'll be here for as long as *she* needs me to be here."

I could see fury insurmountable rising in Daniel. He got up suddenly, too quickly, as though to swing a right hook David's way, but didn't. His face paled before he made a quick dash for the ensuite bathroom. Door slightly ajar, we heard him violently retching and vomiting into the toilet.

"A little too much to drink tonight," David noted, stating the obvious.

"Well, at least he knows how to hang loose," Johnny stated. "More than you'd ever know being all uptight all the time."

"You need to act your age," David replied.

"You need to act your wage - barber slash butcher slash surgeon," Johnny replied, tapping on his gold Rolex watch, flaunting it at David. David frowned in response.

"Enough guys," I requested, tired of the bickering. It was wearing me down.

Heeding my request, Johnny shot up and out of the chair he was in, and looked in after Daniel, leaving the bathroom door fully open. Standing next to him, he held Daniel's tie out of the way as he was sick in the toilet. I felt my stomach churn in disgust.

David sat down next to me, passing a furtive glance towards Daniel and Johnny, the look of disdain on his face very hard to hide. Turning to look directly at me, he said point blankly, "He doesn't deserve you."

Tears in my eyes, I stated, "I'm starting to believe you."

Placing a firm hand on my shoulder, he beckoned, "Don't cry. It's all up from here," he promised. "It has to be. I'm gonna make sure of it."

I laughed mid tears. "And how are you gonna do that,

229

Superman?"

"Ha, ha," he replied. "I've got my ways."

Eventually Daniel left the bathroom, and retired onto the sofa beneath the bay window. "Sorry babe," he muttered. "I just need to sleep this one off," he said.

I hated the way he used the word *sorry* so loosely.

Johnny said goodbye and headed off, promising to come by the next day for Daniel.

Not long after, a knock on the door was sounded and Sharlene came in, medical chart in hand. "Full house I see!" she exclaimed.

"How's the lady?" she asked.

"Better, but I'll let her tell you herself," David said, moving out of the way.

"Hi, I'm Sharlene," she stated, offering her hand. I took it. She held it for a moment before manually checking my pulse. Turning the blood pressure monitor on, she checked the EKG feed. "Babies are looking well, your blood pressure is a little on the low side though," she said, concerned. "Under a bit of stress?"

"A *bit* of stress?" I queried, motioning at Daniel who had made his way back to the bathroom and was hovering over the toilet bowl once again. "That's an understatement."

Sharlene raised an eyebrow in response. "Well, you're going to have to take it easier than you have been. Don't want these little ones to come on out early, now, do we?"

"No," I replied, relieved to hear that the babies were fine, but concerned about my blood pressure.

"Your ob/gyn is Dr George Dimitriou?" she asked.

"Yep," I confirmed.

"He's on tomorrow night but we buzzed him to see if he

could come in and do a brief evaluation. Doctor Foley will see you in the interim, but Doctor George will be here in a few."

I nodded, comforted that Doctor George would be coming by.

"Okay, that's all the checks we need done for now," Sharlene concluded, plotting some figures on a chart before closing the folder that contained my file.

"Doctor Dimitriou?" David asked.

"Yes, the one and only!" Sharlene exclaimed.

"He was my clinical supervisor in med school," David recalled. "Could get a baby out via c-section in 4 minutes flat!"

"George being my ob/gyn, is this a coincidence?" I asked.

"I'm afraid it is, this time," David replied, with a wink. He squeezed my hand, a reassuring gesture in my time of need. "Look, I'm gonna head out for a bit, do the rounds. I'll come back when I'm done. Will you be okay?" he asked.

"I'll be fine," I managed, not wanting him to leave.

"I'll be back in no time," he promised, sensing my anxiety.

"Okay," I said, already wishing him back as he walked out.

George came in not long after. Boy was I was glad to see him.

Motioning over at Daniel, he stated, "Are you the patient, or is he?"

"Tell me about it," I said.

He laughed in response. "Try to reduce the amount of stress in your life," he urged. "I can't emphasize that enough. We don't want these little ones born too soon, now do we?"

"No, of course not."

"Good. We're on the same page." Unstrapping the blood pressure cuff from my arm, he noted, "Blood pressure is on the lower side, but I'm not too concerned. Make sure you get enough rest, and only light duties at home if you absolutely must," he ordered. "I'm also putting you on bedrest for a few weeks, in the hopes that this will encourage you to settle down, reduce the stress and let someone else do the heavy lifting," he stated, motioning towards Daniel.

"Bedrest, meaning..."

"You're working from home, or quitting work for now, altogether," he stated.

"George, you know I can't do that, I've practically been on bed rest the past two weeks already."

Arching a brow, he re-stated, "You need to reduce the amount of stress in your life. You'll have to do something, unless you want to have these babies come early," he stated. "It's non-negotiable."

"Okay, then." I reluctantly agreed with his recommendation.

After George had done his evaluations, he turned to David who'd just returned from doing his rounds. "You're the brother in law?"

"Davenport," David stated, introducing himself to George.

"No introductions necessary," George said, "Class of '96?" he recalled.

"Yep."

"Good to see you mate," he said. "How's the practice back in Aus. Busy?"

"As busy as we can be mate, just taking a sabbatical for the moment, doing a bit of work up here," David explained.

"Well, we need you here, that's for sure. Let's catch up some time, even if it is just for a brew at the local," he requested.

"Sure, no doubt," David replied.

"You know when I first met these two, I knew dad looked familiar," George said. "Didn't know he had an identical twin, did he?"

"No, trust me he didn't." I said.

"Explains why you're pregnant with twins now, hey?" George said, turning to me.

"Exactly," I replied.

"So, everything's all good?" David asked, seemingly irritated at the mention of anything to do with Daniel.

"Yes, mom and bubs are good," he confirmed. "Superwoman here just needs to learn to take it easy."

"Bedrest?" David asked.

George nodded to the affirmative. "For at least 6 weeks."

"Right," David said pensively.

Turning to me, George stated, "It *is* just bedrest I'm asking for. It's not like I'm asking you to give up a kidney," he joked.

David smirked at the comment and I laughed.

"That's more like it," George said. "A little less stress, a lot more laughter," he added. "No strenuous exercise, and definitely no sex," he ordered.

I raised a brow in response. "Daniel's not going to like that," I noted.

David averted his eyes from me when I snuck a look at him sideways. I could tell he was secretly happy.

"It isn't up to him," George stated. "Doctor's orders. Now, get some rest, drink lots of water, laugh much, stress little, and keep the drama to a bare minimum," he said, before heading off. "My regards to Dad," he added as an afterthought.

"Man, this is awkward," David started after George had

left. "Father to be is out like a light, and it's just you and I here, and somehow I'm privy to everything that's going on in your life."

"It *is* awkward," I agreed. "But I'm glad you're here with me."

"Good," he said, heartily. "Hey, do you want to go for a quick walk, catch some fresh air, get something to eat from the canteen?" he asked. "It'll be a while before you get discharged." Motioning at Daniel who was fast asleep, he stated, "It'll be a while before *he* gets up."

I *was* hungry. "Okay," I agreed, quickly getting up.

"Take it slow," David suggested, swiftly carting a wheelchair next to my bed. "You're on bedrest, remember," he reminded me, helping me into the wheelchair. He slipped the blanket that was on the end of the bed onto my lap and stretched it over my legs. I smiled as he did so.

"Thank you," I told him. He nodded in response.

As we went out to the courtyard, I asked, "Aren't you afraid that people will talk?"

"They can talk all they want, for all I care," he replied. "Besides, it's not as though we're doing anything worth taking about anyway," he said. "Not yet anyway," he added.

"David, I wish you'd stop with this wishing we'd be together."

"You know me," he replied. "The day you're with me, the day we're together is the day I'll stop wishing."

"You've got it bad," I stated.

"Tell me about it," he replied. Changing topic, he stated, "So, no sex. For 6 weeks. I don't reckon your old man's gonna be thrilled about that."

"Yep, well, he's going to have to deal with it."

"No sex. That means no sex of the solo kind either," David said as he smiled wickedly, waiting for a reaction.

"David!" I exclaimed loudly, giving him the reaction he expected.

"Why are we having an X-rated conversation here?" I asked.

"We just are," he replied. "Don't friends discuss sex?"

"You know it ain't right," I stated. "Besides..." I started. "Talking about sex is off limits."

"So, what's it like?" he asked.

"What's what like?" I asked.

"We're friends, right?" he questioned.

"Of course we are," I stated, not liking where this was going.

"Good," he replied. "So, what's it like being married to my brother? Was he the first one to pop your cherry?"

I closed my eyes in disbelief. "Are you for real David?"

"I'm very real."

"I'm not discussing my sex life with you."

"Why not, we're friends, aren't we?"

"Yes, but friends don't make each other feel bad," I said.

"Who says I'll feel bad," he questioned. "Who's to say I'm not taking note for future reference for the day that you are mine," he stated.

"David you really need to stop with all this pursuing me," I warned. "I'm off limits."

"I know, I know," he replied, sighing heavily. "I can't help fantasizing about you, and wishing that I was your man." He paused for a moment. "I know I'm sinning every day, breaking that 10th Commandment – to not covet someone else's wife, someone else's life, but I can't help it."

I nodded in response.

"I'm only human," he added, applying the brakes on my wheelchair and taking a seat on the bench opposite the mini water fall in the courtyard. He sat so he faced me directly.

"I didn't lose my virginity to Daniel," I informed him, regretfully. "I lost it by force," I stated, remembering Duayne when I long should have forgotten him.

"I'm really sorry to hear that," he replied, full of empathy. "Really sorry you had to go through that," he said softly, kindness in his blue eyes.

"Daniel was my second," I replied.

"Hm...," he stated, leaning forward slightly. Contemplatively he said, "How I wish I could have been there for you. How I wish I could have been your first."

"I'm flattered," I replied. "Things happened as they did for a reason, though. It's not up to us to second guess the past or the future," I said.

"I guess so," he replied. "I had a plan to see us together," he added. "I didn't have the confidence to approach you properly then. So I'm here, now, and it's too late," he mused. "So, if I prayed for us to be together, irrespective of what the present shows, do you think my prayer would go answered?"

"David, you praying for us to be together would be you praying for things between Daniel and I to come to an end," I stated bluntly. "Prayer is powerful. Please don't do that," I requested.

"I hear you," he said. "It's just real hard for me to continue seeing you being taken for granted. I long to be the one who satisfies your every need."

"David..."

"Alright, I'll stop," he promised. "Can't stop me from

236

praying though, that's between me and God."

I worried for a split moment, before thinking that God wouldn't allow harm to come my way. Still, I remained concerned about David's blind adoration of me, knowing that prayer was powerful.

"So, I know you said we should stop talking about sex...," he started.

"I did. Please stop."

"Okay," David said, somewhat disappointed, but he didn't let up. "So... he said he was a virgin when you were first intimate?" he asked skeptically.

I nodded in response.

"He's having you on," he stated.

"Meaning what?" I asked.

"He's not being honest," David claimed.

"And why do you say that?" I asked, convicted that Daniel had told me the truth.

"Ask him again and listen carefully to his response," David suggested.

"Look," I started. "He hasn't given me any reason to doubt him. I see no reason why he would embellish or lie about something like this."

David smirked in response. "A man in love may do or say anything to get and keep his woman. Ask him again," he suggested. "Just because there was no penetration doesn't mean he hasn't had sex before," he said point blankly.

David. Why do you always have to throw a spanner in the works?

"I'm not trying to hurt you here," he stated. "I just want you to get real where he's concerned. If he demands honesty from you, he needs to be honest."

"I hear you," I replied.

"The thing is, you needing to "respect" and "submit" to him is or at least should be nullified, where there is clearly an abuse of power and position in the marriage," he said, sternly. "Now I'm not saying he's abusing you or anything, I'm just saying that you should only "submit" to a Christ-like husband. Submission involves yielding and giving way. No one's perfect, but he can't start making demands on you like that."

I took what he said to heart. After all, Daniel had promised me he would not be controlling.

"There's no excuse for his behaviour," David added.

"No, there isn't. He's just afraid of losing me," I offered, as an explanation.

"So he should be," David stated. "Holding on to someone too tightly is one sure way to lose them."

I sighed heavily, unsure of what to do next.

"He needs to get right with you," David suggested. "This needs to come from him." Fiddling with the beaded bracelet on his wrist, he added, "For a moment, forget that I have vested interests in this whole affair."

"Kind of hard to forget don't you think?"

"Hear me out," he beckoned. "If he gets right with you, and changes his ways, I'll accept that you'll never be mine, and we can work on maintaining a friendship that supports you and him. I only want you to be happy," he reiterated. "But if he doesn't get right with you, then that's another ball game. He knows as well as I do that all's fair in love and war."

"This isn't about you and him."

"Well, it can be, and it will be," David suggested. "Besides, isn't it about you both submitting to each other - submitting to one another out of reverence to Christ?"

"I guess so," I said, slightly unsure and feeling ill at ease that he was suddenly quoting scripture and starting to know more than me. *He's done his research*, I thought.

"You know I'd submit to you. Willingly," he said.

"This isn't about you," I reminded him.

"I put it to you that it is," he said confidently and as a matter of factly, leaning back into the bench in an effort to get comfortable.

Silence ensued as I contemplated what he had just said.

Sensing my unease, he apologized. "I'm sorry. I can't help how I feel. Me saying this and me being here is probably not helping things."

"I just wish he could see what I see, and feel how I'm feeling. He's taking me back to a place I never wanted to return to. I know I shouldn't let my past rule my future, but somehow this all seems like familiar territory. I refuse to go through what I went through before. Daniel's so called love is not love if it seeks to control me."

David stood up abruptly, and put a firm hand on my shoulder. "I'll talk to him."

"I don't think that's a good idea," I warned.

"Good idea or not, I'll talk to him," he promised, getting up, determined. "A quick bite to eat in the canteen?" he suggested. "You must be famished."

With that, he whirled me around in the wheelchair and we were off again. My heart felt heavy at the thought of David confronting Daniel. It would not end well.

David's plan to talk to Daniel backfired. No surprises there.

"You need to lose this order, and lose your control issues," David suggested.

"You need to get lost!" Daniel replied stubbornly.

"Guys, settle down," I urged. They both ignored me.

"One day she *will be* mine," David said with such conviction and voracity it made me tremble.

"Not in this lifetime," Daniel replied swiftly.

"Gee, I don't know mate. I'm on my knees every night praying for it to happen. I know God answers prayers – question is whether my prayer is in His will," David announced.

A flash of anger swept across Daniel's face. "Don't you dare try to break up what God has put together."

David laughed. "God may have put you two together, but *you're* doing everything you can to throw away what the two of you have. I don't need to break up anything," he announced. "You're doing a pretty good job of that yourself. Temwani and I *will* end up together."

In a swift move, Daniel gave David a hard left hook to the jaw.

David winced in pain.

"Not in this lifetime, *mate*." Daniel repeated.

"Stop this nonsense!" I urged, standing in between them.

Turning to me, Daniel stated, "You're not helping this at all! What is it with you and your so-called friendship with him? Am I not enough for you that you feel you have to be so close to him all the time?"

"Daniel, you know where you and I stand. You *should* know where I stand with him. I'm with you. He's a friend." I wanted to comfort David, but held back, knowing that it would add fuel to the flame. Daniel wasn't having it.

"Well some friend he turned out to be," Daniel stated. "He's doing everything he can to break us up."

"Typical," David stated. "Blame everyone else but your-self."

Sizing him up, I thought Daniel would lunge for David again. Instead, he stood, fists and jaw clenched.

"Daniel," I stated, placing a hand on his shoulder. "Calm down."

"You'll be sorry you knew me, David," he threatened.

David shrugged in response. "We're brothers."

"Not by choice," Daniel added.

A brief tinge of sadness swept across David's face, and he collected himself, patting his disheveled hair down, suddenly self-conscious. "If you say so," he replied, casting a furtive glance my way before turning to go. My heart went out to him and went with him as he walked out the door.

Turning to me, Daniel questioned, "When is this going to end? Are you going to start respecting me as your husband and are you going to start doing as I wish? Do we need to ask for some outside help here to get this right, and do we need to ask the church to pray on this for us? It really is getting to be too much," he said.

"Are *you* going to start respecting me? Firstly, you can't choose my friends. Secondly, I've been praying on a lot of things, and one of the things I been praying on is for you to be a lot less hot-headed and a lot more considerate of others," I replied. "I've also been praying that you become a lot less controlling. You're starting to remind me of Duayne!"

Disbelief shown in his eyes and he shook his head in response. "You're not really hearing me at all now are you. About me reminding you of Duayne, don't you dare compare

241

me to him. We are nothing alike." Abruptly getting up, he didn't wait for my response. He walked out, leaving me alone again.

I broke down in tears as soon as he walked out. I reached for my phone, ready to call David, but hesitated. Daniel and I needed to work things out together.

Daniel's ears must've been burning as he walked back in moments after he'd walked out. His face flushed, it looked as though he'd been crying.

He sat by the side of my bed and held my hand, firmly. Toying with the ring on my finger, he sat there in silence for a moment before stating, "I don't know how I'm gonna fix these problems we're having. Feels like we're so far gone."

I nodded in reply. Looking at me fondly, he wiped a stray tear off my cheek.

"I refuse to lose you to David," he said defiantly. "I'll do whatever it takes to keep you mine," he promised. "I'll risk it all for you," he said, his words sending a chill down my spine.

12

THE CORINTHIAN

As Daniel went on bender after bender with Johnny, I lost track of the number of nights I'd be up waiting for him to return. In defiance of the restraining order, David kept me company in the evenings when he could and avoided Daniel, but one night he decided that enough was enough; he was going to talk to Daniel, yet again. He stayed up that night with me, and greeted Daniel at the door.

"You need to get your act together," David scolded him. "She needs you to be there for her, she needs you to be present."

Daniel, clearly still drunk, shrugged in response. "She'll be right," he said. "She's a strong independent woman, she'll be right. Isn't that what you Aussies love to say?"

Placing both hands on Daniel's shoulders to hold him steady, David replied, "No, she won't be right. For as long as you continue acting like a tool, she won't be right."

Daniel laughed delightedly. "Acting like a tool... that's a new one." He straightened up slightly when he realized I was awake.

"Daniel if you don't settle down, you'll be sorry," David

warned.

"You done making your proclamations? Who died and made you King?" Daniel questioned, starting to get annoyed. "King David."

David frowned. "Don't mind him, he's on his way out...he won't be staying here with you tonight," he stated, turning to me.

"No, no, no, I'm not on my way out, I'm not going any where," he announced. Sighing loudly, he pondered, "Oh, where's Goliath when you need him!" Staring David down, he questioned, "You got your slingshot ready, mate?"

I couldn't help but laugh. David cast an annoyed look my way. "This isn't funny," he stated. "Don't encourage him." Turning back to Daniel, he said, "This is for your benefit, not mine. The sooner you can get your act together, the better it will be for everyone involved."

"Yeah, yeah, yeah," Daniel stated, brushing past David and towards me. He drunkenly tried to steal a kiss from me but I turned away from him.

"David's right," I told him. "You need to get it together." He rolled his eyes in response and I knew there was no point talking to him any longer.

"Look here beautiful, I'm fixin' ta get myself some shut eye right about now. Stop worryin' about me, stagin' interven-tions and all...and just let me be," he requested. Winking at me, then saluting David, he walked off saying "Everything'll look better in the morning."

Daniel gone, David turned to me. "I'm staying here tonight. I'll leave in the morning when he's sobered up."

I said nothing, grateful for his mere presence. This was Daniel's way of getting back at me for continuing to maintain a friendship with David. Trouble is, it would hurt him more than it could ever hurt David or I, in the end.

November came a week later, and Craig reserved some seats at the Bayou for the joint birthday celebration for myself, Daniel and David.

"Well, look at what the cat dragged in!" Daniel exclaimed loudly when David arrived, looking cool and handsome in beige cotton trousers, chinos and a blue polo shirt. "The Corinthian," he announced. "The man about town."

David looked visibly shocked. Turning to me he asked, "He feeling okay?"

Daniel carried on. "Cat got your tongue?"

Craig who had been there before us said firmly, "That's enough mate."

Daniel continued. "Cat ain't got your tongue, you're what the cat dragged in."

Posturing, he announced loudly, "For those of you who don't know, this here is my baby brother. Pity he has no sense of loyalty to family though - every waking moment he's got, he uses it to get close to my woman."

David squeezed my shoulder lightly, and turned to go.

"Leaving so soon?" Daniel queried. "I was just getting started."

Craig stated again, "It's enough mate," and tried to usher Daniel away. Daniel fought him angrily. "You're just as bad. The whole lot of you. Defending this vagabond of a man."

David stood there for a moment, visibly hurt. His face was flushed, and it seemed all eyes were on him.

Craig tried once again to usher Daniel away. "I think you've had a bit too much to drink mate," he said.

"Oh the fun police!" Daniel announced.

"Time to shut this down I think!" Craig thought aloud. "Alright everyone, spectacle is over, barbecue's outside, drinks and music are outside."

A few people immediately took his cue. Quite a few didn't. Daniel continued to resist attempts to be ushered away. "To quote the great Bard, all the world is a stage, isn't it baby brother. And everyone has their role. You played your role pretty well..." He stumbled for a moment, almost lost his balance, then carried on. "Bravo baby brother, my woman doesn't need rescuing, but you're playing the role of the knight in shining armour pretty well. How many of you here can agree his performance is worthy of an Oscar. Or a Golden Globe, or Logie or whatever you Aussies give out for a stellar performance," Daniel said, turning to take a swig of bourbon out of his glass.

David still stood there, motionless, before finding his voice and stating, "He needs to be stopped. He's embarrassing you, he's embarrassing himself and he's hurting me." Sighing heavily he added, "I'm sorry for all this drama."

Without warning, Daniel threw his glass in David's direction, narrowly missing him. Shards of glass peppered the floor as glass hit marble tile. Checking I was okay, David was livid. Motioning to Craig and Jonah, David signaled to the door. They read his cue and attempted to usher Daniel out. Daniel fought them all the way. Just as he got to the door he lunged at David who was caught unawares. Daniel's left hook struck him hard in the mouth before he had a chance to react. Bloodied lip, I could see that it took everything for him to not fight back. "Thanks for that mate, thanks," he said sarcastically.

I left his side in a hurry to get some ice for his lip.

"I suppose I should take a bow," David said a little too loudly. "Man about town he says I am," he stated, half smiling. "And what was it he called me? The Corinthian?" he laughed slightly.

A woman I didn't recognize had her phone out. "Should probably leave," I mentioned under my breath, motioning towards the woman.

"I *will* take a bow," he said, making a sweeping bow. "Don't let this ruin your night," he urged. "Next half hour, drinks are on me," he pledged, winking at the bartender. A friend. Turning to me, he stated, "Not much of a celebration I'm afraid. I'm sorry things had to go so far."

"Don't apologise for him. You've done nothing wrong," I told him.

"Coming here after all this time - I shouldn't have. I should've let well enough alone and things wouldn't be like this," he assumed.

"That's a lie and you know it."

"Well, he wouldn't be drinking himself to death and carrying on like this had I not been in the picture."

"David, you don't know that," I told him. "It would've been some other thing, some other issue... Daniel loves control."

Silence ensued before he stated, "I'll take you home."

"I'm not going back there now. He needs to cool off," I said.

"I'll take you wherever else you'd like to be then," he said, in between applying pressure to his bruised lip. "Man that hurt," he said beneath his breath.

"You're a sight for sore eyes," I stated, fighting the urge to reach out and touch his face. "I'm losing track of the number of times he's swung at you."

"Yep, well..." David said. "I need to make myself scarce. He's not planning on going easy on me anytime soon."

"True," I acknowledged, meeting his hand and offering to hold the ice over his lip. His fingers were ice cold.

"I can manage," he said, though he didn't knock my hand away.

"I know you can," I replied. "I'm just letting you know I'm here for you too."

He sighed in response, before saying "I'll be alright," and taking the ice away from his lip.

Craig returned. "We're going to have to shut this down mate, I've tried to smooth things over but the manager's not happy."

"Understandable," David replied. "How is he?"

Avoiding eye contact with me, Craig stated, "He's out back, having a bit of a chuck up. Johnny's not much help, the pair of them are a disaster waiting to happen."

"What a surprise," I stated, disappointed.

"Sorry matey," Craig stated, embracing me. "We'll have a little get together on your actual birthday. No drama allowed. I'll make sure of it."

"Thanks Craig," David replied on my behalf.

"You alright?" Craig asked, motioning towards the slightly swollen lip.

"I'll be alright," David replied.

"Good," Craig said. "Well, I'll shut this party down, and we can get on with the night."

"Okay," David said. "I'll make sure she gets home okay."

"Great," Craig said, squeezing me gently on the shoulder.

Catching my eye, David advised, "I know my place is small, but I can cook up a meal for you there and you can kick back for a little while before heading back home."

"Sounds good," I concurred.

"Sounds like a plan?" he asked.

"Sure thing. Though the way I feel, I'm not interested in heading back home at all. Not for a while anyway."

"Well, whatever you want to do is alright by me," he declared.

David's one bedroom studio was very minimalist in nature. Cushions on the floor in place of a sofa, and a shikibuton in the middle of the room reminded me of his nature. Calm, simple and uncomplicated.

"Any requests?" he asked, sorting through a sleeve of CDs. "How about some Dru Hill?"

Haven't heard Dru Hill in ages! I thought to myself. "Dru Hill sounds great," I replied flatly, not wanting to let him in on my excitement. *He knew me too well.*

"Dru Hill it is then," he said, picking up on my curtness, and suddenly becoming nervous. "I'll just go prepare something for you to eat," he said. "Make yourself at home."

He came back moments later with a grape spritzer. "I've made up some lentil pasties, as you know I'm a vegan, so unfortunately I can't offer you anything else right now."

"That's fine, David. It's enough that you're offering," I told him. "I'm sure it'll be delicious."

He nodded in response before setting the bottle of grape spritzer on the table and setting two glasses next to each other on the coffee table. His hands shook as he did.

"David, no need to get all nervous," I stated, partly laughing at his sudden shyness.

He stared at me somewhat relieved. "I don't know what just took over me...having you here has sort of brought back memories of me trying to get you to be with me, back in the day."

"I figured that," I said. "I won't bite," I told him.

"I wish you would," he joked, a little more at ease as he poured the spritzer into our glasses. He handed me a glass and sat next to me on the floor. "Cheers," he said, raising his glass for a toast.

"Cheers," I replied.

"To better days ahead for both of us," he declared.

After a few sips I set my glass down on the coffee table. "So, you came all this way to connect with your brother, and to get me to fall for you again. Things didn't work out as planned, so what next?"

"There's still a chance," he said. "Obviously at some stage I'm going to have to accept things may not change, but I'm not there yet."

"David, I want you to be happy. Knowing that you spent all these years longing after me makes me feel sad – you may be missing out on meeting the love of your life," I told him.

"I'm not missing out on anyone else," he stated. "I know in my heart that I'm not. You're here. You're the love of my life," he stated. "You're the only one I'm missing out on at the moment. If I can't have you, I'll just have to find a way to be without you. Alone."

I searched his eyes for reason, and found only love, resolve and determination.

"I admire Daniel," he said. "I wish I had his balls and his courage. I would have made you mine long ago if I had," he imagined.

I smiled in response, but advised, "Don't admire Daniel too much. He hasn't been the best role model of late."

"Yeah, well..." David started. "He's gonna have to fix up before your babies get here."

I nodded in reply. Switching topic, I requested, "Tell me more about you Doctor Davenport. I hardly know much else apart from the fact that you're crazy in love with me."

He smiled. "Apart from you, I'm all work. Med school and dentistry was my ticket out of a bad life," he stated stoically. "I had nothing else at the time, it gave me a sense of belonging, a sense of purpose. I'm not like Daniel, in the sense that he's always felt God was with him and on his side."

"What do you mean?" I asked. "Don't you believe in God?" I thought he did.

"I do believe in God," he confirmed. "I just wonder where He was at those moments in my life where I felt like what I was going through was too much to bear."

Embracing him, I stated, "He was watching over you then, and He's watching over you today. When you wondered where He was, He carried you. I know that for a fact. I've been there."

He nodded his head in agreement, though he seemed unsure. "Those were some tough times," he said. I beckoned him to say more, but he didn't. "There are some things I don't need you to know," he explained.

Fair enough, I thought. I knew he would tell me all in time. Just not tonight. Switching topic, I asked, "How are you liking Texas, you think you'll move here permanently?"

He half smiled. "I'm loving the fact that you're here, but I'm missing Aus. Getting a little tired of Daniel cussing me out and disrespecting me in public," he said.

"Don't blame you," I replied. "I just hope he fixes up before the babies are here."

"My thoughts exactly," David stated, getting up to check the pies he'd made.

The pies were delectable. I should have known that his preparing my meal was another way of him trying to woo me, despite his insistence to the contrary.

"I have a gift that I wanted to give you earlier on tonight, but thought I'd give it to you when I got you alone." He reached for my hand and placed a small red box in it. I hesitated for a moment, and he explained, "An early birthday gift. Open it please."

I opened the box to reveal a jewelled crucifix in gold with embedded pink diamonds. It was a beautiful gift.

The folded note within the box read as follows:

Teme,

Always keep the faith and keep believing and inspiring others. You've been an inspiration to me in more ways than one, and have encouraged me to reach for the stars in everything I do. I give you the gift of my time and attention, my money and resources, my power and influence, and finally, my love and affection. I know it's a long shot, but I'll give you what you ask for and take whatever you'll give. I feel blessed all the same to be in your life, as your friend. Please call on me when you need me (or any of the above). I will move mountains to be there for you.

Always,

David x.

"Thank you David," I said. *Such a brazen declaration of*

love. I paused for a moment before getting him his gift. "I have something for you as well," I told him, reaching into my handbag. "I couldn't get out much as you know, so I made you this." I presented him with a handwoven friendship bracelet. "Your wrist please," I requested, sliding the bracelet on. The deep brown hue of the bracelet complemented his tanned skin. I'd also gotten him a surf watch, so slipped this on as well.

He smiled widely. "Thank you, Temwani. I'm touched," he said, his eyes a little teary.

"You sure you like it?" I asked.

"Absolutely," he said. "Excuse the watery eyes. I'm just touched that you cared enough to get me something."

"Of course I do," I told him.

Examining the watch from every angle, he asked, "Is this one of those ones with a pre-programmed tide chart?"

"Yes, that and then some. Tide height and direction, moon phase..."

"So freakin' awesome," he said, clearly excited. "Thank you Teme, you've made my day."

"And you mine," I told him. As he beheld my gaze, a moment of awkward silence ensued before he reached for my hand and held it. "I can see you're exhausted. How about you get some sleep, and I can take you home in a few hours?"

I nodded in agreement. It was late, and I was beyond exhausted. He swiftly directed me to his bed, where I fell asleep to his eye gazing and the weight of his hand on mine as he knelt on the floor by the edge of the bed. Yet another moment I would remember forever, another moment which I wished would last a lifetime.

The promised get together on my birthday came in the form of a barbecue at Craig's place. Daniel wasn't invited, nor was Johnny. They both kept their distance, respectfully, given how out of hand Daniel's behaviour was at the previous get together.

Jonah greeted me with a firm handshake and a warm smile. His chiseled face and pure handsomeness made his hello all the more disarming. I could see why the other women were swooning over him, but something I couldn't put my finger on told me that there was more to him than met the eye - he was anything but gentle - he was capable of doing great harm. I hadn't had the chance to meet with him properly the night of the attempted birthday celebration. He'd been busy manhandling Daniel and getting him to cooperate.

"So I see you've met our resident muscle!" David exclaimed.

Jonah raised an eyebrow in response to David's comment and turned towards me. "Well, I've finally met our resident beauty," he said, in a way that was both charming and disarming.

David looked from Jonah to me and from me to Jonah. "Yep, she is beautiful isn't she," he acknowledged. "Now keep your eyes on the barbie mate."

"Yep," Jonah replied. "Wouldn't want to get those prawns on the barbie overdone now would we."

I peered over and into the barbecue grill. Jonah nudged me unexpectedly. "Just steak and sausages, no shrimp or prawn as the Aussies call it." I stared back at him blankly and he laughed heartily. "Inside joke."

"Yeah," David replied. "I forgot to laugh."

"Love you man," Jonah said with a candor that surprised

me.

"Love you too bro," David replied with equal candor. It was heartwarming seeing the way they were. Like brothers. Such a shame Daniel and David were at constant odds with each other.

Jonah smirked in response. "So you say, so you say." Turning to me, he asked, "So, can I get you something to drink? A champagne..."

"Nothing alcoholic for me," I replied.

"Hey, you can see she's with child, can't you?" David scolded him.

"I can see that, yes, but I know not all women do the right thing when pregnant, now, do they," Jonah said, flipping over a steak. "But I now know she does," he said as a matter of factly.

"I'll get you something to drink," David said quickly, wanting to avoid the topic. "Won't be a tick."

"Won't be too long," Jonah translated. "I guess you're getting used to the Aussie lingo now, right?" he asked, turning to me.

"Somewhat," I said, considering what I'd heard earlier about him. He was enforcer for the Brotherhood.

"You judge me," he stated abruptly.

"Sorry?"

"Don't believe everything you hear," he warned.

"I don't and I won't," I replied. "I try to go on my instinct, but it's been a bit off of late."

"We are all on the same side," he stated. "I would consider us all to be guardians of all that is good. We just have a different way of doing it."

"I guess so," was my reply.

David joined us again. "Doing what?" he asked abruptly, handing me a lemon flavoured mineral water.

"Preserving all that's good in this world," Jonah said. I could tell by David's reaction that he was pretty thrown.

"None of that talk any more Jonah, we're here to have a good time," he reminded him.

"I'm sure she understands me," he said in response. "I'm surprised you haven't..."

"Like I said, none of that talk now," David said firmly.

"Okay," Jonah replied. Switching topic, he asked, "How many weeks are you now?" he asked referring to my pregnancy. "What are you craving?"

Surprised by his forwardness, I smiled and replied, "30 weeks now." Sneaking a glance at David, I added, "Sticky date pudding, grapes, guava and hot dogs with a lot of pickled relish."

David gave me a knowing wink, while Jonah smiled warmly. "International palate I see. A bit of Aus, a bit of America, a bit of Zambia. Looking at David suspiciously, he added, "I'm guessing Aus is a pretty heavy influence, but I can help you with America."

Stepping in, David stated, "Alright American boy, that's enough flirting to last you a lifetime."

I giggled in response, and David gave me a gentle poke in the side, as though to remind me of something.

"Yeah, yeah," Jonah replied. "Your husband's one lucky man," he concluded. "If only I should be so lucky," he stated.

"If only *we all* should be so lucky," David concurred.

"Well, I can always hook the both of you up," I offered.

"Him yes, me no," David replied. "You know I've only got eyes for one woman," he reminded me.

256

"*You're* in need of a hookup the most," I reminded him. "Daniel's not going anywhere."

David swallowed hard before he spoke. "That may be the case, but I *need* you the most," he replied.

I sighed in response. There was no convincing him otherwise.

"Dangerous games," Jonah warned, gazing from me to David and from David to me. "It'll all end in tears," he predicted. Motioning towards the barbeque, he announced, "These are done. Can I get you that hotdog you've been craving?"

"You sure can," I said. David stepped forward and rolled up his sleeves to help. Washing his hands in the basin, he shook them off dry. He then handed Jonah a plate. Jonah piled on a hotdog and a lot of relish. *A lot.* Just the way I liked it. Handing it to me, he nearly dropped the plate when his eyes drifted and fixed on someone in the distance. *Shania.*

"Watch it mate," David warned, taking the plate from Jonah before noticing what Jonah had noticed. Shania who wore an emerald green swing dress which dipped into her cleavage, was making her way over to us. David gave Jonah a playful slap on the back and stated, "Here comes the hookup." I rolled my eyes at his statement but thought that a pairing between Shania and Jonah might just work. For a time anyhow. Apart from his disarming nature, Jonah seemed to be genuine. If anything, they would be honest with each other about how they would relate.

"Shania," David greeted her with a kiss on the cheek. She greeted me the same, and threw in a hug, causing me to drop my hotdog.

"I'll get that," David and Jonah said in unison.

Shania's eyes flittered to Jonah immediately. She gave him a wide smile which he noticed but tried to ignore, preferring to act composed. I could tell he wanted to smile back. Nervously, he picked up my plate while David swiftly moved to prepare me another hot dog.

She sensed his hesitancy. "I'm Shania," she said, hand outstretched.

He quickly took her hand and shook it with such vigour that his glasses nearly fell off his face. He adjusted appropriately before making his introduction. "Jonah."

"Pleased to meet you Jonah," she replied. I could tell she was smitten.

"The pleasure is all yours," he stated, confidently. David and I exchanged a knowing glance while I tried my hardest not to laugh. *The pleasure is all yours? How bold.*

"You here alone?" Shania asked, a little too direct for my liking, but not so for Jonah.

"You're here with me now, aren't you?" he replied.

"Let's go find you a chair," David said, in a cue for me to leave with him and leave the two of them alone. I could tell straight away that they would hit it off.

A self-assured, beautiful redhead by the name of Claudette appeared midway through the barbeque. In a silk green top, lycra tights and high heels, she was dressed to impress.

Greeting us all with a kiss on either cheek, she announced "Austin's finest is out to play, huh? Might just have to go get me some," she said, scoring the men of the Brotherhood, all of whom were otherwise engaged or occupied at the moment.

"Claudette, the men in the Brotherhood are off limit," Craig stated bluntly.

She tossed her auburn red hair and winked at him. "You

wanna bet?" she asked.

"This isn't a challenge," Craig stated. "It's a warning."

"Whatever," she stated. She wasn't listening. Her emerald green eyes blazing with a mix of determination and rebellion, she spun on her heels and walked away from him and straight towards David and Dante.

"She needs to be stopped," Craig said fiercely, without offering an explanation as to why she was not allowed to mix with the men of the Brotherhood. I watched as Craig stepped to her and pulled her aside. He whispered something in her ear that visibly caused her to recoil.

I watched as her face paled, and she stepped back from him for a moment. Then in indignation, she stated loudly, "How dare you play God like this!"

Craig tried to calm her down, but it didn't work. "How dare you!" she said again. "What, do they know?" she asked. "I'm guessing they don't." I noticed David taking a keen interest but he eventually turned away, lured by Dante's animated chatter. Craig leant forward and whispered something to Claudette again. His arm outstretched ahead of him, he gestured for her to walk ahead of him. She abruptly did, and they were gone. I stood there wondering what had gone down. David made his way towards me and asked the same thing. "What was that about?"

"I wish I knew," I replied.

"Guess we'll find out soon enough," David replied. Glancing at his wrist watch, he mumbled something about the time. "Should be going soon," he advised. I agreed. Daniel wouldn't be too happy if I stayed out much longer. "I'll take you home," he offered, motioning towards Shania and Jonah. It wasn't likely that we'd all be leaving together.

After saying a quick hello to Daniel, David said goodbye to me at the door. Following twenty questions on how the evening was and went, Daniel retired to the living room, and continued watching TV. A re-run of True Detective Season One was on.

I decided to call Shania to check in with her. Jonah had dropped her off at her apartment, after a few night caps at the local. Her excited chatter over the phone that evening was enough for me to see she was smitten by Jonah, and that he in turn was smitten by her. As I washed up the baby bottles I'd bought earlier on that day, I had her on speakerphone.

"Girl, he was so fine. Too fine for his own good," she said.

"Too fine? That's a new one. When is anyone ever too fine!"

"Well, I'd say *he* is. I can't believe he's single," she said. "Those trousers he was wearing were so tight I could see his religion!" she exclaimed.

I laughed in response. Daniel who'd caught the tail end of our conversation stated loudly, "Hey, hey, hey, enough with the dirty talk." Despite his scolding, he came and positioned himself at the end of the kitchen bench, eager to hear more.

"Is that who I think it is, the fun police?" Shania questioned.

I laughed in response. Daniel raised an eyebrow and frowned before turning to go. "You know you ain't right Shania. You're turning out to be a bad influence on this here lady of mine."

"Right," she replied. "Anything else you'd like to say? Wasn't talking to you, I was talking to her. Mind your own business. Bye!"

"Yeah, whatever," he replied, clearly irritated. Since David had been on the scene Shania had taken a strong disliking to Daniel. Probably because Daniel's behavior towards me had markedly changed. Probably because she had a soft spot for David. "I'm going out for a bit," Daniel told me. "I'll be back in a few hours.

I looked at the clock above the photo frames of us on our wedding day. 8 o'clock. I'd given up asking Daniel where he was going. If it wasn't investigative work, he'd be out drinking, and would stay out til he was sober enough to get home, or come home drunk.

"I'm popping out to see Craig," he stated.

The fact that he was alarmed me. They hadn't been seeing eye to eye on a lot of things of late, and dropping in to see Craig may not have been the best thing to do. So late.

"Okay," I replied.

"I'm still here," Shania chirped out.

"I know, girl, Daniel's just heading off."

"Good," she replied. "We can get back to discussing Jonah's religion."

"Shania, come on now!" Daniel exclaimed.

I nudged him and planted a kiss on his lips. "I'll see you later."

"You know, I used to like you Shania. I used to like you a lot," he spoke into the phone, hanging around for a while longer than he should have.

"I used to like you too, until you joined the Squad," she stated.

"I don't get it," Daniel replied.

"The Fun Police Squad," she stated, laughing hysterically.

I tried not to laugh but it was impossible. Daniel frowned before stating, "I'm out. See you in a bit."

A message came through from David as I settled down on the couch, popcorn and remote at hand. I planned to watch a movie until Daniel came back. *Hope you're okay*, the message stated.

All good, I replied. *He's gone out, says he needs to talk to Craig.*

A knock on the door startled me. *It can't be David.* I opened the door to find Johnny standing there. He seemed a bit off.

"Can I come in?" he asked, casting a quick glance behind me. I was in my PJs, ready for bed. "Sorry I came over without notice, and so late."

"Don't be silly, come in," I said. He did.

He slipped off his shoes, and I noticed he wasn't wearing any socks, he was barefoot. He then slipped off his jacket and when he turned to drape it carefully over the coat rack, I noticed vertical scratch marks on his neck. When he turned back to me, I motioned for him to follow me into the lounge room and towards the sofa where I asked him to sit.

"Rough night?" I asked as he sat down.

"Something like that," he replied.

"Daniel's just gone into town for a bit. You happy to hang til he gets back?"

"I'd love to," he said, his tone morose. "Thank you."

He sat there, head in his hands. I noticed the same scratch marks stretch across his collarbone.

"The marks on your neck, rough sex?" I asked, for want of a better thing to say, but knowing that was not the case.

He hesitated before replying. "You know, I wish it were something like that, but it isn't."

"So, what's it like?" I asked.

He shook his head. "I need to leave Michaela. I can't continue to live like this. All the things she says, all the things

262

she doesn't say, the lot of it is doing my head in."

I felt for him. "Sorry to hear that Johnny."

"Don't be. I got myself into this, I just can't see a way out," he stated.

There's always a way out, I thought silently, remembering how I'd felt with Duayne.

"Can I get you something to eat or drink?" I asked.

"Something to drink," he answered. "Whisky, rum, gin, whatever you've got."

"We've got the lot," I told him. "You know Daniel. Help yourself," I insisted.

"Thanks, I will," he stated, getting up. He'd been around our place enough times to know where things were kept.

Daniel came back home in a burst of energy. He made no mention of his visit to see Craig. Happy to see Johnny, he spoke a little too loudly, his tone only dampened by Johnny's sad mood.

"Man, what happened to your neck!" he exclaimed, not hiding his shock.

Johnny shrugged and said nothing.

"Rough sex?" Daniel asked.

"I wish to fuck it was," Johnny replied. "I try, I really do. When Michaela gets into one of her moods, she lashes out, and I just let her do what she needs to do."

"Sorry to say that buddy but I never liked that witch. You're better off without her," Daniel said bluntly.

"I hear you," Johnny replied, taking a big swig out of his glass of whisky. "I know if I go back to her tonight, I'll probably end up staying with her."

"So don't go back to her tonight," I suggested.

"I haven't got anywhere else to go," he advised. "She doesn't trust me with the finances, you know, what with me being... an addict. I usually have 20 dollars to my name at any given time. That and a petrol card."

Swallowing hard, he added, "Leaving her means losing everything I have and everything I've known," he said, his voice cracking.

"I'll get you another glass of whisky," Daniel offered.

"You're staying here with us," I insisted. "No buts. You are."

Johnny half laughed, close to tears. "That won't go down well with Michaela."

"Too bad," I replied. "What won't go down well is her being put in her place. Stay here for as long as you need to. She'll have to come here to get you to go back home."

He shrugged in response but agreed with me. "Okay."

I offered him a hug, which he took, wholeheartedly. One of the babies kicked hard against his belly and he pulled away abruptly, surprised. "Whoa, nelly."

I laughed a hearty belly laugh.

"Someone in there either likes me a lot or doesn't like me at all," he imagined.

"You want kids, someday?" Daniel asked, re-entering the room, bottle of whisky and two whisky tumblers in hand.

"I've always wanted kids, but Michaela..." he started. "Let's just say, she wasn't planning on having any with me - she didn't think I'd make a good father," he recalled painfully.

"That's a rotten attitude to have," I stated. "You're better off without her."

264

"I second the sentiment," Daniel said. "Just need to get you to see that too."

"No one's perfect, Johnny, any other woman would be happy to have you," I assured him.

He shook his head to the negative, disagreeing with me. "Not sure I believe that entirely, but I know I can't be with her anymore."

"Good," Daniel replied. "Cheers to that," he added, raising his tumbler to Johnny's for a toast. "Here's to better days ahead."

"Aye," Johnny replied. "To better days."

Despite the bad influence Johnny and Daniel could be on each other, *and let's face it, they were just as bad as each other,* there was so much love between the two of them, and I was grateful he was in our life. Johnny was the brother Daniel wished he had, the brother David wished he was to Daniel, but would never be.

Johnny stumbled into the living room one evening, after clearly having had too much of something. "Speaking with Michaela today was a mistake. She thinks I'm using, I may as well use," he stated.

"Daniel's not going to be too happy to see you in such a state," I told him. "Not here, not now."

"I know," he said. "I need to get clean."

"That's awesome Johnny, glad to hear it!"

"Just not tonight," he replied. "Or tomorrow night, or..."

"Okay," I stated, firmly gripping him by the wrist. "I'll get you something to eat, and I expect you to settle down. Whatever it is you've had, no more. Give it a rest will you?"

"You're an angel," he stated, clumsily taking off his jacket. "I've just had a few drinks tonight," he confessed.

"Seems like you've had more than that," I noted. Some white powder rested on the tip of his nose. I dabbed it off.

"My bad," he said. "I might've had bit of angel dust too. Angel," he joked.

"Please stop this nonsense Johnny. Enough is enough alright? You can't expect Michaela to support you when you're not even trying."

For a moment he looked hurt. "I try, believe you me. I try. It's hard to measure up when there are all these expectations. From Craig, from Michaela, you..."

"No, Johnny. The only expectation I have from you is that you start caring about yourself enough to want to change."

"You're right," he said sombrely. "I need to get over my weak ass, and everything will change."

"That's not what I said Johnny," I stated. "Nor is it what I meant," I explained. It was late, and I wasn't in the mood to reason with him when he was high, so I directed him to the guest room.

"I don't want to sleep!" he protested.

"I'm not trying to get you to sleep, I'm trying to contain you," I told him.

"I'm more interested in staying up and talking," he said, resisting my attempt to redirect him. "Food first," he insisted, standing firmly in place. "Food first, then I'll go to sleep."

"Okay, you win," I conceded, heading back to the kitchen. He followed.

"I've got a bone to pick with you, Temwani," he said all of a sudden.

"Do you now?"

"Make me up one of your awesome omlettes and I'll tell you more," he promised, planting himself firmly before the kitchen bench.

"You win again," I said, getting busy with the omlette making. The quicker he could eat, the quicker he could lose his state and return to normalcy. Or so I hoped.

"Daniel loves you like crazy," he started. "Everything he does is for the love of you."

"Including going out on a bender with you, like almost every other night?"

"No," Johnny stated. "We haven't done that for a while. Not since that night at the Bayou when he lost it. What I meant was, most of the time he walks around pretty tore up inside about the fact that you might be falling for his brother."

"Daniel knows how I feel about him. I can't spend any more time convincing him that I'm not planning on being with David any time soon," I insisted.

"Any time soon, she says," Johnny noted.

"That came out wrong."

"You have considered it, then?" Johnny questioned.

"You need to get to bed," I advised.

"You *have* considered it," he said again. "Heartbreaker."

"I'm only human," I replied, cut at the fact that he'd called me a heartbreaker.

"So is Daniel. He's not perfect. He's bound to make mistakes. Don't judge him by the yardstick David's set and loves to go by. David's as perfect as they come."

"I won't and I don't," I replied, placing his omelette on a large plate and serving it up with some cherry tomatoes.

267

"Thanks darlin'," he said, before devouring his meal.

"I'm not a heartbreaker," I stated. "He's breaking mine."

"I hear you. Well, at least he's got your back and you've got his. I'm sure it'll all work out in time. Once David goes back to Australia, I'm sure things'll work out."

Once David goes back to Australia? Had he been making plans to leave without informing me?

"You, know, I lucked out with Michaela," he announced. "She doesn't cook, she doesn't clean, she doesn't even put out for me. Anymore that is."

"That's pretty sad," I replied. "How long have you been with her?"

"Six years now," he said. "Long enough to know she doesn't care for me at all. Long enough to know she's been using me. I'm just a meal ticket to her. Now that her meal's running out, what with me not having a job anymore, she doesn't give a toss about me. Probably never did."

"Surely there's *some* love involved? Six years is a long time to pretend, don't you think?" I asked.

"You've seen her, Teme. No fucking love involved whatsoever," he replied, and I cringed at his swearing.

"You did say her tolerating you was some kind of love," I reminded him.

"I know. I've wisened up since then. I suspect she's givin' a little something on the side to someone I know."

"Who?"

"One of the guys who deals," he stated firmly. "Either way, she's no good for me," he stated.

"She's not," I confirmed. "You're not doing right by you either. You're no good for you," I added.

"I know, it's fucked innit it. I want to change but I'm so

caught up in this pain and..." he broke off.

"I wish you wouldn't swear as much, Johnny!" I exclaimed.

"I wish I didn't as well. My life is just fucked."

"Johnny!"

"Sorry. Don't mean to, I can't help it," he claimed. Reaching into his pockets he produced a lighter, some cigarettes and some keys. His keychain had a silver whisle attached, and a black sapphire cross wrapped in angel wings. One which I recalled seeing somewhere else before.

"Can I see that?" I asked, reaching out for the key chain.

"Sure," he said, slightly puzzled.

"Where did you get this?" I asked.

"Some girl passing by cared enough to give this to me many years ago when I was on the street."

I dropped the keys in shock. I'd picked up a similar pendant at the Camden markets many years ago, and had given it to a man I saw sleeping on the streets of Guildford. One afternoon as we walked out of our criminal law procedure lecture, I noticed the swag at his feet. The same swag I'd seen him sleeping in near the bridge, by the cinema complex.

Johnny knelt down to pick up the keys at the same time as I did. In that moment I recalled his face and he recalled mine. *I* had given him that pendant, all of ten years ago.

We spoke without saying a word. I handed the keys back to him.

"What are the odds, ey?" he asked.

"What are the odds indeed," I stated, suddenly overwhelmed with emotion, my eyes watering with tears as I recalled how I had wondered after him for many years.

"You truly are an angel," he said. "Daniel's lucky to have you."

"I'm lucky to know you," I told him.

He helped me get up. "I'm sorry for putting you through this, for involving you in my sorry excuse of a life. As you can see, despite the time gone past, I'm still a bit of a mess."

"No apology needed. I'm glad I'm in your life," I told him.

"You might end up regretting you said that," he warned.

"Then the regret is mine to have," I told him.

"What's with the secrecy and the low voices!" Daniel asked, strolling into the kitchen, startling us both.

"Just taking a stroll down memory lane," Johnny replied, quickly slipping the keys back into his pocket.

"Hm...," Daniel said suspiciously before he was distracted by the empty plate that was in front of Johnny. "Any chance that I can get some of what you made him?" he asked.

"Of course, baby. Of course," I replied. Johnny snuck me a wink which Daniel didn't see. As I prepared another omlette, I worried after Johnny. I worried about the past which was clearly influencing his present. I worried that his drug use would get the better of him, and that he didn't care. He wanted to erase the pain he felt at all costs.

"How are you feeling today, mate, are those nasty headaches you were having gone?" Johnny asked.

"Funny you should ask, yes, they're gone, for today at least," Daniel replied. "Meds have helped."

"Well, they haven't helped me," Johnny replied.

"Hm...?" Daniel asked.

"Meds have helped you, but haven't helped me – I've been left without a drinking partner," Johnny joked.

"Oh, poor Johnny," Daniel replied, playfully nudging Johnny with his fist, an invitation to shadow box.

"Not in the kitchen guys," I warned.

"Well, let's take it outside then," Johnny suggested.

"Yeah, right," Daniel replied. "You won't even make it to there Johnny boy, I'll knock you out cold, straight up."

"Sounds like something Michaela would say," Johnny replied. "Empty threats?"

Another jab to the waist and Johnny raised his fists then swung one at Daniel in retaliation.

"Outside you two," I ordered.

"I was heading that way anyway," Johnny stated. "For a quick smoke."

"Can't stand the heat, mate?" Daniel jived.

Johnny half laughed before attempting a roundhouse kick.

"Outside you guys!" I exclaimed. "Don't be too long," I told Daniel. "Daniel, your omelette will be ready in no time."

"Thanks babe," he stated, weaving past Johnny to give me a quick peck on the lips before heading out front.

"Johnny you promised me you'd rest," I reminded him.

"What with all this excitement? I take that back!" he exclaimed. After seeing the look of dismay on my face, he stated, "Okay, I will."

"Good," I replied as he walked off to join Daniel.

Boys will be boys, I thought, smiling to myself as I wondered about life and how funny it was that I'd met Johnny all those years ago.

13

THE HEALER

When I woke, I checked my phone and noticed I had missed several calls from Shania. I immediately tried to call her back, but David rang me first.

"I need to meet with you ASAP," he demanded.

"Can you come over?"

"Not if Daniel's there. Besides, it's probably better we meet elsewhere. He hasn't dropped that restraining order."

"Daniel's out," I told him.

"Still."

"Okay," I obliged. "There's a small café just a few meters from ours?"

Sighing heavily, he stated, "I forgot, you shouldn't be driving anywhere, being on bedrest and all."

"George went a little easier on me," I told him. "I can drive short distances. He says I'm alright to do a few moderate activities."

"Okay," David said. His tone worried me, I'd never heard him sound this anxious. "Look, I'll just come over to yours. Daniel comes back, I'll just have to handle it."

"Okay. See you soon then," I replied, wondering what had

him all shook up inside.

I turned back to my phone and called Shania. Her phone rang out, so I left a message.

It didn't take long for David to come over. He sent me a text message when he was out front, and insisted on talking outside.

We sat on the porch swing.

"How are you?" he asked, barely smiling.

"I'm okay," I replied. "You don't seem okay," I noted.

His face flushed, he paused for a moment before blurting out, "Shania's pregnant," he said stoically, without making eye contact. My heart skipped a beat. That was unexpected. As I tried to recover from the shock, I realised why she had been frantically trying to get in touch with me earlier.

"I guess that's what happens when you're busy picking them up and laying them down!" I said.

He frowned in response. "Those rumours aren't true," he insisted.

"Well, she got pregnant somehow, and I believe congratulations are in order, given you're going to be a dad!" I exclaimed with feigned enthusiasm. I hadn't expected him to move on so quickly with her, but it was evident that he had.

He frowned in response, failing to share my enthusiasm. "The child isn't mine," he declared.

"What?"

"It's impossible. I think I'd know if I slept with her. The story is I got drunk and slept with her in a moment of passion."

"I thought you didn't drink?"

"I don't."

"How did it happen?" I noted.

"It didn't."

"You're not making sense at all David."

"The baby isn't mine. She wants me to say it is. She doesn't believe Jonah will settle down with her..."

"And she believes you will?" I asked, shocked at the revelation. "The baby's Jonah's? Why didn't you say so in the first place!"

"She came to me threatening to spill some insider information if I told the truth, and if I didn't agree to say I was the father. So, I agreed," he stated.

"Insider information?" I wondered. "You know, secrets have a way of coming out," I reminded him.

"I know, but I've got to keep quiet about some things for now," he advised.

"Well, it's a shock and a half to me," I told him. "I'm happy she's pregnant, but I'm not happy to hear she's pressuring you to pretend you're the father."

He nodded in agreement. "This is not what I wanted, this is not how I wanted things to play out, but she's obviously resorting to desperate measures for a reason. I'll support her as I promised." Abruptly he added, "I guess this is how it's all going to go - you're probably elated that I'll need to shift focus from you and everything you and to her now."

"No. This isn't about me David, it's about you," I stated, knowing full well it was about him and I. Our friendship was going to have to change. Shania was not as liberal as Daniel was. Daniel did not have a choice as I'd decided I would talk to whoever I darn well wanted to, arch nemesis included and irrespective of the restraining order. If David and Shania were to play the happy couple, Shania would not stand to see his attention elsewhere.

"Has she spoken to you about this?" he asked suddenly. "'Cause I find it pretty sus that she's only bringing it up now."

"Okay, like when was she supposed to bring it up? You've been avoiding her like the plague," I noted.

"I suppose," he stated, sounding overwhelmed. "She's beautiful but I'm not in love with her."

"You could grow to love her," I advised.

He shook his head adamantly before stating, "There's always a silver lining. I guess it could be the perfect front."

"Perfect front for what?" I asked.

"Marriage. She said she wouldn't take anything less. Marriage would be the perfect front. It'd keep Daniel off my back and keep me off his radar."

I chuckled under my breath. "What is it with you, Daniel should be the least of your concerns at this moment. Besides, you'll always be on his radar. You're his brother."

"And you're his wife," he reminded me. "As I said, it'll be the perfect front, he'll ease up on being so strict about the time we spend together..."

"David, I'm not trying to keep anything from Daniel. Maybe it will be good for you to move on this way. You being with Shania, I being with Daniel, I'll never be yours."

"Never say never," he stated, flashing me a wink and a smile.

"You're such a hopeless romantic," I replied. "Just think, you'll get to experience fatherhood and married bliss."

"Hm. Not sure about the second part of your statement," he said. After a slight pause, he stated, "Oh man, shotgun wedding it is then, I guess."

"I'll talk to her. Would hate to see you doing something

just for the sake of."

"Don't," he urged. "Just let it be. Things are as they should be. Doesn't change how I feel about you. Won't change how I feel about you. Things will work out for good eventually. She's honed in on me for a reason - she needs my support. I'll give it to her. For now."

"You mean, until Jonah finds out?"

"He won't not unless you tell him," he said.

"*She'll* tell him. You watch," I said, dialling her number straight away.

"Don't," he said, placing a firm hand on mine to stop me. "I can't let her go public with what she knows."

"If you expect me to be on side with you, you need to let me in on what you're on about," I told him.

"I can't," he said.

"Then you can't stop me," I said, dialling Shania's number.

He sighed in response and leaned back into the porch swing.

"Is he with you?" Shania asked, picking up on the first ring.

"And if he was?" I challenged. She didn't respond. "No good will come of this Shania. If you don't give Jonah a chance to step up, you're cheating yourself and the baby out of a chance at happiness."

Silence met me on the other line.

"Shania, are you there?"

She was crying. "I can't talk to him."

"You could just the other week, he's not as bad as he seems," I told her.

"You don't know what I know," she stated.

"I don't need to know what you know in order to know that if he cared enough to sleep with you, he'd care something about the fact that you're carrying his baby," I said.

She sobbed on the line.

"Shania, I care about you. David cares about you. He wants to spare you any embarrassment and to support you nonetheless."

"I know," she stated. "He's a standup guy."

"This isn't fair on him though. It isn't fair on Jonah either," I said.

"Well, tell David I'll manage on my own. It was a mistake to think I could rely on anyone," she said, hanging up.

I called her back immediately and the phone rang off the hook.

"Give her space. She'll turn to you when she's ready," David suggested.

I nodded, agreeing with him.

"I don't want you to hear this from anyone else, so I may as well tell you," he started. "I used to roll with the Brotherhood."

I sat there in silence. I should have figured as much, but I didn't.

"I'm known as The Healer," he said.

"David, all this time...you know, Jude and Ernesto are onto the Brotherhood," I stated.

"I know this," he said.

"*Used to* roll with them?"

"Yes, used to," he repeated. "Past tense."

"I don't know what to say, David."

"You don't have to say anything at all. Just that you still want me around you despite what's going on with Shania, despite what I've just told you about my past," he said.

"You haven't told me anything about your involvement

with the Brotherhood. How do I know you're not putting us at risk?"

"I'd never put you at risk," he promised. "I haven't got anything else to say about my involvement other than that it's over and done with."

"You're not getting away with telling me just that, David," I said, prompting him for more.

"Okay. Tell me what you want to know and I'll tell you," he urged.

"Tell me you didn't torture or kill anyone?"

"I didn't," he said.

"I don't want to know anything else," I told him.

"I'm sorry," he apologised.

"You *will* be sorry," Daniel stated, standing at the bottom stair of the porch. We'd been so enthralled in conversation we hadn't seen or heard him come back. "You know you're not supposed to be here. Please leave," he ordered.

David immediately got up to go. "Take care," he said curtly, giving Daniel a wide berth as he walked down the stairs and headed down the road. I realised then that he'd walked to ours. *Quite a distance to walk.*

Despite Daniel's best efforts to keep me from seeing David, I caught up with him that afternoon. I buzzed on the intercom, and he buzzed me in without talking. I drove along the narrow entrance to the block of apartments and into the undercover parking area. His Airstream and Landrover were parked in the usual spot.

The door to his apartment was open. I walked in and immediately noticed the void. He stood by the window, looking out pensively on the city. His home was bare except for a box, a suitcase and his guitar that leant on each other, in the middle of the room.

My heart sank and I mouthed, "David, you're leaving?"

He nodded to the affirmative, as though talking were too painful.

"When were you going to let me know?" I queried.

Turning from the window, he looked at me with yearning. "I wasn't going to leave without letting you know," he managed. "I just need to get away for a time." Reaching out to me, he stated, "I haven't left yet, don't be so far away. Come over here," he requested, pointing to a space next to him, by the window.

I did. A move I would later regret.

"Give me your hand," he requested.

I wanted to, but couldn't. Daniel had been right all along. The more time I spent with David, the more I would end up falling for him. Again.

"It's only ever been you," he confessed. "Give me your hand," he requested again. "I know it makes you uncomfortable. You're afraid of crossing boundaries he has set," he said, knowingly. I sighed in response, not wanting to be taken in by him, but enjoying his blind adoration of me. "Let's pretend. Just for a moment," he said. "Pretend you're as into me as I'm into you."

Reluctantly, I gave him my hand. His touch was warm and electric. He toyed around with the ring on my finger for a moment, before raising his eyes to meet mine. "I love you Temwani, I always will," he confessed. "It'll only ever be you for me," he said. "I've tried to remember you all these years, while you've tried to forget me all these years," he noted, his blue eyes deep with longing and yearning unfulfilled. "I love you dearly, but it's time I leave you to live your life," he said.

"David..."

"I was wrong for coming here, wrong for wanting to wish and will you away and into my life again," he said, sadly.

"I've only tried to forget you as I felt we couldn't be," I explained. "You left as though you'd never existed. I didn't know what to do with myself when you left. I..."

"Shhh," he said, silencing me with a finger on my lips. For a moment I stood face to face with him, so close that I thought we might kiss. So close that I thought our bodies would touch. Standing there with him, I could feel his breath with mine, the strength of his body interwoven with mine as it was the last time we were intimate, in my fantasies and in my dreams. All those years ago. The last time I gave him some serious thought.

"I can read your mind," he stated. "I know you're doubting your union with Daniel, and I know I'm not looking too bad when it comes to being a suitable alternative. However, as much as I want to just have you for myself, it wouldn't be on for us to turn fantasy into reality. Not while you're still married to him." Toying with my ring again, he stated, "I know you love him, and I know how deeply he loves you. I won't be the one to break you apart," he promised. "But I will be the one who will promise to love you and stand by you no matter what. Placing my hand on his heart, he added, "This heart of mine will forever be yours. I'll wait forever and a day for you to be mine."

Tears filled my eyes. "Why did you stay away all those years? Why couldn't you have found me sooner? It's all so complicated now. I'm married to your brother. He adores me and I love him, but my feelings for you are still there."

"I know, I know," he replied somberly. "There's only one way for us now, and that involves me leaving here, leaving you to get on with it, where he's involved," he said with finality. The tears that threatened to fall, fell. "Hey, hey, hey," he stated. "I didn't mean to make you cry."

"You never do," I replied hastily.

He pulled me in and held me tight. "I'm not going to make you choose between me and him," he stated. "I want you for myself, and if I had my way I would will us back to that night at Broadbeach, the night at the Blues Fest, and we never would have parted ways," he said nostalgically. "I can't, and I need to face facts," he stated. "You being with him, that's facts. You carrying his babies, that's facts. You wearing his ring, that's facts. Only a miracle would see you with me for good," he mused. "Deep in my heart, I know it will happen. Only a matter of time. For now, I'll keep praying for that day to come sooner rather than later."

I melted into him, and wished the moment would last forever. My swollen belly pressed up against him, I felt the twins kick.

"I felt that!" he exclaimed. He tapped on my belly, and one of the twins immediately tapped back. In between tears, I joined him in laughter.

"I'll do everything I can to support you, but I won't be the one to stand in your way," he promised.

"You're still leaving," I reminded him.

"I am," he confirmed. "Only for a while," he explained. "After all that's happened recently, the stuff with Shania, the stuff with Daniel, I need to lay low somewhere for a bit," he decided. "Maybe I can come back for a while after the babies are born? I'm hoping the time away will somewhat dissipate the anger he feels towards me. I'm hoping time will give you a chance to reflect on where you want to be," he said. "I'm hoping time will give me a chance to love you more deeply and unconditionally, even if it is from a distance. I'm hoping time will make me a better man," he concluded.

I shrugged in response, not knowing what to say. I felt deeply for him too, but did not dare make it known as it would give him false hope. I was married to Daniel after all, and my loyalties lay with him.

"Let's sit down Temwani," he suggested. "Time to get off your feet," he stated. "Take a load off," he added. I didn't quite understand what he meant but I followed his cue. I wondered how long it would be before I fully understood his Aussie lingo.

We sat on the floor, a cushion behind my back and the wall. *You're still leaving*, I thought but did not voice my thoughts.

"How have you been keeping otherwise?" he asked.

"I've been fine, knowing you're in my corner," I confessed. "I don't think I would've been able to tolerate Daniel's behavior had you not been here."

"Well, I'm glad I can be something other than trouble for you," he said, looking at his watch absently. "Can I drive you home?" he asked suddenly. "It's getting late and I'm not sure I like the idea of you driving across town on your own, in your condition," he explained.

"Pregnancy is not a condition," I snapped.

"Oh but it is. I'm the doctor here aren't I?" he stated as a matter of factly.

I raised an eyebrow in response.

"Maybe when I'm gone, you can get back to wedded bliss

with Daniel," he said.

"Wedded bliss? It's been everything but," I told him.

"Me being here hasn't helped at all," he acknowledged. "I'm sorry."

"Don't apologise David. Daniel made his choices," I said.

"I didn't make it easier," he said, abruptly getting up. "I know I just asked you to sit down, but can I have this dance?" he asked. The saxophone intro to George Michael's *Careless Whisper* played on the radio.

He held his hand out to me, and I took it. On my feet, he pulled me towards him. Barely above a whisper, he asked, "Can't we just pretend for a moment that I'm yours and you're mine?"

"No, David," I replied quickly. "We can't."

Undeterred, he held my hand in his and led the dance.

With one hand in his, the other on his shoulder, we danced. My pregnant belly forced us to do so slightly apart, and I was grateful for the distance. His presence was overpowering. As we danced, I found myself imagining how different my life would have been had he been in it from the get go.

"It'll only ever be you," he stated, as the song came to an end. "Come, I'll take you home, before it gets too late, and before I make things worse for you."

I sighed in response at his thoughtfulness. Pity Daniel didn't give much consideration and thought to him.

My chest felt tight as we pulled into the driveway. The living room light was on. Daniel was home. Without hesitating, David stepped out of the car and rushed to my side to help me out. "I'll walk you in," he insisted.

"Daniel will be livid."

"What for, it's not as though anything is happening between us, except for friendship, right?" I could tell from the look on his face that he didn't believe his own words.

I shrugged in response. His friendship was seeming more and more like a prelude to a courting.

I put my key in the door, but before I could turn the knob, the door was yanked open.

Daniel stared at David, David stared at Daniel.

"So you finally decided to come home?" Daniel questioned me.

"Mate..." David started.

With a seething glare, Daniel looked David straight in the eye and warned, "There's a special place in hell reserved for a man who covets another man's wife." Motioning for me to get into the house, Daniel added, "Good will always triumph over evil, and I *declare* right now that you will not succeed in taking her away from me."

David shrugged in response. "She's your wife mate, I can't take her away from you. She'll end up leaving you if you don't treat her right."

Enraged, Daniel questioned, "And you would know everything about treating her right, would you?" Before David replied, he added, "Of course you would. You've had lots of experience, haven't you?" he stated as a matter of factly.

"Mate, you don't know what you're talking about," David said defensively.

"Oh, but I do," Daniel responded. "You and I both know what you had to do to put yourself through med school," he started. "Care to let your here lady friend know?"

"Mate..." David started, at a sudden loss for words as he stared past Daniel and towards me. "There isn't much she doesn't know about me. What she doesn't know, she will know in time."

"Yeah, whatever, *Shaman*. I bet you never told Teme about the work you did in the past."

David hesitated for a moment before responding. "That isn't entirely the truth, and it's not as though you're being completely honest with her anyhow," he said. "Care explaining why you spend your Friday nights at Bojangles?" he asked rhetorically. "Isn't this woman who you call yours enough for you?" he asked. "Oh, and you lying that she was your first?"

The color left Daniel's face and he leaned back onto the door post. "That was just business, and our sex life is none of your business."

"Yeah, good save," David replied. "Whatever it was, you can lose your holier than thou attitude and just admit that you don't deserve to be with her."

I was infuriated with the both of them. "Enough already! I can think for myself, thank you very much, you don't need to stand here and defend me. The both of you need to stop fighting over me!" I exclaimed. I could feel the twins kicking wildly in my belly. "Daniel, I'm married to you, grow a spine and stop being so insecure. David, I'm friends with you, stop trying to convince me of how good we could be together! Will the both of you just let me be! Will the both of you just leave well enough alone and just let me live? Let me breathe!"

Daniel threw his head back haughtily and used the opportunity to gloat. Shifting his weight to one leg in a cowboy-esque pose, he turned to David and stated, "Well, well, well. I never thought I'd see the day but she's finally told you to get lost, brother."

David, who by this time was red faced, shifted on his feet uncomfortably. "That's not what I heard," he managed.

"It's never what you want to hear," Daniel retorted. "Here's something else you don't want to hear. You're trespassing on my property. If you don't git in the next few minutes..."

I lost it. "You've got no idea, do you, Daniel. No idea just how much your behavior is stressing me out. No idea whatsoever..."

Daniel interjected, "Don't get all excited baby, don't forget you're carrying my babies," he said in a somewhat pejorative tone, suddenly concerned for the twins.

"You're telling *me* to not get so excited?" I asked.

"Yes, I'm telling you to settle down." he replied, grabbing my arm. I forcefully pulled away from him, shifting him away from his comfortable post by the door.

"Teme..." David started.

"And don't get me started on you. You're here telling me about how bad he is and yet you're no better!" I said, shouting at him for the first time ever.

"Teme, it isn't like that at all," he managed, his head bowed.

"What is it like then!" I exclaimed.

"I needed to put myself through med school. I didn't have the benefit of a lush trust fund like Daniel here did. I worked as a waiter, I worked as a cleaner. I worked as a tantric sex yogi," he admitted.

I nearly fell over.

"None of what I did in the past should be of consequence to you. It's not as though we're together, it's not as though..." David explained.

"You might not be with her, but you're going out of your way to judge me, to make it out that I'm less than..." Daniel said.

"Nope, you're doing that all by yourself," David replied, not taking his eyes off me. "Teme, please don't think ill of me. I couldn't take it if you did. Where I've been should be of no consequence to you. We're not together. Besides, everything I've learned, I wanted to share with you," he said bluntly.

"Please leave," I stated, not wanting to hear his reasons or excuses. I was upset at myself for listening to him and hearing him talk about love and the purity of unconditional love. He knew nothing of that, though the thought of him sharing all he'd learnt as a yogi made heat rise within me.

"Okay," David replied. "I'm sorry for all this. You deserve better," he said, walking off.

"I hope we can now get back to it just being me and you now." Daniel stated.

"It's only ever been just me and you," I told him, walking away from him.

The revelation about David had me reeling. I googled *Tantric Sex Yogi*, and what I read had me clutching my metaphorical pearls. No wonder he was so intense, no wonder his touch was so electric, no wonder his presence was so disarming. Apparently couples instructed by a yogi would reach a deeper level of consciousness, a deeper level of passion in their relationship. Apparently a yogi could make a person climax without ever laying a hand on their body. Apparently some yogis dabbled in the dark arts. I shuddered at the thought, and suddenly became aware of and understood why Daniel had warned me to stay away from David, but was conflicted in my feelings. Regardless of the brush Daniel had tried to paint him with, David had never set out to intentionally hurt anyone, and knowing what he was like, his role as a yogi would've been undertaken at arms length. I believed him when he said he'd only ever has eyes for me.

I slept fitfully that night, and woke up to Daniel opening and shutting drawers noisily. When I looked at the clock, it was a little after 3 am.

"Sorry babe," he said in a strained voice. "We're all out of Aspirin I think."

"I've got some Panadol in my handbag," I replied.

He leaned over the bedroom dresser, eyes winced in pain. In the process he knocked over a few of my cosmetics. He swore under his breath and groaned in response.

"What's wrong?" I asked, leaping out of bed, concerned.

He paused for a while before responding. "I've been having these awful headaches and it seems that no matter what I do they get worse. I've been taking Aspirin..." he clumsily tried to pick my cosmetics off the floor and rearrange them.

I went to his side and urged him to sit down and disregard the things he'd just knocked. He fell to his knees instead, and leant his head against the dresser front. I knelt with him, gently stroking his back.

"Before you ask, no, I haven't been drinking," he muttered under his breath, his hands shaking and speech slightly slurred.

"I'll get you some water," I offered, getting up.

When I returned, he was where I'd left him, eyes closed and in tears. I reached for the Panadol in my handbag, gave it to him with a glass of water and sat with him in silence. "Baby you need to see a doctor," I suggested.

"I'll be fine," he replied. "Just a headache." Tears and his head in his hands told me it was more than just a headache.

"Daniel..."

He winced in pain.

"If you won't go to a doctor, can I get David to..."

"David's the last person I need to see," he said firmly.

"David's a doctor. If you won't go see one, I'll call him. Your choice."

He sighed heavily in response. "This Panadol ain't doin' nothin' for my pain right now. Don't add to my pain by asking David to come around."

"Come to bed, Daniel," I urged, ignoring his request. He refused to budge. I got up and decided to call David.

He was on shift at the Presbyterian, and suggested I bring him in, or he would come by after his shift, all despite the restraining order in place. Daniel wouldn't be pleased, but I wasn't giving him a choice.

When I got back to Daniel he'd fallen asleep where he was. He protested slightly when I tried to wake him and direct him to the bed, but eventually he gave in.

I stayed with him for a while, bedroom pitch black, before I decided to head off and see David.

David seemed surprised to see me standing at his door. "Where's Daniel?" he immediately asked, motioning for me to come in.

"Asleep," I replied. It was 5 am in the morning, and I'd left Daniel in bed.

"You're supposed to be on bed rest. What're you doing driving around town at this hour?"

"I needed to get out," I told him. It had been a few days since we'd last seen each other. He'd kept his distance.

"You sounded worried earlier, everything okay?" he asked.

"Daniel's been having quite intense headaches, he hasn't been able to sleep because of them."

"Does he get migraines with aura?" he questioned.

"I'm not sure," I replied.

"He needs to get himself checked out," David suggested.

"That's exactly what I told him, but unfortunately he refuses to listen, which is not unusual of course."

He nodded in agreement, then in silence, he led me to the living room and motioned for me to sit with him, on a cushion, on the floor. "I'm sorry about Daniel being ill, but I'm glad you're here right now. I need to talk to you.

"If it's got anything to do with what you told me the other night, I don't want to know," I told him.

"That's a lie and you know it," he said. He was right.

"Look, I'm sorry if what you found out about me hurt you. I can explain," he promised. "Do you trust me?" he asked all of a sudden.

"That's not a question."

"Do you trust me?" he asked again.

"Yes."

"Okay," he said. "Sit down, hands in your lap," he directed. "Any pain anywhere in your body?"

"Some pain in my hands - carpal tunnel."

"Okay," he said. "Give me your hands."

"David..."

"Give me your hands."

I placed my hands in his, which felt warm to touch.

"Close your eyes," he commanded.

I closed my eyes, and he held my hands in his. Eyes closed, I felt warmth fill my hands to the point that I pulled them away, slightly startled.

"Do you have pain in your hands now?" he asked.

I wriggled my fingers around. "No," I replied abruptly. My hands felt warm and the pain that had been there moments ago was gone.

"Okay," he stated. "Let's try something," he insisted. He motioned for me to sit closer to him on the floor, cross-legged, directly facing him. He took my right hand and placed it on his chest, so I could feel his heartbeat. He placed his right hand on my heart.

I sat there with him, his hand on my heart, mine on his. "Hold my gaze for as long as you can," he urged. "Feel my heart beating in sync with yours."

I gazed into his eyes and felt his heart beating at the same pace as mine.

"Look into me as I'm looking into you," he commanded, his voice deep and entrancing, his eyes warm and full of love.

We sat in silence, not breaking gaze. In his eyes I saw adoration and love. Love unwavering, love never ending and love unconditional. As I stared into his eyes, I also saw pain. I saw heartache. I saw suffering. I felt tears come to my eyes but continued looking into him. He didn't break my gaze, but reached out to wipe the tears that rolled down my cheek. I gained composure for a moment, and we sat there, staring into each other again. Tears welled up in his eyes when he finally spoke. "I can see pain, I can see fear. I can see what he did to you. I can see what you were before him. I can see who you are now. I can see who you could've been had I not let you go." He moved his hand from my chest to my hand on his chest, and I could feel the warmth radiate through from him to me. As he stared into me, his eyes pierced through to the core of me, and I felt as though I'd been stripped bare, with nowhere to retreat.

"I'm sorry for failing you," he apologized. "Sorry I wasn't there for you when things with Duayne took a turn for the worse. Sorry..."

I tried to speak but no words came.

"I can't take your pain away," he stated, tears falling down his face.

"David, it isn't your job to take away my pain," I replied, crying as well, tasting the salt of my tears on my lips.

"Yours is the type of pain I can't take away. But I can help you open up to love again," he promised.

I shook my head in response, feeling heavy and over-whelmed. "David, your pain runs deep. I didn't realise how much pain you were in. It can't be all over me, this runs deeper."

"We can stop this now," he suggested, wiping tears off his face with the back of his hand. "Let's stop this now," he insisted.

I nodded in agreement, suddenly feeling unwell. Uncrossing my legs, I shifted to lie down on my side, overwhelmed, exhausted and everything in between. David abruptly stood up and offered me his hand. "Not the floor. You'll wake up in a world of pain. Try the bed," he suggested. Lightheaded and dizzy, I stumbled when I stood up, and he braced my fall. "Easy," he cautioned, his embrace warm and gentle.

I lay down for what seemed to be a few minutes but ended up being a few hours. I awoke to the smell of toasted raisin bread and freshly brewed tea.

"Feeling better?" he asked.

I nodded to the affirmative. I felt as though a burden had been lifted.

He brought over a breakfast tray with some brioche style raisin bread, hash browns and some syrup.

"It's just after 7 am," he noted. "Your phone's been ringing off the hook."

I shrugged in response. I had no doubt it was Daniel.

"I didn't want to wake you," he advised. "I took the liberty of checking your messages, just in case Daniel was needing you, what with the way you left him," he stated. "Hope you don't mind. He seems to be fine. Fine enough to send you a few scathing text messages," he added.

"What a surprise," I stated. "I'll be heading back soon enough. He needs to learn to trust me."

"You being here doesn't help I'm sure," David said surprisingly.

I shrugged again, and took a big bite out of my bread. "You're not eating?" I asked.

"No," he replied abruptly. We sat in silence for a moment before he stated, "So, you know I'm leaving. I think it's for the best. These days I can't even look him in the eye when he talks about you. I'm afraid my eyes will betray me. Anyway, I know you've only got eyes for him, and that for as long as you do, I am alone here in love. I know..." he broke off, hesitating for a moment. "I can't help the way I feel about you no matter how I try. You're everything I've ever wanted, you're all I've always wanted." He paused again, then smiled sadly. "Well if not this lifetime then maybe the next. Or will you turn me down then too?"

"You're being so melodramatic David. There are other

women in the world. You can and will find someone else to love," I told him.

"You don't understand. I won't be able to love someone the way I love you," he declared.

"Don't you want to be with someone who will adore you, and love you for everything you are?" I asked.

"Trust me, despite the bravado and flair, I'm not the most loveable person," he stated. Firmly, he added "Trust me, I don't want to be with anyone other than you. And trust me, I know you secretly adore me."

"David," I chided him. "We've talked about this."

"Temwani," he said in kind. "You can't change the way I feel."

I sighed, feeling his pain and anguish.

"With all due respect Teme, you don't know what it's like for me to love you the way I love you. The fact that we're here again, revisiting this, confirms you have no idea. I can't just switch off the way I feel about you. I can't pretend I'm not jealous of you and Daniel and the life you have planned. If you'd only said yes to me all those years ago this would have been our life together. He would have been me."

"But he's not you, and you are not him," I said a little too coolly, though my all felt for him.

"I can't be here anymore," he stated with finality.

"Distance and time might change how you feel," I offered.

"Distance and time will only make me more fond of you," he replied. "I just can't do *this* anymore. Can't be here, watching you with him..." he broke off, running a hand through his tressed locks, despair in his voice apparent. "You don't know what it's like."

I could only imagine what it felt like, but he was right. He loved me with such fervour and adoration. I didn't know what it felt like to love someone so deeply, so unconditionally.

A momentary pause ensued before he stated, "You're not supposed to be here."

"I can be where I want to be," I told him.

"You don't understand. Daniel does not want me to even talk to you."

"Or else what?" I asked.

"Amongst other things, he's promised to ensure that I'd never get to know your kids. My niece and my nephew. As it is, I'm a *persona non grata*. He doesn't want me around. Doesn't feel I should be a part of his life in any way. But I haven't got any family apart from him and you. And them. I can't risk what I've just found. Being here has made me feel real again. It's made me feel alive and it's made me feel whole. But I can't take the risk of inciting him any further. So I'm leaving."

I felt saddened at what Daniel had threatened. He had no right. No right at all. Daniel was all the family David had, and he didn't deserve to be treated like that. "Daniel has no right to treat you like this."

"Oh, but he *is* your husband," he reminded me.

"Don't I know it," I said. "He's acting more like a tyrant than a life companion these days."

"Well, you know where to find me when you get tired of living under a dictatorship," he said winking and managing a cheeky smile. "No seriously, he's just trying to hold on to what's his. Okay. I know we're not together, never have been, and the way things are now, the way things are going, we never will be together, but I'm gonna miss you big time. Gonna miss seeing you, gonna miss being around you, gonna

295

miss having you around."

"David, you make it sound so final. I'm not going any-where, I'm still here. We're friends. I'll always be here for you," I told him.

"Friends we might be, but I'm still completely head over heels in love with you," he confessed. "Staying here, seeing you so happy with him is sorta killing me. Plus, I made a promise to him. Promised that I'd put distance between us."

"He can't control my friendships," I noted.

"Friendship," he corrected. "He's only got qualms about me and you being friends."

"I'll talk to him," I suggested.

"No use," he said. "I've already tried. He's got his mind made up, and he won't be convinced. So, I'm off," he said with finality. "Now I don't know what I'll do without you being around me day to day, but I'll find a way to deal. Had to find a way all those years ago, I'm sure I'll find a way now, somehow."

The reality that he was heading to Australia so soon brought tears to my eyes unexpectedly.

"Come now, don't cry," he urged me. "I'll always be just a phone call away. Call me when you need me, and I'll be right back here, by your side. This isn't the end for us. Our friendship is greater than anything or any one circumstance life can throw in our path."

"David, I wish I could believe you, but I can't. You're what's been keeping me going through the trials and tribulations I've been through. You've been my rock, David."

"Teme, there's a lot of things you don't know about me. Things you shouldn't know," he said mysteriously. "Maybe it's better this way. The lower the stakes, the less pain there'll be."

"David, you know better than I do that in matters of the heart the stakes are always high."

He nodded in response. "True that. Promise me one thing though. Promise me you'll keep happy," he urged. "...and those spiders, make sure you get him to get rid of them humanely - put them outside."

I laughed in between tears. He hugged me deeply and earnestly.

"You'll be alright?" I asked, worried that he was going away for good, despite his words to the contrary.

"I'll keep busy," he promised. "Plan to spend some more time in training, get my orthodontics training down pat. Also considering going on base for a few months. Depending on how things pan out with Shania. I can't stay away for too long, but I'll stay away for as long as I can."

"Any idea where you'd be based?" I asked.

"Afghanistan likely," he said.

I felt my heart sink. "Please be safe," I told him.

"I'll write you every week. Think of you every day," he promised. Unlike Daniel's his promises were as good as gold.

Overwhelming sadness filled me. "I wish things were different for you. I wish you could find happiness."

"Not an easy thing to achieve. My happiness is tied to you," he stated frankly. "And you're bound to him."

I sighed in response.

"I've always been in love with you. I'll take what you can give, so don't worry about my happiness. Happiness is being here for you, in whatever which way you'll have me."

To say I didn't love him would be to lie. I'd be lying if I said I didn't love him. Instead, I said, "David, there are a lot of things I could be saying right now, but they would only complicate matters. What I *can* say is thank you for everything."

As we stood facing each other, in that moment I felt the raw energy between us.

He broke the silence. "You are such a beautiful sight to behold. Remind that brother of mine to watch his step and to cherish you every day and show his love for you in every way. For if he doesn't, I'll be on to him. And quite possibly on to you," he said as a matter of factly.

"You're incorrigible, Doctor Davenport."

He smiled again, that whimsical smile that would always make me melt.

"You'll find someone new," I said, knowing in my heart how hard it would be for him to turn his heart to someone else.

"I won't," he replied. "Please don't start this again - I can't just forget about you. I can move on, try to love someone else but it's only you. It will always be you," he declared. "When it's all said and done, you know I'll be here waiting for you," he said. "I hope you know that, and I hope you remember that." Looking at his watch again, he stated, "Let me take you home. Last thing you need is for Daniel to be in a huff."

My return home started and ended with drama. David left me at the door, not wanting to ignite any further drama with Daniel. As I walked in the door, I found the drama was already lit, my arrival fuelling the flame.

"So, you decided to make your way home. Think you could have called me to let me know you were planning on leaving me alone in the condition that I was in?" Daniel questioned.

"It wasn't like that Daniel. I knew you'd be okay, plus I wanted to get David to have a look at you, or at least get an opinion from him," I told him.

"It was more than that and you know it. You could have called me, but hey, I guess the Shaman had you under his spell," Daniel said.

"Don't call him that."

"Whyever not?" he asked. "That *is* what he is, right? He practices in the dark arts, and has been tryin' to work his *voodoo magic* on you for time."

"You don't know what you're talking about, Daniel," I said.

"Oh, don't I now. Prove me wrong," he challenged.

"I don't have to prove anything to you," I argued.

"I wish you'd lose your sense of loyalty to him. You should be loyal to me and me only."

"Come on Daniel. He's your brother, and he's my friend."

"He's your friend for now, but clearly he'd take more, given half a chance," Daniel declared with certainty.

"You're so selfish sometimes," I told him. "You've wanted nothing to do with him from the start. You won't even give him the time of day."

"Look at this from my perspective for once," he urged. "My brother or not, he's a man in love with you, and I simply don't have the time to entertain any sort of relationship with him."

"You know, you disappoint me. David's got nothing. He's broken. You had a privileged childhood. His childhood was stolen from him." I could tell from the expression on his face, he didn't care.

"Privileged?" he fumed. "Okay, so me being raised by just

my mom, me struggling to come to terms with who I am without a father figure around, is me having had a privileged childhood?" he shook his head. "Oh, the Shaman's got you now."

I rolled my eyes in response. "Daniel, until you start to take ownership for your role in the issues we're having here as husband and wife, I simply don't have time for you."

A look of shock swept across his face. "What the heck is that supposed to mean!"

"It means what it means," I said. "I can't live like this. Love is not supposed to be a battle."

"So, you're walking away from me?" he asked.

"No. I'm walking away from this drama."

"Baby, you can't just leave me," he said, in shock.

"I'm not leaving you."

"What are you doing then! When push comes to shove and the going gets tough, you hit the road. *Every single time,*" he alleged.

"Can you blame me?" I asked.

"No, I can't and I don't. I just know that we need to work things out, here. Together," he insisted.

"You've got issues you need to resolve all on your own," I told him.

"Look," he said. "I know I can be a pain in the behind. I know I can be insecure. I know I'm not the easiest person to love. But leaving me here on my lonesome to work through things isn't going to help," he said.

"You haven't tried it, so you don't know it won't work."

"Oh, but I have tried it. You're hardly home these days," he stated.

"You haven't been to see a counsellor as you promised," I

reminded him.

"Yeah, that," he said flippantly.

"Don't *yeah that* me. The one thing you could be doing to help this, you're refusing to do."

"If we lose what needs to be lost, I won't need to," he reasoned. "If David leaves us be, I won't need to."

I shook my head in response. "You don't get it, do you. We had issues before David turned up. We've still got issues now."

He stood there for a moment, silent, before stating, "I'm out. We can talk about this when you've had time to cool off, and you're trying to be reasonable," he announced. "I'll catch you later," he said, planting a gruff and unwanted kiss on my lips before turning to leave.

Walking away again. I couldn't find words.

That night, I went to bed alone again. If only he knew how much he was hurting me, but he didn't.

Over the next few days, I busied myself with plans to leave. I had three days to get organized to go. David was going to Australia, and I was planning on going too. Daniel would not be a party to any of my plans, and neither would David. I planned to catch up with a friend on the Gold Coast, in Queensland, and had everything organized to that effect. I planned to leave on the same flight as David, but that was as far as it went. We would go our separate ways in Sydney, given that he planned to go on to the Sunshine Coast, while I would remain on the Gold Coast. At least this was the plan.

George cleared me for travel, but was insistent that I return after a short spell only.

"Two weeks maximum," he said, signing my letter of approval for the airline. Two weeks would see me at 34 weeks.

"No travel after you hit 36 weeks. Please try to be back by the 34 week mark," he insisted. "Anything later, and you run the risk of not being able to fly back, or the risk of the babies being born overseas." I agreed, despite knowing that Daniel wouldn't be happy with my plans. All the more reason not to tell him until the very last minute.

Daniel took to drinking in excess the last two nights I had with him before my departure. Johnny was a bad influence, as David had said, though he did ensure Daniel came home every night, and I was grateful for that and grateful for him. I knew deep down Johnny meant well and would've stopped Daniel if he could, but he obviously couldn't. I also knew and had heard through the grapevine that Johnny's relationship with Michaela was on the rocks, which didn't surprise me at all. He'd been staying with us on and off, more on than off. Misery loved company and Daniel was in good company. I just wondered how far they would both go when I was gone, but I was past caring in the end.

The night before I was set to leave, Daniel surprised me by actually being at home in the evening. He was leaning against the corridor wall when I walked in, and it was quite evident he had been waiting for me to get back. He motioned towards the kitchen table and pulled out a chair for me to sit in. He sat at the head of the table, to my left. Johnny wasn't in, it was just me and him.

"I hear you're leaving," he said, his voice somber and steady. "I hear David's leaving, and I hear you're leaving too."

"I'm getting away for some time," I corrected him.

"You can't just leave," he stated, the strain in his voice apparent.

"I need some time away from all of this. Surely you can agree."

"I disagree. Stay here and we can work on this," he begged.

"That's the problem. *You* need to work on this. *You* need to sort yourself out," I replied.

"You *can't* leave," he said again in disbelief.

"As I said, I'm giving you the time you need to deal."

"So you're going to Australia?" he asked.

I was a little surprised he knew, given how hard I had worked to keep my plans a secret. Then again, I shouldn't have been. He had his ways as a private investigator.

"Tell me this isn't true," he said. "So, are you going to tell me your plans? I don't like the idea of you flying so far into your pregnancy. In fact, I don't like the fact that you are leaving at all." After a momentary pause, he stated, "I forbid you to leave."

Of course you do. I laughed in response. "Here we go again."

"Temwani, I *am* your husband. I have a say in this."

"Of course you do," I acknowledged. "You've said your piece. Now it's time for you to accept what I have to do."

"You can't leave," he said again. "This isn't fair."

"Don't talk to me about fairness Daniel," I warned. "You of all people should know that it isn't fair for you to continue to hold me ransom to your views. Your beliefs. Your behavior. Your feelings about how this relationship should be. This is meant to be a partnership, not a dictatorship."

"So, the solution is for you to leave and shack up with my brother?" he asked.

"I'm not shacking up with anyone," I stated. "I'm going

on my own steam, making my own arrangements. Also, for your information, David has done nothing but support me. He's done nothing but support us."

"That's the problem," he stated. "Under the guise of supporting you and supporting me, he's just there, waiting in the wings for me to make a mess of things so he can come through and rescue you. I have a say in this. I *am* your husband, and I'm putting my foot down. You cannot leave," he insisted.

"Watch me," I dared him, getting up to go.

"He'll break your heart," he said, defiantly, grabbing me by the wrist.

"You've already broken mine," I replied, breaking free from his grasp.

Something like pain flashed across his face as he visibly desisted from arguing. Sighing heavily, he asked, "Is this what we've come to? Is this all we have left? Are you really walking away from me after everything we've been through together?"

"I'm not walking away from you. As I said, I'm taking a step back from you and us. You need to sort yourself out. For your own sake, and for the sake of our kids," I told him.

At that moment, my phone rang. Grateful for the excuse it gave me to walk away mid-discussion, I walked over to the lounge and sat down on the sofa. Daniel remained at the table, watching me from a distance. It was Craig on the line, wanting to know where the briefs for the MacKenzie matter were.

"I've got them with me," I advised. "Can't you come collect the brief tomorrow morning?" He wanted to stop by instead, now. I acquiesced, thinking it would be good for Daniel to see that I had support in my plans. "See you in a bit," I said, ending the conversation.

Daniel still sat at the table, in silence. I tried not to notice the sadness in his eyes and averted my gaze from his when he caught me staring. I put my feet up on the foot stool and pretended to be busy, checking my emails.

Eventually he joined me on the sofa.

"I'm sorry for breaking your heart." he started. "Please tell me what I need to do to make things right between us," he begged.

"Daniel, I've told you, time and time again what needs to be done."

"I'll do anything for you," he promised.

"That's what you said last time," I reminded him. "Your word doesn't count for much anymore, I'm afraid."

He nodded, acknowledging what I'd said. "When do you get back?" he asked, slightly hopeful.

"I hope to be back end of August."

"That's a whole month!" he protested, clearly shocked. "Isn't that cutting it too fine, what with the babies due in September?"

"George has cleared me to travel. He says it'll be fine as long as I'm not flying back past the 36 week mark," I explained.

"I see," he said, flatly. I could hear how disheartened he was. "I really wish you didn't have to leave," he added. "What happened to for better or for worse? Are you just going to leave me now without a second thought?" he asked.

"You promised me you would love me and respect me..."

"Yes, and you promised me you would stand by me through good times and bad," he recalled.

"I did," I replied. "I'm not leaving you, I'm taking time out from all of this negativity, uncertainty and your possessiveness. I'm taking time out from this situation."

He dropped to his knees. "Please don't leave Teme, not even for a moment. Not now," he begged. "I'll do anything to keep you here."

"A little too late to be making promises like that," I replied, cooly.

"Teme I'm begging you to stay and not leave," he said, still on his knees.

"I'll be back in good time," I told him. "For now, I need to go," I said, getting up and turning away from him. I couldn't bear to see him on his knees begging. He knew how to tug at my heart strings but I couldn't let him convince me otherwise this time.

He got up from being on bended knee and intercepted me on my walk away from him. "I'll do everything I can to get back right with you. I promise I will. My love will be here for you always. Don't you forget it," he said, stepping to me and planting a deep kiss on my lips. "When do you leave?" he asked suddenly.

"Tonight," I replied quickly.

He shook his head in response. His eyes glistening with tears, he walked away from me and into the next room.

I felt for him, but I wasn't going to let my heart win over my head this time. The flight was leaving in a few hours. Enough time to pack and get a few other things organized. No time to be sentimental, no time to regret. The slamming of a whisky glass on the table in the next room, and the predictable clanging of ice that followed was enough for me to know he was having a drink. *Whatever he needs to get through this I guess.* My one hope was that he'd be different on my return.

Moments later, Craig was over. He knew of my plans, and had arranged for a cab to take me to the airport. Daniel stood in the hallway briefly, curious to see who had come through the front door, before walking away again without a word. In ordinary circumstances, he would have given Craig an earful, but today, he had nothing to say.

"How are you?" Craig asked.

"Good. Looking forward to getting away."

"I see," he said. "How did he take the news that you're leaving?" he asked of Daniel.

"Not very well," I told him.

"Not surprising," he replied. Switching topic, he asked, "That MacKenzie file I was after?"

"It's in the study," I told him, leading the way.

I was just as surprised as Craig was to find Daniel in the study perusing the MacKenzie file. I'd left it on the desk, ready for Craig to collect. Daniel had no reason to be reading it. His disbarment meant he could have no hand in any of the matters we were dealing with.

"You're out of line, mate. Hand me that file," Craig insisted.

"Come and get it," Daniel taunted, closing the binder, placing it on the table and putting his whisky tumbler on top of it.

"You know, you better not ruin that file," Craig warned.

"Or what, Craig. You'll manhandle me?" Daniel challenged. "If it wasn't for me, you'd still be in the UK, working your 52 hour week, a slave to the system. If it wasn't for me..."

Craig cut him off. "Things aren't always what they seem,

mate. I chose you, remember?"

"Are you tryin' to tell me that everything, down to you becoming partner in my firm, was orchestrated by you?" Daniel questioned.

"The power of persuasion – isn't it a thing?" Craig stated.

"You're kidding me, right?" Daniel replied.

"I kid you not," Craig said, haughtily. "You're not as in control of things as you think."

Clearly fuming, Daniel stood up abruptly, and ran a hand through his hair before grabbing his glass of whisky and pouring it all over the MacKenzie file in a circular motion. "Well now, let's see you persuade your way out of this one at tomorrow's hearing," he stated, before giving us both a wide berth and stepping out the room.

Craig and I immediately tried to salvage the file, first with the throw that was strung over the chair, then with some paper wipes I quickly retrieved from the kitchen. We heard the front door slam shut moments later. Daniel had stepped out.

"He can be such a dick," Craig commented.

"You adding fuel to the fire didn't help," I argued.

"He's destroyed the original paper copy of the record of interview," he stated, jaw clenched. "He really needs to be put in his place."

Musing for a moment on what that meant, I remembered that I needed to finish packing – my taxi would be arriving soon.

14

ISLANDS

I got to the airport slightly before the check-in desk opened. *Great*, I thought. *At least I won't have to wait around for long.* I'd planned to check in first, then call David. I'd tried checking in earlier, online, but for some reason the facility was unavailable.

I handed my passport and ticket to the stewardess. "Just one bag Ma'am?"

"Yes," I nodded, hoping an aisle seat was available.

"Ma'am, this queue is for our economy passengers. Please take your passport and ticket to the other queue," she said, motioning towards the business passenger queue.

What was she on about? "Sorry, my ticket is an economy ticket, perhaps there's been some kind of a mistake?" I asked.

"No Ma'am, your ticket's been upgraded to business class," she stated.

"That's news to me," I replied. "Might I ask why?"

"Please take your ticket to the next service desk and we can better assist you there, Ma'am," the stewardess stated, motioning to the service desks to my right.

"It must be some sort of a mistake," I offered, not that I

wouldn't have minded a seat in business, but I couldn't afford one.

"No mistake Ma'am," the stewardess confirmed. "Kindly move to the next desk so we can check you in there, Ma'am," she requested.

I picked up my carry-on bag and suitcase, wishing that I had help to lug the suitcase around.

No sooner than I had thought that thought, did I hear, "Temwani," in an all too familiar voice. *David.*

I turned in the direction of his voice, and he tipped his Akubra hat at me before flashing me his beautiful, dimpled smile. Leaning forward onto the service desk, he was discussing something with a stewardess, who was clearly chuffed that he was talking to her. *Probably flirting with her.* Ending the conversation, he turned and winked at me, then extended his hand, beckoning me to join him.

"To what do I owe this surprise?" he asked. "I'm supposed to be following you, not the other way around," he stated.

"I need to get away," I said.

He turned back to the stewardess, "As I was saying before, it would be sweet if you could allocate her the seat next to me."

"Of course. Will do," the stewardess replied, all too happy to meet his request. She spoke with an Australian accent similar to his. He was flying business class, and now so was I.

"David, I really wish you hadn't gone to that expense," I protested.

"Nonsense," he replied. "Not a thing, not a thing. Time you get used to being treated like the Queen that you are," he stated, taking off his hat and taking up my bags. His auburn brown hair sat just above his shoulders, and after the experience of him healing my pain, it made him look like a guru of sorts. Travelling with him was going to be an adventure. I smiled to myself, feeling the earlier stress I was under, dissipate slightly.

As we walked towards the departure lounge, I noticed people stare, though not the way they stared when I was out with Daniel. With his grand public displays of affection, people stared at Daniel and I as a couple. This was different. People stared at David as he was beautiful. Of course he didn't help the situation none. Constantly smiling, constantly joking around, constantly - calling attention to himself, it was not possible to ignore him. *Such a show off.* He *was* beautiful though.

"So, my brother couldn't even make it to the airport to see you off?" he questioned, slicing into my thoughts.

"No," I replied.

"So, he's still being an ass," David said, disapprovingly and a little angry. "I hope this time away from you will knock some sense into his head."

"I hope so too," I said.

"What was he doing when you left?" he asked.

"He was drinking."

David nodded his head, knowingly, before reaching for his phone. I presumed he was calling Daniel, and he was.

"I don't care how you get here, get here now," he commanded, sternly, speaking into the phone.

I didn't really want to see Daniel at that time, not after how we had left things, and how he had just walked out, but I guess I was going to have to. David had insisted on it.

311

Daniel appeared in the departure lounge, a few moments before departure. Our flight had been delayed. Craig was with him.

"I guess I have you and David to thank for him being here," I said to Craig. Craig nodded before stating, "Just hear him out."

"I wish you were a better man, Daniel," I told him. The sadness in his eyes was apparent, and for a moment I felt guilt at leaving him at this time, but knew it had to be done.

"I'm trying. I really am trying," he insisted. "Though no use in me beggin' you to stay, you're a leavin' no matter what I say."

"You got that right," I said, still peeved off at him yet glad to see him at the same time.

"Whatever you do, just come back to me – just keep me on your mind in everything," he requested. "Just remember the good times we had."

"Good times which are few and far between these days," I added.

"I hear you," he replied, looking a little uncomfortable. Craig stood within earshot, and it looked as though Daniel was now under his thumb somehow. "There's still a lot of good here between you and I. I just need a chance to prove myself to you."

"Well, I'm not staying," I confirmed.

"So you say," he stated. Placing both hands on my shoulders, he added, "Please call me when you get there, I want to hear from you every day. Call me when you're on layover. If you can't bring yourself to call me, well, I'll understand."

I nodded to the affirmative.

Placing a hand on my belly, he stated, "Take care of our

babies. Take care of you," he said, planting a moist kiss on my lips. "I'll be the man that you need me to be when you get home," he promised.

"I'll make sure of it," Craig said abruptly interrupting.

Our final boarding call was announced. David, who remained at a safe distance nodded his head and mouthed, "Time to go."

Daniel sighed heavily in reply. "I'll be missin' you sugarpie," he said, his voice coarse and strained.

As I turned to go, Craig said a little over a whisper, "I'll keep an eye on him. I'll get him clean." Daniel was a law unto himself at the best of times. Any method to get him clean would have to be questionable.

As the airhostess called out a final call for boarding, David shook hands with Daniel and picked up my carry-on baggage. Daniel made eye contact with me again, his eyes still begging me to stay. I couldn't. I had to leave. "Goodbye Daniel," I said, planting a kiss on his lips. "See you in a few weeks."

I knew he watched after me as I walked away, but I didn't turn back until I'd gotten through the boarding gate. I turned to see a man who looked defeated and deeply saddened. *My dear husband.* I gave him a wave before following after David.

The flight from Texas would've felt longer had it not been for David's company. We talked at length about nothing in particular. Politics, music, food. He convinced me to order a vegan meal on the flight, in hopes that he'd convert me. I did. David was persuasive in more ways than one.

The warm, humid and salty air greeted us on arrival at Coolangatta Airport, Gold Coast. David had some business there on Monday, and he'd arranged for us to stay at a friend's. His plans were now my plans, my plans were now his plans.

Marc lived in a Queenslander in Currumbin, a leafy and quiet suburb close to the Northern New South Wales border with Queensland. He was an avid surfer and musician. They knew each other from their days at university, back when David was a chemistry major.

While they caught up on the balcony, I took a long soak in the spa bath that overlooked a lush green forest. Being back in Queensland brought back fond memories. Memories of being out in the sun and sea, and memories of lots of laughter. David was a clown back in the day, anything and everything he said would make me laugh. At the time, I wasn't looking for love. Had I been, David should have been the clear choice. If only. If only David and I had linked up then. If only.

Instead, it was Daniel and I. I truly loved Daniel but wished his behavior were different. As bad as it sounded, I wished he were more like David. Comparing him to another man, his own brother wasn't fair though. *How could he compete? Could he ever measure up to such an expectation? Wasn't Daniel enough until David came along? Had I made a mistake in leaving with David? Was there not the obligation on me to work things out with Daniel before throwing in the towel and calling it quits? Was I in some way contributing to his rising insecurity?*

A sudden knock on the door sliced through my thoughts and made me jump. I'd been so lost in my thoughts that the bath water had gone cold, and my fingers and toes were all wrinkly.

"You okay in there?" David asked from the other side of the door.

"I'm fine, coming out now," I replied.

"Okay," he replied. "Just checking you're okay. Dinner's almost up."

"Thanks David," I replied.

"Not too long in the bath, your core body temperature and the babies..."

"Yes, Doctor David!" I replied, and thought I heard him chuckle before his footsteps were heard going away from the door.

Out of the bath, I stepped into the bedroom and got dressed. The king sized bed in the guest room was expansive. I'd gone to bed alone many a night, but Daniel had always made his way to bed eventually. I'd never slept alone. Tonight I was sleeping alone. I'd be missing him.

A Kookabura sat on the ledge of the balcony, peering in through the glass. I smiled, recalling the Dreamtime stories David had started telling me on the plane. In that moment, I resolved to not miss Daniel, and to focus on enjoying the time away. Daniel had after all made his choices, and he'd chosen not to honour me. I didn't need to spend another moment worrying about whether he was thinking of me or not. He hadn't been thinking of me before I left and he was likely not thinking of me now.

I slipped on a spaghetti strapped cheetah and peacock print maxi dress that flowed and fit snuggly around my belly. It was cool enough to suit the humid weather, beautiful enough to make me feel good about my growing body.

"How *you* doin'!" Marc exclaimed as I walked out into the lounge where he and David were kicking back on the sofa.

David took great pains not to stare at me for too long, before telling Marc, "She's married, man."

315

Marc rolled his eyes at David's statement. "Last time I checked, it wasn't a crime to pay her a compliment, mate," he replied. Not waiting for David to respond, he stated, "How about some dinner? Mostly vegan, but I did up some Barra for you."

"Barra?" I asked.

"Barramundi," David replied. "Used to be your favorite?"

"It still is," I replied. "Sounds awesome."

"I don't know about you lot but I'm starving, so let's eat," Marc insisted. "A bit of a feed then a swim in the surf?"

David nodded to the affirmative. "I'd be in for that. Teme?"

"I'll be catching up on sleep," I told him. *And waiting for Daniel to call me.*

"Sleep can wait," Marc stated. "Have you ever slept under the blanket of the skies, sand as your bed?"

David snuck me a side glance and a wink before stating, "Came close to it. Once upon a time."

Once upon a time. Many years ago, after an evening out on the town with friends, David and I had wound up walking on the beach, and he'd been so bold as to kiss me. It was our first and only kiss. I felt passion rise within me at the memory.

I said nothing in reply, but saw the forlorn look in David's eyes.

"Well, water's nice and warm out, sleep can wait," Marc stated again.

"I'll join you then," I vowed, slightly saddened at the memory of David and I. We'd been friends, and had enjoyed companionship for a time. I wasn't looking for love. Up until that night when he opened me up to the possibility. A few days later, he was gone without a trace. The messages he'd sent me, I did not receive. As far as I knew, he had bounced, but the reality was that I had been very much on his mind, and remained on his mind since that moment we'd shared a kiss. Now, many years later, I wondered about David and the fact that he'd shut off the idea of love with anyone else in order to make himself be available to me. Now that I was no longer available, he still held out hope for us. It had to hurt some, but he didn't seem to mind. He still held out hope for us being together one day.

15

SOMEONE ELSE

"Rise and shine beautiful!" David said loudly, pulling the sheets off me, waking me up from my sleep.

"It's way too early to be up," I protested, pulling the sheets back up.

"You wanted to come with, didn't you? Told you, shoulda gone to bed at a decent hour last night. All those late-night movies..."

"You were up late too. Sun isn't even up yet!" I protested.

"It shouldn't be, not just yet," he said, standing by the window. He wore a fitted blue t-shirt and khaki shorts. Standing by the window he looked picture perfect, as though posing for a magazine. He sounded ready to take on the day, while I was struggling to get up.

"Come on now," he said. "Think of what you'll miss out on. Fresh grapes, peaches, plums, mangoes...there might even be figs. Might even get the chance to drop in to the local for a sticky date pudding," he said, trying his hardest to entice me.

"I haven't even showered yet..."

"You can take a dip in the ocean no worries. Just pack your

togs."

"My what?" I could hardly understand the things he was saying.

"Your swimwear. Just get out of bed already," he ordered, pulling open the curtains. The night light shone bright into the bedroom. "You're beautiful as is," he said.

I sat up, stretched. He stood there for a moment, staring at me. I caught his gaze and he turned away abruptly.

"Sorry for staring, but you're too beautiful for words," he stated. "If you were mine, I wouldn't be able to bear being away from you, not even for a day. Don't know how Daniel does it."

"David, you're such a romantic," I told him.

"Um hmm," he replied, changing topic. "Come on now, let's get going. Ten minutes please. I've prepared something for you to eat on the go. I'll be waiting out front."

The Eumundi Markets were a feast for the eyes. Music was in the air, as was laughter and joy. The warm sun and humidity kissed my face as I walked from stall to stall with David. I loved seeing him negotiate and walk away from a seller, only to be called back to purchase at the price he'd originally asked for. As I walked through the market with him, I caught a glimpse of what life with him would have been like. His shoulder length sun kissed hair, tanned skin and muscular physique gave people a chance to stare. Seemingly oblivious to it all, he didn't let the attention get to him. His attention was on me. At one point, instead of letting me walk around a puddle, he swooped me into his arms and carried me over, surprising me and shocking me all the same. There, as we were, I could feel his love for me, and wondered how we could ever live our separate lives without each other around.

After about an hour of walking around and grabbing a few things, we stopped at a vegan stall for lunch. He was actively encouraging and persuading me to switch to a vegetarian diet. "Sauerkraut and sausage stand is just next door, we can go there after," he suggested.

"This'll be fine," I told him. He smiled his beautiful smile, the one which I would grow to miss when he was no longer around.

"So, I thought we could go and see my dad, Michael, when we're done?" he suggested. "He lives in Maleny. Maybe have dinner with him or head into town for a meal before we call it a night?"

"Sounds good," I replied, eager to know more about him, and in so doing, learn more about Daniel.

After visiting a few more stalls, we left the market, and David drove to his father's.

"You know, we haven't spent much time talking about *your* life growing up," he noted, brusquely taking a quick turn to the left, leaving the tar-marked road for a dirt road.

"No, we haven't. You haven't told me *anything* about your childhood," I added.

"I don't like talking about it," he explained.

"I figured that."

"I guess we better get talking then," he said, somewhat morosely.

"Guess so," I stated. "Tell me more, and I'll tell you more."

His father lived in a quaint cottage in Maleny. The steep drive up to the house was picturesque.

We stopped at the entrance to the gate. David rolled down the window and entered a sequence of numbers on the digital key pad. The gate opened outward and he drove forward. Though the loose gravel was white, the red dirt had in places turned the stones pink.

A Land Rover was parked in the driveway.

David rapped on the door before calling out, "Honey I'm home!"

He then cracked up laughing at the expression on my face which was clearly one of shock.

Michael opened the door, grinning from ear to ear. "Hey, Davey!!!" He gave him a firm embrace and a pat on the back. Eyeing me intently, he stated, "And who is this beautiful creature?"

David smiled in response. "Go on, have a guess!"

"Temwani," Michael stated loudly. "Pleasure to finally meet you!"

He embraced me strongly. I embraced him back.

"Michael. My dad," he replied. "My adoptive father, but my dad all the same," David explained. We went inside and sat on the sofa. Damien, Michael's partner got us all cold drinks, and David got straight into talking about his childhood.

"I constantly wonder about the type of man I would have been had I not been given up," he noted. "I was born with a deformity - a cleft palate. They gave me up and took Daniel in for obvious reasons,"

"That's not the whole story Davey," Michael interjected. Michael was an obstetric surgeon in training at the time. He had been witness to the birth of the first child, and stood by while an abortion was attempted on the second one. One which was attempted but failed.

Daniel, the first child, was given to the adoptive parents at

321

birth, while David, the second child, was to be "disposed of".

"They knew there was something wrong with the second baby. The adoptive mother did not want him, and the birth mother was too out of it to care. They placed him in a bucket in the cupboard and asked the nurse to place formaldehyde in with him to ensure he would not survive," Michael said.

I gasped in shock at what I'd just heard. My heart skipped a beat when I imagined David, a mere infant, defenceless and unwanted.

"I felt for the baby boy with all my heart," Michael said. "Despite their efforts to get rid of him through a post-term abortion, he was born alive, and I couldn't stand to leave him. The nurse didn't get to him. I took him out of that bucket, wrapped him in a blanket, and snuck him out. I raised him with the help of a whet nurse."

David sat with his head in his hands, and I slipped a hand across his knee, reaching out for him. He rested his hand on mine, and I hoped the small gesture was reassuring to him.

"Their birth mother took her life in the weeks following the birth, but not before I had a chance to talk to her. She refused to look at David, and she refused to hold him. She said she mourned the loss of her perfect son, Daniel," Michael said. "I raised David as my own. He always has been and always will be perfect to me," Michael stated. "The surgical repair of his cleft palate took place eventually, but to me, he's always been perfect."

"How did you end up in foster care?" I asked of David.

David looked at Michael, Michael at David. "Oh, you want me to explain?"

"If you don't mind," David stated.

"Well the long and short of it is I messed up," he started.

"Police had a sting operation the night they nabbed me; I was out looking for fast love, cruising, if you know what I mean. Happened to proposition an undercover police officer. Ended up spending 12 months in the slammer," he recalled, running a hand through his deep brown hair. Pausing for a moment, he added, "I'll never forgive myself for the things that happened to David when he was in foster care."

"Dad, that's all in the past..."

"Is it?" Michael asked, walking across the room to gaze through the window. "If it was all in the past, why are you still searching for answers?"

David sighed heavily, then responded, "I'm just wanting closure," he stated. "I needed to know who Daniel was and I needed to make him aware that I was around. I wanted to see Jolène face to face and impress on her how much her decision to take in Daniel and not me changed my life."

"David, your father raised you and he raised you well," Damien, commented. "I know you wanted for nothing when you were growing up."

David agreed. "No arguments there, I don't take issue with the way I was raised, at all, I'm lucky Michael raised me and I'm convinced things happened the way they did for a reason," he said pensively. "I just had this burning desire to get closure," he clarified. "It wasn't supposed to be this way, anyway," he stated. "Daniel wasn't supposed to fall for Teme...anyway, guess that's just how things go," he stated, somewhat sadly.

"Well, whatever the case, she's here with you now. She's in your life. Now, what's this about Jolène?" Michael asked.

"I haven't confronted her about what she did."

"And you will not," warned Michael. "No sense in dredging

up the past," he said.

"No, but if the shoe fits..." David commenced.

Damien chuckled. "She'll have to wear it alright!" he exclaimed. "Nothing like a bit of karma to bite her in the behind," he added.

I presumed that David would tell me all eventually, so instead of pressing the issue, I resolved to enjoy the time we had at his father's place.

"Michael?" I asked, breaking the silence. "Can I raid your fridge for some food to eat? Can I cook up something and possibly bake up a storm?"

The troubled look on Michael's face softened, and he got up and gestured for me to join him in the kitchen. "You certainly can," he said. "Now to you, Temwani. Forgive me for not asking before, but can I take you on a tour around the house?"

"Of course," I said, linking my arm in with his. David, smiling affectionately at me with Michael sent a nod our way before settling down on the sofa and engaging in conversation with Damien.

David received a phone call that afternoon that had him on edge. He pulled over to take it and was clearly distraught when he hung up. Immediately, he asked whether I minded driving to a town an hour away to pick up something he'd left behind. When asked what that something was, he remained tight lipped about it all.

We drove in silence for most of the journey, stopping twice for food and a toilet break. He remained noticeably on edge.

"You need to tell me what's got you so stressed out," I insisted.

"Someone's broken into one of the properties I own. I have

something of value there. I hope it's still there," he said, panicked. He refused to tell me what *it* was.

"No secrets," I reminded him.

"There are some things you shouldn't know at all," he said in response. "Trust me."

When we got to Maryborough, he asked me to stay in the car, doors locked while he checked out the place. It was an old worker's cottage, very similar to the one we stayed in, in Nambour. There were no visible signs of damage or forced entry from the front of the house.

David came back not long after, urging me to go in with him. The stairs leading to the front entrance creaked as we walked up them. A single key opened the deadbolt while another key dabbed with a touch of black paint opened the other lock.

He flipped on a light on entry. The house had a distinct smell of sanded timber.

"Smells nice," I noted.

He nodded in agreement. "Cypress. Floorboards haven't been sealed yet. It's a work in progress."

I hesitated before walking further. "Is it safe?"

"A window in the second bedroom's been broken. Other than that, nothing else has been touched. It's safe. I'm here with you. Just watch the glass on the floor down there," he said, motioning towards one of the bedrooms.

He brusquely opened the wooden blinds in the living room, letting in warm rays of sunlight. Dropping to his knees, he quickly moved the chaise-longue and rug out of the way to reveal a panel in the floor. Popping the panel open, he reached within to reveal a wooden box. I watched with anticipation as he flipped the lid and rummaged through the contents. He sighed heavily. "It's gone."

"What's gone?"

"My notebook," he said, his tone solemn. "It's a notebook with some very powerful information. Part memory, part investigation."

"If it's that important, why would you leave it here?" I asked.

"I didn't think it'd be touched."

"Why not keep it with you?" I asked.

"I couldn't keep it on my person. The information's powerful. In the wrong hands..." he said, his voice trailing off. "Damn it." He wasn't about to tell me what the information was. At least not yet, anyway.

"Craig's not going to be too happy about this," he said.

"Oh David, whatever it is, it's probably not as bad as it seems."

"You're right. It's worse," he said, looking up at me, clearly distraught. Sneaking a quick glance at his wristwatch, he stated, "We should be heading back soon." Placing the box back under the panel and shutting the lid, he moved the rug and chaise-longue back over the panel.

Trying to distract him, I asked, "Can you show me around before we leave?"

"Sure," he said. The house was beautiful and quaint. Decorative cornices adorned the roof, and the skylights stretching across the ceiling brightened up the main living area. Long expansive windows with painted white frames looked out into an extensive backyard. The grass had recently been mowed. "I envisioned having you here with me one day. Just not under these circumstances," he said. "I envisioned this being our home."

My heart skipped a beat.

"I'm still holding out hope that one day it'll be our home."
Pulling the sheer curtains back across the window, he noted,
"Gotta remember to patch up the broken glass before we go."

I lay down on the Queen sized bed, watching him fit a panel
of wood between the pane and the glass, then patch up with
duck tape across the broken glass. "That'll do for now," he
said.

"You're quite the tradesman," I noted.

He laughed lightly. "That's a funny thing to say. I wouldn't
quite call myself a tradesman. I can do most things, and if I
can't I'll give it a go," he said. "That's the Aussie way." All
done, he extended his hand to me. "Come, let's get out of
here," he requested.

Outside, he gave the place a quick once over before we
headed to the car.

"You alright to drive?" I asked, noticing that his hands
were shaking.

"You're in no condition," he stated, motioning towards
my heavily pregnant belly.

"I'm in a better condition to drive than you are right now,"
I replied.

After a moment of hesitation, he handed me the keys.

The skies were a foreboding grey as we drove back. I drove
halfway, and he slept through my part of the drive. He took
over when we got to Gympie, noticeably refreshed but still
on edge.

"Cyclone weather," he mentioned. "Might be time to
consider heading back to Texas," he suggested.

"Trying to get rid of me already?" I asked jokingly.

"No," he replied swiftly. "Just trying to keep you safe. In
more ways than one."

When we got back, he ventured out to the shops to get some food and a few supplies in preparation for when the storm would hit. I used the time alone to take a long, soothing bath. By the time he'd gotten back I'd fallen asleep on the settee.

"Everything alright?" he asked.

"All good," I replied, feeling a sudden urge to clean and prep for the babies.

"Rest up good," he urged. "Babies are notorious for arriving at times like these, when storm season's in full effect." Closing the blinds around the house, he announced, "I've signed up to do a shift at the General tonight. You gonna be okay?" he asked.

"Of course," I replied. He was throwing himself straight into work again. "Are *you* gonna be okay?" I asked.

"I'll be fine," he stated, when clearly he was not. "Let's prep dinner before I go," he suggested.

As we prepped dinner that night, we discussed plans moving forward. "Heading back next week or so's probably the best thing to do," he advised. "Enough time to settle back in, enough time to figure out where things are going with Daniel."

"Or I can stay here for a while longer, have the babies here and then head back," I teased.

He gave me a serious look. "Be careful what you wish for," he said, tossing the salad, then offering me a cherry tomato before placing the bowl on the table.

"I hear you," I replied. "It's been nice, being here with you," I said. "The time away from Daniel's given me pause to reflect on everything."

"You think you'll be happy to go back to him, pick up where

you left off?" he asked. The sun-dried tomato and mushroom sauce was just about ready, as was the pasta.

"Of course not," I replied. "If he's to get right with me, a lot of things are going to have to change," I stated. "For one, he needs to learn how to be a lot less controlling."

"Ain't that the truth," David chimmed in.

"And a lot less insecure," I added.

David nodded in response. "That'll help heaps."

Dinner was ready. We sat at the butterfly table, and held hands across the table to pray. Prepared to say grace, I was surprised when he took the initiative and prayed over our meal, for my health and for the health of the babies.

It warmed my heart that he was becoming such a Godly man. As I placed salad on his plate and then mine, I asked point blankly, "Do you still wonder whether God is on your side? Not so long ago, you mentioned that you were not sure. How do you feel now?"

Without hesitation, he said "I *know* He's on my side. It's just a matter of me working in with whatever plan he has in store for me and my future."

I nodded in response, wishing I was so clear on what the future held for me.

"Forgiveness is another thing," he added, putting way too much salad dressing on his lettuce, tomato and baby spinach salad. "I don't know where that notebook's at, but the information within is enough to open up a world of hurt and pain for so many people. At the time that I started it, I was in a place where I felt so vengeful, so consumed with hate. Now...," his voice trailed off.

I squeezed his hand across the table. He squeezed back. "I don't feel much of anything at all now," he stated. "Still so

329

many problems to be solved, and still so many unanswered questions."

"What kind of questions?"

"The question of who my father is, for one. The question of what to do with the information I already know about him," he said. I grew curious and wanted to know more. Reading my mind, he added, "And no, I don't want to talk about him. Not just yet anyway." Changing topic, he said, "So we book the return flight to Texas tonight, okay? Leave next Friday or so? Anything after then is cutting it too fine."

The thought of going back to Texas had me conflicted. On the one hand, I wanted to get back to Daniel and see whether there was a chance to salvage our relationship. On the other hand, being here with David was a dream. The time we'd shared left me feeling renewed, refreshed and ready to take on whatever challenges would come my way. I didn't want it to end.

David snapped his fingers. "Earth to Teme, earth to Teme," he joked. "Let's make the most of the time we have left," he urged. "We could go out tonight to the local for a bit, but it don't make sense to go anywhere else anytime soon. I've still got my shift at the General, and I dare say the storm will hit real soon."

"Okay, well, we can book the tickets tonight and take it from there," I agreed. David wanted to come back with me, to help along the way.

He washed up after dinner while I put some clothes in the laundry, and folded a few others.

"Karaoke?" he asked as he emerged from the kitchen.

"Would love to," I replied. He raced over to the TV unit, knelt down, propped the drawer open, and pulled out a microphone before proceeding to set up the TV for karaoke.

"Marvin Gaye and Diana Ross - *You are Everything*?" he asked, smiling widely.

I nodded my head in approval. We went through most of Marvin Gaye's album, followed by a few other Motown classics save for the Temptations.

"Why not?" he asked.

"Daniel. He hardly listened to any hip hop, soul or R and B but he loved the Four Tops and the Temptations." I clarified.

"I see," David said. The Four Tops and Temptations were your thing," he acknowledged.

I nodded in response.

Not phased, he asked, "How about The Commodores? Can't go past them!"

"Go for it," I told him. I loved hearing him sing, and couldn't think of a better way to spend the time we had left.

All was going well that evening up until the moment I received a text message from Johnny.

Hope you and the babies are well, he said. *Look, I know David loved you first, but Daniel is your husband and he's willing to change anything and everything to get back right with you.*

Johnny please stay out of this, I replied.

Too late. Daniel's as close a friend as I'll ever get and I care about you both. I won't stand by and watch a good thing fail, he said.

It isn't up to you to work at us fixing our relationship, I replied.

When do you get back? he asked, sidestepping my statement.

Hope to leave next week, I told him.

He's falling apart here, Johnny replied.

I paused before replying. *He did this to himself.*

He's only human, Johnny replied.

"Everything okay?" David asked, concerned.

"Yep," I replied, deciding not to text Johnny back.

"Daniel?" he asked.

"No. Johnny. He says Daniel's falling apart with me being gone," I explained.

"Hm," David replied. "He knew what he was doing when he did it, and he needs to straighten up before the kids get here," he reminded me. "Give him a chance to really miss you," he advised. "Maybe then he'll appreciate what he has."

I agreed.

"Come, let's do this," he urged, keen to get back into karaoke and keep my mind off things. "It'll all work out in the end," he said.

16

A NEW DAY

David was dead right about the possibility of the babies arriving in the midst of a storm. The contractions started through the night, while he was on shift at the General. *I can't be in labor already*, I thought, *the babies are only 35 weeks old.*

He returned to find me in pain, walking around the house when each contraction hit. Though he suggested a trip to the hospital, I preferred to wait it out and see where things would lead. "Now's not the time to be stubborn," he stated, clearly concerned. "Rest for now, and we can call into the ER for a check-up in a bit?"

"David, I'll be fine," I replied. "My body's just doing its' thing," I said, though a little concerned about how early I was having contractions.

"Could just be Braxton Hicks, but just in case they're not…"

"I hear you," I replied, very aware of his concern.

"The safest place for you to be is in the hospital," he added.

"David, will you stop?" I requested. "If it gets too much I'll let you know, it's probably nothing," I promised.

"Okay," he stated, reluctantly. "Would you at least let

Michael come by and give you his opinion?" he requested.

I rolled my eyes in response.

"Please?" he begged, the concern in his eyes apparent.

"Okay," I obliged.

"For now, take it easy," he insisted, motioning towards the chair.

"Do I have a choice?" I joked.

"No, you don't," he replied.

"You're starting to sound an awful lot like Daniel," I said.

"Oh, don't get me started," he stated. "You can be too stubborn for your own good sometimes."

"I understand your view though, and I respect how you feel. I'll go in for a check-up this afternoon?" I asked. "Just after I finish painting that back door."

He sighed heavily in response. "Do I need to hide the paintbrushes and paint to get you to stop?" he asked. "No waiting. Let's do it now," he said, clearly concerned.

"Alright."

The weather was not the best. Strong winds were brewing outside, and by the time I got my bag together, it was hailing. "I'm not sure we'd make it alright. I'll call the ambulance instead. Don't make sense to go out right now," David said.

I leaned against the wall, feeling every contraction run through me.

"Breathe," he suggested, a tender hand on my shoulder. I held his hand as another contraction hit.

"I don't think this is a trial run, it feels like the real thing," I told him.

"I'll time them," he suggested, motioning for me to lie on the sofa for a moment. "Can I check how the babies are doing?" he asked, offering to palpate my belly and determine the babies' position.

I nodded in response, another contraction surging through me like a wave.

"Breathe," he said again, hand on my belly this time. He knelt on the floor next to me, waiting for the contraction to come to an end before he checked the position of the babies. "One of them is head down and engaged, the other...slightly at an angle above, but head down too. Good babies," he remarked, smiling his beautiful smile.

Another contraction hit, and I gripped his hand. The pain was excruciating. It felt as though my insides were being ripped to shreds, and my back hurt terribly.

"With the spacing between your contractions, I think you're in spontaneous labour," he stated, rolling up his sleeves before he held my hand again. "I also think you're in a lot of pain."

"You think?" I interjected. "Tell me something I don't know."

He ignored my sarcasm. "Being in water would help with the pain," he suggested. "Hot towels on your back would help too."

"I can try the shower, but the thought of all that water going to waste..."

"The bath then?" he asked.

"Yes," I said, trying to remember some of the things I'd learnt in my online hypnobirthing class. I hadn't had a conventional pregnancy. Daniel hadn't been there, and I'd had to see George on my own several times. The big day had come and Daniel wasn't there. I was on my own again.

"Darling, I know it's hard, but let go of any negative thought, any negative thinking," he urged. "Focus on the moment. These babies. You."

"Okay," I said, reassured by his confidence and mere presence.

"The bath it is then," he said, getting up quickly. "I'll be back."

I heard the bath running and I tried to rest for a bit, in between contractions. He came back a little flustered.

"Okay?"

"A tree's down at the front, driveway is blocked," he said.

"Oh," I replied.

"Ambos can just pull up at the front, just means we can't drive anywhere ourselves," he said. "You're doing well so far," he observed.

"I have a doppler in my suitcase, can you check and see how they're going in there?"

"A doppler?" he asked. "What are you doing with a doppler?"

"My doula recommended I get one to check on the babies from time to time," I explained.

"Your doula?" he asked accusatorially. I knew he wouldn't like that, so I'd kept it from him. "Keeping secrets now, are we?"

"You're a doctor David."

"What's that got to do with anything?" he questioned. "I don't see why you kept having a doula from me? I'm for anything that would help. Some things, such as you using a doppler outside consulting with a doctor may not be helpful."

"I knew you wouldn't be happy so I kept it from you," I explained. "Your reaction shows you're not happy."

"Okay. Let's not fight," he said.

"No one's fighting here, you don't know what a fight is,

336

until you see Daniel and I in action."

"Yeah, I hear you," he said briefly. "I'll go get that doppler."

He came back with the doppler and a glass of water with a straw.

Lifting my shirt, he applied a gel to my belly and listened in. All seemed okay.

"I'm happy for you to labour away for a while, up until the ambos get here, but hopefully we won't be waiting here for much longer. We need you to get to the hospital." Wiping the gel off my belly with a tissue, then rolling my shirt back down he advised, "I might call Michael and see whether he can give us a lift. Neighbours are away, and I can't get in touch with the guys on call at the General."

"Isn't the General just 20 minutes away?" I asked.

"It is. But I'm being told access roads are blocked off due to flash flooding. Might be easier to get to Buderim Private if we go Rosemount way, down the mountain."

I felt a little anxious, then he held my hand again. "It'll be fine. Babies are doing fine," he said. Though he was calm, I could feel the anxiety in him. "Time you get ready to hop into the bath," he said, helping me up. Another contraction hit and I leaned into him. He held me close, applying counter pressure to my back until the contraction waned. We stood there for a while before he asked, "You good?"

I nodded in response. "Thank you."

"My pleasure," he said. "It truly is an honour." Offering me his hand, he stated, "Come. The bath awaits."

He leaned over the bath, emptying some water and refilling with hot water as the water he'd put in previously had cooled down.

Another contraction hit, and I leaned against the wall again. He met me there, and beckoned me to lean into him, applying counter pressure to my lower back again. Once the contraction had waned, he tended to the bath again.

I stripped down to my bra and underwear, remembering I had a bikini packed in my suitcase. I stopped short and decided to go get it.

"Wait, wait wait, where are you going?" he asked.

"To get my bikini from the suitcase."

"I'll get it," he offered.

Had Daniel been with me, I would have stripped down completely, but David wasn't Daniel, and I didn't want to be a temptation.

He returned in no time. "So you have me rummaging through your undies now," he said. "Daniel's not going to like that."

"That sounds all wrong," I laughed and he winked.

"Go on," he urged, turning his back.

I changed quickly and got into the bath. He knelt by the edge, encouraging me to breathe through each contraction.

"Better?" he asked.

"Much better," I told him.

"Well, I'd love to see you naked but now's obviously not an appropriate time," he said, half serious.

"David!" I exclaimed, flinging a little water off my finger-tips and onto his face.

He laughed heartily, wiping the water off with the back of his hand.

"Credit where credit is due. At least you're being honest," I said. "At least you know how to make me laugh."

"That and then some," he remarked. "I'm completely

wrapped you've gone into labour and I'm the one to support you through this."

I could only smile in return.

"I've got a bone to pick with these babies though. They couldn't have chosen a better place or time to look at coming into the world!" he said sarcastically.

"That's Daniel all over," I commented. "Marching to the beat of his own drum, going against the grain."

"That's so funny," he laughed. "Funny but it's true." He glanced at his watch again. "Speaking of Daniel, I rang him. He's not in Texas. Apparently he hasn't been there for days. Must be on his way down here," he guessed. "I left a message."

It was reassuring, but disturbing in ways. If he'd been out of Texas for days, he'd been lying to me when we last spoke on the phone. The contractions suddenly felt stronger and unbearable. I decided to come out of the bath.

"You've been in the bath all but five minutes, are you really done?"

"Yes," I replied curtly. The contractions had changed, and I wanted to be elsewhere as the water didn't appear to be helping.

When I stood up, my waters broke, and not long after, I felt the urge to push. David's face suddenly turned pale. "That's a lot of blood now. Ambos should be here by now but they're not. It's probably easier..." he broke off, helping me out of the bath.

"Where to?" he asked.

"Anywhere else but here," was my response.

"Okay," he said, handing me a towel, and nervously scrambling for a few more.

339

"Need to keep you warm," he said. "Try to rest for a bit while we wait for the ambos or Michael to come around."

He threw a few towels onto the bed and encouraged me to lie there on my side. "Breathe through them. Breathe," he urged, as another contraction hit. He was getting increasingly concerned but said very little and maintained a calm demeanour.

I couldn't lie there on my side, so sat upright, at an angle. He hopped onto the bed, and sat next to me, encouraging me to lean into him.

"I feel I'm going to be sick," I told him, making a dash to the toilet.

When I finished, he was there at the door, looking in on me. "You're doing amazing," he said, offering me his hand and leading me back to the bedroom.

On the bed, he sat behind me and braced my pain. With each contraction I leant into him and he held me, encouraging me to breathe deeply and work with the pain to help the babies descend. Birthing was an incredibly intimate experience, one which I'd hoped to share with Daniel, yet here we were, David and I, juxtaposed against all odds, juxtaposed in an intimate life changing moment, in time.

I suddenly felt the urge to push and stripped off my bikini bottom. I threw a towel across my legs for modesty. David caught the fleeting moment of nudity but said nothing. There was no doubt that the babies were coming out now.

A very strong contraction hit, and I called out David's name. Caught up in the raw energy of it all, he jumped into rescue mode and encouraged me to push.

"I can see the top of a baby's head!" he exclaimed excitedly. "Okay," he directed. "I'll tell you when to push, it can't happen too quickly…"

"Don't you dare tell me when I can push or not! I'm the one giving birth here!" I shouted.

He smiled lovingly. "I hear you."

A few expletives later, he announced, "Okay I'm gonna give it a go."

I listened but didn't hear. "Breathe through this, breathe through this, your body knows what to do," I heard him saying under his breath.

Josiah was born first. David immediately placed him in my arms. Adalia followed closely behind, screaming her lungs out. Our babies were beautiful. When I looked at them I saw Daniel, through David. The ambulance arrived not long after the babies were born. I shivered in shock while David, shirtless, kept me warm, his body pressed up against mine. A thermal blanket covered us all. He held one baby while I held the other and encouraged me to initiate breastfeeding.

"You are simply amazing," he declared, tears in his eyes as he held me and the babies close.

"I'd shower you with passionate kisses right now if you were mine," he stated, wiping tears out of his eyes. "But this'll do," he said, planting a kiss on my forehead and embracing me tightly, squeezing me, Adalia and Josiah in the process.

I parted from him only when I separated from the babies. He remained with them, feeding them some of the first milk I'd expressed.

My body ached, I felt tired but otherwise felt fine. The babies I'd longed for, the babies I'd carried were finally here. A manifestation of the love between Daniel and I. Pity Daniel was not there. I tried ringing him several times, but somehow he did not respond. He had not been in contact in days. In his absence, I was grateful for David's presence, and his love. Steadfast, unconditional and ever present.

"You alright?" David asked, sitting in the nursing chair, rocking Josiah in his arms.

"I'll be okay," I told him, suddenly in tears.

He carefully got up, placed Josiah into the twin bassinet with Adalia and made his way over to me on the bed. "It'll be okay," he assured me. "Babies are healthy, you were amazing. For 35 weeks they're doing extremely well. Daniel will get here soon I'm sure."

Tears rolled down my face. I was happy, but suddenly felt overwhelmed with the blues.

"And if he isn't here soon, I'll be there." He wrapped his arms around me, held me tight and said nothing further. It was what I needed at the time, and I was grateful for it. I was grateful for him.

I fell asleep and woke to him sitting on a stool at the head of my bed. He smiled widely at me but looked tired. "Have you gotten any sleep?" I asked.

"No, I was hoping I could get some shut eye now you're awake," he stated.

"Some sleep, then we look at an early discharge?" I was sure he and I could manage the babies at home. "I have a few stiches, is all. I think we can manage on our own."

"A few stitches yes, but a world of hurt if you don't take it easy while you can," he told me.

"Please," I begged. "I just want to be home."

"Oh, so you consider my place home?" he asked.

Tears fell down my face. "Home is where you are David."

342

Touched, he held me as he had before. "We'll see what's possible," he stated. "Try to get some sleep. I'll sort something out," he promised.

I awoke to David sitting at the head of my bed staring into me. "Hi Temwani," he said. "Bags all packed, we can hit the road when you're ready. Managed to get an early discharge."

I was overjoyed.

"We'll manage," he reassured me. "We just have to kangaroo care the babies, keep them warm and monitor any changes. Other than that, they're good to go." Glancing at his watch, he stated, "I'll go home, do a bit of a clean up then come back and get you. How does that sound?"

"Sounds good," I told him.

Back at the cottage, Adalia was unsettled. For reasons unknown, she kept crying, without abating. No matter what I did, she continued. Without words, David took her in his arms and rocked her. He hummed and she stopped complaining instantly. I sighed in relief, very grateful he was there with me, but sad it wouldn't last. Daniel would be on his way soon, and who knew what terror would be unleashed on David for having been there for the birth of our babies.

Eventually both of the babies got back to sleep. David prepped me a meal before insisting I slept. He promised to wake up with me when the babies woke.

The next morning after breakfast, we sat on the patio enjoying the warm rays of the sun.

"I got something for you," David said. "Close your eyes."

I could feel the cold metal of a necklace against my skin. He adjusted the clasp at the back. I opened my eyes.

"Did I tell you it would be okay to open your eyes?" he

343

asked. "Keep them closed please."

I felt a pendant dangle on my skin. "Now open your eyes," he said. A beautiful pink sapphire heart shaped pendant with a singular blue and baby pink gem within. "The blue is for your son, the pink your daughter," he stated.

"It's beautiful!" I exclaimed, but knew Daniel would take issue with it.

David sensed my hesitancy. "Daniel's not going to like that I got you another gift, but hey, I'll take my chances. He doesn't like anything I do."

"That is true. But he's not here yet. I'll keep it on for a while yet."

"Alright," he replied. "I'm glad you like it."

"I love it. Is this another one of your creations? Did you make it yourself?" I asked.

"That I did," he replied. "Temwani, I met you when you were just coming of age. I thought you were amazing then. I think you're even more amazing now."

We sat there on the balcony for what seemed like forever, talking about everything and nothing. I loved how with him there were no unreasonable expectations – he just allowed me to be.

"So, Daniel's on his way over. Flight gets in tomorrow morning. I guess you and the babies'll be heading back with him as soon as they get cleared to fly?"

"I guess so," I replied. "The nurses said it wouldn't be for another two months or so."

"That'll be about right," he agreed. "Might have to take on some portable oxygen to help them cope with the drop in oxygen levels," he said pensively. "Safest thing of course would be to stay here for as long as you need to," he advised.

"Is this Doctor Davenport talking, or is this David Daven-port, I want to keep you for myself, talking?"

He laughed heartily in response. "A bit of both darling."

Darling. Sweet words just rolled off his tongue so effort-lessly.

"You're such a charmer, David."

"I'm only after a way into your heart," he said. "If I have to charm my way in, I will."

I laughed again, but realized quickly that I needed to be careful with what I said with him. I wanted him in my life forever, in the only way that he could be. As a friend. That said, I didn't want to lead him on. "You had me from the moment you professed your love for me," I replied. "I just..."

"No need to explain," he said. "I know how you feel."

He wore his heart on his sleeve most times. It wasn't hard to see that he preferred to live with the expectation that one day I'd be his, than the reality that I was married to Daniel and would never be his.

"I also know I need to get real," he said. "But in my heart of hearts, I truly believe one day we will be," he said. "After all, here you are, and here I am. Closer than ever. A far cry from what we were when we first met. At least we're friends now."

"True," I replied.

"Anyhow, I'd rather be your friend, than your ex or your could have been," he said.

"I feel the same way," I told him. "I just don't expect you to be waiting for me, forever."

"Forever is such a loaded word," he stated. "Forever can change in a moment," he said, in a way that sent chills down my spine, as I remembered the last time the word forever

345

was mentioned to me. *I will love you forever* Daniel had said, on our wedding day. "I prefer to say forever and a day. Or better yet, always."

"I do like the sound of always," I told him.

"Same," David said. "Anyway, let's not worry about the future, it isn't in our hands."

I nodded, agreeing with him.

"Just know I'll always be in yours," he declared.

I smiled, thinking of how he never missed an opportunity to profess his love for me.

With both babies still sound asleep, we continued to sit on the veranda, talking. Our afternoon was idyllic up until a dark blue Commodore sedan with tinted windows pulled up. Daniel wasn't coming when he said he was coming; he was here now.

David stood up immediately, though not as shocked as I was. Daniel opened the gate for himself, and strode past David to me, with no more than a nod in his direction as acknowledgement.

"Baby, baby, baby," he said, planting a kiss on my lips and cheeks. "I missed you like crazy sugarpie..."

"We were expecting you, just not this soon," David stated, interrupting.

"Got here as soon as I could," Daniel replied barely turning to face him. "The babies?"

"Fast asleep," I replied. "Got an early discharge yester-day."

"I see," Daniel replied. Looking at David, he added, "Don't you all hug me at once. I finally got here despite the floods and despite the fires."

"Good you're here," David managed. "I'll get your bags,"

he said.

"Won't be staying," Daniel replied sharply.

David stopped in his tracks, and shook his head.

"Got their passports all sorted, it's time my wife and kids came home," Daniel added.

"Settle down, mate, will ya? This isn't about what you want, it's about what's best for them," David argued.

"Thanks, *mate*, but this is my family and my household and as head of this here household I will do what I think is best," Daniel said.

David paused for a moment before responding. "Well, good luck getting clearance to fly. Babies haven't even had oxy sat tests done."

"Like it or not, I'm taking them home. Shouldn't even be here in the first place," Daniel fumed.

Turning to David, I stated, "Forgive him David, he really is grateful that you've been there for me. At least he *should be* grateful."

"You're alright," David started. "Don't need to apologize for him being an arse."

Anger flashed in Daniel's eyes. I could tell another punch up was likely.

"Did you come bearing gifts?" David asked.

"What's it to ya," Daniel replied.

"Simple question," David insisted. "Did you come bearing gifts?"

"What I chose to do or not do is none of your business," Daniel replied.

"So, no flowers, no push present, no nada?" David asked.

"As I said, what I choose to do or not do is none of your business."

"You make it my business when you come out here acting the way you're acting..." he stopped mid speech. His phone was buzzing vigorously in his pocket. He'd set it to vibrate earlier, so any ringing would not disturb the babies. "Hmm, yep. Hmm..." he muttered into the phone, eyeballing Daniel. "I didn't hear the phone ring...right. Right. When was this?" he asked into the phone, now glaring at Daniel. "Right. I'll call you back later." Turning back to Daniel, he asked, "You mind telling me what possessed you to go over to my father's place and act the way you did? What gives you the right to get up in his face and..."

"Are you kidding me?" Daniel asked, standing up face off with David. "Some kind of a father he was, too busy feeding his homosexual lifestyle to care about raising you the right way. Your stint in foster care happened because of him."

David stood there for a moment, holding space, then in one swift move, he threw a hard punch which landed on Daniel's jaw. The punch left him holding his hand in pain. Daniel gathered himself together before standing up and launching for David. David ducked and swung for Daniel again, clearly enraged. Sooner or later this was bound to happen, and at that moment, I had no time for it. I got up, went inside, locked the front door behind me. With all the commotion, the babies had woken.

I threw on a cardigan and decided to leave. Irene, the midwife, was bound to be home, and she was only five minutes away. I knew she wouldn't mind a visit. I scooped both babies up, put them in the carrier and headed for the car.

As I drove up the driveway, Daniel was still throwing punches, while David was largely ducking them and avoiding

348

him. I drove off without a second thought, and left them to it. With both the front and the back door locked, neither one could get into the house. As I turned the corner I saw them stop for a moment, likely in shock that I'd taken off suddenly, but I had no patience or concern anymore. The tension between them was tiring, and they had to have it out sometime. No time like the present.

I stayed at Irene's long enough to make cornbread to accompany the stew dinner she'd prepared earlier. She helped nurse the babies, and I was very grateful for her help. After dinner had passed, I decided to look at my phone.

Eight missed calls. Six from Daniel, one from David, one from Michael.

I listened to the message from Michael first. "Congrats on the babies. I'm sorry I couldn't get there but I hear Davey managed just fine. I'll catch up with you in a few. Now I hope you get this message before he heads over... David's brother is on his way over. He's on the warpath."

Knowing Daniel was on his way over would not have changed anything at all.

The six messages from Daniel were urging me to return home with the babies right away. He was hungry and tired apparently. David's message encouraged me to come back soon.

When I returned they were both a sight for sore eyes, but seemed to be more at ease with each other than when I had left. David nodded in acknowledgement at my return, and helped with the babies. Tenderly, he lifted Adalia out and cradled her before handing her to Daniel, who was unsure of how to hold her. He cried tears of joy as he held her, before moving on to hold Josiah. "I hope you're nothing like your old man," he joked, breaking the ice. We all laughed.

I reheated last night's dinner for Daniel. He devoured the pasta heartily as though he hadn't eaten in days. Dabbing pasta sauce off his chin with a napkin, he turned to David and stated, "I'm gonna need to defer to you, mate, for a lot of things – you're in the know as far as my babies are concerned."

"No worries at all," David responded.

"I'm sorry about earlier. I'm very grateful you were here, and that this beautiful wife of mine and babies are fine," he acknowledged.

"I wouldn't have had it any other way," David replied.

"I bet you wouldn't have," Daniel replied sarcastically.

I rolled my eyes in response. "Here we go again."

Daniel heeded my statement and said, "Look I know your feelings for Teme won't just disappear overnight, but I respect the fact that you were able to respect me and honour us, even if this meant losing her to me."

David sighed in response. "I hear you."

"So, I feel it's right we turn over a new leaf now, and start working with each other instead of against each other," Daniel said, surprising me.

David nodded in reply.

"Speaking of which, Craig," Daniel started. "He needs to be stopped."

"I'd stay away from Craig if I were you," David cautioned. "I wouldn't advise messing with him."

"He's messed with me, I'm messing with him," Daniel vowed.

I got up to check the babies, and they were fast asleep. I

thought it appropriate to broach the subject of the missing notebook with Daniel. He might be able to help.

"David, the notebook that went missing, anything Daniel can help with?" I asked.

David frowned slightly before stating, "Whoever's got it went to great lengths to find it."

Pushing his plate to the side and setting his hands in front of him, Daniel stated, "This notebook. You really need to hide things properly."

A puzzled look on David's face and Daniel added, "Yes, I have it."

"Well, thank goodness for that," I stated, relieved.

"Don't be too relieved," Daniel warned. "A few pages are missing. It's clear someone else got to it first," he suggested.

David got to his feet and paced, clearly distraught.

Daniel got up and put a hand on his shoulder. "Look, for what it's worth, I'm truly sorry about the life you lived in comparison to the one I lived."

"I don't need your sympathy," David replied curtly. I knew he didn't mean that.

"Look, I'm here to help," Daniel said.

"Firstly, how did you get the notebook, and why the suggestion that someone got to it first?"

"Craig had copies," Daniel stated abruptly.

"That's not news," David stated. "He knew about it."

"Okay," Daniel replied. "How about this for news – one of our father's henchmen had it as well."

David shot him a look of disbelief. "What?"

"Our father? Birth father? One of his henchmen had it," Daniel stated.

It took me a moment to register what he had said. The look

on David's face was one of shock.

"What are you on about?" he finally managed.

"As I said. Someone else had it, and I'm pretty sure they weren't too pleased about the contents," Daniel stated.

Panicked, David admitted, "I've been trying to identify our father all these years. You're trying to tell me you know who he is?"

"Not yet unfortunately," Daniel replied. "I'm close though."

I heard the twins crying in the distance. "I got this," Daniel replied, heading for the nursery.

David looked at me and I looked at David. The look on his face said it all. Daniel had opened up a can of worms and there was no telling what would happen next.

David made himself scarce that evening, heading out to give Daniel and I a moment together.

"I'll be at the hospital," he said. "I'm sure there'll be something for me to do there."

I felt for him, and knew he'd secretly been counting on Daniel not being there for me, so that he instead could be there for me. I couldn't blame him. After sharing the birth experience with me, we had reached new heights in our relationship, which could only be explored further as friends. He looked in on the babies before he left. "I'm only a phone call away," he reminded me. "Get as much rest as you can, I'll look in on them when I'm back, bring them to you when you need me to..."

"I'm here now," Daniel reminded him. "I can take it from here."

"Good," David said stiffly. "I'll see you later on," he added, before leaving in a hurry.

Turning to Daniel I stated, "You know, you don't need to be so hostile towards him. He has been here for me when you were not."

"I know this," Daniel replied. "He needs to know you're mine, not his."

"I think he knows that," I said in his defence.

"Oh, I'm not sure he does," Daniel argued as David walked back in. He'd forgotten the keys.

"Keys would help," he said. "See you later." He walked off humming a tune I recognized as the Supremes' *Someday We'll Be Together.*

"Hm," I noted. *He still held out hope that I'd be his one day.*

Daniel waited for the door to shut before stating, "I missed you. I'm sorry I wasn't there for you."

"I missed you too," I replied, though the truth was that David had kept me so busy the only time I got a chance to miss him was in the evenings when I went to bed alone.

"I've got something for you," he advised, standing up and reaching into his pocket. He produced a ring. "Give me your hand," he requested. I did.

"Love covers over a multitude of sins," he said, quoting the Bible. "1 Peter 4:8. Temwani, you've loved me so much. You've forgiven so much. You've stood by me through all those spurious claims which led me to lose my licensure as a lawyer, you've carried me when I should have been carrying you," he concluded. "This ring, please accept it as a symbol of my eternal love for you. Always remember how much I love you and will continue to love you, come what may." He placed the eternity ring on my finger. "In my stupidity, in my selfishness and in my self-centeredness I almost lost you.

353

I'm not losing you again. You're it for me, baby. I don't ever want to be without you," he said.

My eyes welled with tears as I recalled the doubt that had racked my mind in the time I'd spent away from him. I knew now I didn't have to doubt him, he'd promised to love me forever, and so far, as far as our love went, his word was good.

"I'm sorry you had to put up with me the way I've been. I'm here now, I'm sober, and I'm willing and able to be all the things you need me to be," he promised.

I cupped his chin in my hand, the stubble on his face giving him a rough, rugged yet handsome look. The Queensland sun had bronzed his skin and hair giving him a summery beach look, not dissimilar to David's look, save for the shoulder length locks David sported. Staring into me intensely, he leaned in for a kiss.

"I missed this. I missed you," he stated. "What is it, six weeks before we can... you know, have relations again?"

I tried to hide my surprise, but truth was, I wasn't surprised. "Yes, give or take six weeks," I told him.

"Well, that's a relief," he replied. "I'm finding it hard as it is, your body all blossomed up and all." He noted my discomfort and stated, "I'm sure we can work on building our relationship in other ways."

"We're going to have to," I replied, recalling how uncooperative and impatient he had been at that, when I was on bedrest.

"I'm a new man," he said, noticing my unease. "But I'm not blind. Your body's blossomed into something else – some kind of super perfection. Hope you won't fault me for admiring the goods from a distance."

"I won't," I told him, laughing under my breath.

"Good," he replied. Looking around at the house, he noted, "So, this is where you were when I was back in Texas, all on my lonesome." Looking at the bassinette and plush baby toys and swing, he added, "I see he spared no expense for our babies."

I sighed. *He wouldn't have had to if you were here.* "David loves our babies as though they were his own," I advised.

"I can see that," Daniel said, gently touching my cheek. "I can also see how much he loves you. I don't blame him, I just wish...I don't know," he started, getting up to pace the room. "If he wasn't so much in love with you, he wouldn't have asked me to rescue you and we wouldn't have met. I guess I just wish I could love you without the threat of you being stolen from me. By him. 'Cause let's face it. He is the better man."

"That won't happen," I promised him. "I'm yours. For a lifetime."

"Is that all?" he joked.

"Daniel. You know what I mean."

"I do. You've got me for a lifetime and beyond," he joked. "If I die today, I'll come back and haunt you."

"That's not very romantic at all."

"Hauntings are not supposed to be romantic," he acknowledged. "How old is this house?" he asked.

"Stop it Daniel," I cautioned as he smiled away, cheekily. "Life is for the living."

"So let's live," he ordered. "Let's do what we've always wanted to do. Together. No time like the present. When you recover, let's make it happen. Mexico, Brazil, Zambia, let's make it happen."

I grinned, warmed by his new lease on life. I wondered how

long it would last.

"Let's get you to bed," he suggested. "I'll set your bath with some Epsom salt, apparently it'll help you heal better. Quicker."

"Of course," I replied. "The quicker I recover the better it will be for you?"

"Yes, but not just for me. It'll be good for us. For the babies."

"Right," I replied, glad he was here with me nevertheless.

I woke to hear one of the babies cry out in the night, then soft hushing. I turned in bed and noted Daniel was fast asleep. *David.* I lay in bed for a moment longer before getting up slowly, the stitches making it difficult for me to move quickly and without pain. David met me at the bedroom door, Josiah in his arms.

"Get back into bed, I'll bring him to you," he whispered.

I did as he said, and sat upright in bed, feeding cushion on my lap.

"Lie on your side," he suggested, casting a furtive glance at Daniel who was fast asleep. Once I did, he helped me position the pillow behind my back and placed Josiah in my arms. I positioned Josiah correctly for a breastfeed and silently thanked David.

"I've moved the bassinet into your bedroom," he whispered. This would make it easier for me to get to the babies. He sat in the corner of the room, by the lampshade, partly asleep, waiting for Josiah to finish eating.

Daniel stirred in his sleep and eventually woke up to Josiah nursing in bed. Rubbing the sleep out of his eyes, he stated, "I don't think this is a good idea, they should be getting used to sleeping in their own bed."

David who was kneeling by the end of the bed now stated, "Don't be a dick. This is what the babies need right now, this is what your wife needs right now."

"That's our call to make," Daniel said. I happened to agree with David but was too tired to argue.

"I'll just be in the lounge. Sing out for me if you need me," David said, getting up.

That moment was a sign of things to come, and evidence that Daniel and I were perhaps not as attuned to each other as we initially thought we were. Where parenting was concerned, we were polar opposites, and this would become apparent over time. What would also become apparent was the fact that David and I would have been the perfect pairing.

It was a few weeks before we flew back to Texas. David's initial insistence on remaining in Australia didn't last long - he insisted on returning to Texas for a few weeks to help out. Daniel initially refused, but my insistence won him over. There was also the steadily unfolding drama with Shania that needed to be dealt with. Apparently Jonah had discovered that she was pregnant, and did not believe her claim that the baby was David's. Word was he was making plans to be with her longterm, but in her stubbornness, she was refusing to be with him for as long as he continued to remain a part of the Brotherhood.

17

CALLING IT IN

Daniel's behaviour on our return to Austin, Texas was in many ways somewhat erratic. He supported me and the babies the best way he could, but what worried me the most was his state of mind. The investigative work on the Brotherhood and his birth father had him driven to the point of obsession.

One night, he left in the early hours of the morning without an indication of where he was going and when he was coming back. When a few hours passed and he hadn't returned, I worried.

I called him on his mobile phone several times. *Pick up Daniel, pick up*, I thought to myself. His phone rang out. Twice. Three times. The fourth time, I left a message. I got up and turned the kettle on for a cup of tea. The kettle whistled what seemed like a little louder than usual. *Something was wrong.*

I called Daniel again. To my surprise, he answered. "Hello?"

"Daniel, baby, it's me. Where are you?"

He muttered something I could not understand.

"Daniel, wherever you are, I'm coming to get you. Daniel,

say something..."

He sobbed over the line.

"Daniel, please tell me where you are, I'll come and get you."

A slight pause then he said, "Craig..."

"Daniel, tell me where you are." I was met with silence on the other end of the line. "Daniel..." I started again. The line went dead. I called him again and the phone rang out. I speed dialed Craig.

"Not to worry," Craig said. "Anything stand out when you talked?" he asked.

"He sounded off," I said, nearly in tears.

"Okay, not to worry. I'll call you back," he insisted.

Moments later he rang back. "I found Daniel," he said, with bated breath. "I need you to come now. He's in a bad way." Before I'd had a chance to ask more of him, he'd hung up.

Johnny was staying with us again, so I left him with the babies. A quick call to Sadie, our newly appointed babysitter, would ensure she'd be there with him in no time, so he wasn't alone. I also contacted David who was all too happy to come over.

When I got to the office, Daniel was seated on the couch, his hair, face and clothes visibly wet. He sat motionless, staring into the distance, eyes glazed as though he were under the influence of some drug.

"Daniel," I called out. He turned slightly to face me, managing a half smile before looking away.

"I just need to get some sleep," he said. Visibly gaunt, he had lost a lot of weight over the past few weeks. He shivered, cold. A towel lay strewn across the couch, he had on a blue suit shirt and grey trousers which were soaked from the rain. He'd taken off his shoes.

"Daniel, let's go home."

"Alright," he stated. "I'll save you the embarrassment of being here any longer than you need to," he added.

"Daniel..."

Craig appeared.

Immediately taking me to the side office, Craig asked, "You okay?"

"I'll be fine."

"Is he okay?" Craig asked rhetorically. "Doesn't look it." Stating what I feared, he said, "I think he's suicidal."

Shaken, I said, "He has so much to live for, at least this was what I thought."

"Take tomorrow off," Craig insisted, writing down a name and number on paper. "Give Scottie a call," he insisted. "Ask him to come by." Noting my concern, he added, "He's one of the best. He's discrete." I looked at what he'd written down. Scottie was a psychiatrist.

"Thanks," I managed, filled with sadness. That Daniel would even consider leaving me and the babies saddened me.

"I am here, you know," Daniel said in the distance.

Ignoring him, Craig insisted, "Leave your car here. It's late. I'll take you home." After a slight pause, he said, "Or you can stay here, overnight. I'll be here with you."

After the way he'd treated both Johnny and Daniel, I didn't trust Craig, so I called David instead. He was there in a heartbeat and took Daniel and I home. He offered to stay the night, an offer I graciously accepted.

Daniel said very little other than complain about his head hurting, which David put down to a migraine. When we got

360

home, Daniel jumped straight into the shower and then into bed.

I sat up with David and Johnny in the early hours of the morning, while Sadie looked in after the babies. David advised against calling Scottie, saying we needed to have a very good reason to call a psychiatrist. "I don't see why Craig is jumping the gun and asking you to call a psychiatrist. I don't know why he's saying Daniel's suicidal. Daniel loves life."

"That he does," Johnny confirmed. "Craig's speakin' out of his arse as per usual. Pay him no mind."

"We can't just ignore what he has to say," I cautioned.

"Of course not," David said. "Calling Scottie right now isn't the right thing to do though."

"I hear you, David, but if he's under distress somehow, we need to act appropriately," I said.

"Of course we do," David agreed. "Something here just doesn't sit right with me."

"Johnny, Daniel hasn't been taking any drugs in our absence?" I asked.

Johnny almost scowled at me. "I'm not *that* bad you guys."

"I didn't mean to suggest you were," I apologised.

"That's alright," he said. "I know I'm a bad influence. But no, he's been good. He hasn't touched a drop of alcohol since you left," he said. "Nor has he touched any drugs. he doesn't do drugs, you know this."

I sighed in response. "Well, this investigating he's doing is as good as a drug. He's obsessed. He's barely sleeping, he's hardly eating..."

"I'll evaluate him," David suggested. "Discretely. I'll also get a colleague to do the same. Discretely. We agree not to

361

call Scottie at all at this stage," he insisted.

"Alright," I agreed.

"Aye," Johnny agreed.

When I went in to check on Daniel, he had gone out again. He'd gone out through the patio adjoining the study.

At 1 am in the morning my phone rang incessantly. I didn't recognize the number. I didn't pick up the phone on time and it stopped ringing. Daniel still wasn't by my side when I woke.

In the distance, I heard David's phone ring. He picked up, and spoke in a hushed tone. "Right, right. Will be there as soon as I can."

My phone rang again. It was Craig this time. "My apologies for how early this is, but Daniel's been picked up and he's been committed to a facility," he said.

It took me a moment to gather my thoughts. "What?" Had I heard him right?

"Texas State Hospital," Craig stated firmly. "He's been involuntarily committed."

I tried to get more out of him, but he refused to say any more over the phone. I quickly got dressed and ready to go.

"This all doesn't make sense to me," David said frankly when we were in the car. "Daniel's not on the edge, he's not...I don't believe he is..." he mentioned before insisting on driving in silence.

At the hospital Daniel seemed in good spirits when we saw him.

"The food's decent," he claimed. "Milk and juice will be my staples though. Not sure I can hack this food all day every day," he said, referring to his mashed potatoes and pureed meat.

"What happened?" David asked.

"I don't know how I ended up here," Daniel replied. "I went back to the office last night, tried to get a bit of research completed, had an excruciating headache, fell asleep. Got up, looking for water, I don't remember much else. Somehow I wound up here."

"Craig called it in?" David asked.

"He must have," Daniel replied.

"Apparently you were behaving strangely earlier on," David said.

"According to who, Craig? He was in the middle of reviewing merger contracts when I confronted him. I..." he broke off, wincing in pain. "Is it me or is the light flickering."

"You confronted him? About what?" I asked.

Daniel stared at me oddly, not able to recall.

"The light isn't flickering," David interjected. "Nurse, can we get an evaluation done by the doc?"

She looked at the chart. "One's not due for another two hours."

"Please get one done sooner than that. Query migraine with aura," David said as a matter of factly.

Puzzled, she looked at him blankly.

"Doctor Davenport," he replied. "Max Facial,"

"Oh, I see," she said, giving him a brief once over.

I interrupted her gaze. "Lawyer and the patient's wife."

"I'm on your side," she said softly, writing something down on Daniel's chart.

"Good to hear it," David replied.

"I'll get the doctor to see him now," she said with finality.

"Paging Doctor McIntyre," she announced over the inter-com.

A familiar face turned up. Scott. The last time we'd seen each other was at the barbecue Craig had thrown for my birthday. The one where I'd met the members of the Brotherhood.

"Scottie!" David exclaimed, feigning surprise.

"I'll just be a moment," he announced, gesturing for us to make an exit. "Grab yourself something to eat or drink in the canteen. I'll be there in a moment."

I quickly said goodbye to Daniel. Struggling to hold back tears, he reluctantly said goodbye as well.

Scottie ate as though he hadn't eaten in hours. David ate nothing, while I sipped on a strawberry milk.

David shifted uncomfortably in his seat before stating, "Something's not right here. Daniel shouldn't be here. Who called it in?"

Scottie swallowed the food in his mouth before stating, "Craig."

"Of course," I said, shaking my head.

"Look, I know how you feel. I've looked at his notes, and I can say that he *was* brought in as a precaution. There were a few issues of concern in the lead up to his admission," Scottie stated, before taking a huge bite out of his blueberry muffin.

"What issues of concern?" David questioned. "He was fine when I last saw him, both last night and two days ago."

"Aren't we all fine up until we're pushed over the edge?" Scottie asked. "He's been under a phenomenal amount of stress, it's no surprise that it's all come to a head now."

David frowned deeply. "This doesn't feel right, mate. This

here stinks to the high heavens. I don't believe for one moment that Daniel should be here."

"Believe what you will matey, he's here. He wouldn't be here if there wasn't cause for concern," Scottie insisted, still savouring his muffin.

I sighed in response, carefully contemplating what Scottie had said. Daniel had been under a lot of stress lately. Finding out he had a brother, finding out Jolène wasn't his birth mother, missing the birth of his children, facing the loss of our relationship.

"He's right," I agreed. "Scottie's right. Daniel's here, and he's here for a reason."

"I'm glad we're on the same page," Scottie said.

"Who says you're on the same page? 'Cause *we* are not on the same page," David announced. "The fact that Craig called this in..."

"Okay, I can see we're not getting anywhere," Scottie interrupted. "I'll let you make *your* own observations once *I*, the resident psychiatrist, have drawn *my* own conclusions."

David refrained from saying anything further, while Scottie stuffed the remainder of the blueberry muffin in his mouth, wiped his hands on a serviette and tossed it in David's direction.

"Come on man!" David exclaimed. "I see you've not changed, always tryin' to get a rise out of me."

Scottie half smiled, "You ain't seen nothin' yet," he announced.

"Hm.." David stated.

"Let's make this happen," Scottie said, getting up.

I remained seated at the table moments after they'd both gotten up. David offered me his hand. I felt like crying but

I couldn't, I felt like my world was caving in, but taking his hand changed things. For a moment.

"We'll make sure he's alright," David said with firm resolve.

It hurt my heart to see Daniel where he was. So helpless, so defenceless.

"I'm doing okay," he insisted. "Enjoying the quietude."

"We can take you home then," David said.

"Home?" he questioned. "I'm not interested in you babysitting me, I'm afraid," he stated, casting a furtive glance at David and I.

"Daniel..." I started.

"Go on now and get some rest," he advised. "I'll still be here tomorrow. Kiss the babies for me."

Reluctantly, we left.

David and I sat in the car for a moment before he started the engine. "I won't go in and see him next time. He obviously doesn't want me here."

I sat there, contemplative. The mental health facility looked eerily beautiful from the outside.

"Teme," David called out. "You alright?"

"I can't believe he's in here," I said. Tears came without warning.

"Come now," he urged. "Don't cry. You're not alone. I'm here with you."

I dug into my handbag for some tissue. He wiped tears off my cheek as I did. "This is but a moment in a lifetime of moments," David insisted. "He's in safe hands, Scottie's an excellent doctor. However, I don't agree with the commit first and watch and see approach they're taking solely on the advice Craig's given them, but if he has to be anywhere, he's in good hands here."

I found the tissue. "Scottie, how do you know him?" I asked.

"Met him in my third year of med school. I did a six month exchange in Louisiana. He was the psychiatry registrar at the time.

"Interesting," I noted.

"Look, I know what I just said about him being in good hands, but I just feel ill at ease leaving him here," David confessed. "He's my twin, my brother. I can't shake the feeling that something is wrong."

"Okay," I replied.

"I'd like for us to go back in and talk to Scottie," he suggested.

We did just that. Scottie seemed surprised to see us again. David went straight into his concerns.

"I hear you. I understand where you're coming from," Scottie said. "I just feel you're not being objective."

"Can I have a moment?" David asked, turning away from Scottie, and to me.

"Sure," Scottie said. "I'll give you a few minutes on your own, and I'll be back." With that, he stepped out of the room.

"Does Daniel have what's called an Advanced Medical Directive in place? Has he appointed you Power of Attorney?" David asked.

"I don't know," I replied.

"Well, if he has, we can override some of the decisions they're making here, get them to change strategy."

"I see," I replied, suddenly feeling overwhelmed. "Change

367

strategy, how?"

"Whatever it is they're diagnosing him with, I need them to run a battery of other tests. It could be possible the symptoms he's experiencing are a sign of something else," David suggested.

"Like what?" I asked.

Before he got a chance to answer, Scottie was back.

"All good?" he asked.

"No, we just have a few questions," David stated. "You've done an assessment. What's the diagnosis?" he asked.

"Bi-polar disorder," he said quickly.

"Is that what Craig's told you?" David enquired.

"I'm the doctor," Scottie stated. "I did my own observations, and this is what I've come up with."

"What you've come up with, with a bit of persuasion and input from Craig, no doubt," David said.

"Look, David. You're not being objective. I suggest you let me do my job, and you take a step back."

"Did Craig mention anything about capacity?" I asked point blankly. From the look on Scott's face, he had.

"Well, he did express concern about that," he stated briefly. "He had his reasons."

"Okay," David said. "You need to do some talking here," he insisted. "If you don't, well, I'm no longer a part of the Brotherhood, and this can go as far as you want it to go. Teme's no longer working for the District Attorney's office, but she's best mates with the fellas who are."

Scott frowned slightly before stating, "What do you want?"

"For you to put aside everything that Craig has told you, and for you to run a series of other tests."

"I can't just do that," he replied.

"Well, if you don't, then I can't help what might happen next," David threatened.

"Okay," Scottie replied, sneaking me a side glance.

"I'd like you to do an MRI," David suggested.

"An MRI?" Scottie questioned.

"Yes, an MRI," David repeated.

"Do you suspect a tumour?" Scottie asked.

"Just do an MRI, will you?" David insisted.

I must have had a look of alarm on my face which David picked up on.

"Don't mean to be alarmist," David stated. "What Craig suggested aside, which I highly doubt is the correct diagnosis, I'm just a little concerned that we may be missing something."

"Such as?" Scottie asked.

"I don't like speculating, but I feel pretty strongly that it could be some sort of a tumour. This is consistent with the lack of responsiveness to treatment for his migraines and the loss of certain faculties. It might also explain the persistent pain he's experiencing and the constant left hemiplegic migraines. Time is of the essence here. Please get this done as soon as," David insisted.

It took a while for David's words to sink in. *Tumour. Time.* I truly hoped that was not the case.

"You can't hold him here any longer than you have," David reminded him.

"I know this," Scottie replied. "I'll have to discharge him, have the tests done through neurology."

David nodded in response, noticeably calmer. "So, we're free to take him home in a bit?"

"Of course," Scottie stated, unhappy with David's insistence. "I'll get the referrals organised."

"Right," David replied, deep in thought.

"I'll discharge him on a low dose of Topamax. Hope this will decrease and altogether halt those migraines."

"Good stuff," David replied. "Appreciated. Hope there're no hard feelings."

"Well, no," Scottie said. "He needs to have that MRI done."

"Pleasure to meet you again Temwani," Scottie said, extending his hand out to me for a shake.

"None of that golden handshake business mate," David joked, encouraging me to drop Scottie's hand.

"Ah, funny," Scottie replied. "Good one."

Daniel's effects had been put aside for him. The clothes he'd worn on admission had been laundered and pressed. The only thing missing was a pair of shoes. He was not wearing any the day he was involuntarily committed.

"How are you feeling?" David asked.

"Good," Daniel replied quickly.

"He's on your side you know," I reminded him, aware of the ever present animosity.

"I know," Daniel said reluctantly. "It's been a pretty isolating experience," he admitted tearfully, pausing as we got to the gate. The guard nodded goodbye before authorizing the gates to open.

I noticed Daniel's hands were shaking.

"You okay mate?" David asked, concerned.

Daniel hesitated for a moment before responding. He looked faint. "I just need to take it slow. Wish I wasn't so emotional," he said, leaning his back against the corridor wall.

"Keep moving," the guard commanded.

"Not much longer," David encouraged, as he helped Daniel regain his balance.

I stood at the entrance of the facility with Daniel, as David went to bring the car around.

"I missed you," I managed, embracing him.

"Missed you too," Daniel said, leaning in for a kiss. "I'm so sorry for all of this."

"Please don't apologize Daniel. The important thing is you're on the mend."

"I'm not sure about that. I don't feel too crash hot at the moment," he stated. He was sweating profusely now.

"You don't have to worry about us, we're alright," I promised.

He smiled ever so slightly. David was back. "I need to stop being so insecure and all," he acknowledged. "You are married to me, after all, and you have given me two beautiful babies. Everything else, my past, Craig, all bygones."

David held the door open for me. As I got in, I noticed Daniel looked a little worse for wear. Instead of getting into the car, he sat on the curb, head between his legs.

I got back out. "When did you last eat?" I asked, offering him a granola bar. He waved it away. David stopped the engine, sat in the car for a moment.

"The sooner we can get you out of here and out of the heat, the better off you'll be," he suggested.

Daniel quickly got up and made a dash for the hedge, where he was sick. I made my way over to him, stood there with him. I offered him a tissue which he gladly took. He was shaking, and looked as though he might faint.

I turned to look over at David, who was on the phone. I

371

gestured for him to come over. He nodded in response, but motioned at the phone.

"Please sit down Daniel," I ordered, noticing he was having difficulty staying on his feet.

He turned to respond, and muttered something unintelligible before collapsing in front of me and hitting the pavement, hard. I fell to my knees, terrified. David rushed over.

"Keep him on his side," he ordered, checking Daniel's pulse. "Daniel," he called out. "Daniel, can you hear me?"

Daniel stirred slightly. He grimaced in response. His head was bleeding from the hit he'd taken to the pavement when he fell. "Daniel, can you hear me?" David asked again, as Daniel drifted in and out of consciousness.

The paramedics were there in moments. Daniel was placed in a head brace, and onto a stretcher.

The shock of seeing Daniel so helpless had me in tears. I wanted to ride in the ambulance with him, but was not allowed to. David firmly placed a hand around my waist and quickly led me to the car to save further argument. We followed the ambulance bumper to bumper until we got to the Presbyterian Hospital. I thought to call Jolène at that moment, and did.

David and I waited in the lobby before being told where Daniel was. Triage was complete, he was conscious and being admitted for observation. Jolène arrived not long after.

I detected the animosity between Jolène and David from the moment she arrived. I suspected it was because she hadn't gotten over missing the birth of her grandkids. On arrival, she gave a casual nod to David, and embraced me.

David took her cue and maintained a distance. "I'll go get us all some coffee and tea," he muttered under his breath before heading off.

"Please tell me that the two of you will stop this nonsense of constantly fighting. You need to get it together for your own sakes and for the sake of your babies. What happened anyway!" she exclaimed.

I discussed Daniel's admission to the mental facility, and explained how he suddenly collapsed when we were leaving. She cupped her mouth in alarm. "Oh, my poor baby. Why didn't anyone call me when he was first admitted!"

"He specifically did not want you to know," I offered.

In tears, she asked, "Is there anything else I'm not being told?"

"His treating doctor is doing a series of tests. He's no longer convinced Daniel's bi-polar."

"If he's not bi-polar, what is he?" Jolène asked, worried.

"It might be a tumour of some sort," I replied.

She gasped loudly, outwardly expressing the shock I felt inside. "Well, is it? How soon will we know?"

"He hasn't had the tests done yet. I assume he will be having them done now."

David returned with two coffees and a tea.

Jolène immediately launched a scathing tirade directed at David. "You did this to him. He was perfectly happy until you came along. You did this to him!"

I tried to calm her down, but she was not having a bar of it. "You put him through so much stress, and you won't lay off making moves on his wife. What kind of a brother are you David! Certainly one who doesn't care too much. Go back to where you came from, go back to Australia!"

An orderly approached, cautioning Jolène. "Madam, you will have to leave if you don't stop this right now," he warned.

"Why don't you ask *him* to leave! *He's* the one that's wreaking havoc on my son's and daughter in law's life!"

David frowned in response, handing me the coffee and tea on a tray. "I'll be at the front, moving the car. Daniel's in good hands."

Turning to Jolène he stated, "Sorry you feel that way Jolène," before walking off.

I handed her the coffee. "That wasn't called for, Jolène."

"Oh, but it was. Someone needs to put the fear of God in that man, he needs to step off and get a life of his own. One that doesn't involve you being the centre of it."

I wanted to argue back, but was too exhausted to. Daniel was my main concern now. David came in a clear second. Maybe Jolène was right. All the stress of David had culminated in this. Though, as I recalled the past, we had problems before David showed up. While David's presence had not helped, Daniel had been forced to step up his game because of David.

Moments later, David sent me a text message. *Okay?*

I wondered where he was. *3 o'clock, by the bay windows,* he texted back.

I turned to look, and Jolène caught and followed my gaze. She gave me a dirty look in response.

"You know, I only have eyes for Daniel," I stated. "So you can stop with all the accusations and the judgement."

"Could have fooled me," she fumed, giving me the once over. "Now's as good a time as any to convince me otherwise."

I laughed in response. "You're not being serious, are you? Daniel is laid up in a hospital bed, fighting for his life and all you can say to me now is that you hope I'm not having feelings for his brother?" She shrugged in response. "Give it a rest will you? He *is* family." I made my way over to David, not waiting for her response.

"What are you up to, and why didn't you come back earlier?" I asked.

"Trying to keep a safe distance between myself and Mama Bear. Not trying to enrage her any further, and get clawed or anything," he replied.

I giggled at the "get clawed" bit.

"Besides, you need time with him. Without me hanging in the background like a bad smell," he said.

I sighed. "I hope you're not taking everything that's being said about you to heart."

"No," he stated unconvincingly. "Even if I was, I'm a big boy. Comes with the territory. She'll be right."

"As long as you're okay," I offered.

"Yep," he replied, abruptly changing topic. "I might head off and check on the babies?"

"You would do that? Sadie said they'd be fine, she said she'll top up the expressed milk with formula, if worse came to worse."

"Daniel's not going to like the sound of that," David guessed.

"Nope. No choice though," I replied.

"Although...how about you express some milk now and I can shoot it back to them? It'd be easy enough to get some bottles and a pump organized for you. I could go by maternity and ask the question," he suggested.

I pondered for a moment.

"Or better yet, I can bring the babies back here for a feed, you can nurse them, then express what you can and I'll make sure they get back home in time for their bedtime routine?"

It warmed me to see that he was thinking like a father. He'd had enough practice, those first few weeks in Australia.

"Okay, sounds like a plan," I agreed.

"Great," he said, and he was off.

18

PATHS COLLIDING

David was helping me label the bottles of expressed breastmilk in the kitchen when Jolène burst in.

"White Trash," she stated.

"Excuse me?" David asked.

"Every moment I turn around, here you are again," she remarked.

David slammed the pen down on the table. "Will you just stop with your holier than thou attitude already? I've just about had enough of your judgement."

"I'll stop when you leave my son's family alone," she challenged.

"Your son's family? This is my family too. In fact, my bond to them is closer than yours will ever be. How about we have it out then?" David replied. "Since you insist on badgering me every chance you get." He stood up to face her. "Your son is my brother. My blood. Blood is thicker than water. You're water."

"You've always been more trouble than you were worth," she stated, with disdain. "We don't need you here."

"Why is it that you're so desperate to have me gone? Can

it be that I'm a living breathing reminder of the guilt you felt all those years ago when you refused to adopt me too? How about we tell him how you were part of the process that forcibly removed us from our birth mother, and that in the end, you took him but chose to have me terminated?"

Jolène's face turned pale.

"Yeah, that's right," he concluded. "You insist on having me gone because I'm supposedly tearing this family apart. Yet you won't admit why you really want me gone. You won't admit how much hatred you feel towards me. Well guess what. I've made something of myself. This baby that was left in the dumpster has made something of himself," his face flushed, he challenged, "How about you tell your "son" just how much you cared about him all these years when you let on that he was an only child. How about we start telling the truth around here."

"You will do no such thing. He is to never find out."

David laughed sarcastically. "He's not stupid. He'll figure it out for himself anyway, if I don't tell him first."

"You wouldn't dare," Jolène challenged.

"You don't know me," David stated. "Never have, and never will."

Jolène cast a look my direction. I was equally as shocked at David's admission, if not, more so, as Jolène had known all along that David had survived the attempted termination. *All these years.*

She turned to me. "You know what, Temwani? I'd be glad if this relationship you have with my son falls apart. You've been nothing but trouble. If only he had his heart set on a southern belle, not someone like you. You people are always so much drama..."

"You people? What the?" David exclaimed, as shocked as I was. "You're on thin ice now," he warned.

I was enraged at what she had said but found no words in that moment. Two words rung in my mind. *Dumpster baby.*

"Blood is thicker than water," David stated again, motioning at the door. "Your so-called grandkids are my blood too. Like it or not, that's facts."

Realising the error of her ways, apologetically, Jolène stated, "I don't know what came over me..."

Sternly, David replied, "You've said your piece. Now, get out."

"David, I'm..." she started.

"Out," he ordered, cutting her off.

"David, for what it's worth, I'm sorry..."

"Jolène, out please." He didn't care to listen to her apology.

She gave him the finger on her way out. He kissed his teeth in response.

Amidst the indignation, I could see the anguish in his eyes. I wondered how long he would have kept the whole of his story a secret from us all. From me.

"I didn't mean to keep secrets," he said apologetically. "Thought I'd go to the grave with that one, but I had my back against the wall with nowhere to go. Been wearing my heart on my sleeve lately, and it's not a good look." Running a hand through his sun kissed auburn brown hair, he turned to me in jest, "Cat's out of the bag now, and I've opened up a huge can of worms."

"You sure have," I said softly. "I can't imagine what kind of a life you've had David. Are you okay?" I asked, arms outstretched to hug him.

"No, but I'll be alright," he replied. "I'm a big boy,

remember?" he reminded me as we embraced. I could feel the pain he felt inside. "Daniel's the one we should be worried about right now."

I resolved not to ask any more questions on the matter, at least not while we were waiting on the medical team to give us an indication on Daniel's condition. Emotions were running high in more ways than one, and I didn't want to add further anguish to the situation.

"I'll take these bottles back home as planned, and bring the babies back with me for a real feed," he planned. "You need to be here when he comes to and regains consciousness."

"You sure you'll be alright?" I questioned, finding it hard to hide my concern.

"I'll manage. It's been just me all these years and I'm fine. About Daniel, I don't know how to feel. I'm feeling a little cut up inside at the thought that this could be something far worse than it is. We've wasted a lot of time bickering and being mad at each other."

"You and me both," I replied. The last bottle was done. I placed them all in the carrier bag, ready for David to take with him.

"You're not alone, David. I'm here with you and here for you – I'll never let you walk alone from now on," I assured him, standing up to embrace him again.

"I so needed that," he mentioned, when I hugged him. "Thank you."

"Thank you for being here for me, the kids, and Daniel once again," I replied, noticing that Jolène hadn't gone far; she stood just outside the kitchen door.

"Don't mention it," he said, before heading off. "Anything changes, call me please." He kissed me lightly on the cheek, to Jolène's aire, and was gone.

It was hard seeing Daniel laid up in a hospital bed, wires and tubes all round and on him. He was asleep when they allowed me to see him.

I squeezed his hand and leaned in to kiss his cheek. He stirred in his sleep.

The nurse came in. "He's stable now," she stated. "You're Temwani, his wife?"

I nodded to the affirmative.

"The doctor will be in to talk to you in a moment. He's been drifting in and out of consciousness, and we need to run a series of tests – we're hoping to get your consent."

"Sure," I replied.

She handed me the forms with a pen.

"He's a lawyer?" she asked.

"We both are," I replied.

"I can't imagine what you're going through. My brother's a lawyer too, and I know his brain is everything."

I smiled in response, at a bit of a loss as to what she meant.

She sat with me at Daniel's bedside. "It's my role to advocate on his behalf and on your behalf as his family. Don't let anyone push you into doing anything you don't want to do," she stated.

"His brother's a doctor," I mentioned. "They aren't all bad," I added.

"I didn't mean that, of course they're not," she corrected. "It's just in circumstances like this, there is the right thing to do according to the medical team, and the right thing to do according to the patient."

Clarifying further she stated, "Your husband here has

a DNR or Do Not Resuscitate order on file. He has also requested no transfusions and no medical assistance that would serve to prolong his life."

It took me a moment to process what she'd just said. "I wasn't aware of that," I managed.

"Not too many people are," she stated. "The other thing is he's appointed you Power of Attorney in the event that he's not capable of making a decision on his own behalf."

I looked at Daniel lying there. His head had been shaved to allow for placement of electrodes. His beautiful chestnut brown hair was almost all gone. Thoughts back to the order, I realised I loved him deeply, but wanted to wring his neck. *How could he have a DNR order in place when he had a family and children who wanted him alive?*

"Is there a date on this DNR order?" I asked.

"Should be in the notes," the nurse said, flipping through a few pages before stopping on one. "Seems like it was done just last month," she stated.

I was livid. Had he done it himself, or had he been coerced to do it by someone else?

A brief knock on the door sounded before it was opened. "Doctor Collins, here. Alright for me to have a chat with you?" His English accent was quite apparent. "Hey Melissa," he added, greeting the nurse.

Turning to me he said, "Look I'll put it plainly. He's doing better, just a mild concussion after the fall, but we need to run some scans. A CAT scan and MRI to be precise." Talking a mile a minute, he added, "He has a Do Not Resuscitate order in place. He has a few things in place which would not allow us to proceed further. But you're Power of Attorney, what you say can override this and let us proceed."

I nodded in agreement, understanding full well what he was suggesting.

"I'm in the business of saving lives," he stated. "Not wanting to pressure you or anything, but time is of the essence here. The sooner we can get those scans done, the better."

"I hear you," I stated. I was certain that the tests should be ordered to find out more about his condition, but reluctant to go against Daniel's wishes unless it was in relation to saving his life.

"Would you like a moment to consider?" Melissa chimed in.

"There is not much to consider Melissa. It's either a yay or a nay," Doctor Collins said sharply.

"Of course there is much to consider," she stated. "Five minutes, and you'll have your answer."

Annoyance flashed across Doctor Collins face. "Okay," he conceded. "I'll check in with you then."

Before leaving, he did a brief check on Daniel, and browsed the notes. "Time is of the essence," he reminded me.

I stepped out of the room to call the one person I knew would help me make sense of the situation. *David.*

He picked up after several rings. I could hear the babies in the background. "Teme," he said in his deep velvety voice. "You alright?"

"Not really, there's a bit of an issue here at the hospital," I told him.

"Pray tell."

"Daniel has a "Do Not Resuscitate" order in place," I stated, crying into the phone.

"Okay," David said, sighing into the phone. "He *should* pull through this. Talk to him about it when he comes to. Maybe not straight away of course...but talk to him, sometime soon. I'll talk to him," he vowed.

"Okay," I managed.

"Just hang tight, I'll be there shortly," he promised.

I stared at the phone long after the dial tone was gone. *A Do Not Resuscitate order. What was he thinking?*

I fed the babies as we sat waiting for Daniel to come to. I authorised Doctor Collins to enable IV fluids and medications that would help relieve pain when Daniel came to.

"He's stable now," the doctor said. "I do need to keep him in overnight, for further observation. The MRI and CAT scan can be done while he's here."

I thanked him for his quick action, and sat with David in the feeding room, comforting the babies. They had grown so much in just a few weeks. In their innocence they were unaware of the drama unfolding in our lives.

"David, what do you plan to do about the fact that... well, you know that...you've known for some time that Jolène chose to abandon you and order you be terminated. Any plans to report that and press charges?"

"No," he stated abruptly. "I know what happened, she knows what happened, the people that matter in my life right now know what happened, and that's all that matters," he explained. "Reporting stuff will only lead to me needing to delve further into the details of my personal life, and I'd much rather keep that a secret."

"So it was a meaningless threat?" I asked, reminding him of what he'd said earlier.

"No, I do plan to tell Daniel," he replied. "Eventually.

Or you could tell him on my behalf," he suggested. "I'm not exactly his favorite person at the moment," he added. "Telling him will at least get him to see that I am not out to hurt him. I'm only wanting to connect with the only sibling I have."

"I hear you," I replied. "You were saying that blood is thicker than water, but sometimes friends are closer than brothers," I told him.

"I hear you," he echoed. "I *feel* you, friend."

Daniel came to and initially refused to have the MRI and CAT scans done. He also refused to remain in hospital any longer. Doctor Collins compromised by referring him to the outpatient clinic, where he would have the scans done no later than a week after discharge.

"Why are you resisting so much Daniel?" I asked.

"I feel fine. I don't know what y'all are worried about. Migraines are migraines. That's all this is."

"It may be more than that," David stated, "Better to know than to not know," he said.

"That's your opinion," Daniel replied. "I feel fine, and I can't wait to get back to normality. I've seen enough of the inside of hospitals to last me a lifetime."

Examining his head in the rear view mirror he asked, "And who allowed *this* to happen?"

"It had to happen Daniel. You were bleeding pretty badly and you needed to be stitched up," I explained, noting his dismay that his hair was almost all gone.

He frowned deeply. "I suppose it doesn't look too terrible," he said.

"Would you have preferred a mohawk?" David asked.

385

"No!" Daniel exclaimed.

I laughed at the voracity of his response. "To be honest a crew cut looks pretty good on you," I told him.

"As long as you like it, that's all that matters," Daniel replied.

"So, you go for the scan this week?" David asked.

"Yeah, sometime this week," Daniel replied.

"The sooner the better," David advised.

Daniel nodded in agreement as we pulled into the driveway of our home. The kids were lying on the grass at the front, on a play mat while Sadie and Johnny chatted away.

Immeasurable joy swept across Daniel's face as he dashed over to kiss both babies and tickle their little bellies. David caught my eye and smiled sadly. "Hope he'll be okay," he said. "His bloods weren't looking too good."

"Please continue to stay with us just in case he isn't okay," I insisted.

"No problem," he replied. "I'll just head off and get some more gear," he mentioned. "If you need me to get anything from the shops, let me know."

"Alright," I replied, and he said goodbye, giving me a kiss on the cheek and a wave to the others.

I silently thanked God for David's presence in my life, and for bringing Daniel out of the hospital and back home again. My one hope was that he would agree to the additional tests recommended by Doctor Collins. Sooner rather than later.

"Will you be needing me tonight?" Sadie asked. "Babies seem settled enough."

"They do," I replied. "No, we'll be fine tonight."

"Okay. Then I'll see you Sunday then?" Sadie asked.

"Monday," I corrected.

"A night cap, Sadie?" Johnny proposed, strolling into the room from seemingly nowhere.

"Not tonight," she replied. "The Sabbath."

"Oh okay," Johnny replied, flatly and somewhat disappointed.

"Will you come with me to Church on Saturday?" she asked. She was a Seventh Day Adventist.

"No," Johnny replied firmly. "I don't think God wants to see me in the state I'm in."

"That's where you're wrong," she said, slipping on her coat. "He wants you to come as you are."

Johnny rushed to her side to help with her coat. "I'll come one day," he promised. "I'll clean up real good before I do."

"Come as you are," she repeated. Giving me a kiss on either cheek she said goodbye. "Take care Johnny," she said, squeezing his hand lightly before heading out.

"She's a gem, isn't she?" he noted.

I nodded, agreeing with him. "She's right about God," I confirmed. "He'll meet you where you are."

"I'm not sure I believe that," he said. "I'm not someone worth saving."

It saddened me that he felt that way.

"Enough about me," he said. "Tell me, what are your plans moving forward, now the babies will soon be better able to manage without you? Planning on going back to the firm?"

"Working with Craig's going to be a challenge after the way he's treated you and Daniel, but yes, I'm planning on going back. We need the money. Plus it's Daniel's firm too, Craig can't just take it over completely. He needs to be reminded of that."

"Good luck," Johnny remarked. "Craig doesn't like being reminded of anything."

"I hear you," I told him. "He can't stop you from having a career though. He also made the unilateral decision to let you go, when he should've consulted Daniel or myself. This being the case, he needs to accept that you'll still be working with us."

"I'm not sure I can hack being in the office with him, you know, after the things he said and the things he threatened..."

"You don't have to be in the office with him," I told him. "Work from here, or I'm sure we can set you up in a serviced office. I can swing some work your way, and we can split my workload if you're willing?"

Intrigued, Johnny asked, "And you think he'll go for that?"

"He doesn't have to know."

"Okay," he said after careful thought. "Sounds like a plan. Though he won't be happy when he finds out."

"*If* he finds out," I corrected.

"*When* he finds out," he replied.

19

AFTER FOREVER

It was the night of our anniversary, and we sat at the Bayou Restaurant across from each other. Despite the happy occasion, Daniel didn't seem happy at all. "This is not the time or the place," he stated, motioning over towards Jonah and Shania.

The fire and passion between them was clear. Shania and Jonah were at it and refused to quit. Jonah spoke in a low, monotone voice, while Shania was very expressive and loud. He was trying to calm her down.

"Someone needs to get them to stop," Daniel said, peering over his menu. "They're putting off the other patrons."

"You're the one who loves laying down the law," I reminded him.

"Whatever," he said annoyed. "Any idea what that's about?" he asked motioning over at them.

"It's a long story."

"Does that story start and end with Shania being pregnant with David's baby?"

"Shania's not expecting David's baby," I replied. "Your brother's baby," I corrected.

"Yes, he *is* my brother, you don't need to over emphasize the point."

"Don't I?" I questioned.

"We might be blood, but I can tell you now I've got friends who are closer," he said unconvincingly.

"Like who?" I challenged.

"We're not doing this here and now, are we?" he asked, not amused. "Besides, I thought the story was that she is carrying his baby..."

"That's just it. It's a story," I confirmed. "She's not carrying his baby. Jonah's the only one she's been with."

He raised an eyebrow in response. His disappointment that Shania and David hadn't become an item, was evident. "Well, it's only a matter of time that it happens."

"David's not like that and you know it," I said.

Daniel rolled his eyes at me. "Straight to his defence again, I see."

I ignored Daniel's comment, trying to be at peace with him. It was our anniversary after all.

Jonah and Shania's fighting had reached a new level. "I don't need anything from you, and I don't expect you to be there for me. I will do this on my own!" she declared, loud enough for all to hear.

"No you won't," Jonah replied before suddenly announcing for all to hear, "I'm not an honorable man, for if I was, I would not have put this beautiful lady in this situation. But I will do the honourable thing now," he promised. Dropping to one knee, he asked, "Shania Lee Thompson, will you do me the honour of becoming my lawfully wedded wife? Will you marry me and make me one of the happiest men alive?"

Almost as shocked as Shania was, I gasped in response.

Daniel cast me a worrying look. In the short time that I'd known him, I didn't think that Jonah was marriage material. Then again, what *was* marriage material? He was clearly smitten by Shania from the get go, and would apparently do anything for her now.

"Whoa," Daniel said, his reaction delayed. "I guess they're in love, ey?"

In between tears, Shania uttered an elated "Yes." It seemed as though the whole restaurant burst into applause. Jonah got up and embraced her with such might she nearly fell. He braced her fall then kissed her fully, for all to view.

"Aw," I said.

"Get a room," Daniel mumbled, looking away and onto the menu.

"You've become such a grouch lately," I noted as he slammed the menu shut and eyeballed me. "I also see you're very disappointed it's Jonah rather than David," I mentioned.

"You've become so judgmental," he replied in kind. "How do you expect me to feel, David constantly interfering..."

"How is he interfering?" I asked. "Calling you out on the many lies you've been telling me lately? Calling you out on all the things you've been keeping from me? Trying to get you to acknowledge him as your brother after all those years he spent looking for you?"

"He knew I was here in Texas all this time. He only chose to come forward as the stakes were getting high."

"Whatever," I replied.

"We're not doing this," he said.

"Doing what?" I asked.

"Arguing."

"Who says we're arguing," I said.

He shook his head at me. "This is the problem. You refuse to see things from my perspective."

"You're kidding, right?" I replied. "All I can see is *your* perspective," I told him. "This is all about how insecure *you* feel about David, how you think one day he will snap me away from you, how you think I'm just going to throw what we have away for greener pastures."

"Well, aren't you?" he asked.

"Of course not," I replied, nearly not believing myself. David had become such a big part of my life of late, I didn't see my life without him in it. "I made my vows to you," I added, understanding his concern.

"Vows," Daniel repeated. "I want your love and affection, not your obligation," he said. "Wish they would hurry up with the service here," he said switching topic and impatiently looking around for a waiter or waitress. "I guess we should give our regards to the future Mr. and Mrs."

I felt for him. Obligation was not what I felt for him. Love was all it was, but he wasn't to be convinced. "We definitely should," I agreed.

"Maybe we could offer to take them down to the pad in South Texas one weekend next month, or just give them directions and the keys?"

I sighed in response, glad he was sounding more like the Daniel I fell in love with and less like the selfish, bitter man he had been of late.

"Maybe we could go there ourselves and get away from it all – reconnect?" he suggested.

"You mean, get away from reality? Get away from...the fact that you still need to get those tests done? Get away from... David?"

His eyes narrowed at the mention of David's name again. "I'm big enough to admit that getting away from him is part of it," he confessed. "I feel I haven't had you to myself since..." he broke off. "Well, since a long time anyway."

"You can't blame him for the way you're choosing to relate to me," I said. "You're the one who's being insecure," I reminded him.

He tapped his fingers on the table, impatient. "Where is that waiter," he asked, before adding, "We're not doing this. We're not fighting over him and I and you, again."

"Okay," I said turning from him to look over at Shania. Jonah had her hands in his across the table, and they spoke to each other with much emotion and warmth. I was happy for her, but envious of the future ahead for her with him, so full of promise.

"How did we get to where we are now?" I asked. "We used to be so happy once."

"Things happened. Things changed," Daniel offered. "Life happened. I changed. My wounded ego happened," he said. "I'm sorry I haven't been the man I promised to be," he apologized. "I'll do anything I can to get right with you."

I knew better than to hold him to his word.

He reached for my hand across the table. "I mean it," he urged. "Life is too short to do otherwise," he said with a finality I'd never heard before.

"I agree," I said.

"Moving forward, I want to be at peace with you," he said. Reluctantly, he added, "Even if that means making peace with him."

Why the sudden change of heart? I wondered.

He rapped his fingers on the table again, impatiently

waiting for service. "If we're not served in the next 5 minutes, we're out of here," he threatened.

I rolled my eyes in response. *Typical.* "Give them a chance Daniel. Besides, if we go home now, that sort of defeats the purpose of going out for dinner on our anniversary, right?"

"I suppose," he said, clearly still annoyed.

"You haven't answered my question. Why the sudden change of heart?" I asked, curious.

"I know now that I can't get past him if I want to get to you," he said. "I also can't afford to alienate him. You'll be...the babies'll be..." he started, hesitating. "I need him to be there for us."

Strange. I wasn't sure if I was hearing him right. "Daniel..."

"Please, let's just go," he requested. "I've had enough of waiting, I'm done here."

I could see I wasn't going to win with him. "Okay. Let's stop for a moment, congratulate the soon to be Mr. and Mrs. Jonah Hughes."

Somewhat distracted, he concurred, "Right."

"Try to be happy for them," I urged.

I could tell he wasn't as he got up.

"Daniel," I said in a slightly raised tone, startling him somewhat. "Be happy, or else."

"I'm trying," he replied, stopping me in my tracks. "I'm really trying," he said. "It's hard to be happy for everyone else when I'm dying, Temwani," he said abruptly. "This'll probably be our last anniversary dinner. I wanted things to be perfect tonight, but so far... anyhow, the docs, they've given me 6 months to live," he said.

I felt as though I couldn't breathe. *Every hope, every desire, every dream would no longer be. With him.* I fought for words to say but nothing came.

He sat back down and urged me to as well. "Temwani," he said, his voice deep and reassuring. "I'll be okay. You'll be okay without me. The babies will be okay without me. We all have to go sometime. We all have to leave this life here behind someday."

The waiter finally appeared. "Sorry guys, what can I get you."

"We were just about ready to leave!" Daniel exclaimed, and got engaged in small talk as he placed our order. He ordered a bottle of champagne and a spritzer for Jonah and Shania, seeming upbeat all of a sudden.

"Jonah doesn't drink," I mentioned bluntly.

"Oh?" Daniel asked, surprised. Turning to the waiter, he stated, "Okay, well, if you tell the gentleman and lady that their meal is on me, that'll do it. Throw in a fancy desert for them both," he requested. The waiter topped up my glass of water before leaving.

Daniel reached for my hand across the table and squeezed tightly. "Say something, baby."

Still in shock, I muttered, "There's nothing I can say that'll make this better, there's nothing I can say that'll make this alright." Tears threatened to fall, and I decided to excuse myself from the table.

I went into the Ladies, locked myself in a cubicle and cried. *How long had he known? He'd had those tests done after all. Had David known?* I thought to call David, but my phone was in my handbag, which I'd left at the table. *David would know what to do. He always knew what to do.* He might even be able to refer Daniel to a friend. Daniel was dying. *This could not be the end of our story. This cannot be the end.*

After a while, I decided to freshen up and step outside for a moment before joining Daniel. Stepping out through the back door, I stood under the eaves and stared up at the night sky.

"You're doing it again," Daniel said, stepping out of the shadows, startling me slightly.

"Doing what?" I asked.

"Standing me up," he replied. "Remember our wedding day?"

I laughed in response, despite my sadness. "I was fashionably late, is all."

"Come here," he urged, embracing me, pulling me into him. "Remember our first dance?" Pulling me close for a slow dance, he sang the opening line of Nat King Cole's *When I Fall in Love.*

I held him tight. "Brings a new meaning to the word forever," I said tearfully.

"I know, I know," he said, slightly above a whisper. "You're it for me. You're my forever after."

I couldn't see his tears in the moonlight, but I could feel them on my cheek, his face pressed up against mine.

"Should we call it quits, and head home?" he asked. "Or can you brave the crowd for a while longer? I ordered our favorite desert – strawberry vanilla cream cake..."

I lit up despite the sadness that befell my heart. "Of course." If it was going to be our last anniversary, it had to be perfect.

We held each other for a moment longer before we decided to go back in.

Sleep didn't come easy that night. Though the kids slept peacefully, I tossed and turned, unable to come to terms with the fact that this man before me, the man I loved deeply, might not be with me for much longer.

We went to see the oncologist who'd originally made the diagnosis, the next day, together.

Doctor Menzies repeated the diagnosis for my benefit. A brain tumour. Likely inoperable. Daniel nodded stoically at the diagnosis. "How long do I have again?"

"Six months tops," he said. Daniel sat there, unmoved. My eyes welled up with tears. He reached for my hand and held it firmly.

"But if we excise the tumour completely there's a likelihood that you'll be able to come out of this with many years ahead of you," Doctor Menzies advised.

"Well, God hasn't failed me yet," Daniel stated.

"Mr Brennan, the prognosis isn't good. I'm afraid you're going to need to be realistic here," the doctor said.

"Who says I'm being unrealistic?" Daniel piped in. "I'm just making a statement. God hasn't failed me yet. I'm sure he's not about to fail me now."

Doctor Menzies laughed nervously. "You're optimistic, I'll give you that. Not sure I can match your optimism though."

Ignoring him, Daniel stated, "So, where do I sign?"

The doctor looked perplexed. "The surgery might render you unable to function. The chemo might not work and might just kill you in the process."

"Alright then," Daniel replied. "I'm seeking a second opinion. You won't be hearing back from me." He got up and motioned for me to follow after him. Stunned, I got up as well.

We walked in silence to the car, then had it out in the parking lot.

"How can you be so casual about this?" I questioned in between tears. "The doctor's just told you you've got 6 months left to live and you're acting as though you've got all the time in the world to work through this..."

"Come on now, have some faith," he said embracing me. He held me for a moment before stating, "I'm doing what I do best. Putting blind faith in my Heavenly Father. I'll get that second opinion, won't hurt."

"Daniel, we can't take silly risks and stand firm on morals. You're dying. If we can save you, we should. Not just for your sake, but for our sake," I told him.

"This isn't a silly stance. I need to...never mind," he said. "I just thought you'd understand. I live by what I believe, and that's all there is to it."

"How do we do this?" Daniel asked when we got home. "I prefer this were on a need to know basis. I don't need anyone's sympathy, and I know for a fact there'll be people who'd be glad I was dying."

My heart felt heavy at the thought that he'd be gone and certain people would be happy he were gone. My heart felt heavy at the fact that he'd be gone.

"I made a list," he said. "Johnny first. Then Colleen. David already knows. Craig already knows."

"I can't do this now, Daniel," I stated.

"We're going to have to sugarpie. What I need right now is to be surrounded by people who'll rally behind me and support you and the babies without a question. This has to happen sooner rather than later."

I tearfully acknowledged that he was right.

Johnny met us at the front door when we got home. He'd

been up with Sadie, watching a movie. The babies were fast asleep.

He instantly knew something was wrong. I left him and Daniel alone in the kitchen, and Daniel told him the news. Johnny cared deeply for Daniel, and I knew the news broke him.

I found them sitting in the kitchen, in silence. Johnny sat head bowed, Daniel fixated on a space in the distance.

Sadie walked in behind me and broke the silence. "Why the long faces?"

"Daniel's leaving us," Johnny said cryptically. "Inoperable brain tumour."

Sadie gasped in response. "Oh no," she cried. "Oh no." I reached for her and we cried together.

Daniel got up and announced, "Guys, it isn't over yet. I've still got to get a second opinion, and besides, six months is six months. It's not six days. Still enough time to enjoy all that there is to enjoy."

Johnny got up and slipped an arm around Sadie and I. "Well, we'll see to it that it's the best six months of your life, Daniel," he promised. "Look out."

I smiled sadly, knowing the next few months would likely not be the best six months of his life.

We stayed awake together through the early hours of the morning, writing down a few ideas, discussing the possibility of overseas travel and plans for the babies. I fell asleep in Daniel's arms, resting my head against his chest, the sound of his heartbeat lulling me to sleep.

Sadie and Daniel were out first thing in the morning, while Johnny and I remained at home.

"So, he's all busy making plans for life here without him.

It's almost as though he's at peace with leaving so soon, and leaving us all behind. I guess it must be done. I just can't stand to see him like this," Johnny confessed. "I offered to drive him to chemo and he refused. I'm at a complete loss as to how to support him, how to...," he turned away, tears streaming down his face.

"Johnny," I called out, beckoning him to turn to me. "I'm hoping and praying that he pulls through this. He's strong. He's got faith, he's..." I stopped mid-sentence, in tears, realizing I was just as scared and just as distraught as Johnny was.

"He's only human and you're just as fucking scared as I am," he said in between tears. "Pardon my French," he said.

I laughed nervously in response. "Your French was never crash hot Johnny."

He laughed in between tears. Deep in my heart, I had doubts that Daniel would survive this. I feared losing him. Overwhelmed with sadness, I fell to my knees and Johnny braced me. We held each other and cried, longing and praying for more time with the man we loved in different measures but equally.

David came by a few hours later but didn't stay for long. "I'm sorry Temwani," he said, sorrowfully.

"You've kept your distance," I noted.

"I came by when I could. Daniel doesn't want me around," he mentioned. "He claims I'm robbing him of his remaining time with you."

"I can't believe you two are at it again," I replied, amazed their animosity still continued.

"We're not. At least, I'm not. He's pretty angry at the

situation in general," he explained. "He's always been angry at me. Nothing's changed."

I shrugged in response.

"I've given him the details of some colleagues that may be able to help. A second opinion on the course of treatment would be useful," he said.

I heard Daniel pulling into the driveway. David suddenly chose to bolt. "I'll be seeing you soon, I'll give you a call later," he promised, quickly exiting through the back door.

Daniel walked in moments later and threw the car keys down on the kitchen bench top.

"I can't believe this is happening to me," he said indignantly. "To us."

"We'll try everything," I promised.

He ignored me. "I've tried to be all that God commands me to be, yet here I am. I'm not perfect, but I try. A lot of good that's done me. He's answered the prayer of an unrighteous man over the prayer of a righteous man," he said angrily. "This isn't fair."

"You're the righteous man, and David's the unrighteous man? You're being a little dramatic baby."

"It's the truth," Daniel insisted.

"Daniel, it isn't all about you and David. It really isn't. God's not playing favorites," I told him.

"You don't know that. David's gotten everything he's prayed for. So far," he replied.

I tried to reason with him, but he refused to listen. "This isn't fair," he stated again.

"I'm sure God isn't picking sides and choosing your brother over you."

"Well, it certainly feels like He is," Daniel stated, overwhelmed with sadness. "It's as though David's sacrifice is somehow greater than mine."

I pondered his statement for a moment. I disagreed. I knew that all prayers came before God, and if they were in His will He would make things happen.

"So, nautical dusk is setting on me, and a new dawn is rising on him, right?" Daniel asked rhetorically, clearly hurt and struggling to come to terms with the fact that there would be no future for us, together, once he was gone.

I shook my head, disagreeing with him. "That's not how it is," I said.

"Isn't it? I think that's exactly what it is," he replied. "I'll be gone and you'll be free to be with David. Some form of poetic justice this is," he said, his statement filling me with sadness. "Next time you see him, tell him to face me like a man. Tell him to walk out the same door he walked through. Tell him to stop slinking around and hiding away. Tell him to face me like a man."

"He didn't want to face you today as he says you're pretty angry with him."

"Why shouldn't I be!" Daniel fumed. "I've got six months left to live, and he's got his whole life ahead of him!" he yelled.

I went to bed that night, my heart heavy laden with sorrow. I mourned for Daniel though he was not yet gone, and cried silently for the moments which we were to have which were no longer ours to dream for and hope for. It wasn't fair, this I knew, but I also knew that David had been through a terrible time from the beginning. Was this a form of justice that we could not understand yet?

As the days went on, and we got opinion after opinion

confirming the original diagnosis, I couldn't tell. When I spoke with David, my anger would often spill out into our conversation. "You prayed for this," I reminded him.

"I prayed for you and I to be together, I didn't pray for *this*," David promised. "I never asked for *this*."

I could tell he was hurting, but his hurt at that moment was the last thing on my mind. I felt a sense of guilt at the time that I'd wasted being angry at Daniel. I decided to make up for this by being completely devoted to him, and shutting out all outside noise and intervention. Disconnecting from David was part of that plan.

Throughout that week, David called and I did not pick up. He sent numerous messages when I didn't. I ignored the messages he sent for a whole week, and didn't return any of his calls. Inevitably, he turned up at the office one afternoon, forcing me to talk to him.

"If you don't want me here, you just have to let me know," he stated. His blue eyes looked sad, his voice strained. Not dressed up in his usual casual attire, he wore a black sweater, corduroy jeans, loafers and an air of sadness. "I'm not trying to be a thorn in your side," he declared.

"Aren't you? Isn't this what you wanted? For Daniel to be out of the picture, and for me to be available to you?" I asked angrily.

"Temwani, please," he pleaded with me. "I never asked for my own brother to have terminal cancer," he said, his voice wavering. "I'm torn up inside about all of this."

"You're obviously not too torn up inside if you're here insisting that I talk to you – if you were all torn up inside, you'd appreciate that I can't waste any more time entertaining you and the thought that we will eventually be together," I stated.

He winced slightly at my statement as though in physical pain. I refused to hold back. "You're a doctor right? Why haven't you been busy thinking of ways to save him other than refer him on to other colleagues?"

In that moment, he sighed heavily and appeared exasperated. Shaking his head, he asked, "Don't you think I've been trying? He won't listen to me; he doesn't want to hear anything I've got to say. He thinks the universe has somehow conspired against him to get him out of the picture and to make you available to me. He's calling me names, saying I'm an unrighteous man who's trying to make amends with God and putting my love for you on the line as a sacrifice... How am I supposed to help when neither one of you will let me help?" he asked. "I love you Teme, you know I'll do anything for you. He's my brother. He's part of me. He's a big part of me. It's killing me inside that the both of you are shutting me out."

Hearing him plead his case and hearing him tell me that he loved me and was trying the best he knew how to help Daniel made the tears come unexpectedly.

"Aw, don't cry, Temwani," he begged. "Please don't cry. I'm sorry," he apologized.

"It's not any one thing you said," I replied, in between tears. "It's... well, I never thought that this could happen. What'll become of me and the babies when he's gone? How will we survive?" I sobbed.

"Hey, hey, hey," David said, tenderly pulling me in for an embrace. "I'm here for you. I will continue to be here for you. You're not doing this alone," he promised.

I melted in his arms, forgetting my anger at him, and grateful that he was there, once again.

404

"I see you're wearing my gift," he noted, referring to the pink diamond embedded crucifix on my neck. "A reminder for you to keep your hopes up and keep believing."

I nodded in response.

"I guess I was out of sight but not out of mind," he said jovially, despite the earlier sadness.

I shook my head in response. "You're incorrigible, Doctor David Davenport," I stated.

He smiled widely and hugged me tightly. "I missed having you around, missed seeing you," he stated. "But I promise to not make this about me," he said. "He needs you right now, and I won't stand in the way of what he needs. I need to talk to him face to face and let him know that I'm not here to stand in between the two of you."

"He's pretty angry right now," I warned.

"I can understand why he would be," David offered. "But when is he never angry when it comes to me?"

I laughed, he was speaking truth.

"So, you going back to him this arvo, like right now?" he asked. "I figured I could come with," he advised.

An image of the last punch up between them filled my mind. "You got your gloves on?"

He smiled in response. "Trying the non-violent approach this time," he said.

Easier said than done. Daniel was in the living room, watching a re-run of the X-Files when David and I came in. "What a surprise," he commented, shaking his head in disbelief. His anger was quite apparent.

"No need to get all riled up Daniel, he's just here to talk to you," I explained.

"I see nothing has changed," Daniel presumed. "He's

clearly convinced you to be on side with him."

"Hear me out," David pleaded. "Hear me out, will you? Five minutes of your time then if you want me to leave, I'll leave," he said.

"Oh, this better be good," Daniel said, standing up to face David.

"I'm really sorry about everything. I'm really sad about your diagnosis," he started. "I didn't ask for this. I wouldn't wish this on anyone. I don't know how to be there for you when you don't want me around. I need you to know that I'm not here to cause you distress. I want you to know that I'm here to help you and your wife out in any way possible. I will be here to take the babies off your hands and give you time together, I will be here to take you to your appointments...I *will* be here in any way you want me to be here. You don't want me to be here, say the word and I'll be gone."

Daniel stood akimbo, and appeared to be open to what David had said. "Okay then," he started. "We need to talk."

"Go for it." David stated.

Motioning towards me, Daniel said "Alone. Without Teme. Just you and me."

Unsure, David stated nervously, "Okay?"

"There's only one way that things can be made right between you and I," Daniel announced. "Let's talk, and I'll tell you how," he said, making his way to the patio that flowed off the study. "Close the door behind you," he commanded, as David stepped out onto the patio with him.

I wanted to eavesdrop on their conversation but I didn't. Instead, for a moment, I stood there, watching them in heated discussion. Surprisingly, the conversation did not seem to be confrontational. The expression on David's face went from embarrassment to shock and disbelief. Daniel seemed largely unmoved, though it seemed he was trying hard to conceal his emotion.

I heard the babies stir in bed on the monitor. Reluctantly, I left the two brothers to discuss and air out their grievances with each other, all the while resolving to find out what they had been talking about.

When I came back, David was standing with his hands in his pockets, leaning up against the kitchen bench for support. "I'm heading off now," he stated as a matter of factly, eager to leave in a hurry. Daniel was sitting back on the sofa, watching the X-Files.

"Everything alright?" I asked. David nodded to the affirmative but his eyes betrayed him.

"I'll see you tomorrow morning," he stated abruptly. "I'll come by on my way to work."

Not taking his eyes off the screen, Daniel chimed in, "Thanks for stopping in, and see you tomorrow."

Tomorrow? I wondered. *One moment they couldn't stand each other, the next moment they were making plans to meet again? Odd.* I hugged him goodbye, and wondered at the quick change from animosity to being amiable with each other.

Daniel kept me wondering. When I tried to find out what had transpired between the two of them, his response was, "It's complicated. You'll find out in good enough time."

I texted David, and his response was very much the same. "He will tell you in due course, leave well enough alone for now." Annoyed, I sent him an upside down emoji in response.

While slightly dismayed at the secrets being kept from me, I knew I could corner either of them at any given time, and get them to spill the beans so to speak. David would be easier to break than Daniel, who'd recently become an expert at keeping mum. I resolved to do some digging in the morning, when David was over.

20

THE PACT

The next day, David was in our home, bright and early. I offered him tea which he refused. He sat at the kitchen bench watching me prepare breakfast. He offered to help and I declined his offer. I knew how much he liked my cooking, so despite the offer, I continued prepping breakfast. Daniel was still in bed, he'd struggled to get up that morning.

David lightly tapped his fingers on the kitchen bench top laminate, somehow impatient. "Has he been in to get a second opinion?" he asked of Daniel.

"He's gotten a third and a fourth," I replied.

"About his treatment plan *and* the diagnosis?" David asked.

"If you're asking whether he's explored all possible options, then no," I replied. "He doesn't want to do anything that he's not been commanded to do," I stated. "Apparently God doesn't want him to do anything that will involve extending his life."

David's expression shifted from disbelief to anger. "He's got to be kidding." Standing up he asked, "That's a nonsensical way of thinking. Doesn't he think that God has given doctors the capacity to think of ways of prolonging life, and that this might actually be for his benefit? Doesn't he think that God would want him to stick around for his children?" he asked.

I shrugged in response. "With Daniel it's always been a matter of watching, waiting and praying," I said. "Right now we need to pray. I've tried to convince him otherwise but he's not interested in changing his perspective. Not now anyway."

David shook his head in reply. "He wouldn't want to wait around too much longer, time is of the essence."

"And *His* timing is perfect," Daniel said, suddenly appearing at the door. Walking up to me, he planted a full kiss on my lips. Lately, all his public romantic overtures felt as though they were for show. I saw David look away. Knowing how deeply he felt for me, I knew it still hurt him deeply to see me with Daniel.

I prepared a fruit platter, toast and beans for David which he ate heartily, as though he'd not eaten in a while. Daniel slowly devoured his bacon, eggs, toast and beans.

Putting his fork down, David stated, "Mate, now's not the time to stand on principle. Now's the time to take action and hope that God will guide you in making the right decision when it comes to your treatment. Doing nothing is not an option," he warned.

Daniel finished eating before saying anything. *The suspense. Typical of him.* "What makes you think God is not guiding me now?"

"I find it hard to believe that God would want you to do nothing and leave your beautiful wife and kids behind," David said.

Daniel caught on to his words. "Beautiful, that she is," he agreed. "You prayed to be with her, didn't you? What makes you think God is not trying to grant you your prayer request?"

A flash of regret shone on David's face, and he cast a side glance at me. "I didn't pray for this to happen to you. I didn't..." Stopping mid-sentence he said, "I agreed to what I agreed to yesterday, but I didn't agree to this..."

"What did you agree on yesterday?" I asked, feeling I would finally get the answers I longed for.

"Sugarpie," Daniel started. I knew I would not like what he had to say already. "I've asked David to fill my shoes when I'm gone," he said point blankly.

"Meaning?"

"I've asked him to take the kids in as his own. I've also asked him to see to it that you're well taken care of when I'm gone. He's to take my place in your life when I'm gone," Daniel confirmed.

It felt as though I was hearing things. I took one look at him, and one look at David. "So, you're already gone now, are you?" I asked.

"Sugarpie, results is in. I *will be* gone soon. We all have to go somehow, someday," he said, with finality. "I can't think of a better person to fill my shoes than David," he stated. "At least with the kids," he explained. "I'm sure in time his charm will wear you down, if it hasn't done so already. I want you to find happiness when I'm gone," he said. "With him."

"Baby, you're not even trying to stay alive!" I exclaimed, in tears.

"No, that's not what God's intending," he replied.

"Please stop this," I pleaded. "Why don't you just stop for one minute and consider that your ideology may be at odds with what God wants. For once, just admit that you may be wrong?"

I looked over at David for backing and he averted my gaze. *He had tried.* I was in this battle alone.

"Don't I have a say in this? How can you two be sworn enemies one day and the best of buddies the next?" *Something's amiss* I thought.

"This is what you've both wanted for the longest time, isn't it?" Daniel questioned.

I rolled my eyes at the suggestion. "You're not going to make David feel guilty for wanting what he has. He's only human."

"And so am I. Flesh and blood. And as you know, flesh and blood doesn't last forever. Ashes to ashes, dust to dust," he stated. No sooner than he said that did I hear Josiah crying through the intercom. It was only a matter of time before Adalia was crying too. Instead of getting up as he ordinarily did, Daniel commanded, "David, you know the deal. Time to show me what you're made of."

David nodded to signal his agreement, then made his way down the hall. I could see he did so with a heavy heart. *This isn't fair on him,* I thought. Turning to Daniel, I stated, "This isn't right. You can't just abdicate your responsibility for your own children."

"I'm not abdicating anything baby. I'm merely letting things play out the way they should and the way they would, when I'm gone," he insisted.

"Daniel, you can't act as though you're already gone..."

"Well, I will be," he said dismissively.

I could hear the babies cooing over the monitor. David had worked his magic.

"Go with," Daniel urged.

"They're still your kids," I reminded him.

"Of course they are," he replied. "Go join him."

I planted a kiss on his lips before I did as he said.

David had Josiah in one arm, and with the other arm, rocked Adalia in the cradle. She was smiling at him delightfully.

"You okay?" I asked.

"Never better," he replied. "I love these kids as though they were my own."

"Someone loves you!" I noted, "I've seen how much she smiles at you."

"Yep. She's not the only one who has me wrapped around her finger," David said with a wink.

"Incorrigible you are," I remarked.

"I bet she's Daddy's little girl now," he guessed.

"She definitely is," I confirmed.

Motioning towards the baby monitor, without words, he reminded me that Daniel was probably listening in on the other end. I reached for it and turned it off.

"He's not going to like that," David noted.

"I'm not liking how he's behaving," I admitted.

"You and me both," he replied. "So you said earlier, it's a matter of watching and praying?"

"You heard me," I said.

"Can I come to church with you on Sunday?" he asked suddenly.

Taken aback at his sudden interest in going to church, I quickly replied, "Of course you can." For a moment I tried to figure out his game but quickly realized that this time, there might not be any game. Daniel had not been coming to church of late. He complained the music was too upbeat, he complained the preaching was too much about prosperity, and too little about rules to live by.

"I don't want to cause you any trouble," he added. "I'm happy to meet you there and we can go in separately? Just wanting to go with someone I know."

"Daniel probably won't be there, but even if he is, you'll be coming there with us," I promised. "It'll be just me and the babies otherwise," I advised. "We'll go together."

"Okay," he said, nodding in relief, though he seemed troubled.

The morning that David came to church with us was the morning that the band was short of a member. The person who sang lead. David offered to sing.

"You can read music?" the preacher asked.

"Yes," David replied.

"Familiar with our worship songs?"

"I can't say I am," he admitted. "I'll try my best."

As David sang the words of *It Is Well With My Soul*, a hymn penned by Horation Spafford, I felt my heart soar with every note he reached despite the sadness over Daniel and the fact that he was dying. I still remained at a loss as to how to feel and how to be moving forward. The babies and I would need to live without him somehow, for he wouldn't be coming back.

The pastor picked up on my sadness, and tried to get me to stay after the service. David read me well and assisted with a quick exit.

"You alright?" he asked, in the car.

"As alright as I can be," I told him. The babies were cooing away in their car seats, oblivious to everything that was happening around them. David checked their seat belts one last time before starting the ignition.

"I thought we could take a quick trip to the grocery store and I can pick up a few things for lunch and dinner?" he asked.

"As long as we don't take too long," I replied. "I worry about leaving Daniel alone at home for too long, despite him saying he'll be okay."

"I hear you," David replied. "He's asked me to take you and the kids out though."

"Oh," I said. *Playing matchmaker again.*

"We don't have to if you don't want to," he stated. I could tell he'd be disappointed if I said no.

"Okay, let's," I told him, all the while thinking of Daniel and all the things I could possibly do to help him.

We drove in silence until we got to the local neighbourhood grocer. "I'll quickly pop in, won't be a tick," he said, rolling down the windows, turning for an instant to smile at the babies. "Or should I take them with me?" he asked. "One in the pram, the other in the sling? Or both in the sling if you come with?"

Adalia was already squirming in her seat. Josiah didn't seem to mind either way, he was fixated on something through the window, in the distance.

"Let's put them both in the sling, wear them down," he suggested. Reluctantly, I agreed. With Daniel being ill, I didn't feel like facing the world and putting on a smiley face.

Josiah in my sling and Adalia in David's, I absently followed David through the store as he methodically picked out a few items and hurriedly put them in the trolley. "Have you considered putting the babies on solids yet?" he asked, pausing at the baby section. "They're nearing the five month mark," he stated. "I can make up a few things for them, we can get some of these fruit and vege pouches here for when we're out and about," he suggested.

"We thought we'd wait til six months or so, I'm happy to exclusively breastfeed until then," I told him.

"I know you are, but you'll need your strength," he advised. "It won't hurt for them to have a breastfeed replaced by a small meal. Adalia's definitely keen, I've had to stop her from grabbing food out of my hand."

"I guess we could look at them starting on solids soon," I replied. "See what Daniel thinks."

"Moving on already, I see," Jolène stated from behind us, causing David to startle then turn sharply in her direction.

He scowled in response. "Ignore her Teme. We're not playing your game today Jolène," he announced turning his back to her.

She ignored him and cast an endearing eye at the babies. Josiah gave her a toothless grin and reached out for her. "May I?" she asked, reaching out to hold him.

Reluctantly I took Josiah out of the sling and she held him. He giggled away when she rocked him and tickled under his chin. A lone tear ran down her face. "Looks just like his dad did at this age, save for those cute cheeks, cocoa skin and gorgeous locks that come from you no doubt. I miss Daniel," she said. "He's refusing to take my calls, refusing to even let me in the door, but he needs me. Please talk to him Teme, please convince him not to shut me out. He needs me now more than ever. I can help him get through this. He wants me to make nice with the both of you. I was't prepared to do that, but I'm now prepared to put my differences aside and do just that," she promised.

"Well, you can't blame him for feeling the way he feels. He feels you betrayed him. He can't get over what you did to David - he says he's not prepared to entertain any discussion on you being in his life, and the life of our kids," I informed her.

"And that's his call to make," David added, examining a packet of millet flour before putting it into the trolley.

"David, you of all people who grew up without a mother should be encouraging him to keep me in his life!" Jolène retorted.

David shrugged in response.

"Enough has been said already Jolène," I snapped, taking Josiah back off her. She reluctantly let him go and tried to be friendly with Adalia who flat out ignored her. *Daddy's little girl.* "I'll say something to him. Don't get your hopes up. His mind's made up," I said.

"Okay," Joléne said, defeated. "Send my love to him."

"You alright?" David asked as she walked away.

I nodded to the affirmative.

"You don't look it, Mama," he remarked.

Mama? "You've never called me that, David."

"What, Mama?" he asked.

"Yes, *Mama*," I replied.

"I've gotta call you something other than baby, sugarpie or sweet lady or... Can't I just keep on calling you Darlin' or Mama?" he asked.

"I suppose," I replied.

"Good," he said, conscious of the fact that Adalia was starting to complain. "Let's wrap this up. I've got just the thing to make you happy again," he promised.

The thing to make me happy again involved him taking a detour instead of heading home. Daniel had planned a picnic in the park. A chance for Daniel and I to connect, and a chance for David to bond with the babies.

Daniel wasn't hungry so ate very little.

We left David on the picnic rug with the babies and went for a short stroll.

"What if you survive?" I asked. "What if all this distance you're placing between yourself and us is not necessary?"

"It'll be necessary whatever the outcome," Daniel claimed.

"Baby, if you survive, I'm sure you'll be possessive to a fault. You've never wanted to share," I reminded him. As we sat on the park bench, in the distance, David rolled around on the ground, causing the twins to explode in contagious laughter.

"This is different," he reasoned. "I can spend the remaining time jealously hoarding your affection, jealously holding on to everything and everyone, or I can learn to let go. I'm going to have to let go in the end. Perspective is everything," he said, thoughtfully.

"I'm not sure I'll be able to let go of you," I told him, hugging him deeply.

"I didn't ever want to have to let you go, but it looks like I'll have to. Better you outlive me than the other way around. I won't get a chance to miss you then," he said.

Tears filled my eyes, and he quickly sought to lighten the mood. "I'm sure you won't miss my voracious appetite for sexy time," he said abruptly.

I laughed at the suggestion.

"You can go back to quiet and peaceful evenings, knowing I won't be there pestering you at all different times of night asking for you to give me some sugar," he said. Taking off his sunglasses, he asked, "Speaking of which, do you want me to give you any more babies?"

His question took me by surprise. "I..."

"You hesitated there for a moment," he noted.

I nodded. "If you were staying on, it'd be a firm yes. But you're leaving, and I don't want to spend the remaining time with you all laid up in bed with morning sickness, or on bedrest for some reason or another. Josiah and Adalia are enough for me. I also want you to know all our babies. If you can't be there to welcome them into the world with me, I'd rather we didn't have any more," I explained.

"Fair enough," he replied somewhat disappointed. "I guess you could always have more babies with Dave," he said point blankly, putting his sunglasses back on.

"Baby, don't be like that," I said. "I only want to be with you. You're it for me."

"Things change, baby, things change. Plus you don't have a choice. I've asked him to take my place. No negotiation," he reminded me.

"You can't make me love him," I stated.

"I don't have to make you anything. You already do. You're just too stubborn to admit it," he said.

"I told you how I feel Daniel. I..."

He silenced me with a finger on my lips. "Let's not quarrel. Let's talk, let's walk, let's make plans to have sexy time later, while I still can," he said, pulling me in for a deep imploring kiss before we walked back to David and the babies.

When we got back, Adalia was trying to prop herself up on two feet, and in that moment, Josiah moved from sitting position to a semi crawl.

"Is he...?" Daniel asked, dropping to his knees.

David bolted upright. "He's definitely on the go!"

Josiah giggled delightfully and crawled towards David first, then took a detour for Daniel. I fell to my knees as well, tears of joy streaming down my face. Happy the babies were growing, but sad that Daniel would miss a lot of milestones. From a distance, David saw my sadness and nodded his head at me acknowledging my pain.

"It'll only be a matter of time before this one starts walking," he said, getting up, holding Adalia's hands in his and walking her around. "She might just skip crawling, I reckon," he predicted.

"I'm just hoping I'll be around long enough to see much more," Daniel said sadly, scooping Josiah into his arms. "Let's go home," he said. He had his sunglasses on again, so I couldn't see his eyes, but from the tone of his voice, I knew he was crying.

Sleep didn't come easy that night. We stayed up talking long after we should have gone to sleep.

"Pray for our kids," Daniel requested. "Promise me you'll never cease praying for them," he urged. "There are so many things in this world... so many matter of things... promise me you'll never cease praying for them."

"I won't," I told him. "They are always in my prayers."

"Please make sure that Josiah is gentle and kind. Don't let him take after me, bein' all hot headed all the time. Tell him to mind his language and to be kind. He better not be using words like I command you ta, I order you ta... them's fightin' words. And Adalia, she's gonna be a heartbreaker. Make sure she knows it ain't just about lookin all purty and

420

all. Make sure she takes after you and knows she needs to use her brains over beauty. And David..." he started. "You know I have too much to say about him. I've said most of what I feel already. I want you to be patient with him, I want you to take the time to get to know him. I didn't do a great job of showing him how much I loved him as a brother, but I'm showing him now. Behind that smile, that laughter, there's a lot of hurtin' that needs a healin'. Between you and him, there's a lot of lovin' to be had. After I'm gone, I want you to move on to someone new. To him."

I shook my head in response. Knowing how David felt about me, it wouldn't be hard to see us in the relationship Daniel envisioned. What I couldn't envision was loving someone else the way I deeply loved Daniel despite our differences.

"I'm not asking him to replace me," he explained. "I am asking him to look out for you and the kids, and I figured he's loved you so long, ain't nothing wrong with goin' ahead with a good thing," he said, stroking my cheek and gently shifting a curly lock that was out of place. "Don't tell me you ain't got feelings for him, 'cause that'll be a lie."

I didn't respond to his comment on my feelings for David. "This isn't how our story was to end," I told him instead.

Easing back into his pillow, he stated confidently, "Well, maybe it *was* meant to end this way. I can't envision living without you, so I think it's fated and appropriate that you should outlive me."

Sadness swept over me. The years without him. The children growing up without their father. All the milestones he would miss. The hopes and dreams we would never achieve now. "Daniel, I wish you weren't so practical all the time," I said.

"Can't help who I am, sugarpie," he replied. "So, in summary, you have my blessin' to go on after I'm gone. And please don't tell me you won't. There's a lot of lovin' to be had, a lot of lovin' to give and receive. A lot of happiness still ahead for you and the kids, and David," he assured me. "As for me, I've got my forever. You'll be my last, you'll be my forever," he promised.

I pulled him close to me and hugged him with all my might. This man that I'd come to love, cherish and adore would be gone soon. This man that I felt God had handpicked for me was leaving my life, never to return again. I knew that my love for him would never end, despite the passage of time. He would always hold a place in my heart. Still, without the promise of a future with him, I felt I would die. I'd never imagined getting through tomorrow without him.

21

SILVER RAIN

The rain was coming down lightly but pounded down on our tin roof. We sat in the living room, with the babies on the floor, happily rolling around and enjoying a fleeting moment of freedom. It wouldn't be long before they would be scooped up for a feed. Josiah didn't mind playtime coming to an end for the sake of food. Adalia on the other hand did.

"Raining again," Daniel noted, deciding to step out on to the veranda, barefoot. Arms in his pocket he stood, staring in to the trees and other foliage beyond. His white t-shirt and gray tracksuit bottoms were getting pelted on by the rain but he didn't seem to mind. He stood there motionless, in deep thought.

Flashing me a boyish grin, his trademark dimples ever present, he requested, "Come join me if you dare." Motioning to the kids, he noted, "Just for a moment. They'll be fine."

I smiled, and took a step towards him and stood there with him. He pulled me in and held me tightly. "I'm already missing you and the little ones," he confessed. "The time I've been given just doesn't seem long enough," he added. "When

I first met you, all I could think of was the lifetime of love we would spend together. I should have known nothing's guaranteed," he stated. "Not for me anyway."

The rain came down a little harder this time. He embraced me whole, then stood behind me against the balcony railing.

"I'm missing you already too," I confessed. "I can't imagine what my life will be like without you in it."

"Well, for now you don't have to worry about that," he insisted. "I'm still here, and I'll be present in every way that I can be. That's a promise. I don't want to miss any moment to share what time I do have left in this life, with you."

My heart felt heavy at the thought that the moments we shared would soon be coming to an end.

"I love you Daniel, I love you so much," I sobbed.

"And I, you. Beyond words," he said. As he cried and I cried, our tears mixed with rain.

Daniel's wedding ring fell into the sink one morning, as he helped me rinse the dishes I'd just washed by hand. All the weight he'd lost meant the ring was now too big for his finger. I added it to the necklace I wore with the crucifix David had given me on the birth of the twins.

We held each other by the kitchen sink.

"Leaving this here earth is not something I'm ready to do just yet...doc says I have three to four months now, I'm hoping I'll have eight months plus. I'm hoping for a complete recovery but you and I both know that the likelihood of that happening is slim."

I nodded, noting he'd changed his mind about therapies that could possibly extend his life.

"That experimental method, the one being offered in

Switzerland - I'm prepared to go for it now. Forget what I said about not wanting to do anything to prolong my life. I have to go for it...what do we have to lose?"

"Your life, Daniel, it could take you away from me in the blink of an eye," I told him. "It's too risky."

"Or, it could extend my time here with you and even see me fully recovered," he argued. "Now, isn't that worth a shot, sugarpie?"

I shrugged in response. I didn't want to lose him, period.

"The cost is out of reach, but David said he would help where he can," I offered.

"David's only one man," Daniel replied. "I'm not trying to burden him with this. The fact that he'll be there for you when I'm gone is pretty big in itself. We need to do this on our own steam though, he's already done too much."

When I'm gone...those words both saddened and troubled me.

"Alright," Daniel said suddenly. "We just need to liquidate a few things. Not the house, but maybe the cars and the boats."

"We can let go of the house," I told him. "I'll be okay. We'll be okay."

Daniel sighed before replying. "I don't know that. I won't be there to see that you and the babies will be okay. Leaving you the house is the best I can do." After a brief pause he stated, "Could always ask Craig to pay me out of the partnership we have at the firm."

"That's an idea," I said, hopeful.

Daniel called him that night, and Craig outright refused, citing the rules of incorporation, questioning Daniel's capacity to make decisions, and the fact that the firm was the legacy of Adalia and Josiah.

"Craig said no," Daniel told me, hands trembling as he put his mobile phone down on the bedside table. "He says the business is a legacy for you and the kids. I have to agree with him there. I'm dying, I'm gonna die. No use prolonging things and leaving you and the kids worse off."

His words saddened my heart. *No use prolonging things?* I instantly hated Craig for playing God with Daniel's life and for refusing to help when he very well could. Daniel read my mind.

"Don't be upset at Craig. It's my decision in the end. I won't be seeking any experimental treatment now, I'll just let things run their natural course," he said.

It was all too much for me to bear. Craig had to be dealt with, Daniel needed to survive. I couldn't survive without him.

After much dispute, Daniel urged me to let it go.

That night, David was on shift at the hospital, but I called and managed to speak with him not long after Daniel had gone to bed. He recommended we see another specialist. Consulting with the doctor he recommended would cost several thousand dollars. David had some money put aside and offered to help, given Daniel was not keen on the idea of remortgaging the house. He knew that the cost of chemotherapy had eaten into our savings, leaving us with not much left over. Not being able to dip into the funds Daniel had invested into the firm meant we couldn't do anything else other than rely on David. Thankfully, David was able to assist.

The next morning, rain was coming down hard. For a moment it looked like tiny silver slithers. "Do you see that?"

Daniel asked, looking out the open window.

"I did. Looks a lot like..."

"Silver," he stated.

I mused for a moment at how good he was at completing my sentences and reading my mind. *If only we had more time.* I really didn't know how I was going to manage with him gone.

"Lord knows I need something like a silver bullet to kill this sickness that's taken a hold of me," he said sadly. I slipped my arms around his waist and embraced him. His weight had plummeted and he was looking noticeably gaunt. I rested my head on his shoulder.

"I wish my three to four months were a year, and a year fifty years," he said, longing for a different outcome. "I can't believe this is how we are going to end. I can't believe this is how it will end for me and you. I can't believe I won't see our babies grow up. I can't..." he broke off, unable to continue. "I can't even give you the thirty plus years I promised you. Can't even give you three years."

Tears in our eyes, we embraced for what felt like an eternity. Our eternity. I imagined seeing him again someday, but knew there'd be no recollection of time or place in eternity, in heaven. There would be no tears.

"No tears," he said, as though he'd read my mind. "No tears for me. Promise me that you'll find happiness when I'm gone," he insisted. "Promise me that you'll keep your heart open to love, with someone other than me. David"

"I can't promise you that, Daniel," I said tearfully. "You're it for me."

With the limited time we had, we loved deeply and fully. It was hard to come to terms with the fact that he would be gone in a matter of months, but we gave it our best, we tried. It was all we could do.

We tried not to argue, but at times it was inevitable. Our few arguments evolved around plans for the future. He wanted to discuss how the kids would be raised. Where we would live. He wanted to discuss the possibility of me finding love after he was gone. I wanted to do no such thing. I could not see a future without him. I was determined to remain alone once he was gone.

As time went on, Daniel came up with a list of last wishes. On that list was the hope that I would find love again and remarry.

I was livid. "We only have a few months left and all you can come up with is this? Can't you see that I do not want to be with anyone else, ever?"

"Have you considered David?" Daniel asked. "I've seen the way he looks at you. He's always loved you. He'd be my obvious choice."

"Your obvious choice? You think I'd be happy about you choosing my future spouse?" I asked.

"So you *are* planning on moving on after I am gone," he stated, forlorn.

"Daniel please don't put words into my mouth."

"I'm not. I just want you to consider the fact that I expect you to find happiness after I'm gone," he explained.

"Why must you be so controlling? What gives you the right to insist on my happiness after you're gone? Who says I will find happiness again after you're gone?" I asked.

"You're being melodramatic Temwani. There *will be* life

after I've gone. You *will have to* find happiness. With David. And when you do, I can be at peace knowing that he'll look after you and the kids. I don't want to see you unhappy and with some loser like the one you were with when I first met."

I held back words of anger.

"Whatever you've got to say, I can take it," he assured me. "I'm sorry for coming across as controlling, but you know me. I want to ensure you're well taken care of when I'm gone. This isn't easy for me. I don't want to imagine you with someone else. But if I had no choice but to picture you with someone else, that person would be David."

"I don't think you know him nearly as well as you think you do," I replied.

"I know him well enough to know that there isn't anything he wouldn't do for you and the kids. And that's what matters to me," he declared.

I shrugged in response. It was as though he were already gone. Planning my future without him. I admired his strength and resolve, but my heart felt weak and as though it would fail without him.

"You'll be fine," Daniel stated. "David'll see to it that you are."

"Your brother loves women a little too much," I suggested.

He gave me a sly smile. "I can assure you he's only ever had eyes for one woman, and that's you. You of all people should know that." After a slight pause he added, "It is possible that he needs you more than I do at this stage. We have lived. We have loved. I'll be yours eternally. Life is for the living. He needs you. He'll need you more when I'm gone," he insisted.

I refused to accept his outlook. He impressed upon me that part of honouring his memory meant honouring his wishes.

"Daniel, neither one of us believes in polygamy. You won't share me now. Why share me after you're gone?"

"I won't be sharing you," he clarified. "My time here on earth will be done, and you'll be free to love someone else. I prefer that that someone else be him."

"This isn't fair," I said. "You're putting me in an impossible situation."

"I don't follow. The situation is clear. He'll be here, I won't," he stated.

I was crying now. "You feel you've got the right to micro manage my future. You think me being with David will solve everything. You think..."

"I don't just think. I know. I know David will love you and hold you the way that only I could. I know that in time *you will* learn to love him," Daniel stated. Wiping the tears off my cheeks, he beckoned, "Don't cry sugarpie, please don't cry. I need you to be at peace with my wishes. I need you to be at peace with the way I'm choosing to leave."

He tried to convince me that what he was asking for was not extraordinary. He cited a traditional Zambian custom that required the surviving brother of the deceased to take on the figure head role, and to adopt the surviving children.

"Daniel, that is not my tribal custom and neither is it yours," I argued.

"Yes, I know that, but that is what I want to happen and I do wish you would consider my wishes."

I rolled my eyes in response.

"Please take this seriously," he insisted. "I have nothing left to give you when I'm gone. I want you to be happy, and I want you to be taken care of. This is one way for me to ensure that it'll happen," he argued.

"Baby you're so sure that I'll find happiness with David. So sure. What if I don't want to move on to someone else after you? What if you're it for me? You *are* it for me," I declared.

"Please don't be so shortsighted," he cautioned.

"Don't patronize me Daniel," I replied. "This is another way of you controlling me."

"How am I patronizing you? How am I controlling you? I'm merely looking out for you. I care a lot about what'll happen to you and the babies when I'm gone."

"Daniel, I'm not a child. I can take care of myself and look out for myself," I replied.

"Of course you're not, and of course you can," he agreed. "These are my final wishes though. I hope you can at least attempt to honour them."

"I wish you'd stop with the guilt tripping. You weren't thinking of me when you went and did up that Do Not Resuscitate order," I reminded him.

"I am *always* thinking about you, Temwani, *especially* when you think I'm not. You misunderstood my intentions behind the DNR order. When I'm on my way out, I'll just be a shadow of who I was. I don't want you to feel obligated when it comes to me. I don't want you to feel you have no choice but to care for me," he explained.

"When it's my time to go, I want you to let me go," he said.

As painful as it was to hear this, I had to respect his wishes.

The chemo was starting to take its toll. Daniel remained in bed for the most part of the day, too sick to get around.

Johnny was a great help, despite his ongoing issues with Michaela and the uncertainty of knowing where he was at any given time. "I might not be much use to anyone at the moment, but I promise to be of use to you and him. Anything you need done, I'm your man. You've been there for me, it's time I repaid the favour," Johnny stated.

He was there for me as promised. When David was not here, he was. When I stayed up late, crying over Daniel as he lay in bed, too zoned out on medication to move, too sick to do anything other than rest, he stayed up with me.

In moments of lucidity when Daniel would regain vigour, Johnny was there, infusing him with energy and excitement over discussing muscle cars, music and the latest crime drama.

He was there. He was there in ways that David could not be for Daniel.

When Daniel got sicker, while David helped care for the kids when not at work, Johnny was there.

David didn't hesitate to make his feelings about Johnny known. "I hope you know what you're doing," he asked of Daniel one afternoon as he did a quick check up on him.

"I don't understand," Daniel stated.

"With Johnny. I hope you know what you're doing," he said again. "All these medications, unlimited access to oxycodone..."

Daniel rolled his eyes in response. "I know what you're alluding to, but I'm not concerned."

I witheld my comment in the matter. Johnny and David were at odds with each other, most of the time. David's comment was not surprising.

Johnny who'd overheard David's comment got annoyed. "I have feelings and you're hurting them real bad right now. I am more than just an addict you know. I have done things I'm not proud of, but who hasn't? I'm a work in progress.

Aren't we all? I'm trying to do my best. My bestie's dying. I'm doing everything I can to help out. I'm doing everything I can to support them two - they've been there for me when no one else was. So don't you come up in here judging me and trying to keep me from helping out. You've got no right."

David cleared his throat before announcing, "Johnny, I know you. Given half a chance I'm sure you'd pinch Daniel's drugs. We can't take that risk."

"He stays," Daniel insisted.

David turned to look me in the eye and searched my face for an answer. "He stays," I echoed. "I need him here."

"Alright," David said, clearly unhappy. "Don't say I didn't warn you."

Johnny scowled in response to David's statement and stepped out onto the veranda for a cigarette.

"Johnny's a responsible addict," Daniel said casually, adding fuel to the flame.

"You're kidding me right?" David stated, alarmed. "Clearly you're not thinking straight at the moment. I don't want him anywhere near the babies."

"Newsflash baby brother. The babies are mine, and I feel perfectly fine with Johnny being around them," he said.

"Okay," David said in reply. "You're enabling him. A high-functioning addict is still an addict. Stop glorifying his behaviour and stop enabling him."

"No one's glorifying anyone's behaviour. Johnny is Johnny."

"What kind of a friend are you, Daniel! If you wanted what's best for him, you'd hear me and heed my advice." Turning to me, David stated, "I hope you don't agree with him."

"I agree with you both, to a point," I replied. "Johnny's only human. He's doing the best he can. I don't feel he'll do anything to harm any of us intentionally. I also trust when he says he won't use around me and the kids."

"You trust him?" David asked as Johnny walked back into the room with new vigour.

"I've been in the next room for half an hour, and I've come back and you're still at it. Talkin' about me. Can you Adam and Eve it?"

David frowned slightly before Daniel thew in, "English mate. Speak English."

"I say we chew the fat about whatever issues you got with me," Johnny challenged. "Right here and right now."

"I have no issues with you mate," Daniel confirmed. "Neither does trouble and strife here," he added, referring to me. I rolled my eyes at the attempt at cockney slang.

Johnny laughed in jest. "I see we speak the same language!" he exclaimed. Turning to David, he asked, "So, Davey D. What's it gonna be?"

"I'll reserve my judgement and hold my peace for now," David said.

"Getting that stick out of your arse is what you need to do," Johnny suggested.

"Be nice Johnny. Be nice," Daniel said.

"I'm not in the mood for niceties at the moment, especially not where haters are involved," Johnny replied.

"You know, you never apologised for stealing my prescription pads and for forging my signature on those oxy scripts you did out," David stated.

Johnny shrugged. "I tried to call you, but you refused to take my calls."

"It figures," David said. "You nearly ruined my career."

"Water under the bridge?" Johnny offered.

"That remains to be seen," David said sceptically.

"Okay, guys, lighten up," Daniel intervened. "You both need to make nice. We need the both of you here. Just maybe not at the same time."

David nodded in agreement, while Johnny arched a brow and stated, "This is where you leave, Davey D.?"

"I'll be around," David said, turning to go. He gave Johnny the once over before muttering under his breath at Daniel, "Don't say I didn't warn ya'."

"You're gonna have to get along. Both now, and when I'm gone," Daniel insisted. "I want you both to be a permanent fixture in this here woman's life," he said.

"I hear you," Johnny and David said in unison.

I knew they'd both be there for me in spite of their differences. *When I'm gone*, those words echoed in my ears. I felt deep sadness inside when I thought of the fact that Daniel would soon be gone.

"I'm still here," Daniel reminded me, squeezing my hand.

Johnny folded his arms and rested his head on the kitchen bench top. He was exhausted.

"Go to bed," I suggested.

"I'll be fine," he told me. "I'll stay up with you a while longer."

"Go to sleep Johnny. Your eyes are hanging out of your head. Get some rest while you can."

He sat up abruptly, filled with energy. "Thank goodness you told me that, I better keep these eyes in my head. Almost lost them."

I laughed a little too loudly and Josiah, sleeping comfortably in the sling, grimaced in his sleep.

Johnny laughed sleepily at his own joke before getting up to go. "Goodnight," he said, planting a kiss on my forehead. "Sing out if you need me."

I did. That night, Daniel woke up trembling, feverish. Trying not to wake the babies, he tried not to yell. "I can't see. I can't see!" he cried.

"What can't you see?" Johnny asked. "Can you see me in front of you? What am I wearing? What colour's my shirt?"

After a moment of hesitation Daniel replied, "What're you doing wearing my Kiss t-shirt!"

"Didn't get round to doin' me laundry yet," was Johnny's reply.

"Not the Kiss t-shirts mate!" Daniel exclaimed.

"Okay, so you *can* see," Johnny acknowledged.

"It's all a little blurry," Daniel said, calmer than he was moments ago.

I breathed a sigh of relief, but silent tears ran down my face at the thought of him losing his vision.

"Probably a side effect of the drugs you're on. I remember the doc saying it might happen," Johnny said. "We'll get David to have a look in, and see whether Doctor Josefine and Doctor Smith can come by tomorrow.

Daniel sighed and shook his head in disagreement. "I can't do this. I can't not be able to see anymore. I can't," he sobbed. I pulled him into my arms. He'd lost so much weight I was afraid to hug him too tightly for fear I'd hurt him.

Johnny remained by Daniel's side, his face not showing his fear and sadness though I knew he was breaking up inside. "You're still here, mate. You're still here. The meds have

436

shown promise. Despite the side effects they may make you better. I'm sorry we can't do or say anything else to make this better."

Wiping tears off his face, Daniel acknowledged his fear of dying. "I'm terrified of dying. I'm terrified of what kind of future I'll leave behind for Teme and the kids."

"Don't be," Johnny said. "David's as good as they come. I'm here. As long as I've got life in me, I'll be here for your wife and kids. Your family will be well looked after."

"Yes, but financially..." Daniel started.

"We'll build our own law practice, Teme and I. Keep Craig at bay. With David, as long as he keeps on keepin' on, he's set for life. Your family will be set for life."

Daniel nodded in reply. Adalia and Josiah cooed over the monitor and I got up and out of bed to check on them. As I did so, I heard the front door unlock. David was back.

I planted a kiss on Daniel's temple and left him with Johnny.

I flipped on the corridor light, startling David slightly. "You're back earlier than planned?"

"Rescheduled the surgery to tomorrow. A bit of a hold on the dental prosthetics," he explained, slipping off his shoes then hanging his coat up on the rack. I took his lunchbox from him.

"Everything okay?" he asked. "What's happened."

"Daniel's in a bit of pain. He's also having trouble seeing," I told him, nearly in tears.

He gave me a quick embrace before heading straight for the master bedroom with his medical bag.

Daniel was asleep, and Johnny sat at the edge of the bed. That he was distraught was apparent.

"Get some rest, buddy," David advised, making his way over to Daniel. He'd brought his stethoscope in with him.

"I'll be alright," Johnny replied.

"Get some rest," David repeated. "While you can."

Johnny headed his advice, opting to sleep on the settee in the corner of the room instead of in the guest room.

David snuck me a strange look before putting his stethoscope on and checking Daniel's heart rate then blood pressure. Daniel opened his eyes for long enough to let David do his observations.

"Blood pressure's on the low side," David acknowledged. "He's had some pain relief?"

"He has," I replied.

"He needs to be in a hospital," David said under his breath.

"He doesn't want that," I argued.

"He doesn't need that," Johnny stated. "It's tough enough as it is, him going in for chemo treatments and all."

"I appreciate what you're tryin' to do here but trust me. He'll be better off in a hospital," David insisted.

"I may as well give up on life if I'm to resign myself to life in a hospital," Daniel replied.

David paused for a moment before announcing, "I'll arrange for in-home care, then."

"We can't afford that," Daniel said.

"*I can,*" was David's response. Before Daniel had a chance to argue with him, he stood up and left the room.

Daniel swung his feet over the edge of the bed and attempted to get up but failed. He got up too quickly and Johnny hurriedly braced him before he fell over.

"Where to mate?" Johnny asked.

"David needs to know that I don't want to invest in anything that will merely prolong me being here without an improvement in quality of life. I don't want him wasting his money on me," he explained.

"I hope you're not back onto that Do Not Resuscitate stuff," I told him. "I thought we had an agreement?"

"Sugarpie you know as well as I do that we can't afford more aggressive treatment so I've made the decision to opt for hospice care. Here at home. If my health is to worsen, I just want you to do what you can to make me feel comfortable. No trips to the emergency ward. Do not resuscitate means do not resuscitate."

"This isn't fair Daniel," I said, my heart racing. "David's doing all he can to make that experimental treatment possible. Please don't let go of life now. We need you to do everything you can to get better."

"You need to let me go," he said callously. "Life's for the living, and the way I'm living now, I'm as good as dead."

Johnny stood up abruptly and walked away from us, pacing near the bedroom's bay windows. He was distraught and in tears, as was I.

Daniel's painful words struck me hard. I found myself without words to say in response. He had gotten better for a time, but his health had declined seemingly overnight.

"This is not how I want to leave you and the babies," Daniel said, squeezing my hand.

I'd wished for many things but in that moment I wished I could've breathed new life into him. That his pain be ended and that his life would begin again.

"Temwani," David called out from the room adjacent, interrupting the moment I had with Daniel. "I need you to help me sort out something," he called out.

"I'll be back," I told Daniel, reluctant to leave his side. Johnny returned to Daniel's side.

David was vigorously tapping away at the computer's keyboard when I joined him. "I'm putting my house in Maryborough on the market," he announced. "I reckon it'll sell in no time. The money we make on the sale will help fund any and all treatments required by Daniel," he said as he typed away. "I need you to look over the contract of sale. I've got a template, I just need you to give it a quick squizz before I send it back to the agent for the buyer."

My heart sank as I thought of his beautiful cottage in Maryborough. The freshly laid cypress boards, the beautiful cornices and decorative ceilings. He was prepared to sell it all to pay for a course of experimental treatment that might not even work. If he needed help looking it over before sending it to the buyer's agent, it meant he'd already commenced the process. I'd misjudged him. He was prepared to do everything he could to help Daniel.

When Daniel woke the next morning, he made a request regarding Johnny. "Whatever you do, please look out for Johnny. He's the baby brother I always wanted and overall he's an awesome friend. As for Michaela, let's hope he leaves her. For good. She doesn't deserve him and he'd be better off without her."

I nodded, agreeing with Daniel's feeling in principle, though neither one of them was innocent. Johnny's behaviour and Michaela's reaction to that behaviour was largely to blame for the friction and drama in their lives. Siding with Johnny was fair enough but he needed help. Desperately.

"I know what you're going to say. Give him a chance. If he had a chance to live a different life, one away from her, he'd be a different man."

"I hear you baby, but he does need help, and it's got to come from him, and him only," I reminded him.

"True that," he replied. "No harm in trying to help him make that change."

I acknowledged his request with a nod.

"Please," he said again.

"I'll look out for him," I promised.

Daniel was violently sick that evening, and we put it down to the new course of medications he was on.

Johnny and Sadie tended to the babies, while I stayed up with Daniel. David was to come by later, as he had been doing over the past few weeks.

"I can't do this," Daniel complained. "I'm not getting any better," he said.

"Sometimes it has to get worse before it gets better," I told him.

"I'm embarrassed to have you see me like this," he told me.

"Baby, don't be," I said, planting kisses on his forehead which felt hot.

"No more doctors," he protested. "Please," he begged. "No more doctors."

I drenched a face cloth in a bowl of cool water, wrung it, and applied it to his forehead. He closed his eyes and rested momentarily. I thought to call David and to see whether his medications could be adjusted or changed.

"No more doctors," he said again, barely above a whisper.

"Okay," I told him, tears I could no longer contain running down my face.

"I don't want to live like this," he added. "No more doctors."

I fell asleep and woke to the surprise of Daniel holding me in his arms. He'd fixed himself up to a seated position and in that moment looked and sounded better. "I promised to carry you, to take care of you, and to be there for you, but I'm failing," he stated.

"Daniel, none of that matters now, none of that matters. You've been there for me when I needed you."

"That's a lie and you know it," he said, suddenly imbued with energy. "I admit I was an ass for the most part, but I hope you know I've always loved you. If I had my way, I'd do anything to ensure I'd be here for you. I don't have my way. I haven't got the means to ensure I'll be here for you. This is it," he said.

"I'm not giving up hope on you getting through this," I told him, "I'm not..."

"I'm accepting that this is my fate," he replied.

The digital alarm on my phone vibrated lightly. He was due to take some pain relief in the form of pills, his corticos-teroids and anti-seizure medication.

"I've taken the pain relief," he stated. "I'm not taking the other meds," he advised.

"Daniel, you can't just stop..."

"I can," he told me. "This isn't living," he said. "Not for me, and not for you. I feel this is the end."

"Those pills you don't want to take will keep you alive," I told him.

"This isn't living, and I don't feel alive," he stated point blankly, holding me close to him, preventing me from getting away, for I was only getting away to get him those pills. "Look, I'm not in pain," he stated. "Not right now anyway," he said. "I won't be in pain when I let go," he announced. "Not sure how long this'll last, but I want to stay up with you. I want to hold you, thank you for everything you've been to me in the short time we've had together." He held me tightly, head nuzzled against mine.

I couldn't hold back tears.

"This is how I want it to end," he said. "No more doctors. Me, you, the babies. If I haven't got the rest of my life ahead of me with you, this is how I wish for you to remember me."

22

FOREVER LOST

It was more of the same the next morning as Daniel continued to refuse to take his medication.

"Teme, I need your permission to let go. I don't think I can do this anymore. I can't take you seeing me like this. I can feel my body getting weaker and weaker. I need your permission to leave," he said. "Everything within me aches."

"I've organized to be with you 24/7," I told him. "Please just rest. I know you want to do more, but you can't. Please just rest. The more you rest, the better you'll feel..."

"I'm afraid of sleeping," he confessed. "I'm afraid that if I sleep, I won't wake up. I want to go when I'm ready, but I feel I won't be when I do."

I ached for him.

"I...," he started, then trailed off. He reached for the sick bag on the side table and held it over his mouth, in anticipation of getting sick. He wasn't sick. "I can leave knowing he'll be here to look after you and the kids. I can leave knowing I will see you all again one fine day."

That morning, he requested that we organise travel to South Texas.

We took our final trip together to South Texas. Loaded the houseboat up and packed enough supplies to last us a week. Something within me told me this was where he wanted it to end, and that this was where it would end.

Daniel insisted on David coming with us, if only to man the boat, as he was too unwell to do so. I instinctively knew it was another way for him to bring us together. His treating doctor had offered to come as well.

"This is how I want to remember us," Daniel said. "I'll never forget the first time I took you out on this here boat, and you were so afraid of love. So afraid of giving," he recalled. "I'm glad I was able to convince you to let go of the past, and to love again. To give again."

Our first evening on the boat was our last. We slept, the babies in between both of us. Adalia curled up to Daniel as she usually did in sleep, while Josiah slept soundly nuzzled up against my bosom.

"Tasmania," he said, barely above a whisper. "I want my heart to remain here in Texas. I want my body cremated and my ashes scattered in Tasmania."

It felt as though my heart had stopped. I couldn't bear to hear him talk about his death as though it were just a matter of course. My husband, the brilliant defence lawyer and investigator that he was, the amazing father that he was, reducing his death to a mere formality that needed to be planned.

"Let's not talk about that," I begged.

"Please," he said, "Please promise me you'll honour my wishes."

"Daniel..."

"Please, if at all possible..." he insisted.

"Okay," I said reluctantly.

"Thank you. I love you so much sugarpie," he said, squeezing my hand before drifting into sleep. I watched him sleep, and watched his chest rise and fall as he breathed in and out. I watched him sleep, fearing I would fall into a deep slumber and miss his last breath. I thought of all the moments we'd shared, all the moments we'd laughed together, all the moments we'd cried together. All the joy he'd brought me. I remembered how beautiful he looked to me the day we married, and how his warm and generous heart had found space to love me the night we first met all those years ago when things in my life were falling to pieces. I thought of all the tears I'd shed over him, and the empty life I'd have to lead alone.

Adalia woke me up from sleep, whimpering and groping for Daniel but when I reached out to him and reached out for him, he was gone. He'd taken his last breath, and in that moment, he'd left us. I cried a million tears.

I never would have imagined we would end up here. The day after he died, a bouquet of sweet pea flowers was delivered to me. A handwritten note stated:

Adieu my love. Thank you for the moments we shared, the beautiful babies we made and the life we led. You filled my life with so much bliss. Find happiness when I'm gone. Adieu.

David helped with the funeral arrangements. The night before, we sat together, beside ourselves. It seemed there was so much to do in such little time. I knew Daniel would've wanted to keep it simple. He hated frills and pomposity.

"I need to say something that'll honour him tomorrow, I just don't know where to start. I didn't do a very good job of honouring him while he was alive," he admitted, bowing his head and clearing his throat. "Now he's gone, I hope he knew how much I admired him and how much I looked up to him," he said, pressing his eyelids shut with his thumb and middle finger, as though that would prevent tears from falling. It didn't. "I..." he started, before breaking off in tears.

I squeezed his shoulder gently, imploring him to lean into me. I cried with him, not having any words of comfort to offer. For there was no comfort to be had in the pain of losing Daniel. No comfort to be had in the fact that he was gone.

Sitting on the sofa that I'd shared with Daniel in the years, months and days gone past, I rested my head on David's shoulder, and he wrapped his arms around me. We sat for moments, pondering the day ahead and the days that were to come, without Daniel, in silence. The babies were asleep. They were much too young to realise their world had changed overnight, though I had an inkling that Adalia was very much aware that Daniel was gone. She proved my point true when she woke up crying yet again. Rocking her back and forth, she refused to settle in my arms.

That night, David offered to settle her, and after very little protest in his arms, she went back to sleep. When he attempted to put her back in her cot, she protested dramatically. He decided to stay up with her curled up in fetal pose, on his chest.

"She can sense your sadness," he said. "Our sadness," he corrected. "Get some sleep, he urged. "I'll watch over you."

Too tired to argue, I listened to him and did as he'd suggested.

447

"I'll bring them both to you when they're ready for a feed," he said. "Try to get some rest," he insisted. Afraid for a moment that he'd fall asleep as well, he read my mind and stated, "I won't fall asleep. I'll put her back in bed the moment she's sleeping deeply."

I took a long lingering shower before bed and cried inconsolably for Daniel. I had prayed and pleaded with God to give me more time with him, which He did, but he was gone now. Having Daniel in my life forever was not in His plans. The last conversation I'd had with Daniel, he had urged me to find comfort in the fact that we'd known each other at all. The lyrics of George Michael's *A Different Corner* came into my mind. *Had things not happened the way they did that fateful night we never would have met.*

I'd loved George Michael for years. Without the promise of another song, another melody, my heart was crushed when he'd passed away. I'd loved Daniel for a time that felt like an eternity but not long enough. Without the promise of another kiss, another smile, another tomorrow, my heart felt it would die.

David rapped lightly on the the bathroom door. I'd been in the shower for ages, and the skin on my fingers and toes was beyond crinkly. I turned off the tap and reached for my towel on the rack, before stepping out onto the bath mat.

"You okay in there?" he asked, his voice deep, low and reassuring.

"Yes," I replied, opening the door, towel wrapped tightly around me. He was leaning on the opposite wall, Adalia now in the sling around his chest. I peeked into the sling. She rested in fetal pose, hands under her chin, her left cheek flush against David's chest. Unexpectedly, David said, "She knows he's gone." He flinched slightly at his own words. "She's accepting me as a substitute, which is good," he added, his voice trembling slightly and trailing off. "He's left some big shoes to fill," he added.

I felt the tears fall down my face, hot, and unabated. He reached out to me, squeezed my shoulder lightly then hugged me sideways, taking care not to wake Adalia. "How about I make up some chamomile tea for you, and put on some music for a time? Might help you sleep."

In between tears, I nodded to the affirmative. Planting a kiss on my forehead, he paused and uttered some words of reassurance. "We *will* get through this."

I made my way to the bedroom and turned on my Spotify playlist. George Michael's silken voice soothed me in my pain.

Getting through Daniel's funeral was going to be tough.

I fell to my knees when the casket was lowered into the ground. I felt my soul go with Daniel. David knelt down with me, wrapping his arms around me and comforting me. "Come now. I'll take you home," he said in a firm, reassuring voice. I saw tears rolling down his face despite the strength in his embrace. I had lost my husband, while he had lost his brother, and was trying to be strong for us all.

As we walked to the car, I noticed Johnny leaning against a tree. Grief weighed heavily on him. He and Daniel had gotten very close in the last year. I knew it would be very difficult for him to get on with life without Daniel being there. They were best mates, and had been like brothers should be. David nodded in acknowledgement to him. "You alright mate?" he asked.

"Alright's not anything I am at the moment, but I'll get there," Johnny said, before leaning into me for a hug. "Sorry he had to leave us so soon," he said, bringing me to tears. "Don't worry about me, I'll get through this somehow."

Losing Daniel hurt more than I thought it would. Though we had grown apart just before the twins were born, after his diagnosis, I learned of his love for me which was undying and whole. Pleasure and pain.

Going home without Daniel hurt equally as much as losing him. Without him, the home we'd shared together felt cold and empty. But there were memories of Daniel in every room, and I couldn't be anywhere else.

Johnny felt differently. "I'm heading back to the UK for a bit, need to clear my head a little...I know Daniel would've wanted me to stay on to help you manage the firm, but I'm just not sure I can do anything competently around there with him being gone. Not to mention, with Craig being the way he is."

I also wanted to carry on Daniel's legacy at the firm, but I too felt incapable of anything meaningful now he was gone.

"Right, guys," David said, stepping in, his voice unwavering. "I'm sure Daniel would've wanted you both to carry on the legacy. Take the time that you need off, but come back once that's done," he advised. "Remember you're doing this for Adalia and Josiah as well."

"Just a bit of pressure there, David, right?" Johnny noted.

"Don't mean for it to come across that way, but it is the truth. Apart from Craig, he left you both in control for a reason. Honouring his wishes is the best way to keep his legacy alive," he mentioned.

"We'll find a way to make it happen, won't we Teme," Johnny stated.

I nodded in response.

"I gather you're going to Tasmania then?" Johnny asked.

"Yep, just need to do a few things for Daniel," David answered.

"I'd come, but you know how I feel about that place," Johnny stated. "I'm not ready to confront my past just yet," he said cryptically.

David nodded in reply. "I'm not ready to do that either, but this is about honouring Daniel's wishes," he said. In addition to scattering his ashes over the Tasman sea, Daniel had wanted David to formally adopt our children and for them to take his name.

Overwhelmed with grief, I stood against the wind and let the salty water from the ocean spray merge with my tears. Daniel, the love of my life, was gone. David and I released Daniel's ashes over the edge of the ship's bow, and that was it. Daniel was gone.

As my heart heaved with sadness, David stood there with me. An ever present constant in my moment of need.

He stood there with me, held me and said nothing, but his silence and presence spoke volumes.

When dawn arose I gazed at the horizon. Tasmania beckoned me to start again, to find purpose anew, to find happiness, but without Daniel I felt lost. Tasmania called but I couldn't stay. Not now. Staying in Tasmania meant leaving Texas. Something I couldn't do just yet. For in Texas, it felt as though Daniel were not yet gone, and there was unfinished business to tend to. The life we had led, the love we had shared, the house we had lived in were all in Texas. I couldn't leave now.

A day in, and I refused to stay in Tasmania much longer. As beautiful as it was, I asked David to make arrangements for us to return immediately to Texas. The ship docked at the port of Devonport, and we drove to the airport hotel, in readiness for the flight leaving the next morning. All the paperwork regarding the kids would have to wait, David would deal with it in his own time.

Though I'd completely thrown my all into loving and cherishing Daniel in his last days on earth, I felt love for David. His love was all pleasure. There was not a moment I could recall where he had set out to hurt me. Every moment was tender – he loved with his all, holding nothing back, love unabashed, love without bounds. We weren't an item, yet he acted as though we were.

As time went on, I feared that his love for me would wane. However as time went on, his love for me grew, and my fondness for him changed my outlook. Perhaps I could grow to love him deeply one day, as Daniel had so wanted. Perhaps losing Daniel had to happen, in order for me to be with David.

Not wanting to move on so quickly after Daniel, I avoided moments alone with David for fear that he would sense I was falling for him.

He cornered me one morning in the kitchen. Hands on my shoulders, he asked, "How are you keeping?"

"I'm..." I started, but found no words to express how I felt.

"I hear you," he replied nevertheless. "You know how I feel about you," he added. "I want you to be free with me. I *will* be here for you, whether you want to be with me or not.

Daniel's wishes aside, I need you to take as long as you need to grieve."

"It feels like I'll be grieving for a lifetime," I said.

He drew me in close for an embrace. "I know how much you loved him. I know how much you still love him. I just didn't realise how much he loved you in the end. I don't know if I could have done what he did, openly ask for another man, yours truly, to take care of you and the kids. I'll never be him – I'll always be the man who's deeply in love with you – the man who's always loved you, and always will love you. But right now, I just need you to be – do whatever it takes to just be. The kids need you, I need you," he said, warming my heart.

I took his advice, but I grieved deeply, seeing Daniel in dreams, most nights. At first I didn't sleep. I couldn't sleep. So much to do, so much to get used to, now that I was alone. Later, I couldn't wait to sleep. I reassured myself with the possibility that I might see him in dreams.

David was a constant, helping where he could. I was ever thankful for the help offered by him. The twins were used to having him around, making the transition a little easier. Still, there were the moments when they would cry out at night, and Daniel was not there. David did what he could. He helped rock the babies back to sleep, but Daniel was not there. This reality hurt me deeply, and it was at these moments that I felt alone in my grief.

I saved my tears for the moments I was alone. In the shower. In the rain. In bed. I cried myself to sleep. I never imagined that losing Daniel would result in such a feeling of void in my life.

I was very grateful for David being around. Yet every so

often, in the early morning light, when I caught a glimpse of him out my window, heading out for his morning jog, I would mistake him for Daniel for a split moment. That split moment would be enough to send my whole day into disarray. *Would I ever be over Daniel?* I didn't want to forget him. I couldn't forget him, and saw him everywhere he was not. *Would I ever smile again? Would I ever find happiness again?* He had repeatedly urged me to find happiness when he was still alive.

Sensing my hesitance with him, eventually David largely kept his distance emotionally, said very little, and kept his usual banter and laughter at bay. I could see he was grieving in his own way. I felt for him. I'd lost my husband, my better half, my forever lover. He'd lost his brother, and despite the somewhat acrimonious relationship history between them, he seemed to be struggling with the loss.

He cooked up a storm most nights. I ate what I could.

"Please eat a bit more than you're currently eating," he urged one night. "Not just for yourself, but for them. Remember that you're feeding them too," he said, reminding me of the fact that I was breastfeeding and needed to ensure adequate nutrient intake.

A flower and handwritten note arrived every week without fail. Daniel had arranged 52 different floral arrangements, and had completed 52 different notes to accompany the flowers. Every Friday was a new sunrise for me, and I eagerly awaited each floral arrangement and each note.

Two months passed, and the twins were fully on solids. David went to great lengths to ensure all they ate was home-made and not store bought for convenience. Daniel would have been pleased.

When not helping out, David spent time at the dental clinic and hospital. He managed three days a week, the other two days were supervisory in nature, which gave him time with me and the kids. I managed a file here and there – Craig was a big part in ensuring my legal career stayed on track despite the time off.

Jolène's decision to contest Daniel's will hit me like a slap in the face. That she was not going to succeed was irrelevant. I was more hurt at the fact that she refused to see that his love for me had been real.

Daniel's Last Will and Testament was unambiguous and unequivocal. "To my wife and the love of my life, apart from the individual bequests I have made to others, I give her one hundred percent of my estate."

Nowhere in the Will was there any mention of Jolène. Though Daniel hadn't openly expressed his displeasure over her role in ordering that David be killed at birth, he had clearly expressed it in death. She was not to benefit in any way from anything he had. His Will made specific reference to the children, and mentioned his intention that she not have a role in the children's lives.

The news that Jolène was persisting on contesting the Will had me a little shocked, though not worried about the outcome. The shock came from the reel of emotions I felt at having to recall the animosity between myself and her in Daniel's last days, and the feeling that the children were not acceptable to her.

Craig allayed my fears, and brought out the big guns so to speak. Daniel had done a video in which he read out the terms of his Will. Such was the nature of the indisputable evidence that we had against Jolène.

"I heard about Jolène," David stated, later on that day. "You alright?"

"I'm fine," I replied. "I'll be fine."

"She's got the nerve," David stated, angrily.

Grief. A single word to surmise a myriad of emotions and memories. Some days the memories evoked laughter. When he was with us, Daniel was always casting light on darkness, shining rays with such abandon on everyone's fragmented lives. He was gone now.

Some days the memory of him stirred up ambition. He was the embodiment of *carpe diem*. Other days, hearing John Legend on the radio caused pause. There was no true love story without music and the rise and fall in tempo he had once said. No true love story without some pain. Yet other days, a fleeting memory of the times we shared over the years caused a pain unequalled, one that failed to subside, unifying and familiar to all of us who knew him. Gone too soon. Never should have gone.

He lived well, gave well, and loved well. We all missed him well.

The flowers that Daniel had arranged every week were eagerly anticipated week after week. The arrival of his flowers, and the mere anticipation of reading each note ignited passion and zeal for life within me. He was gone, but it was as though we were loving and living together in an alternate plane.

The last flower, last week of the year came with a note that saddened me deeply:

Sugarpie,

I will always love you. I know you'll always have the memory of us on your mind, but I want you to find happiness now. Please do not mourn me any longer. Find happiness my love. This'll be my last flower to you, my last love letter to you. You were my all, and you will always be my love.

Always,
Daniel.

Though I knew it would be my last letter from him, I yearned for more. I was heartbroken the weeks nothing came. Daniel had left a big void in my life, seemingly incapable of being filled.

Eventually I took his advice, and I turned to David, who despite his feelings for me was my friend, my confidant and my eventual destiny. He was all too happy to find ways to fill the void.

To commence, he suggested that we start remembering Daniel in a different way. By looking into his past and piecing together as much information as we could, we could grow to know him more, and create a record of the past for the kids to look at in the years to come.

Every Friday evening, we sat down together and went through old photos of Daniel, school awards and books. Despite the friction experienced between he and Jolène in the end, Daniel was loved, and had been loved by her. She loved him as only a mother would love her child. Deeply.

As we went through Daniel's belongings, I felt a deep sadness for David who had had everything but the idyllic childhood. He tried to pretend it didn't matter, but I knew it did. I carried this intimate knowledge of David's pain with me, and resolved to be a part of making the difference to him one day.

23

THE WAKE

I stood on the sidelines and scored the room for familiar faces. There weren't any. Not yet anyway. Shania had promised to join me but backed out at the last minute. *Some friend she'd turned out to be.* Though it's not as though I'd been there for her. She and Jonah had their forever after, Daniel and I didn't. I tried to be a friend, but I kept my distance. Since Daniel had gone, I hadn't felt like doing much at all.

I really didn't want to be there, but had agreed to as the function was in memory of Daniel. The people that had failed to honour him when he was alive had chosen to honour him in death, through the creation of a foundation in his name, to raise awareness of brain disease and ailments of the mind in the legal profession.

The waiter offered me a spritzer, which I accepted. I made my way to the balcony, where a few of the other waiters and kitchen hands had gathered. One of the waiters recognized me. "Teme!!!"

"Long time, me love you long time even still!" he said.

I chuckled in response, laughter only lasting for a moment.

Malik called out, "Hey Teme." I acknowledged him with a nod. It was a few moments later before he approached. Greeting me with a kiss on the cheek he asked, "How've you been?"

"I'd be lying if I said I was okay," I stated.

"I'm sure it's not easy," he said. "Daniel was a standup guy."

"So everyone here says, yet no one gave him the time of day when he was with us," I reminded him.

"Water under the bridge, ey? We're honoring him today," he replied.

"Better late than never, I suppose," I replied. The mood was stifled. Malik shifted uncomfortably, at a loss as to what to say.

A familiar figure approached. Craig.

"Why does this feel like a wake?" I asked.

"Maybe it is a wake of sorts," he replied. Despite the issues we'd had in the lead up to Daniel's death, his presence was reassuring.

He placed a hand on my shoulder and drew me in for a hug. "Anything I can do, let me know."

David turned up not long after. He looked handsome in his suit, but seemed uncomfortable, as though he wanted to take it off immediately.

He greeted me with a kiss on the cheek and an embrace.

"Is it just me, or does it feel like this is just a show to save face?" David asked.

"It's not just you. They didn't give him the time of day when he was alive, and probably feel terrible about that now that he's gone," I said. We stood there for moments in silence.

"Kids are okay today?" he asked.

"They're doing fine, though I hardly got any sleep. They were pretty restless last night," I told him.

"You know you can call on me anytime to help out, don't you?" he reminded me.

"I do."

"So why don't you?" he asked.

"I'm not trying to lead you on," I replied.

"Hm. Leading me on, how?" he asked.

"Giving you the idea that there's a chance for you and I when there isn't." I stated.

He wasn't convinced. "I'm not sure you believe that, now do you?" he asked. "There's nothing to stop us being together now, but ourselves."

I looked at him squarely. He was the splitting image of Daniel, save for the scar on his face, and the more muscular tone. The look in his eyes was another difference. Where Daniel had looked at me with love and adoration, and of-tentimes criticism, David looked at me with lust, longing, yearning, and admiration. When he held me, I felt I would melt in his arms. He caught me staring, and I quickly averted my gaze from him.

"Can we not talk about this now?" I requested.

"Sure," he replied, all too willing to honour my request. "I hope it's a consolation to you that I'm here with you, and that I'm here for you," he stated.

"It is," I assured him.

"Hey Davey D!" someone exclaimed loudly from behind us. I turned to see a sharp dressed lanky built man in a grey suit. The platinum blond hair and blue eyes dancing with excitement were a dead giveaway. "Me love you long time mate!" *Johnny*. I almost didn't recognise him. It had been a while since we'd connected.

David laughed gregariously in response. "Hey Johnny," he responded, and they knocked fists.

"And who is this beautiful creature?" he asked. "Or should I be saying, *What is* this beautiful creature?"

I laughed heartily in response.

"Joker," David replied, laughing as well. "Of course you know Temwani, my late brother's wife."

"Your current or future squeeze, by the looks of it," Johnny stated, taking my hand. "Enchantée," he said in a strong cockney accent. "We have met before."

Of course we had, he and Daniel were best friends, and had spent many an afternoon burning down the back streets and stirring up dust in his '67 Pontiac. It had been a year since I'd seen him. Though he'd been in contact every so often from London, nearly a year of silence had gone between us after Daniel had left us.

David glared at him in response to his comment about me being his current or future squeeze. "We're good friends," he corrected.

"Yep, I buy that," Johnny replied. "For what it's worth, you look great together," he said, winking at me. "Daniel would have approved."

Quickly switching topic, David asked, "So where's your other half, Michaela?"

"That's a story and a half," he replied. "I'm here on my own."

"Hm..." David wondered aloud.

"Well, she thinks I'm using again," he explained.

"And are you?" David enquired.

462

"Well, I wasn't then, but I am now," he confessed. "She thinks I'm still using so I may as well use."

David shook his head. "That's no good, man..."

"Yeah, yeah," he said dismissively. "I don't need to hear your criticism."

"Well, if you let me finish, you'd see it was support," David explained.

Johnny stood there for a moment, considering what David had said, before saying, "You know, there's a really cool joint that's just opened up, thought we could all check it out later."

"Maybe," David said, less than enthusiastically.

"I'll be up for that," I offered.

"Good," Johnny stated.

I saw the displeasure in David's eyes, so suggested instead, "Maybe we could get together at my place after this?"

Johnny glanced quickly over from me to David then to me again. "Sounds like a plan. Whatever you'd like to do, I'm down. You are after all, the guest of honour here," Johnny reminded me. Glancing quickly at his watch, he muttered something about needing to disappear for a bit. Purposefully avoiding David's glaring gaze, he mentioned he'd be back, before heading off.

I used the moment he was gone to question David over his response. "Why are you being so judgmental, David?"

"Not judgmental," he argued. "I'm just worried for him, is all."

"At least show some support."

"I hope we're not going to regret having him over tonight," David said, warily. "Can I get you something else to drink?" he asked, changing topic.

"I'm fine," I replied.

"I knew you were fine as, the moment I met you. I called it first."

I threw my head back in laughter. "David! Back to your flirting again!"

He laughed with me before stating, "I want you to consider coming back to Australia with me. You don't have to do this on your own. I can take care of you and the kids."

"I don't need you to rescue me," I replied.

"No, I know you don't. I'm not rescuing you. I'm being here for you. I'm continuing to be here for you. Just wanting to make it official."

I sighed, pondering the thought. "It's not that easy. Visas, starting my career over in a whole new place..."

"Well if you agreed to be my wife, things wouldn't be that complicated," he suggested.

Wife. That was such a loaded word nowadays. Daniel had gone, but I was still *his* wife. Here stood David suggesting I move on and become his wife. While I had thought of David and I being together some day, I hadn't considered the prospect of us getting married. "You make it sound so easy. It isn't," I told him.

"It can be," he urged. "It could be an arranged marriage of sorts. I could get you and the kids to Aus, and you could grow to love me."

"If only it were that easy," I stated.

"Please give it some thought," he suggested.

"I can't move on after Daniel," I confessed. "I can't move on so easily."

"I didn't say it'd be easy," David explained. "I just...well I thought...," he started. "Never mind."

I stood there on the balcony, the cool breeze kissing my

464

cheeks. I trembled slightly, surprised at the cool weather in the middle of summer.

David noticed. He quickly took off his suit coat and slid it around my shoulders.

"All good?" he asked, pulling me in to him for comfort.

"I wish I could say it was," I stated, tears rolling down my face, unabated. "I feel so lost with Daniel being gone," I confessed. "I didn't realize how much I'd miss him until he was gone."

David wiped my tears with a handkerchief from his suit pocket. "I hear you," he stated. "You and me both."

We stood there for what seemed like an eternity. The lights over the city of Austin were beautiful.

"Come live with me in Australia. We can remember together, and I can help you forget your pain," he stated.

"You make it sound as though you have some remedy to heal my pain," I said.

"Perhaps I do," he said, leaning into me. He embraced me tightly, then planted a deep kiss on my lips.

I did not resist his advances. He kissed my lips fully and wholly, his passion apparent, sending chills through my body. I kissed him back, running a hand across the nape of his neck and through his auburn well tressed locks. He sighed in pleasure, chasing my tongue with his, then stopped mid kiss. "Maybe not the best place to be intimate," he stated, motioning towards the crowded room behind us, and through the glass doors.

I shrugged in response. He slid his hand around my waist, pulling me closer to him. It felt so good to be held, but in my heart of hearts I longed for Daniel still. Still, David was here with me, and there was no denying that it felt good to be held by him.

"I'm not expecting you to get over Daniel so easily," he admitted. "I'm asking you to be open to the possibility of giving us a go. This *has* been a long time coming, you know."

"I hear you, David." *Daniel would have wanted this anyhow*, I thought to myself.

"I'm glad you do," he said. "Daniel would have wanted this."

The hairs on the back of my neck stood up as he stated aloud what I'd thought.

"You know I want this," he added, tracing my lips with his finger. "I've wanted you for the longest time ever."

I imagined that if this was all about sex he would satisfy his longing and be done with me. I wasn't prepared to have that happen after Daniel. If I had to move on after Daniel, I had to be sure that it was for real, and not just for a time. It never seemed as though it was just about sex with David. He'd made that clear the first time we met, all those years ago, when we were young.

"I love you Temwani," he suddenly declared. "I adore you," he added. "I love everything about you."

"That's a tall order," I stated.

"How so?" he questioned.

"Well, I'm not the most lovable person. Look at how many years I've had you chasing after me."

He laughed in response. "Are you kidding? You're a dream. Have you heard Jill Scott's *He loves me?*"

I had.

"Well, I love *you* from top to bottom. I love every inch of the body that I have yet to explore. I love your mind, I love your spirit, I love your being. I love you."

I smiled in response.

"Of course, there are the things you love that drive me around the bend, like your love of mackerel and kippers, your love of all things Peter Sellers, Geoffrey Rush and George Michael."

"Hm, do I detect a hint of jealousy?" I asked.

"No, no, mama," he replied in jest. "Actually, truth is I'm jealous of anything that holds your attention. I've been longing for so many years for you to put your attention on me," he confessed.

Poking me gently, he stated, "Only you my dear could convince me that the jitterbug was a cool dance," he said, taking my hand and beckoning me to dance the jitterbug. He spun me around once, and after a few dance steps, I ended up in his arms again.

I smiled and laughed, forgetting my earlier sadness. "I love you too David," I whispered.

He squeezed me so tightly I thought I would burst.

"Our work here is done," Craig announced, slightly below a whisper, appearing seemingly out of nowhere. I wondered what he meant.

"I'll see you both in Australia," he stated, thumping a fist with David and embracing me briefly.

Johnny stood nearby, fidgeting with his phone. "Yes, score!" he exclaimed. He was playing a game. "So, I'm just about done socializing here. How about we leave now?" He seemed rather restless.

"I think we leave when the guest of honour decides to leave, ey?" David stated.

"Well, I'm starving, I could meet you at yours?" Johnny suggested.

"You're in no condition to drive, Johnny," David pointed out.

"Driving?" Johnny questioned. "I'm not driving. Haven't driven in months now," he replied.

I wondered why that was. *Something related to drugs or drink* I concluded. David kissed his teeth in annoyance. "You either come with us now, or not at all," he ordered.

"I think I'll take a taxi," Johnny replied somewhat apprehensively. "What's the address again darlin'?" he asked, turning to me.

I handed him one of my mommy cards. He turned it over, and laughed gregariously. "Love the pink elephant!" Turning to David, he stated, "We both know the proverbial pink elephant in the room is just waiting to get out!"

Irritated and impatient, David asked, "You heading off now?"

"Yep," Johnny replied quickly. "No need to get your panties in a twist," he said cheekily, eyeballing David.

"Whatever," David said under his breath, dismissively.

"See you soon darlin'," Johnny said, turning to me. With a quick peck on the cheek and a wave, he headed off.

Not a moment after he had walked away, David asked, "Is this all about him and what he needs now, or this about me? Are you trying to avoid me?"

"Avoid you how?" I asked, feigning non-comprehension.

"I've just asked you to start your life anew with me in Australia, you haven't given me an answer, and you're going out of your way to be hospitable to Johnny - even inviting him over," he explained. "What's the deal?"

"David, he looks like he's down on his luck. He's smiling and joking around, but I feel he's in a bad way. Besides, Daniel would have wanted this," I added. "You remember how close they were in the end. What do you have against him anyway – I thought you two grew up together?"

"Nothing I want to talk about right now," he replied, not doing a very good job of hiding his disdain for Johnny. "And yes, we did grow up together. But right now I'm just trying to keep you from harm."

"Oh?" I queried. *The same old excuse that Daniel used to use.*

"You wanted to say something?" he asked.

"No," I lied, a little unnerved that he could see through me to the point he almost heard me.

"Okay," he replied, unconvinced. "Look, we still have a moment or so before he gets to your place. How about we leave now that way we have some time together before he gets there?"

I smiled. "Sounds like a plan, though when are we not together these days?"

"True," he replied. "Though being with you now will be a whole lot different than it's been lately," he replied. "What with us being an official item now."

He was right, though I hoped we wouldn't lose our friendship, I found myself looking forward to exploring a relationship with him on another level. At the same time, I also found myself wondering whether moving on after Daniel would ever be possible.

"I'll drop you off, then head out, change and get a few things for the night," he mentioned.

When we got to the house, all was still. Sadie sat on the couch watching something on Netflix. I peeped into the twins' bedroom. They were both sound asleep.

"Thanks Sadie," I said, grateful she was in my life. The

kids adored her, and her presence was a constant to us all. She was there without judgment and without demand. She stood up, gathering her belongings.

"You can stay, or you can hang around for as long as you want to," I assured her.

"I'll leave at the end of this," she promised, motioning towards the movie which was on pause.

"Great," I replied. "I'll be in the study," I advised. "David will be coming back soon, so will Johnny."

"Johnny?" she asked, surprised. She hadn't seen him for as long as I had. "Alright, I'll let them know where you are."

David was over not long after. I heard him drop his overnight bag then hang his coat on the rack by the door. Shoes off, he sauntered into the reading room, where I sat on the lounge, gazing out at the moonlit sky. Daniel had loved looking at the stars, and this was one habit I was not able to break now he was gone.

"Hey David," I greeted him, sitting back from the telescope.

"Hey," he replied, making his way over to me on the lounge. "You know, at any given time, you could see shooting stars in the night sky, where I grew up," he recalled. "Not long after we met, I used to climb up on the roof and just lie there, looking up at the stars, wondering where you were." Nostalgically, he added, "The moment I heard you were gone, I resolved to find you. I didn't know if I could, but I resolved to try," he remembered. "I dreamed of the day we would both look up at the night sky and know we were finally together again. And here we are," he said, his words warming my heart.

470

I was distracted by some noise outside. Equally alarmed, David stood up to investigate. "Probably Johnny," he predicted. He was right. Johnny appeared out of the darkness and by the study's sliding door.

"Anything to eat?" Johnny said a little too loudly.

"I can do up an omelette or eggs benedict?" I offered.

"Sounds awesome," he replied. "I did get something to eat, but that was ages ago."

"You mean, an hour ago, right?" David's continued displeasure at Johnny's presence was unnerving and quite apparent.

"Yep, Doctor Cranky Pants," Johnny replied to David's displeasure, causing him to frown. I held back laughter.

Johnny said he'd be off to the toilet so left us momentarily. I confronted David immediately.

"David, what's your deal!"

"I don't want to be the bearer of bad news but once an addict, always an addict," he stated.

I cut him off. "Pretty unfair, don't you think?"

"He's clearly high," he replied.

"That may be the case, but don't you feel he needs our help?"

"He needs help, that's for sure," he replied. "I don't think it's something you or I should be getting into."

"Isn't he a good friend?"

David shrugged. "I'm not prepared to deal with the drama he brings again," he stated abruptly.

I waited for him to elaborate on what he meant, but he didn't.

"I bet he's using in the toilet," he predicted. Without a further thought, he headed towards the bathroom.

Curious as to whether he was right, I followed after him.

He was right. Johnny sat on the floor, head leaning back onto the toilet rim. A used needle lay strewn on the floor, the wall slightly blood stained. His eyes were closed, he looked peaceful. "What the heck, Johnny," David chastised him. "Johnny!" he called out. Johnny stirred slightly but didn't open his eyes. "Johnny!" David said even louder. I hoped he wouldn't wake up the children.

Johnny's eyes remained closed. David got down on his knees, carefully moved the needle out of the way and slapped Johnny on the left cheek, hard.

"Fuck!" Johnny exclaimed, groggily.

"Get up," David ordered. "You're not doing this here."

Johnny attempted to rise to his feet but failed. He banged his head on the sink and David braced his fall.

David tried reasoning with him but Johnny refused to listen and refused to budge.

"I'm out," Johnny announced eventually, angrily walking off. He slammed the door on his way out.

David stood up to go after him, then paused. "He's so off his head he couldn't find the front door."

He was right. In a huff, Johnny had walked out of the bathroom, into the living room then into the prayer room.

I suspected it would be a moment before he walked out again in a huff and tried to locate the actual door, but instead, we were met with silence. Five minutes passed before I went after him, wanting to check on him.

David motioned for me to remain seated. Disobeying him I got up and rapped on the door of the prayer room. "You okay in there Johnny?"

"Yes," he responded, his voice faint. It sounded as though

472

he were sobbing. I opened the door. He *was* sobbing.

He sat, back against the wall, crying uncontrollably. I turned on the light, entered and sat next to him in silence. David stood at the door. I acknowledged his presence with a nod, and we tacitly agreed that we would sit with Johnny.

"Mate, I'm sorry for the tough love. I just don't want you to go back to...you know what I'm talking about," David said, a little subdued.

"I'm a colossal fuck up," Johnny cried. "I'm too far gone to ever get over this," he said. I sat there with him as he cried, bracing his head in his hands. In between tears, he looked up and noticed the hand posted notes and prayer outlines on the wall. Many written by Daniel, many written by me after Daniel had left us.

"Can I pray for you?" I asked.

"Don't waste your breath," he muttered. "I feel God's given up on me a long time ago."

"You mean, you've given up on you, right?" I stated. He stared at me deeply, before looking away, in shame.

"I'm sorry guys, being the fuck up that I am I've brought my issues here and involved you. I'm truly sorry," he apologised.

I heard Josiah call out for me in his sleep. "I got this," David said quickly, leaving Johnny and I in the prayer room.

"Can I pray for you?" I asked again, hand on his shoulder.

After a moment's hesitation, he nodded to the affirmative.

I prayed that the chains that had him enslaved would be broken. I prayed that his heart would be filled with hope and his body would be filled with health. I prayed that he would once and for all be free of all that bound him and kept him enslaved.

473

As I prayed, he sobbed. By the end of it, he sat motionless, staring at the wall. I offered him a tissue which he gladly accepted.

"This isn't in your hands any longer. You don't have to do this on your own," I told him.

"I really miss Daniel," he said, echoing my sentiment. "I don't know that I'll ever stop missing him."

"It'll get better," I told him. "You'll see."

I lay some fresh sheets on the guest bed. I was determined that Johnny would stay with us for a few days.

"What are we doing here?" David asked suspiciously, returning from having checked up on the twins.

"Johnny hasn't got anywhere else to go. He needs to stay here," I told him.

He shook his head in disapproval. "I don't want you taking his issues on."

"And why's that?" I asked. "He hasn't got anyone else in his corner. He really wants to kick this habit for good," I explained.

David sighed heavily. "You sure about this?"

"I'm very sure," I replied. "I have to help him."

"You've got a heart of gold, I tell you," David said. "Tell me what I need to do to help and I will," he offered.

"Good," I replied. "Great to have you onside. He needs to stay here, come off what he's been on. He can't afford treatment in a centre," I explained. "Michaela won't have anything to do with him, so we can't count on her support. He hasn't got anyone else."

"He can't stay here," David stated, concerned. "Not with just you and the kids here. It's not safe," he added.

"The only person he's a danger to at this moment is

himself," I stated. "He can't be alone. Daniel would have wanted us to help him out. I thought you said you were willing to do anything to help?"

After an awkward silence, David replied, "I did. I will."

"I'm expecting you to stay here with me," I told him, boldly.

He didn't succeed at hiding his surprise. "I can dig that," he said grinning widely. "You know I'm happy to do whatever where you're involved."

I know. I smiled back.

Johnny sauntered into the room, wearing a t-shirt and shorts that once belonged to Daniel. I smiled sadly, recalling Daniel for a moment. Daniel who was so full of life and so willing to help out others in need. Had he been here, I'm certain he would have helped Johnny. "Some juice?" I offered.

"Yes thanks," Johnny replied simply. He appeared restless and anxious.

David surveyed him from a distance. I could still sense his hesitation.

"I don't want to put you guys out," Johnny said, suddenly panicked. "I'll be gone in the morning," he promised.

"We don't want you to be alone, Johnny," I stated. "You're staying here, getting clean as you promised."

I still sensed David's hesitation. "David, the only person he's likely to be a danger to, is himself."

"Thanks for the offer Teme, though I tried this before, it was hard, and it didn't work," Johnny interjected.

"To a point it did work," I countered. "You stayed sober for two whole years."

He nodded profusely, finishing the last of his orange juice.

"Fresh sheets, bucket by your bed, full use of the ensuite, we'll check up on you from time to time," I told him.

"Right," Johnny replied. Pupils dilated, his blue eyes seemed black.

"Try to get some rest," David suggested. "We're not giving up on you."

Johnny turned to go, breaking down in tears. "You don't know how much this means to me," he stated. "Thank you."

"Don't mention it," I replied.

"Guess I have old mate to thank for you taking a liking to me?" he asked.

I laughed lightly. "Yes, Daniel thought you were a riot. He once described your energy as infectious. I'm so glad we have you back."

Johnny smiled briefly. "In the short time I knew him..." he started. "He was a stand-up guy. God rest his soul," he said sadly, his eyes watering up. "Look, I'm gonna try and get some rest," he stated, turning to go.

The next morning, we had a visitor. Owen. David had invited him over to discuss Johnny and plans moving forward.

"Teme, you remember Doctor Collins?" David asked.

Of course I did. Owen was one of the doctors on the medical team supporting Daniel on his discharge from the mental facility. He'd also been at the wake.

"Owen's a good friend of mine," David stated. "We go way back," he added. "Med school days."

Owen held out his hand for me to shake. "Nice to see you again," he stated. "You look well this morning," he noted. "My condolences," he added. "It isn't easy, but keeping busy helps."

"Thanks Owen, it meant a lot that you were there yesterday," I said.

After a moment of silence, Owen stated, "So, I'm here today to see what I can do to help. I'm a recovering addict. You name it, I've tried it. I've been clean 10 years now and counting."

Clearing his throat, David explained, "I think Owen'll make a good sponsor for Johnny."

I nodded in approval, hoping Johnny wouldn't think it too forward to be staging an intervention in such a manner.

Johnny sat on the sofa, television volume on low. Formula One was on again.

"Johnny, you know Owen?" David asked.

Turning to face us, he said, "I vaguely remember him, yes."

"I'd like to be your sponsor," Owen said. "We've got a lot in common."

"If you say so," Johnny said, turning back to Formula One.

"Johnny, please," I begged.

"Alright," he said. "I'll give it a go."

Owen stood at a distance and purposely dropped his keys.

Johnny noticed. "You drive an Aston Martin?" he asked.

"Only on special occasions. I've got the old girl in the garage for the moment, just needs a little bit of detailing," he said.

Johnny bolted up. "What year?"

"She's a 2013 DB9."

"Convertible?"

"Yep," Owen replied.

"Totally sick!" he exclaimed. "Guess we do have something in common!" he acknowledged.

24

WITH HIM

David moved around the house hurriedly and purposefully. I tried following him around to see what he was doing but he asked me to leave him be. "Go sit down," he requested. "When I need you, I'll sing out for ya'," he said, waving me away.

I then sat in the living room with Johnny. *Formula One. Again.* He read my mind and laughed aloud. "How 'bout I watch this later?" he proposed.

"Don't worry about it. Had enough practice sitting through this with Daniel," I said.

"Sounds painful," he joked, grinning from ear to ear. It was hard to be down around Johnny. His smile lit up the room like a spark.

As he attempted to change channel, I insisted, "Leave it on. It's all good."

"Okay, if you insist," he said.

David pranced into the living room, in a burst of energy. "Johnny, you reckon you and Sadie'll be alright with the kids for a few hours or possibly a night?"

"Yep. Why?" he asked, sitting up, suddenly alert.

"Just going across the border to pick up that Pontiac '64 of Daniel's. And to have a night out under Mexican skies with this beautiful one," he said, referring to me.

"I'm comin' with you, no two ways about it," he announced, getting up abruptly. He stood a neat 6 foot 2, making David look short in comparison. *Not afraid to be the third wheel*, I thought to myself.

David hesitated for a moment as though he were contemplating the third wheel factor, before stating, "Alright then, in fact you might just be the person I need to come with." Turning to me, he said, "Pack an overnight bag for yourself. Let's leave in an hour?"

I immediately thought of the kids. Save for the night I spent in hospital, keeping a vigil over Daniel, I hadn't spent a night away from them. "Not sure I can bear being away from the kids."

"Okay," David replied. "How about..."

"How about we ask Sadie to come along, and we both can mind them?" Johnny proposed.

David eyed him suspiciously.

"What!" he interjected. "I'm practically their Godfather. Spent a lot of time with them when Daniel was around."

Not convinced, David shook his head in response.

"Sadie'll be very happy to come along," Johnny said, with conviction. In that moment, I was convinced that Johnny had intimate knowledge about what Sadie would and would not like to do.

Passing a furtive glance at me, David nodded to the affirmative. "We stay a few nights then?"

"It's just across the border, we can stay however long we want to or need to," Johnny suggested.

I glanced at Johnny warily. I hoped he was not going to use the opportunity to score.

"No, I know what you're thinking, and the answer is no. I've come too far to go back now," he said. "42 weeks and 2 days. And counting," he added.

It was hard to believe he had been living with us for that long. It had been a year, 42 weeks and 2 days since Daniel had gone.

"I won't be in your hair for much longer," he stated, as though he'd read my mind.

"No one's asking you to leave," I told him.

"I *will be* leaving but for other reasons," he said, before indicating that he wanted to talk to me in private.

David eyed Johnny suspiciously as I walked with him into the prayer room for a quick discussion.

Door closed behind us, Johnny pulled something out of his pocket. A ring. Barely above a whisper, he stated, "I'm going to ask Sadie to marry me. I need your help to pull it off."

I didn't try to hide my surprise. "Whoa Johnny. Congrats?"

"Yes, I believe congrats would be in order, but hold off on the celebration as she hasn't agreed yet," he said, obviously concerned and not entirely sure of what Sadie's response would be. "I'm taking a huge risk, but I figured it's a risk worth taking. I've spent the last few years making stupid mistakes and taking harmful risks. I think it's high time that I took a risk on real love."

I'd seen the way they looked at each other, but hadn't been aware of the romance that was blossoming between them. They'd obviously kept it well under wraps, and in my busyness, I'd failed to notice much at all.

"Say something will you?" he insisted.

"You never saw fit to marry Michaela."

"I was too up myself to care for anyone other than myself back then," he confessed. "Besides, some support she turned out to be. I don't need someone like her in my life," he said with such clarity it made me assured that the decision to wed Sadie was the right one. "So, I need your help pulling this off," he requested again. "I need you to help with a few of the logistics," he said. "Going over across the border is a start. She won't know what to expect. I also need you to help me with this," he said, running a hand through the platinum blonde blur that was his hair. "I need to have it cut and dyed back to my natural colour, dark brown," he said, talking a mile a minute.

I smiled at him. "Of course I can help."

"Good," he said. "I'm really grateful. You're a true friend," he said, squeezing my shoulders, and giving me a tender hug, reminding me for a moment of Daniel. They hung around each other so much in the final days, their mannerisms were shared.

"No worries at all, Johnny," I managed, tearing myself away from the memory of Daniel. It still hurt.

"I been doing a lot of thinking about where I want to be 10 years from now, and I know it's married, with kids, and clean. This is my first step in getting there, and I've got you, Daniel and David to thank for it."

Our time in Mexico was a blast. Sadie accepted Johnny's proposal and they returned engaged and in love. On our return, David and I agreed to leave the house to them while we went back to Australia for a few months. Some time away to start anew.

481

Daniel had left his interests in the firm to me, and I had insisted on Johnny being a partner in his absence. Craig was not too happy, but he had to deal with it. I'd arranged it so that Johnny worked away from the main office in Austin. He used Daniel's study to work files and met clients at their place of business.

While the threat of a relapse always loomed, I trusted that Johnny was in a better place than he'd been before. With Sadie, I knew he had a new hope. A new dawn was rising for him.

Johnny's goodbye a few mornings later took me by surprise. He placed his hands on my shoulders and stated, "You've seen me through some tough times. You and Daniel stood by me when everyone else bailed or sat on the fence. I'm eternally grateful. You've been an angel to me," he said with some sadness in his voice which I quickly picked up on.

"You give me too much credit Johnny, you got yourself through this. You were strong enough to withstand what came your way. You've been an amazing friend and support to me." I paused before asking, "Why do I get the feeling you've got something else to say?"

"I don't know how to put this, however I do, it'll be difficult," he predicted.

"Just tell me," I insisted.

"This here is goodbye," he said.

"What?" I questioned.

"I'm going underground for a time. This is goodbye for now."

Goodbye. So much finality in one word. I thought of how close Johnny and I had grown over the years, and how his brief stint back in the UK had left me feeling empty and alone, after Daniel had gone. David had always been there, but with Johnny there was a longstanding history of never needing to measure up and never needing to be anyone other than ourselves.

"The expression on your face - I'm not dropping off the face of the earth. This is just for a time," he said. "I can't say much, but Jude will always know where I am, and I'll always know where you are."

I sighed deeply. After a brief pause he added, "I'll be fine, you don't have to worry about me." Placing his hands on my shoulders again, he said, "Let me worry about you for a change."

Johnny being gone, I died a little inside, though I knew I would see him again someday.

David was all too happy to fill the void, and comforted me in my misery.

So on that early morning in September, we said our bittersweet goodbyes with the promise that Johnny and Sadie would be safe, together. As we said goodbye to beautiful Texas, I braced myself for the adventure that awaited us in Australia.

The Aussie sun had tanned his skin a deep golden brown. "A Virgin Colada?" David asked, suddenly interrupting my thoughts and standing a little too close to me. He'd been in the surf, and I could nearly taste the salt on his skin.

"Sure," I replied, dropping my pen. What was meant to be resisted was becoming irresistible. He caught my gaze in that moment and gave me a wink, knowingly.

"I called it first," he said smugly. "You'll be mine one day and I'll be yours."

"Incorrigible," I stated for want of a better word.

"I find it hard to believe you've been celibate all these years."

"I know how to keep myself happy," he interjected, giving me a left eye wink. "Don't need nobody but me," he said, a little too proudly.

"I didn't need to know that," I replied.

"Oh yes you did!"

"No, I didn't."

"Yes you did."

"No, I didn't."

"Yes you did," he stated. "Hopefully it will increase the amount of empathy you feel for me, and cause you to not even think of letting me suffer any longer."

"David, you're incorrigible!" I told him again.

"Hm, got a nice ring to it. David Incorrigible Davenport."

I rolled my eyes in response. "You don't know when to stop, do you."

"Oh yes I do."

"No you don't"

"Yes I do."

"No...David!" I exclaimed. "Give it a rest will you?"

He laughed. "Glad I can make you smile. I'll stop annoying you now," he promised.

We lived in a quaint workers cottage in Nambour, on Queensland's Sunshine Coast. I fell in love with the place the first moment I saw it, the time I had left Texas for Australia with David. The same cottage where I'd birthed the twins.

Daniel's presence was still there. I remembered him there, the punch up David and he had gotten into at the front, and

484

the few short weeks we'd spent there waiting for the babies to mature enough to travel back to Texas.

David stressed all the work he could do to the place, while I envisioned restoring the house to its original glory. A browse through the archives at the Nambour Library revealed the house had been constructed in 1840.

"Guess what I found out today," David said, smugly. "Peter from down the road said this place had been a "House of Love"," he said. "Used to be purple."

"You serious?" I asked, a little shocked.

"When am I ever serious," he joked. "Yes, I'm serious."

We both laughed heartily. For a moment I forgot to miss Daniel.

Those moments became days, and those days became eventually became weeks. Still, I thought of him daily, with each day remembering him in light.

We spent our sunny days at the beach.

"Check this out," David beckoned. "Am I or am I not awesome!" he exclaimed, stepping back to admire his workmanship - a castle made of sand that he'd carefully constructed with the kids.

"You are awesome," I confirmed. Just a little vain too," I added.

"Vain, no, not me. I just love myself," he claimed.

"Same thing, isn't it?"

"No ma'am. Not the same thing. I need to love myself so you can learn to love me," he philosophised. "Deeply."

"You could have been a philosopher," I noted.

"Could have been? I AM." He posed akimbo, then turned to me, hand under chin in a plato-esque pose.

I laughed helplessly in response to his behaviour.

"So, is it working?" he asked suddenly.

"What are you talking about?"

"Me loving me more so you can learn to love me," he stated.

"David you're incorrigible," I responded, averting eye contact.

He caught my eyes. "It is working," he suggested. "Can't even answer my question," he noted. "Your eyes betray you."

"Oh David, must you must continue to insist..."

"Yes, I will continue to insist," he confirmed. "You will learn to love me one day, and we will be one."

I did love him, I just was not prepared to admit it fully yet, for fear of where it might lead. Despite the kisses we shared here and there, loving someone else fully meant leaving the memory of Daniel. I wasn't prepared to do that.

He snapped his fingers in front of me, startling me slightly. "You went somewhere, just then, didn't you. Thinking of me I hope."

"David, you are too much."

He smiled deeply and laughed lightly. "One day you're gonna love me," he declared. "So deeply."

My heart skipped a beat at the thought. Loving him was easy. Getting over Daniel was hard.

Changing topic, he said, "Surf's up. Good time to head into the water, catch some waves," he suggested. "The babies, all slipped, slopped and slapped?"

"What?"

A pregnant pause ensued before he clarified. "Do the babies have sunscreen on?"

"Why couldn't you just say that initially?" I asked.

"Why couldn't you just understand me initially?" he

486

teased.

I rolled my eyes at him. "No, they don't, not yet," I told him, envisioning Adalia trying to escape. She hated putting sunscreen on, but the Queensland sun was unforgiving.

David seemingly read my mind. "I'll get to it then," he said, planting a kiss on my forehead before tending to the babies.

Fun in the surf only lasted so long. It was uncomfortably hot. I sat under the beach umbrella, watching David carry each child close enough to the shore to feel the water lapping against their little feet then retreat back as the waves encroached further. His energy and zest for life warmed me and filled me with passion for living, but I missed Daniel. Had he been here, he would've complained about the weather, complained about the heat. He would've wanted to be on the water instead, in his boat. I missed him.

"I say we take the kids out to the park after," David said. "Want to come with us, or would you rather be home?" he asked.

I didn't feel like doing much of anything else, so I shook my head to the negative. The loss of losing Daniel still weighed heavily within me.

"I understand," he said. "We'll go home," he suggested.

Josiah flashed a toothless grin, his cheeks edible. "Dadda," he said.

David responded by kissing him on the forehead. "It's complicated little man," he stated, seemingly unfazed.

"He just called you Dad!" I exclaimed excitedly, before the sadness hit again. Daniel was gone.

"He's just sounding out a few words," David said in an

attempt to ease my sadness.

Adalia kicked in the pram.

"He doesn't need to call me Dad when he's older."

"Daniel would've wanted him to," I reminded him.

"It's whatever really," David said. "I know what he means to me, and he knows what I mean to him. We can sort it out in time," he said. "He can call me whatever," he confirmed.

"Daniel should've been here," I said, tears threatening to fall. "I really miss him," I stated.

"I know. You and me both," David said softly. "Temwani, just know, I'll be whatever you want me to be for these kids. I'll be whatever you want me to be for you. You know how I feel about you. I worship the ground you walk on."

"You shouldn't," I cautioned. "I am but a mere mortal."

"You're a goddess to me," he replied.

That he loved me so much was endearing. Yet I felt conflicted. Despite the fact that it had been over two years since Daniel had left us, I couldn't bring myself to even imagine seriously being with someone other than him, even if that person was David.

We got home, and I couldn't wait to get to bed, for most nights, I saw Daniel in dreams. He was usually wearing white, and was surrounded by a yellow aura.

I woke from my dream that night my face wet from tears. In the dream I was walking towards him. As I got closer, he walked further away. I got closer he went further. I desperately tried to keep up with him. In desperation I called out his name. He then stopped and turned to face me. "Life is for the living," he said. Arms outstretched, he beckoned an embrace. I melted in his arms, the warmth of his glow all consuming. "Live," he whispered. "Live again," he stated, before turning to walk away from me again.

I followed him, and saw he was walking towards a pond. His face turned from me, he threw rocks into the pond. The water rippled in effect. "You promised me you'd find happiness," he said.

I tried to speak but no words came.

"You promised," he said, suddenly turning towards me. His hair was a burnt auburn from the sun that seemed to glow within him, his skin a golden brown. "Find happiness. You promised," he repeated.

I awoke up with a start. David stood at the doorway, and for a moment I mistook him for Daniel. Without a word, he sat on the edge of my bed and held me. "It'll get better," he promised.

I felt deep sadness within as I recalled that Daniel had said similar words when we'd first met, and when I was in so much pain. More than two years on, I still found it hard to envision things getting better without him.

25

A COURTING

I still missed Daniel. I would always miss him. The notion that our love would transcend space and time was real. I could feel it within. There would never be a time that I did not recall the memories we had and the love we shared. My reality was also real. David was a living breathing being who had professed his love for me decades ago. Being Daniel's twin, he was a living replica of the man I loved and would continue to love, eternally.

It was hard being around David at times. Most times. Many times he reminded me of Daniel, other times he showed me how different they were. In the beginning, I hated myself for entertaining the notion of loving David one day. I resisted any move by David to bring us closer, hoping he would distance himself from me. Instead, being who he was and had always been, he came closer to me and used every opportunity to discover me and uncover my weaknesses. I wondered how long it would last before his patience in waiting for me wore thin.

I didn't have to wonder long. One evening he came to me, visibly agitated. The kids were asleep, he had just returned from a shift at the hospital.

"Bad day?" I questioned.

"More like bad days," he said, throwing his bag into a corner of the living room.

"Tell me about it?"

"It's been a while since Daniel left us. I can't pretend any more. I'll be straight with you. I need to get this off my chest," he said. "Daniel said a lot to me while he was still around. I've tried my best to be a better man. Brigades, I'm a youth pastor now, who would have thought," he said. "I love the kids. I consider them to be my own." He paused for a moment. "And I love you. I've always loved you. We share a kiss here and there, but you won't be mine," he said. "You'd think I'd know by now that there will never be a place for us," he said sadly. "I still believe..." he broke off, his voice wavering.

"My brother had one final request," he said after a momentary pause. "There's something I need to show you," he said.

He sat next to me, opened up a well-worn letter from Daniel. Apparently it had been given to him as part of the reading of Daniel's Last Will and Testament.

Please ensure that she finds happiness, preferably with you, the note read.

"I've had this letter checked for authenticity..." David confirmed.

"I saw him in a dream the other night," I interjected. I explained how Daniel had seemed sad and troubled that I had not found happiness in his absence.

"I see," David stated, stoically. We sat in silence for what seemed like an eternity. David broke the silence. "I don't want to be pushy, he said. "I only want what's best for you.

491

You know how I feel. You know how I've always felt. But I feel that if there is absolutely no chance for us to ever be, I should probably allow you to find someone else who would make you happy. After all, I have a duty to help you find happiness."

"What makes you think I want to find someone else right now? Daniel was it for me," I said.

Something like pain flashed across his face. "Alright then," he said.

"I'm sorry, David."

"I'm running on empty here," he declared. "My love tank's running dry and I need to fill it up."

"David you keep on asking me to give. I feel I have nothing left to give right now. I gave Daniel my all. You can't expect me to offer you what I gave him."

He stood motionless, clearly shocked. "There are a lot of things I deserve. I don't deserve that," he said abruptly. "I'm not asking you to give me anything I wouldn't give you myself. I'll put it to you bluntly. He's not here anymore, I am."

Sorry I'd said what I did, I replied, "Look, I didn't mean to hurt you."

"Well you did, and you meant every word," he said. "Apart from my help here, would you rather I be gone?" he asked. "I'll do whatever you prefer, whatever you want of me. I'll honour your wishes, if it'll make you happy."

"I don't want you gone, David."

"Then what is it?" he questioned. Not waiting for my response, he mentioned under his breath, "Stupid of me to think there'd ever be anything between us," he said, head between his hands.

"I'm sorry David. I didn't mean to hurt you," I said, placing a hand on his. He squeezed my hand back, and turned to face me directly.

"You'll always be forgiven," he promised. "I love these kids as though they were my own. I truly do," he confessed. "I love work. I love this home we've made together, and the things we do together to forget. And I love you. I always have and always will. But this isn't enough for me." He struggled to find words for a moment, then got up and paced. "You might see this as pretty bold. It is what it is. I can't make you forget him. I don't want you to forget him. But I want you to try to be present here with me. I'm trying to keep my head above water. I'm smiling to keep from crying. I..." he broke off.

I didn't know what to say. *I can hardly save you from drowning if I'm drowning myself*, I thought. "David, I'm here for you. I might not be here in the ways you want me to be, but I'm here for you, and I'm here with you. Isn't that enough?"

He stared at me blankly for a moment, lost in thought. It was clear that my words had appeased him. Momentarily at least. "It is, for now," he managed. "Thank you. You always did know what to say." He sat down again and leaned back into the sofa, his exhaustion apparent.

"Tough day?"

"It was a dog's breakfast."

I made him a cup of almond hot chocolate while I plated up dinner.

"What's for dinner, chef?" he asked, in a lighthearted way.

"Basmati rice and stewed vegetables," I replied. "I also made your favorite. Cornbread."

"Awesome," he replied, scoffing down the food immediately I set it in front of him. In that moment, he reminded me of Daniel. I smiled to myself.

Dinner finished, he lingered at the table for a while instead of getting up as he usually did to help with the dishes. Reaching for my hand across the table, beckoned me to place both my hands in his. I did.

"Let me love you," he requested. "I'll show you how good we could be together."

"David..."

He held me silent with a raised hand. "Darlin' I've told you how I feel. You know how I feel. I feel I can't do this anymore. With every day that passes I live with the hope that you will one day love me the way I love you. I'm taking this here friendship and making the best of it. With every day that goes by I find myself lusting after you, wanting more of you. I'm effectively living in sin. I can't do this any more. I feel I will just explode from the pressure of keeping a lid on my emotions. Prayer has helped, but I'm only human."

"David you're asking me for more than I can give."

"I'm asking you to give what you can. To find it in you to love me as more than just a friend. Three words for you lady, gimme your love. Da me tu amor."

"That's actually seven words, David."

"That's just being pedantic right there," he joked.

"Well I'm right and you're wrong. I guess you fell asleep when the class learnt to count to ten," I joked.

"Ha ha, very funny. My maths is pretty advanced if I must say so myself."

"If you say so, genius," I replied.

"We have so much fun, don't we?" he noted. "I don't want this to end. I want more but I'm afraid of losing this. I'm afraid of losing what we already have."

"You'll find someone else someday, David."

"Please don't start this again - I can't just forget about you. I can move on, try to love someone else but it's only you. It will always be you," he insisted.

I said nothing in reply, but later consoled him with a kiss. At that moment I wasn't ready, but would need to get ready to be with him.

Craig was in town a few days later, and he used the chance to give me a piece of his mind on the state of affairs as it stood between David and I.

"You need to face facts," Craig advised. "Do you know how hard it is for a man to stay committed to someone who doesn't return his affection? How long has he been into you - twelve years now?"

"I'm pretty sure he hasn't just been waiting on me all these years."

"But what if he has?" Craig asked.

"He has had other things to do in that time other than focus on winning me over, I'm sure."

"But what if he hasn't? Wasn't it he who sought you out after so many years? Isn't he still here waiting on you?" he observed.

I shrugged in response.

"The thing you need to do now is decide on whether you want him to be a part of your life. It's obvious he wants more than friendship. If you can't give that to him, you need to cut him loose. If you don't you might end up losing his friendship as well."

"I'm not sure that will ever happen. We're linked inextricably. I was married to his brother," I argued.

"That is not in question. The point I'm trying to make is

495

you will have to cut him loose if you care for him. Surely you want him to find happiness, even if it isn't with you. That's if you care for him."

"Of course, I care for him," I retorted, a little angry that Craig was being so blunt. He was right though.

"Could've fooled me," he replied. "This man has gone through so many changes and done so many things to get you to notice him. He's even playing house with you, and raising kids that are not his own."

"I didn't force him to."

"My point exactly. He is where he is with you because he wants to be with you. This man is completely devoted to you, and if you're not in the slightest devoted to him, cut him loose."

"I hear you."

"He is a good man, you know," Craig said. "Better than most. Myself included. Daniel was a standup guy, second to none." Craig recalled, with a look of pain in his face that seemed a little put on and exagerrated. "He's gone now. He would have wanted you to move on. With David."

"I hear you," I said again.

"I'm being serious. You shouldn't do this alone," he advised.

"I *can* do this alone," I stated.

"You shouldn't," he urged, pouring himself another whiskey. "You mind?" he asked.

"Why would I?" I replied.

"Get some sleep," he suggested. "I'll wait for David to come back."

I did as he said but tossed and turned in my sleep, worried I was mistreating David and his goodness.

In the days to come, everything Craig had said continued to weigh heavily on my mind. Angie, a friend from the local playgroup who I'd agreed to meet up with for coffee noticed.

"How are your beautiful babies?" she asked.

"Good, they're doing real good."

"They in care at the moment?"

"No, David's been with them while I'm at work during the day, it's been good so far. He works evenings."

"Doesn't give you much time for yourselves or each other," she stated.

"It's not as though we're officially together..."

"But you could be, right?" she asked.

I couldn't believe my ears. *Everyone had an opinion on what David and I should be.*

"We can all see it - eventually he'll win you over, or eventually he'll walk away. He's only human," she reminded me.

"I see your point."

"Girlfriend, he has his needs. I'm not suggesting that you're not meeting some of them. I mean you're offering him companionship and friendship. But given your history, or should I say, his history of being completely enthralled in you, with that comes the expectation that someday you will give in to him and spend the rest of your life with him," she assumed.

"I'm pretty sure he's clear there isn't a future with me, not in that way anyway."

"That isn't as clear cut as you say it is. He speaks of you in such high regard - he speaks of you as a man in love would speak of a woman he is completely devoted to."

"I know what I feel," I told her. "I know what I could

497

be doing but feel on some level I'd be betraying Daniel," I explained.

"Yes, but you're going to have to make a decision sooner or later. Probably sooner rather than later, before the stakes get too high."

"The stakes are already high," I thought aloud.

"Damn straight they are." Angie replied. "What do you have to lose anyway? He's completely devoted to you, this much I can say."

Despite the let down of not being able to take our relationship further, David got busy trying to please me and win my heart over. He started by buying me flowers every Friday, as Daniel had done. His actions warmed my heart.

"You liked the flowers?" he asked one morning.

"I did. Thank you David. I know how you felt about Daniel and the things he did for me. I know that you're not trying to replace him."

"I'm not," he confirmed. "I just want you to be happy," he insisted. "I'm prepared to go to whatever lengths necessary to make that happen, even if it means picking up where he left off, without the expectation that we will be together someday," he said. Choosing his words carefully, he added, "I also know how much you value quality over quantity. I want you to know that though I am busy trying to get things going with work, ministry and all, I am here for you, and I will take time off just to be with you and the kids, whenever you need me. I want us to..." he broke off, hesitating to continue. "My time is your time," he said.

"David, I'm sorry if I've ever made you feel uncomfortable

– you've walked in and taken on the role of father and provider while I've been so...too busy mourning Daniel. I feel I haven't been there for you at all."

He shook his head and I saw the love in his eyes despite his clear anguish. Placing both hands on my shoulders, he added, "Don't apologise, sugar, honey. Me being here with you and me being there for you is more than I could have hoped for. I'm grateful for what I can get," he said.

"David, you have such a big heart. You fascinate me, your love for me and the babies is just awe inspiring," I stated.

"And you thrill me," he said in response. His eyes beholding me deeply, he added, "I adore you. Please let me be there for you," he requested. On the steps of that old Queenslander we embraced. The strength in his embrace melted me whole. We stood there for a moment, and for that moment time stood still. Craig was right. Keeping him at bay might mean that I would eventually lose him. His love had become too deep for him to consider anyone else, and too deep to even try. I knew right then I needed to let him know how I felt, and move forward.

Suddenly red-faced, he admitted, "I'm not doing a very good job of hiding how I feel these days." He quickly let go of our embrace and stepped away from me in an effort to conceal the fact that he was aroused. I noted the obvious and quickly looked away, not wanting to embarrass him further. Deep passion for him stirred within me as I noted the clear embarrassment on his face. "I'm sorry," he managed.

I smiled at him, feeling for him. All was forgiven. After all these years, and after all this time, this man loved me. The man loved me, despite my reluctance to be with him, despite the brokenness he must have felt in this heart when he watched me live and love another.

"What are we doing?" he questioned, interrupting my thoughts. "We started this journey with a kiss, back in Austin. We travelled all the way here to start again, but the way we're headed isn't clear. Meanwhile, I still love you. I still want you," he confessed. "Teme, this can't go on - it's becoming harder and harder for me to fight this desire for you. I know I promised I would lay off and calm down, but it's only you I'm after. Only you," he professed. "And you not wanting me is sort of doing my head in now. Like, for me this isn't infatuation. This isn't just lust. It's love. Always has been and always will be."

I silenced him by planting a kiss on his lips.

He stood there, stunned.

"I'm ready to be with you now, if you'll still have me," I told him.

He seemed dumbfounded. "What?"

"I want to be with you," I said. "Properly. Officially."

Still shocked, he asked, "You sure?"

"David, I've never been more sure about anything," I told him. "I'm sorry if I ever made you feel like you were less than. I'm sorry for taking your friendship for granted, and I'm sorry for making you wait so long to be with me. I've come to the realisation that I need you, and don't want to be without you."

His blue eyes glistened in the yellowing street light, and he took a step back as though to admire me. After giving me the once over, he then reached out to hold my hands, and I held his. His hands were shaking. "I can't believe this is happening, finally. I've waited for this day for so long. I can't quite explain how you're making me feel. You've just made me so happy," he said. We stood there holding each other before we let go. He and I were finally together for keeps.

26

VIOLETS ARE BLUE

I t seemed nothing could go wrong, but he'd let me down, and I wasn't going to let this go easily. I'd given myself to him after much resistance, and he didn't get to treat me this way.

"So, David, we've been together for a few weeks now, and I thought it was all good. But I heard through various sources that you were in the market for a new woman. That you were finally free to love," I said.

He frowned, as though the mere thought disgusted him. "What are you talking about?"

"Claudette took it upon herself to advise me of the fact that you were apparently making plans to settle down, that you wanted kids, and a family of your own. You even went so far as to tell her that you were sick of living in Daniel's shadow, and that though you loved me and the life we have, you want more."

"Trust Claudette to take things out of context," he said, running a hand through his hair.

"And there were photos. She showed me details of your travel itinerary, and told me about your secret visit to Western Australia, where you apparently stayed in an old mining town. She mentioned that the area you stayed in was teeming with women who were after one thing and one thing only – pleasuring men. She showed me and told me enough to make me believe that all this time you've been stringing me along. All this time you've been playing me for a fool."

He shook his head in response. "So, after all this time, after everything I've done for you and the kids. After everything, you're taking her word against mine?"

"After all *you've* done for me and the kids?" I asked. "Sorry to make you feel obligated David!"

"I didn't mean it to come out like that..." he said.

"I thought I knew you David, but I realise now that I don't know you at all. If you wanted to move on to someone other than me, you could've let me know. I would have happily gone on loving Daniel, moving on to no one else after he was gone. He was after all, the love of my life. The passage of time won't change that. I was stupid to think I'd be more to you than just a conquest. I heard about the string of women you had at your beck and call before we met..."

"Are you done?" he asked. "I can't take this from you. All I can hear is how disappointed you are in me. All I can hear is how much of a screw up I am."

"Well, you are screwing up, royally. How can you say you are not!" I exclaimed.

"Have you ever stopped to ask any one of those women exactly how I treated them? Have you ever stopped to ask any one of those women exactly what I did with them? Because until you have, you can't judge me," he stated. "I'm no Casanova. I'm a one woman man. You're the only one I've ever had eyes for. All other women be damned. Have you stopped to think for one minute that it could all be lies? Have you stopped to confront whoever it was that told you this?" he questioned.

"Don't be ridiculous David. Of course I haven't asked and I cannot go around asking any of those women anything of the sort."

"Okay. I know I have a bad boy reputation. But you of all people should know how much you mean to me, and that I would not risk anything for what we have. I'm not a slut. I'm not a male gigolo. I'm not a womaniser. It's all a front," he stated as a matter of factly.

"David, I wasn't born yesterday," I said curtly. "The best thing you can do for me right now is to admit that you never had any intention of settling down with anyone, let alone me, as you love yourself too much to give up being so selfish."

He shook his head. Something like pain flashed across his face. "Teme, you're hurting me," he said, beckoning me to stop in my tracks. "You're really hurting me."

I felt my heart sink. I had not set out to hurt him.

"Look, I've made a fool out of myself for far too long. I'm never going to be like Daniel. I could never replace him." His voice strained, he turned away from me. "I screwed up royally when he was alive. Instead of being there for him, I made things difficult for him. I coveted after you instead of supporting you and him, when you were not mine to begin with." He paused for a moment, in thought. "I'm still screwing up. Now that I've got you, I really don't know how to keep you on side. I'm not trying to hurt you, but it feels like you resent me, and you're going to great lengths to hurt me..." He turned away brusquely, averting his eyes from me in shame.

"I'm going away with the kids for a few days," I told him, suddenly. He didn't seem surprised.

"I understand," he said immediately. "Don't stay away too long," he urged. "When do you leave?"

"I'm leaving tomorrow," I told him. It felt as though I were running away, again, except this time from David, not Daniel.

A flash of disappointment went across his face. He stopped pacing and sat down on the sofa as though to catch his breath. "I guess I haven't given you much incentive to stay," he said. After a momentary pause, he begged, "Please don't leave me now, Teme. Not even for a moment. I can't go back to living my life without you."

I sighed in response. "You meant what you said, David," I reminded him. "Plus, I haven't exactly been fair. The kids, you and I became a family overnight. I thought you could deal..." I started. "Daniel thought you could deal..."

"I hear you," he replied. "I just wanted you to love me for who I am, not who you expect me to be. I will never be the man that Daniel was, but I can give you more of what I have. More of what I am. That's if you'll still have me. I love the kids. I love them as though they are my own. But I want you to carry my babies. I want to be the only one you lust after, the one you desire and no one else. I want to give you my name."

"David..."

"Wait here, just a moment," he said suddenly. "There's something I want you to see."

From the top of the bookshelf, he retrieved some papers. Drawings and sketches. He unfolded one and rolled out the other onto the dining table. It was a blueprint of sorts. "Daniel started building this before his health took a turn for the worse. He wanted me to finish it off for you," he explained. "It was hard keeping this from you, it's been hard keeping secrets from you."

"There shouldn't be any secrets between us," I reminded him.

"No, there shouldn't be," he said, regrettably. "Unfortunately, there have been, and I'm truly sorry." I wondered what else he knew of that I had yet to find out. He handed me a note written on Daniel's trademark parchment paper. It read:

My Dear Brother,

Thank you for all that you have been to her. I know it hasn't been easy, but you're a stand-up guy. If she hasn't tired of you by now (she shouldn't, deep down she adores you, and if you wear her down with your charm and your kindness and adoration for her, she will find it within her to love you), I hope you will work up the nerve to ask her to marry you. This garden arc is for the both of you, in hopes that it'll be a daily reminder of how lucky you are to still have life, and how lucky you are to still have love. I beseech you to find happiness with each other.

Daniel.

P.s. Anything or anyone else and I'll come back to haunt you.

David smiled ever so slightly. I burst out into laugher which was short lived. How presumptuous of Daniel to assume that I would fall so easily for David. "How presumptuous of him," I stated aloud.

"Playing matchmaker again," David concluded.

506

I nodded in agreement, pondering the letter and visualising the garden arc he had mentioned in it.

David placed his hand on my shoulder and squeezed gently. "You okay?"

I nodded my head to the affirmative. He placed the letter in my hand and added, "For what it's worth, I still do want you to love me and I still do want you to marry me someday. I just want it to be what you want too." He didn't wait for my response before adding, "You know I wish I could say I want you to love me for me, and not out of loyalty to him, but I can't. After all these years of wanting you and yearning after you, I just want you in any way you'll have me. I'll take anything. I really wish you didn't have to leave. I feel once you do, there'll never be a chance for us again."

I stood there, touched by the sincerity in his eyes and the adoration in his words. No response I could've come up with would equate such a declaration of love. He was beautiful, the light dancing on his auburn brown curls, his lightly stubbled chin giving him a rugged look. "My Aussie dream," I accidentally said aloud.

"Sorry?"

Embarrassed, instead of explaining myself to him, I leant forward to kiss him. I could feel him melt the moment my lips touched his. As briefly as I had kissed him, I pulled back. He seemed stunned, somewhat gasping for breath.

I hadn't meant to kiss him, not then, and not like that, but I did. I had.

Taken aback he uttered, "Please don't hold back now, I'll take anything."

I tried to explain but failed, my head reeling from the kiss. "I didn't mean to…"

"I see," he said, a little too quickly. Switching topic he stated, "Alrighty. I need to show you something, are you ready for the big reveal? Ready to see the arc?"

Not waiting for my response he took my hand in his. Passing by the kids' room, they were still sound asleep not unusual for them after a late night last night. He led me through the cottage's back door and down the stairs. At the bottom of the stairs stood an archway with a cascade of climbing and rambling roses. On either side of the stairs was a bed of roses. The smell of the roses was so strong, so fragrant and overpowering.

"This is beautiful!" I exclaimed. "When did you..."

"You're a deep sleeper when you do get to sleep," he stated affectionately.

"Give me your hand," he requested.

"You are already holding my hand, silly!"

"Your hand in marriage," he corrected.

It wasn't possible for me to hide my shock at his sudden proposal.

Dropping to one knee he stated, "Please do me the honor of becoming Mrs. David Davenport." Fumbling slightly he took a beautiful pink diamond ring out of his pocket and held it in the palm of his hand. "So, what do you say - we spend the rest of our lives together? Make it official?"

"Oh, David, it's complicated." I replied.

"Life is complicated. The love I have for you is simple and pure," he confirmed. "Is this about Daniel? Or is this about you not loving me?"

"No, David, this isn't about me not loving you, and its not about Daniel." I replied.

"Then what is it?" he asked, clearly taken aback.

I ran a hand through his auburn brown hair which glistened in the sunlight. His bronzed skin shone and he seemed to glow. A smile crept up the corners of his mouth when he noted me taking him in.

"You don't know how much I've longed for you to just touch me, how I've longed to hold you," he confessed.

"David, I..."

"Temwani will you *please* take a chance on us? Please marry me," he requested. On one knee he asked again. "Will you marry me?"

I had thought about this for time. I knew that it would eventually happen, and that it might have happened a long time ago, had I not left Australia all those years ago. I had imagined that it might have been David and not Daniel. But it was not so. I was alone in thought for much too long.

"Please don't do this to me again," he begged.

"Do what?" I feined ignorance.

He frowned slightly. "What you've been doing for the last 12 odd years or so. Leaving me hanging."

Without further hesitation, I stated, "I will. David, I will marry you. I'm yours."

He sprung from his knees so quickly he almost toppled me over. He quickly braced me and kissed my lips fully and deeply. Pure joy shone on his face. "You beauty, I love you so much." Planting kisses on my lips, he pulled me into his arms for an embrace. "You've made me so happy," he said. "Now that I've got you, I see no sense in beating around the bush."

"Meaning?"

"How soon can we make this wedding happen?" he asked.

I laughed heartily. "You're incorrigible, David."

"Oh how I love you Teme," he declared. Reaching for my hand again, he slipped the engagement ring on my finger. It was a slender gold band emblazoned with a pink princess cut diamond and several smaller pink diamonds on either side of the ring. "Hope you like it," he said. "Pink diamonds. My trip to Western Australia," he explained. Claudette had been dead wrong about David. He only had eyes for me.

Holding my hand up to the light, I stated, "It's beautiful!"

"As are you," he said, kissing me fully again. I felt myself melt in the passion of his kiss and strength of his embrace. He sighed deeply as our lips locked. In between kisses, he whispered, "I can't wait to give my whole to you." Stopping suddenly he questioned, "That's if you'll have me. Flaws and all?"

He was referring to the horrific scars on his body, inflicted at a time he was defenceless and unable to stand up for himself.

Tears came to my eyes. "David, I love you completely. I love you wholly. Daniel will always be on my mind and in my heart, but I love you completely and wholly. I want all of you. I'm touched by how much you love me, and by how long you've loved me. I can only hope that my love will be enough for you."

Face to face, and close as though we were dancing we stood there on the stairs, fragrant roses all around.

"Trust me, whatever you give me will be enough," he said with certainty. "Can't believe we're finally going to do this after all this time," he said somewhat nostalgically. "I've spent so many years..." he broke off. I was surprised to see tears in his eyes. He quickly averted my gaze before stating, "I'm sorry. Me getting emotional is not a good look."

"David, you're incorrigible. Since when were you not ever concerned about your looks?" I said sarcastically.

"Like never?" he joked.

"Thank you for choosing me," I said, leaning into his strong frame, embracing him tightly. He pressed his hand into the small of my back, and I felt a tingle through my body. I finally felt open enough to love him. I'd noticed it many times before, but as he stood there in front of me and I gazed in his eyes, the lust in his eyes seemed more apparent than ever. Standing so close, I could feel him undress me with his eyes.

"Cold shower for me," he stated abruptly, as though he'd read my mind. "I'd ask you to take one with me, but that would defeat the purpose," he stated, smiling brazenly.

"I'm not a virgin, you know," I stated openly.

"Clearly you're not mamasita," he said jovially. "You're a mother to two beautiful babies, clearly not the result of an immaculate conception. Just trying to keep this conventional, for the sake of it," he added.

"There's not a lot that's conventional about what we have here," I reminded him.

"Come now, there's plenty conventional about our love story, right?" he said sarcastically. Boy meets girl, girl runs away from boy, boy follows girl half way across the globe, boy finds girl is betrothed with his brother, boy still loves girl, boy moves halfway across the globe to avoid seeing girl happy with someone else, girl asks boy to come back, boy loves girl even more, girl is widowed, girl runs away from boy then girl comes to love boy, boy and girl get married."

"That was a mouthful but that pretty much sums up our story," I laughed. "For a long time I wondered why Daniel had to go when he did. I'm realising now that in leaving, he's opened it up for you to be with me."

"True that, but it's not as simple as it sounds. I've still gotta get through to those who love you. With your parents, your Mom loves me, but your Dad has taken a strong disliking to me from the beginning."

"Mom loves you cause you're a charmer. She knows you'll make me happy. Dad dislikes you cause he thinks you're only after one thing. He also thinks you're a bit of a jock, being a surgeon and all."

"He's talked to you about me?" he asked, surprised.

"Yep, he thinks you're only interested in "getting into my pants"," I said, throwing my head back in laughter. It wasn't funny at the time, but it sounded funny, telling David and seeing his reaction.

"Shocka," he replied. "What did you say? I hope you told him he was wrong."

"I tried to tell him he was wrong but he wouldn't listen," I replied. "I'm sure he'll come around eventually," I predicted.

"Now, there is a little modicum of truth in that - I do want to get into you, but that's not all," he said, defensively. "You know as well as I do that I want all of you. Part of you just so happens to be that rockin' body of yours, and yes, I'd be lying if I said I didn't want that too," he confessed, winking at me.

I love this man. I cupped his chin in my hand and leaned in to kiss his lips. Lightly at first, then with growing intensity.

He pulled back for a moment. "Man, it's getting so hard to fight temptation."

I smiled in response. "Not for much longer now," I said.

He nodded his head in agreement.

"Okay, so I want to do this the right way," he said. "Do you think your dad's opinion of me will change once he finds out about my plans in ministry?"

I shrugged in response. "He'll come around. You shouldn't feel you have to work for his approval."

"I hear you," he replied, sounding unsure. "I just want things to be right. I'm sure you'd like him to walk you down the aisle."

"I would, yes," I replied. "But if he doesn't want to, that won't stop me from marrying you."

He held my hand firmly. "I love you, my future Mrs. Davenport," he declared, raising my hand to his lips for a kiss which sent tingles down my spine.

"I love you too," I replied, looking forward to being his wife.

27

FOREVER AFTER

He looked dashingly handsome in the tuxedo he tried on. Dashingly handsome but uncomfortable. "Don't like it?" I asked.

"It's pretty flash. I like the look but can't wait to get out of it," he said.

"I can see that!" I exclaimed.

"Sorry darl'. But I'll wear it on the big day," he promised.

I straightened his collar then adjusted his neck tie, the way Daniel used to, after a busy day at work. Suddenly, I felt overwhelmed with sadness, and unexpectedly my eyes brimmed with tears. In that moment, as David stood there, all suited up, I saw a glimpse of Daniel, as he looked the day we got married.

David noticed the tears immediately. "Come now, I didn't mean to upset you. I just want to make you happy."

"It's not that," I managed.

"I see," David said solemnly. "I'm not trying to replace him. Though easier said than done when I look just like him." He paused for a moment, then loosened his neck tie. "How can we best honour him, yet make this our own?" he

514

pondered. "How about we forgo the tuxedo? Maybe even rethink the ceremony?" he proposed.

The tears still came, unabated.

"Are we doing this too soon?" he asked, loosening the buttons on his shirt and comforting me, wiping tears away. "Do you even want this?"

"Of course I want this," I managed. "I just don't expect to break down like this every time I see a glimpse of him in you."

"Which is like every time you see me," he acknowledged. "But it is to be expected. I know how much you loved him. How much you still love him."

The tailor walked by. "Is everything okay?"

"Yes," David replied, coming closer to me as if to shield me from prying eyes, though it would have been quite apparent to all that I was crying. "We'll sing out if we need any help." Turning back to me, he smiled nervously, beckoning me to stop crying. "We'll make this work. Make it our own. I really want you in my life forever. If it's not now, you need to let me know when. You know I'll be waiting for you no matter what."

I shook my head fervently. "Oh David, you've already waited so long!" I exclaimed.

"And it's been worth it," he replied, tenderly wiping the tears that rolled down my face. "You won't be able to convince me to leave you alone. Not after I've been loving you for what seems like my whole life."

"You mean obsessing over me?"

He laughed heartily. "I say love, you say obsession - you say tomato, I say tomaato."

"David you're incorrigible."

515

"My lady, I've been pursuing you for just over a decade now," he added.

"You mean stalking?" I joked.

"I say pursuing, you say stalking - I say tomato you say tomaato."

I laughed earnestly. "No I *don't* say tomaato, I say tomato," I replied.

"Too funny," he said in response.

"Oh how I love you David," I said, surprising myself. I had not expected to fall for him so deeply.

He flashed his perfect teeth through a dimpled smile. Leaning in for a kiss, he whispered, "I still can't get over how sweet your lips taste. I can't get over everything about you. I can't be without you. I'll take you however you'll have me."

Muffled whispers sounded on the other side of the change room. The store clerk and tailor had been listening in.

"Good show?" David asked, feigning annoyance. He peeped past the cubicle door, made eye contact with the store clerk.

"So sorry, so sorry," she said, apologetically. "You just seem so perfect together."

"Right..."

"And you'd make such beautiful babies - her caramel skin, your bronzed skin..."

"Right..." David stated, as though he'd heard it all before.

Turning to me, he whispered, "If we don't leave soon they'll be planning our golden anniversary. So let's G-E-T-O-U-T."

I laughed heartily. He knew just how to make me smile.

He stole a lingering kiss from me before hastily changing

out of the tuxedo. He then stood staring at himself in the mirror, undershirt and boxers on only. Flexing his arm and chest muscles he joked, "Man of Steel, ey?" He proceeded to pop and lock to a tune only he could hear.

I couldn't help but laugh yet again. Such a man-child he was. "Stop messing around will you? Still got to meet with the pastor in a bit."

The stigma of getting married again as a widow was real. I called my family and friends to announce the news. "Isn't it too soon?" most said. "Why does it have to be his brother?" was the standing question.

My sister Keyla offered, "So you're finally giving in to his brother. I hope you know a lot of people won't take your relationship seriously. Are you trying to somehow relive your experience with Daniel?"

I cut the call mid speech during that conversation. She didn't call me back.

Surprisingly, despite all the advice offered previously, Angie was not supportive either. "I encouraged you to be straight with him and to cut him loose if you were not interested. Marriage is a big step. Don't you think you're moving too fast?" she asked.

It seemed everyone failed to realise that I'd known David for a long time. That we'd met momentarily years before Daniel and I were even an item. It seems everyone refused to see that I could find happiness after Daniel.

I received an urgent voice message from Renata, the pastor's wife, regarding the meeting we had scheduled with the pastor that evening. She wanted to meet with me prior, over coffee.

I took the children with me to the meeting. They napped in the pram while I sat and had coffee with Renata.

"How have you been keeping?" she asked. The mood was somewhat stifling.

"I've been well, just keeping busy," I replied.

"Okay, no sense in me beating around the bush with this," she started. "I have my concerns about the fact that you plan to marry David."

A little shocked, I responded, "Why's that?"

"I've been praying on this. We've all been praying on this. I don't feel that he's the one God is commanding you to be with. We all feel that the person he commanded you to be with has gone, and you should remain celibate to honour his memory," she suggested.

I put my cup down, astonished at the suggestion. "Renata, you didn't even know Daniel. No one here knows him the way I did. He encouraged me to have a relationship with David, knowing he wouldn't be with us in the end."

She nodded but carried on. "As I said, we've been praying on it."

"You must not know David too well to even suggest that he is not the right one for me," I said.

"I know David enough to know that he's bad news," she stated. "Pastor Petherick and a few of the other men noticed a pattern of scars on his body," she started.

Shocked, I questioned, "Yes, and what about that?" She was referring to his back and truck that was marked with scars from physical abuse.

"We are waging a war against powers and principalities. David's marked and rising influence in the church, and the marks on his body point to only one thing. If you love these children, and you fear God, do your best to put distance between the two of you."

"You're joking, right?" I questioned, amazed at the sudden change of view. Yesterday he was a pillar in the church. Today, he was reduced to mere rubble. "I assume Pastor Petherick will no longer be open to officiating the marriage then?"

Renata nodded in response.

I stood up and left, not wanting to waste another moment talking to her.

David was pacing the floor when I got home. Josiah and Adalia were asleep. He greeted me with a gruff but affectionate kiss, helping me get the twins out of their prams and into the playpen. "How are you?"

"Been better," I said. I explained the day's drama. Explained that the news that we were getting married had been met with a lukewarm reception from the friends we did have left. "I know how Daniel felt about the possibility of us," I mentioned. "I'm not sure the rest of the world will be as enthusiastic about our union. We've already lost a few friends over us being together..."

"Yep, and some friends they turned out to be, bailing on you and I when we needed them the most," he reminded me. Livid, he swore. "Excuse my French, but fuck them. Fuck the lot of them."

It was odd to hear him swearing. He had had some drama of his own that day. The word had gotten out that we had plans to marry. As a consequence, he had been told that his position as youth pastor was no longer certain.

"You know, I can understand that they want me to be a

father figure to those kids, and to guide them through their trials. I'm not a bad person. I'm not a bad influence on anyone. What I don't understand is how my personal decision to finally marry the woman I've been in love with for quite a large chunk of my life is cause for concern and reason to cast me as unsuitable for the role. You'd think we were committing a crime," he fumed.

I nodded in agreement but reminded him of the time that I'd been given the cold shoulder at church in Austi, Texas as a result of the tumultuous relationship with Duayne. How I'd been branded a harlot and felt a sense of shame over something that I did not perpetrate.

He asked me whether I was having second thoughts about being with him.

"No," I promised. "No second thoughts. Just rethinking the whole wedding ceremony idea."

"Like should we even have a ceremony? Should we even bother with the rest of the world?" he asked, disillusioned.

"David, I've never heard you talk like this before," I told him. "We've come too far for you to give up now. I'll be proud to marry you, and I won't marry you under the cover of darkness just because people can't accept us being together."

"I'm sorry, I'm somehow losing faith now, quite a few things haven't worked out the way I planned, and I'm not certain those things are for me anymore," he said candidly, clearly upset.

"David, you're a perfectionist. Life isn't perfect, you have to step back and see the beauty in imperfection." I suggested.

"So, if you say there's beauty in imperfection, there is beauty in what we have here, it's not perfect but it's right," he stated. "But I don't see the beauty in this," he said, motioning towards his mouth, cleft palate repaired, the only evidence a scar. "Or my many scars. Or the fact that I lost my brother, you lost your husband and father of your kids..." He paused for a moment in deep thought. "I don't see the beauty in that imperfection, in your unhappiness. Unless of course you were meant to find happiness with me," he guessed, contemplative. "In that case I can say there *is* beauty in imperfection and your theory wouldn't be too far off at all."

I smiled at his reasoning. "David, to me you're perfect."

He smiled back. "Flattery will get you everywhere my dear," he joked.

"I'm being serious David. Your love for me is perfect. Unfailing, you never gave up hope after all these years, you have been my strength, my unfaltering strength when I was weak," I said. "I only hope that I can be the same and more for you," I added.

"I can only hope that I can measure up and be the man you want me to be," he said with an air of sadness .

"You are everything I want you to be, David," I declared.

"Thanks baby. Though, why do I feel like I'm letting you down here? My plans for the church, our plans to get married there..."

"All I want right now is to marry you, the venue, the company, all those things don't mean much to me anymore."

"But of course they still do," he argued.

"They did. A long time ago. Before we came to be. My outlook has changed now."

He hesitated before responding. "Okay, so we downsize, or we do something pretty low-key," he suggested.

"My thoughts exactly," I concurred.

"Now, the church. They won't even let me minister to the youth group any more," he said, clearly distraught.

"I'm a firm believer of the fact that if it's not for you, it won't happen. What if the plan is for you to start your own church?" I asked.

He stepped back and looked at me squarely. "I'm not sure such a big plan is for me," he said.

"And why not?" I questioned.

He pondered for a moment. After a while, he stated, "Okay, I'm listening."

"What if God is calling you to start your own church? What if every negative experience you've had has been to give you strength to serve and carry others?"

"I hear you."

"What if you could use your power to heal to bring glory to God?"

"You know how I feel about that," he stated. "I'm enough of a pariah as it is," he said.

I felt for him. "David, you're anything but. You're a man after God's own heart, as your namesake in the Bible was. Give it some thought. I'd help you. We could set the world ablaze with your passion and love for humankind. Not to mention, your gift."

He agreed, though somewhat apprehensively.

"Now, for the wedding, how about we just make it you and I?"

He shook his head to the negative. "You deserve better than this, darlin'," he said.

"I don't need a huge wedding to tell the world I'm yours," I told him.

"You deserve better," he stated, turning away. "I'm being

serious. Anything you want, I'll try to make it happen. I let you walk away from me the first time, I'm not letting you go this time." Hurriedly he said, "Look, I can call up Craig, I'm sure he'd be happy to officiate for us. If you wanted a big and lavish wedding we can plan for that, but how about we get this show on the road now?"

"David you've waited long enough for me to come around. I'm happy to do whatever," I replied.

He did call Craig. The one person that we could count on for support was Craig. David put him on speakerphone. "I'd be happy to officiate your union," Craig confirmed.

When we told him of the lack of support elsewhere, he said, "This is your decision. It's your life. If Daniel had not wanted you to move on after him, Teme, he would not have said what he said to me or to you David, while he was still with us. His final letter confirms it all. He wanted you both to move on. With each other."

We married in a low key ceremony on the beach. We did away with the tuxedo and wedding dress. David wore a white suit shirt and khaki shorts, while I wore a sheer blue shift dress. Pail and shovel at hand, the children played in the sand as we recited our vows to each other. And so I became Mrs. David Davenport.

28

PLEADINGS

David seemed on edge that morning as we sat on the patio watching the world go by. Motioning to the father and child walking by, he mentioned, "See the way he's embracing her? I wouldn't doubt that something inappropriate was going on."

What a strange comment to make, I thought.

"I hate my past," he said suddenly.

"That's a strong statement to make!" I exclaimed.

"There are a few things in my past that I'm not proud of," he said. "Good and bad. I was a bit of a hedonist in the past, constantly seeking pleasure above all else. I still seek pleasure, but not in the ways I once did. Fixating on the prospect of one day meeting you again and convincing you to give me a chance again kept me somewhat grounded. I say somewhat, as there've been moments when I lost it. The moment I saw you all those years ago, I felt so strongly about you. When I realised you wouldn't be mine, I set out in search of the perfect means to make you mine. The initial plan didn't work. You left Aus. Took me a while to find you again. I joined the army, knowing it would take me places, then I only looked forward to the day you'd be mine. Here we are. A dream come true to me."

"And me," I told him. "I admire you David for how patient you've been all these years. How full of love you still are after all this time. I admire how you kept hoping when there seemed to be no hope. I love how you are filled with so much desire to serve others. How you put yourself last when it's all too easy to put yourself first."

"I'm not a saint. You're painting me out to be one," he protested.

"Well, you've been one to me," I told him.

"I suppose, to have waited for you all these years, I would have had to have had the patience of a saint," he joked.

"Funny," I laughed.

"Indeed," he replied.

After a brief pause, I asked, "Please tell me more. About your past."

The phone rang and he got up immediately. "I need to take this," he stated, walking away from me.

I heard him talk for a moment, then heard silence. Curious, I decided to check on him. I peered into the living room and saw he had his phone on the table. The speaker on the other end was still talking, yet he sat, motionless without response. I couldn't quite make out who he was talking to. After a while, he stated, "Yep, still here."

Following a series of monotone responses to the affirmative, he stated shakily, "Can't do this right now." Startling slightly when he realised that I had just walked into the room, "Look I just can't," he said more forcefully, and ended the call. His hands were shaking, his face pale.

"You okay?" I asked. Clearly he was not.

"All good," he lied.

"What was that about?"

"Nothing for your pretty little head to worry about," he replied a little too quickly. Changing topic he asked, "Need anything from the shops? I'm just heading out for a few things." He was still visibly shaken.

"No, can't think of anything at the moment."

"Alright," he stated, quickly getting up. "Will be back shortly," he said, planting a kiss on my cheek.

"David, you okay?" I asked again.

"I'll be fine," he promised, walking out the door.

In his abrupt departure he'd left his phone on the table. I checked the last call, and recognised the number. *Craig.*

Our doorbell rang that afternoon. An unexpected visitor. "Craig!" I exclaimed. He'd brought Khadija with him, a friend from the UK. He wore a white polo shirt, blue denim jeans. "Hey Darling!" he exclaimed, roses in tow. He seemed refreshed. Khadija wore a sheer cream dress, and looked stunning. I wondered whether there was a thing between them.

"Aw, look at these babies!!!" she remarked, the moment she laid eyes on Josiah and Adalia.

David outwardly appeared happy to see Craig, though there was a decidedly hostile undercurrent between the two. While Khadija and I sat inside in the front room chatting, David and Craig stayed out on the front balcony. Craig talked, while David nodded mostly. Neither of them realised the side window was ajar and we could hear them.

"Well, the Royal Commission is inviting oral or written statements on what took place at the orphanage," Craig announced.

"The abuse you mean," David said a little too loudly.

"Yes," Craig said sombrely. "I was thinking we could..."

"I won't be making either," David announced.

"It'll help."

"How?" David retorted, now standing and pacing.

"He's still around you know, there hasn't been enough evidence to commence proceedings against him," Craig said.

"That's not on me."

"No, but your testimony can help," Craig insisted. "It's the least you can do, given you got away eventually."

"Haven't got time for this," David said. "I haven't gotten so far just to go back there again. I've..." he stopped, his voice cracking.

"I got you," Craig assured him, placing a firm hand on his shoulder.

"I want to go back to Tas, but not like this, and certainly not for that," David said.

"If you don't say anything, he might continue doing what he's been doing all these years. Your testimony could be what helps put him away. You might not have a choice. As I said, it's the least you can do," Craig stated, turning slightly and acknowledging my presence with a nod. He'd realised Khadija and I were listening in.

"Sorry, but I couldn't help but overhear what was being said," I offered through the open window.

"You shouldn't know any of these things," David said, turning to leave.

Craig stopped him from walking away. "You need to talk to her," he urged.

"Not right now," David said, pushing past Craig, in a rush

527

to get away and be alone.

As abruptly as David had gotten up to leave, Craig decided to go. I said a quick goodbye to Khadija and wondered after her. I knew I'd be seeing her again sometime. The emotional connection and chemistry between her and Craig was quite apparent.

I gave David some space, but after a few hours decided to prompt him to tell me what had upset him.

"I'm not ready to talk about any of that, right now," he claimed.

"When *will* you be ready. This is clearly upsetting you, yet you won't let me in on what's got you so riled up." I said. "If you ask me, you're being pretty selfish at the moment."

"Selfish?" he looked surprised. "Trust me, I'm being anything but. I'm trying to shield you from this all. As I've said before, you shouldn't know certain things."

I was livid.

David pressed a finger on my lips to silence whatever tirade was coming his way. "You're a beautiful, hot angry mess at the moment," he declared suddenly.

How dare he. "Don't you dare patronise me," I replied.

"I'm just stating a fact, don't hate me for being honest," he said.

"I really wish you would stop joking around for a moment and just be serious."

"You know, way back when I used to be known as *the* Joker. I can't quit," he declared.

"You're really making me mad, David," I warned.

"Okay darling, if you feel like fighting, let's have it out then take it to bed. I'll give you the best fight you've ever had."

Hands on my hips, I was fuming and at a loss for words.

He stood directly in front of me so that we were then head to head. Standing intimately close to me, he whispered in my ear. "I'll give you something to shout about and I'll make you forget you were ever mad at me," he promised.

"Okay," I said. "I'll wait for you to tell me when you're ready."

I couldn't stay mad at him for long and he knew this. I caved in to him and abandoned my questioning of him.

As the days went by, I waited for him to open up to me but it seemed as though he made every effort to avoid talking about his past. With each day that passed, the distance became more and more apparent. We spoke generally and about future plans, but he was otherwise largely absent and distracted.

I cornered him one afternoon on his way out to work. He had been quiet the whole morning. "You need to talk to me Dave."

"I can't," he said immediately.

"Why not?"

"Because there are some things about me that you just shouldn't know," he replied.

"There's nothing you could tell me now that would make me love you less," I told him.

"Wanna bet?" he questioned. "I just can't," he repeated. "Not right now anyway."

"If you don't tell me, I'll find out. I already know you were speaking with Craig. I already know it's about the Royal Commission into child abuse that occurred in religious institutions. In Tasmania."

"Keeping tabs on me now, are you?" he replied somewhat angrily.

"No, you left your phone on the table after you last spoke with him. I also overheard you last time he was here," I mentioned. "Was that the last time you spoke with him this week?"

"I see," he replied. "No, spoke with him today as well."

"Okay," I stated, beckoning for him to tell me more. "I'm open to hear what you have to say," I reiterated.

"Not right now," he replied. "I'll tell you tonight," he offered. "Once the kids are in bed."

He didn't. The children saw to it that he didn't; Adalia's behavior in particular was unreasonable. Getting her to comply with anything that evening was a mission and a half.

"Has she been in your handbag again, eating sweeties?" David asked point blankly. On investigation, she had. The box of Tic Tacs in my handbag were half empty despite having been bought the day before. David laughed to himself, not surprised in the least before stating, "I have just the thing."

He searched through his backpack and came up with a packet of Fishermen's Friend. "You've ever had these before?"

"Fisherman's Friend? I have. A little mint won't deter her."

"This isn't just a *little mint*. This is the *original* Fisherman's Friend. A bit of liquorice, a bit of...just try one," he suggested, handing me one.

I almost instantly spat it out. David laughed gregariously in response.

"She'll be in for a surprise. I dare say she won't be in your bag looking for sweeties again, after this."

530

I smiled but grew annoyed at the fact that he had tried to avoid talking to me about Craig and the matter related to the Royal Commission. *He had to tell me now or else.*

"David, you have to tell me what's going on now, or I'll go straight to Craig and find out," I threatened.

His eyes narrowed and annoyance flashed across his face. "I don't want to talk about it," he retorted.

"You *need* to talk about it," I told him. "Tell me what you can," I requested. "I'm your wife, David," I reminded him. "You're safe with me."

Lengthy silence ensued before he sat beside me on the couch and took my hands into his. "I'm ashamed of my past," he stated. "The Mission for Boys, back in Tassie was where it all went down. I stayed there after Michael got taken away. I met Craig there. Johnny and Edwards too. I..." he broke off. Swallowing deeply, he continued, "I ran away a couple of times. I couldn't take what they were doing to Johnny and Raphael, and I couldn't take what they were doing to me. I promised to go back for Johnny and Raphael and I didn't. Not on time anyway. I couldn't go back when I said I would. Craig stayed there for as long as he could. By the time I went back, Johnny, Rafe and Craig were in the UK."

"How old were you when you left?" I asked.

"I was twelve."

I sighed in sadness. "Where did you go?"

"I was on the streets for some time, then just before I turned fourteen, I got taken in by a baker. Lived with him and his wife for a couple of years, then she died, and he passed not long after," he said, painfully recalling the memory. "I stayed on to run the bakery when it was taken over, then..."

He sat there in silence before abruptly adding, "I left Tas

531

for Queensland, moved to the Goldie, linked up with Craig again. Then I met you. The rest is history."

I felt an overwhelming sadness for him. When we'd first met all those years ago, I did not know his story. I did not know that his love for me was not just infatuation. I did not know that in chosing to love me, he had decided to take a chance on something he'd not experienced before, something that had rarely been shown to him. I did not know the depths he would go for love. I did not know the extent to which he would sacrifice for a chance to be with me, in love.

"I wish I knew all this David," I told him.

"You know now," he replied. "I was afraid you'd look at me differently. I haven't told you what happened to me, I don't know if I ever will."

"Of course I look at you differently," I told him, and watched him stiffen slightly before I explained. "I look at you differently, and I love you more."

"I don't need your pity," he said, getting ready to stand up.

"This isn't pity," I told him, beckoning him to remain seated. "This is reverence. This is love. For a man who has spent his whole life looking out for others and putting himself last."

"I'm not sure Daniel would have agreed," he replied. "I know Johnny would not agree."

"Johnny forgives you. He once told me that he looks up to you but knows he'll never measure up. We all love you much more than you think," I told him.

He smiled slightly. "Well, I can't rest until I feel I've atoned for having left Johnny and Rafe behind."

"I understand where you're coming from, but atonement is not what you need to be thinking of. You were just a child.

You did what you could," I told him.

"Craig seems to think I need to atone. He's wanting me to testify before the Royal Commission, to tell them what happened at the Mission. He's of the opinion that this will make up for the fact that I left Johnny and Rafe behind. He says it's the least I can do."

I kissed my teeth in annoyance. "Craig's a trip. How dare he try to force your hand!"

"Well, truth is, I can't testify even if I wanted to. I'm not trying to relive what happened to us there. Craig never experienced the worst of it. He doesn't understand why I won't talk about it."

"I'm sorry David," I replied, squeezing his trembling hands. "You don't have to talk if you don't want to, but it's my understanding that talking will help others, and will help put whoever did this to you away."

"It won't help. Especially when the men and women who did this to me are above the law," he said.

"How so?"

"Our father."

I felt a shiver run down my spine.

"He owned the Mission, he knew about what was going on, and from what I've heard he was a willing participant and oversaw the whole operation. The people who did what they did are still at large."

What a bombshell. I felt sick to my stomach at the thought.

"So, where do we go from here?" I asked.

"Nowhere. This goes nowhere. Daniel tried to rock the boat, you saw where that landed him," he reminded me.

"Daniel knew about what happened to you at the Mission?" I asked, surprised. He hadn't said anything to me at all.

"He only knew as much as I told him," David explained. "Enough to have him convinced that our father was the enemy. Only then, I did not know he knew who our father was."

"So, you know who your father is now?" I asked.

"I'm not absolutely certain, though I might do," he advised.

"Sounds like you do know but you're avoiding telling me," I remarked. "I thought we weren't going to have any more secrets between us?"

"This is different. I want to leave things be for the time being. For your safety, and for the safety of the kids," he explained.

"Okay," I replied.

"Okay?" he asked.

"Okay," I said again. "I trust your judgement. I trust you know what's best for us all."

"I know that, but I know you, baby. I know you'll find it real hard to leave things be, or "leave well enough alone" as Daniel would've said," he stated.

"I know," I replied. "This is different though. I'm not trying to put any of us in jeopardy. I can't guarantee I won't have a word or two for Craig though."

"Fair enough," he said. "Before you do, remember Craig doesn't like to be challenged or confronted. He's always held a soft spot for you though, so... all I can say is tread carefully."

"I will. He won't know I'm coming," I promised.

David smirked in response. "If you say so. Craig's got eyes and ears everywhere."

"No matter. He needs to be spoken to," I insisted. "So, Daddy Dearest. Did he raise any of you?"

"He did," David replied abruptly.

His answer surprised me. "You've known this for how long?"

"Not long," he assured me. "Not long. A few days now."

I sighed heavily in disbelief.

"He raised Jonah," David revealed.

Yet another bombshell. Shockwaves ran through me.

"Right about now is the time to leave things be," David cautioned. "You know what you know now, please leave things be."

"Craig has obviously known all about this?" I assumed.

"More than likely," David concurred. "Tread carefully." After a momentary pause, he held my hands in his and brought them to his lips. "I love you darlin'. Thanks for loving me through this all, and for accepting me for me. I want us to focus on us now. On increasing this family of ours. I want us to have a baby of our own. I want us to forget all of this background drama and just focus on us."

"Babe, you've just dropped the biggest bombshell on me, and you seem completely unaffected," I observed.

"Mamasita, I've had to live with this for a long time. It doesn't affect me the way it used to. I've got love now. I've got you."

"You sure starting a family right now is the best thing for us to do?"

"I can't think of a better time to do it," he replied. "We can start our own legacy, our own pride. A piece of you, a piece of me. You know what I mean."

I smiled widely at him. "I do."

"So, are you on board?"

"I definitely am," I replied. "When do we start?"

"Kids are asleep, right about now is a good time," he stated, fondly planting kisses on my lips and cheeks.

"I love you Doctor Davenport," I said in between kisses.

"And I you," he replied. "Let's do this."

Queensland was in the throes of a local election and we felt stuck in the middle of it all. Resentment at all that was foreign was at an all-time high, and I quickly found myself a casualty of that struggle. Bargain Makers was conveniently located for a last minute dash. That morning the attitude of the store clerk threw me off guard. "Open your bag right now," she yelled. "Open it up so I can see the contents."

Okay? So you think I've lifted something from the store? I did as I was told but left the shop feeling shocked and wronged. I understood security concerns, but there was a way to be, and that was no way.

David was livid when I relayed the experience to him. "Redneck. Why can't folk just act right. Doesn't take much. Shame on her." He paced briefly. "You know it's moments like this that I consider the possibility of leaving town."

"Baby, if I chose to leave every town based on my experiences I'd go everywhere and stay nowhere," I told him.

David nodded tacitly. "I get it. But at least with a place like Tassie we'd largely be left alone to get on with our lives. The kids would benefit from the freedom. We'd benefit from the culture. What's not to love about Tas?"

"Tasmania is beautiful," I agreed. "But would we be able to truly start afresh? The bad experiences you had there growing up - will you truly be able to go back there, and be largely unaffected?"

He paused momentarily, deep in thought. "The experi-

536

ences I had will always be a part of me. It's the extent to which I'll let those experiences impact on the rest of my life," he stated, running a hand through his hair. "On our lives," he added.

"What if you're not over it at all? What if being in Tas triggers painful memories?"

"For you and the babies, I'm willing to take that risk," he declared. "Need to face up to my past sooner rather than later."

I felt for him.

"If you don't like where we are I would gladly leave here with you," he vowed.

"David, I value your perspective. This shouldn't be all about me though. However if you think Tasmania is the place we should be, let's do everything we can to get there," I suggested.

His face lit up. "I'm glad you feel that way, darling. Cause I've spent so much time tryin' to get you on side, so much time building up my confidence just to be able to convince you to be with me, and no time thinking of how I would deal with you being with me, around me, not just in my head but in my bed. I don't feel I'm being much of anything to you these days besides trouble. I'd like the chance to show you something different. Something beautiful. I feel we can find that in Tassie."

"Don't be so hard on yourself," I told him. "You don't have to be anything else. Just be."

"The problem with me just being, is that I just *be* a terrible lover, a terrible friend and and a hopeless romantic," he stated.

"David..."

"I'm hoping I won't lose you, feels like I've waited an eternity to be with you."

I couldn't help but smile. "So, it has been an eternity," I agreed. "Just know I'll be spending the next sunrise, and the one after that, and the ones after that, with you."

"I appreciate you saying that," he said.

"I mean it."

"I'm terrified of losing you," he confessed.

"I'm not planning on going anywhere without you," I told him.

"I hear you. At the same time, I can think of all the ways I'm not measuring up to expectation," he said.

"Let go of that sense of expectation," I advised. "I am living my dreams with you."

He suddenly turned and hugged me with such force I thought I would burst. "You always know just what to say."

I hugged him with equal force. "So, Tassie, we make it happen?"

"Sure thing," he replied.

Tasmania it was then. We said goodbye to Queensland in the weeks that followed. Instead of driving to the Port of Melbourne and sailing over via the Spirit of Tasmania, we flew. Two hours later we were in Hobart. A cool arctic breeze greeted us on arrival. David had warned me about the cold, but I welcomed it after the uncomfortable humidity of Queensland.

29

IN HIS NAME

A faint pink line shone on the pregnancy test strip that morning. David and I grew quietly excited. We imagined who the baby would look most like. I secretly wondered whether my babies with David would look like my babies with Daniel. Our happiness was short-lived when I miscarried 10 days later. I felt broken, punished, and wronged. Had it been a mistake to start anew with David so quickly? Friends and family had not believed in our union - they felt I hadn't mourned Daniel long enough. They failed to acknowledge that even Daniel had endorsed our union. I felt punished. Had I moved on too soon, though it had been over two years since Daniel had gone? I felt wronged. Didn't I deserve happiness? Didn't David deserve happiness? I started second guessing myself. Perhaps trying for a family with David was simply not the proper thing to do.

There we sat, David and I, in tears. His strong shoulders which carried so much seemed weak and heavy with the burden of our loss. Still, he held me, with such force I felt I would melt. Despite his own sadness, he carried me in my grief.

"We need to try again," he said. "We need to pray hard for this one. It will happen in time. It will happen in His time." After a lengthy pause, he stated, "Look, let's not rush, let's take this time to get to know each other more, and to focus on our other babies. I'm struggling to come to terms with this now, but I have faith it will all come together in time, when we least expect. Just have to live through this in the meantime."

"Just have to get through this in the meantime," I agreed, in between tears. He kissed my forehead, then rested his chin on my head. The collar of his shirt was wet from my tears. I sighed, somewhat relieved in the knowledge that I had him, and that he would go everywhere with me.

Following our loss, for months we tried to get pregnant again but couldn't. Eventually we sought the opinion of Adrian, an obstetrician referred to us by Michael.

Tests did not reveal an inability to conceive, but rather, that we might have difficulty conceiving.

"You are aware that there was significant damage to your testicles that could've possibly impacted on the capacity for you to conceive?" Adrian asked David.

"I wasn't aware of the extent of the damage," David replied.

"Have you heard of testicular torsion?" Adrian asked.

"I'm a doctor, I have, though I'd be surprised if *she* has," David joked, referring to me.

Adrian laughed awkwardly. "Well, I'll explain for her benefit, and for yours. It looks like you sustained some significant trauma to the testicles, likely as a teenager. Perhaps a sporting injury?" Adrian presumed.

David swallowed deeply and didn't answer. From his

reaction, I could tell that the trauma wasn't due to a sporting injury. I imagined that the trauma would've been sustained when he was either in the orphanage, or living on the street.

"If that trauma had been dealt with promptly, as in, if you'd had surgical intervention, there would've likely been no lasting damage. But because you didn't have surgery at the time, permanent damage has occurred and this has resulted in reduced sperm production," Adrian said.

David stared off into the distance. "What are the options?"

"I'd still recommend you try to conceive naturally," Adrian suggested. "There is still capacity for you to conceive. The fact that you miscarried is proof of your capacity to conceive. It may just take longer than usual."

"I'm sorry," David apologised, turning to me.

I felt for him. "You don't have to be sorry, David. None of this is your fault. We'll get through this together," I told him. His deep blue eyes glistened with tears that threatened to fall.

"I'd recommend you reduce the stress in your lives, take some time out of the busy lives you undoubtably lead. In the meanwhile, David, I'd like for you to take some multivitamins which are proven to help sperm mobility. Temwani, keep doing what you're doing, and you'll get there in the end."

We drove in silence on the trip back. "David, you okay?" I asked.

"I'd be lying if I said I was," was his abrupt reply. "I'm really cut at the fact that you're missing out on having another baby because of the condition I have," he stated. "So much for me being able to make you happy."

"David. I hope you know there's much more to our relationship than us having kids together," I said.

"I know, but I've dreamed about us having a family of our own for the longest time. I've dreamt that our kids would fill our home with laughter and joy and pretty much everything in between. I never dreamed that it wouldn't be possible," he said, brusquely turning off the highway to stop at the petrol station.

"You okay?" I asked, worried that he wasn't. His hands were trembling, and it looked as though he were about to be sick.

"I just...I can't drive right now," he explained, pulling into an empty parking bay next to the air pump and water.

"David..."

He retched open the car door and was sick on the ground, by the front wheel.

I offered him some water, which he declined.

"I'll drive," I told him, offering him water again. He accepted the water this time, taking a swig and spitting it out. "You okay?" I asked again.

"I'll be okay," he replied. "I've got you by my side, I'll be okay."

I got out of the car, made my way over to his side and embraced him fondly. His chest heaved as silent tears fell from his eyes. I said nothing, just held him.

"It's getting on," he said, red-eyed. Wiping tears off his face he stated, "I could use something warm to drink, maybe we could stop here at the servo for a bit then hit the road again?"

"Of course," I told him. "I'll move the car first," I said, noting a driver behind was waiting to use the air pump.

"Just a moment," he said, pulling out the hose and dousing the cement where he'd been sick.

My David, my love. Too considerate of others.

We popped into the café for a moment, where we ordered some tea and vegan pies to go.

"This whole area used to be bush," he noted, speaking of the land that the petrol station now stood on.

"Lots has changed since way back when, huh?" I said.

"Lots has changed, lots has remained the same. I'm still an emotional wreck," he said, his voice cracking slightly as he spoke.

I sat with him in silence and thought of possible solutions. *Matthieu.* "Adrian suggested we take some time away. Maybe we go overseas for a week or so?"

"I don't know," he said. "I don't feel like doing much at all now." He was feeling stuck. I knew the feeling all too well.

"How about we go to Paris and we get in touch with Matthieu?" I suggested.

I'd piqued his interest. "Matthieu?"

"Yes, Matthieu Bodard."

"How do you know him?" he asked, slightly shocked.

"How doesn't anyone know him? I did some research on him after Daniel did his little bit of digging into your past as a yogi. He's an expert in trauma counselling - sexual trauma counselling."

David nodded in acknowledgement. "I happened to work with him for a short period of time."

"So, he's more accessible than we think, yes? We may be able to contact him on a whim and he can help us?" I guessed.

He nodded again.

"So, what do you say, we make this happen?" I asked. "If anyone can make this happen for us, he can."

He seemed rather hesitant. "I don't know whether I like

the thought of someone else getting into our bedroom issues, but I'm willing to give it a go."

"How soon can we leave?" I asked. "We can make arrangements for us to leave for Paris tonight."

"That's... sudden," David remarked.

"It is," I replied.

"I guess, this has to be done. I can't stand a moment longer living like this. Loving you like this."

So, Paris it was.

We stayed in an apartment in Montmartre. There we learned to love differently and love more deeply.

We arranged for Josiah and Adalia to be in a vacation program while we were busy with Matthieu, then for a sitter to stay with them until we returned home.

Matthieu had long blond hair which he kept up in a ponytail. His green eyes were a shade of emerald, and were warm and kind. His eyes beheld David and I in high esteem from the first meeting. The feel of his hand on mine when he greeted me was electric. He radiated positive energy and love unadulterated. "David has been looking for you for a long time. I'm glad you found him," he said.

And so began our journey of love, discovery and healing. Paris was an awakening of sorts. David and I connected on a level neither of us had experienced before. As a city, Montmartre had an energy unlike other places, one which enthused us with a new appreciation for life, love and an alignment with tenderness. In Paris we learnt to love, learnt to let go of the past, and learnt to hold on to each other.

Matthieu's teachings and instructions seemed counterintuitive. "No sexual intimacy unless initiated by him," he told

544

me. "No discussion about the past unless the discussion is initiated by him."

We therefore refrained from sexual intimacy, opting to grow closer in other ways. In the place of sexual intimacy, Matthieu advocated increased eye contact, increased conversation, and deeper spiritual and emotional intimacy. He advocated connecting on a subliminal level. He encouraged us both to be laid bare, and to lay our hearts, souls and minds bare before each other.

While David didn't reveal the details of the trauma he'd experienced at the orphanage, he grew to understand the extent of my love for him and that it was limitless. There was nothing he could reveal that would make me love him less.

At the end of the journey we were burning in desire and deep longing for one another. We knew then it was time to return home, and we did so with a renewed sense of belonging to one another, and a desire to be quenched only by one another.

The return home signalled a return to a different life, one with a heightened awareness of who we were as individuals and what we wanted to be as a couple. A desire was borne within us both, a desire which charged us both with ensuring each other's happiness and cultivating peace in our hearts and souls.

When we got back, it became apparent that David's internal wounds had yet to be healed, and that for as long as they remained open, I would feel his pain within myself as if it were my own. The connection we had formed meant he was I and I was he.

"I don't want you to have to walk through this pain with me," he told me.

"David, I'm walking through this pain with you, and I'm not letting go of your hand," I told him. His eyes beheld me with such reverence and endearment it made me cry.

"I knew all those years ago you'd be the one. I wasn't wrong in waiting for you all those years. You'll always be the one for me," he said, embracing me fondly. As Daniel had said, there was a lot of loving to be had between David and I. This was just the beginning.

The safety that our relationship offered meant that for the first time, the extent to which he'd been harmed as a child was brought to the surface, and for the first time, he was able to heal.

"Baby, let's eat," I urged, beckoning him to sit down with me at the table. In the weeks that followed Paris, he had become painfully thin, working overtime and beset with worry over what the Royal Commission would reveal. Sleep did not come easy - he had nightmares most nights and would wake up in a cold sweat, memories of the past at the forefront of his mind, causing turmoil in his heart.

I tried to get him to eat. "David, I've made your favorite – cornbread and creamy mushroom soup."

His eyes lit up at the mention of his favourite meals.

"I'll do this up every night just to get you to eat, shall I?" I asked.

"You do enough sweetheart, more than enough. Don't trouble yourself with worrying about me," he replied glumly.

"Asking me to not worry about you is like asking me to not breathe," I replied. I reached across the table for his hands, and said a short prayer over our food.

"And may we be truly grateful for this food and for all you

546

have given us," he added. "Amen."

I watched him take a bite into the cornbread and sigh with reckless abandon. "Heavenly," he said.

"Good," I stated, wanting him to eat more.

We ate in silence until he spoke.

"I'm sorry I've been keeping you at a distance these last few weeks," he said, placing his fork and knife down. "I'm struggling to come to terms with something I've learnt."

I felt my heart leap in anticipation. I assumed it was something relating to his past.

Swallowing hard, he stated, "I found out who my biological father is."

"Oh?" I asked, surprised.

"Um hm," he replied, clasping his hands in front of him as though he were about to pray. "He's a minister," he said. His eyes not leaving mine, he added, "He's the last person I expected to be related to."

"Well, if he's a minister – I guess you have something in common?" I asked.

"That's one thing. We are otherwise unsimilar," he insisted.

Unsimilar. I could see he was struggling with something else, something more sinister. Reaching across the table to hold his hand, I asked, "Dave, baby. Please tell me what's got you so shook up inside."

After eating a few more morsels of food, he wiped his mouth on the serviette and announced, "Thank you for the food. It's delicious. I can't have any more though, I'm stuffed."

"You're welcome," I replied. "Though, you will be stuffed if you keep letting whatever it is that's bothering you, eat you up inside."

The corners of his lips formed a smile and he laughed lightly. "Touché," he replied, remaining tight lipped on whatever it was that had gotten him down.

"You *are* going to tell me what's been bringing you down, right?" I probed.

"My father's a bad man," he stated. "Evil incarnate," he said, with such voracity I shuddered. "He's done terrible things, and I'm ashamed to be related to him," he managed. "I don't want him anywhere near you or the children, and I certainly do not wish to be associated with him."

I pondered on what he'd just said, and I felt great pain and sorrow for him. The father that he'd been looking for for so long was finally known to him. The father who'd played a part in abandoning him as a child. The father who'd literally left him for dead.

David sat there at the dinner table, distraught. Reaching for his hand across the table, I smiled. My smile served the purpose of disarming him, and as a result, he had a puzzled look on his face, what with me smiling at a time like this. I decided to sing the first stanza of Dusty Springfield's *Son of a Preacher Man*.

"Aw, baby!" he exclaimed, joyful. "You're an angel. I guess there's something good that comes with being the son of a preacher, and being called to Ministry. I've managed to convince you that I'm alright."

"Baby, you've always been alright with me," I confirmed. "Way before you became a minister, you were alright with me. Just took me a while to admit it."

"Well alright then," he replied, flashing me a dimpled grin that I hadn't seen in a while. Despite the joy and healing that he brought others, he'd been sad for a very long time. *At least he's smiling now*, I thought, trying to imagine what he must be going through.

"I'm here for you," I told him. "God's always been there with you and there for you," I added.

He nodded in agreement. After a slight pause, he said, "I hit the jackpot when I first laid eyes on you, and now that we're finally together, I just know we can overcome anything that comes our way. Thank you for loving me, flaws and all. I just wish my past was different."

"It's made you who you are. I don't hold it against you. I'm here for you, the good and the bad, baby," I told him.

"I can't describe this in words, but I'll try," he started. "The way that I feel - I feel a sense of assurance in me, that no matter what I do, no matter who I turn out to be, God will always have my back. He has always had my back. I look at you, I look at the kids, and know he's always had my back. Even those times I felt alone, He was there. I may not have felt it at the time, but He was there, guiding me to this life, guiding me to you." His eyes welling up with tears, he stated, "I've found my happiness, and nobody will take this away from me."

My heart warmed at the mention of our love. I loved him out of the fullness of my heart. He adored me, and had from the start. His love was pure, and wholesome, the only expectation being that I accept him for all that he was, and all that he wanted to be. I didn't have to be anyone else, and I didn't have to do anything else for him to love me. Ours was not the love of romance novels or movie screens. Our love was written in the stars and was real. I never knew all those years ago that we would end up here. In love, like this.

A charming, well-dressed man walked into the office that Saturday afternoon. Sandy auburn blond hair, and sea blue eyes, he oozed of charisma. I recognized him as the pastor of Faithbound Church.

"Good afternoon," he greeted. "Is Pastor David around?"

"He's just gone out to do a bread run with some of the other guys, I'm expecting him back shortly. Do you mind waiting?" I asked.

"Not at all," he replied, flashing a perfect set of teeth and dimples in his cheeks.

"Sorry, how rude of me not to make an introduction," he stated. "I'm Pastor Declan, Faithbound Church."

"I'm David's wife, Temwani," I replied, holding out a hand for him to shake.

"Wonderful to meet you," he said, shaking my hand. "Your reputation precedes you."

"Does it now?" I asked, half smiling. "Only good things I hope."

"Only good things," he replied with a wink and a smile. Though he was charming, there was something disarming and unsettling about him.

"Care for some tea or coffee?" I offered.

"Thank you, but it's much too hot of an afternoon for tea or coffee," he said. "I'll take a cold drink if you're offering?" The streaks of auburn running through his sandy brown hair stood out.

I thought of the sweet tea in the fridge that David refused to touch, saying it was some kind of sweet. Daniel had loved it.

"How about some sweet tea, water or juice?"

"I'll try the sweet tea," he said, touring the room. He stared hard at the family photo on my desk. "Beautiful family," he noted. "How old are the kids?"

"They're almost three years old."

"Lovely," he replied. "Children are a blessing from God," he said. "I see your husband's a bit of a rock star!" he noted.

"That he is," I said in response. David had quite the following on social media, with women hankering after him left right and centre, but I wasn't worried about him. I knew where his heart was. His heart had been mine from the start.

Pastor Declan smiled in response. He continued staring at the photos on the wall. Motioning at a photo of Daniel he asked, "His late brother?"

"Yes," I replied, a little uneasy about how much he knew about my family.

"My condolences," he added. "It must not have been easy to lose him so young," he said, with sadness that surprised me.

"No," I replied. "David's support meant everything though."

Awkward silence ensured before I asked, "What brings you to our neck of the woods?"

Pastor Declan appeared to think carefully before he replied. "I'm here to talk to David."

David rushed into the room in a mood. Startled by Declan's presence, he asked, "What do you want?" I was a little shocked by his tone and his unexpected reaction. His behaviour felt a little untoward.

Pastor Declan stood up to greet him. "That's no way to greet your old man."

Old man? I thought. *David and Daniel's father?*

"Get out!" David commanded.

551

"I've come to see you, son. I see how well you've done for yourself. Welcome home," Declan said.

I saw the color leave David's face.

Approaching him, and placing a hand on his shoulder, Declan announced, "Sorry I stayed away for so long, son. Welcome home."

David abruptly stepped away from him. "You have some nerve coming here."

"David, I know who I am and I know who you are. I knew Jolène, I knew your mother. I *loved* your mother. I'm your father. It's time you realise we're family. You, me, your lovely wife here and kids. Welcome home, son."

"You might've loved my mother, but pity you didn't love me. Leave," David ordered. "Get out and leave."

Declan smiled awkwardly in response. "I'll be seeing you."

David turned to me after Declan walked out.

"So, that's your father?" I asked.

"Don't. I don't want anything to do with him. I'm ashamed to be related to him," he said adamantly.

"Surely he's not that bad, he's a pastor now..."

"He's always been a pastor!" David exclaimed.

"David..."

"Don't," he cautioned. "Don't try and convince me otherwise. Don't try and look at his good side. There isn't one. This man is pure evil."

A chill ran down my spine at his mention of the word evil.

"Please," David begged. "I'm just looking out for our family. I have plans for us that don't involve him. Please honour my wishes."

I faced him directly and gave him a warm, strong embrace. "I submit to whatever plans you may have for us as a family.

I trust you. I know that amidst all the confusion in our lives, the love you have for us is driving you."

His face lit up. "I truly struck gold with you," he replied, planting a kiss on my forehead and embracing me with equal force. "I can overcome anything with you and God by my side."

30

THE FIRE

In the days and weeks that ensued, Declan constantly and consistently tried to contact David, while David ignored him and refused his requests. At one stage, Declan even came to our house, and requested to see the children. David was livid, and promised to file a restraint order against him. This was all talk. It didn't happen.

Otherwise, he threw himself into his ministry. Overnight, David became a superstar of sorts in the church. He preached with such fire, and such passion, that the church of 40 soon grew to a church of 200. Not long after, we were fighting for space and wanting to host sermons in a different location.

We celebrated his success one night by going out for dinner and a show at the local theatre. Four years ago I couldn't have imagined myself being happy with anyone other than Daniel. Now, David took love to the next level, and when I was with him, I was overjoyed.

As we walked out of the theatre, the evening air was chill yet moist. David put his arm around my waist as we walked past the crowd, and past the bustle of the city. Our slate grey RX-7 was parked quite a distance away, so we walked the scenic route, past the shops that were adorned in Christmas decorations and lights. Walking the same streets many years ago, I'd felt fear and rushed through to get to the other side. Walking the same streets now with David, I felt secure, at ease, confident about the future, simply because he was in it.

David held the car door open and waited for me to get in. He stole a kiss from me before I did. "I'm the luckiest man alive," he declared. "You're absolutely beautiful, you're a dream," he said. "Let's hit the road, and we can get to being alone together."

I smiled in response, settling into the car, and waiting for him to get in. As we drove the brightly lit streets and onto the Southern Outlet, we were filled with Christmas cheer. Another year, this time, together. Our first Christmas as a married couple.

I heard the truck before I saw it ploughing into our car. I felt a scream rise in my throat, but it did not eventuate. David kept his hands on the steering wheel, trying to readjust to stop from going off road. The truck seemed to accelerate as he did so, pushing the RX-7 off road. A loose log that came off the back of the truck shattered the glass on David's side and he let go of the steering wheel in shock. Shards of glass pelted his arm.

"Lord help us!" I said under my breath as the car started spinning. I felt my head rolling with the motion. David used his other arm to push me back against the seat. The car continued to spin out of control until it came to a sudden halt. We'd hit a tree. My world blackened out for a moment. When I came to, the paramedics were there, disengaging David from his seat, putting him on a stretcher and whisking him to the hospital. They tended to me too, but I was in a better shape than David was. I shook and cried inconsolably. I didn't want to face losing him too.

David came to once we were in the hospital. The doctor spoke with him firmly. "David, you've lost a lot of blood...and your blood type is rare. We're not in a position to get the amount you need right now, but we'll ring around our local blood banks and hopefully we'll strike gold. But for now, we need to sit tight and wait."

Over the next hour or so, David drifted in and out of sleep, barely conscious. Apart from a few head nods, he did not speak. He tried to, but motioned to me that his chest hurt. I sat by his side, holding his hand.

The doctor returned much later. "An anonymous donor has given us the exact amount of blood you need."

"Anonymous?" I questioned.

"Yes, anonymous. The blood is a perfect match."

"Thank God for whoever he or she is," I said aloud, truly grateful.

It was a little after midnight when I decided to take a stroll down the ward. David was still in an induced coma, and I hadn't left his side until now. It had been hours since I'd last eaten and I was famished. The nurse on duty had tried to encourage me to eat earlier but I'd refused.

The ward was cold and dim and smelt sterile. A very young looking orderly walked past and nodded his head at me in acknowledgement. I nodded back at him, and wondered after him. Was he a medical professional in training as David had been all those years ago? I wondered how many nights David had paced halls like this, pondering the condition of a patient or considering if anything could have been done for someone that was so far gone. Thank goodness David was not so far gone. I couldn't bear the thought of losing him, after having lost Daniel. The moment I thought that, a partially open door slammed shut, from wind, presumably. I picked up my pace slightly, aiming to get back to David's side as soon as I could.

At the end of the long corridor was a vending machine. *Forget the canteen. A bar of chocolate was just what I needed.* I punched in the letter and number for a Twix, entered OK then inserted my card. When the machine pushed the chocolate bar forward and tossed it down, I noticed a reflection of someone else in the glass, behind me. Blinking intentionally, I looked again. There wasn't anyone else there but me. In my tiredness, I was probably seeing things. I collected my chocolate bar and made my way past the nurses' station and back into David's room.

The nurses and doctors were in the room opposite, having a meeting of sorts. Devouring my Twix, I turned my mind to David's anonymous donor. I wondered who he or she was. I thought of thanking them with a gift but no gift I had in mind would have been sufficient. Once David recovered, we would try to locate the donor by stealth, and thank them in person.

"You alright there love?" one of the nurses asked, interrupting me in thought.

"Only just," I replied.

"Doctor Davenport's lovely wife?" she asked.

"Yes," I advised.

"Your husband will be fine," she assured me.

"I hope so," I said.

"Trust me, he will. Have you eaten? Something other than chocolate?" she asked, referring to the empty chocolate wrapper in my other hand, the one that wasn't holding

David's. "We've got something more substantial in the mini fridge down at the end of the hall. I can show you?"

I let go of David's hand, then got up and walked with her in silence until she spoke. "You'd be getting pretty hungry by now I gather, though you're only a few weeks in. Baby's already pulling the strings."

I had to pause to understand what she'd just said. *I was pregnant.*

Realising the error of her ways, she apologized. "You didn't know, did you! Sorry. The doctor was supposed to have a chat with you, but somehow in all the drama, he must have overlooked it."

"Never mind, you all just saw the results before I did," I said.

"Something like that," she replied.

I felt a flutter in my belly. Whether from quiet excitement at the prospect of carrying David's baby, or the quickenings, I couldn't tell. David and I were finally expecting. He just had to come out of this.

"Dad just has to pull through now," the nurse said, reading my mind.

I nodded in response.

"Come now, chop chop, get you something to eat now before it gets too late. You've still got to rest now haven't you," she said.

I smiled as she walked away. *God bless nurses.*

The noodles, salad sandwich and orange juice filled a hole.

As I stood by the sink, washing up after myself, I noticed the door of one of the patient rooms was slightly ajar. A man in a wheelchair turned abruptly to close the door. I lost my grip on the bowl I was holding when I looked straight at the man and saw myself looking at someone that looked an awful lot like Daniel. He started straight at me, and I looked away hastily, before blinking and looking back again. In the spit second that I looked back, the door closed, and I pondered for a moment whether I'd imagined it all. *I must have.* The last time I'd been in hospital for an extended period had to do with Daniel. My eyes welled up with tears, suddenly, as I remembered him. Years on, and I was still seeing him everywhere.

Still, curiosity got the better of me. Deciding to walk that side of the corridor on my way back to David's room, when I got there I stood outside the door for a moment. If I knocked, what was the worst thing that could happen? Whoever it was would open the door, and I'd be assured it was just a lookalike, or no one at all, and it'd be confirmed that I'd imagined it was Daniel.

Hand on the door, I prepared to knock, but a deep voice from behind startled me. "Doctor Edwards," the man announced, in a white coat, patient pad in hand. "Friend of the patient?" he asked suspiciously.

Startled, I replied, "Uh, no. Just passing through."

"Hmmm...," he stated before saying "David's wife?"

Every doctor seemed to know him. "Yes," I replied.

"I'll catch up with you in a moment, once I've done my rounds up this end," he promised. "Good to see you're up and about," he added, placing the patient record folder back on the wall and squirting some hand sanitizer on his hands. "David will pull through. He's a fighter."

I felt tears well up in my eyes but I held them back. "I lost my first husband, I can't lose him as well," I stated. Doctor Edwards nodded in response, as though he already knew.

Stealing a quick glance at his wristwatch, he advised, "He's due for a status check right about now, I'll walk you back up to his room."

I was grateful for the company, but it sounded more like an order than a favour. He had given me a suspicious look when I stood in front of that patient's door, and perhaps this was his way of ensuring I left well enough alone. We walked in silence then he spoke again. "Dave and I went to the same school, back in the day, when we were coming up," he claimed.

"School school or med school?" I asked.

"School school," he repeated, laughing heartily. "Primary, secondary then he opted for dentistry before med. I went for med then dentistry. He left the Mainland for here as I was heading there, then we met again when he returned for his max facial training. "Class of '04," he added.

"I see," I stated. David hadn't mentioned Edwards, but that didn't surprise me. He hadn't been an open book about his past. "Well, we'll have to get you over to ours sometime soon," I insisted.

"I'd love that," Edwards said. "Though I'm not sure Dave would be too happy to see me. We had a falling out a few years back."

That's why he hadn't mentioned you in great detail, I thought, realising we'd reached David's room. We headed in, myself first, Edwards directly behind me. Reaching for the hand sanitiser on the end of David's bed, Edwards squirted a small amount on his hands again before doing a quick physical on David. "BP regular, stats okay..." Edwards thought aloud. The machine had done a reading of David's heart rate and pulse, but for good measure, Edwards put on his stethoscope and pressed the dial on David's chest. I thought I was imagining things when I saw David frown ever so slightly when the dial was placed on his chest.

"The anesthetic is wearing off. He'll be up shortly," he said as a matter of factly. Without warning, he asked, "He's got a heart murmur?"

I stared at him blankly, not sure whether it was a question or a statement.

"Sorry," he said, acknowledging that I didn't know. "He has a heart murmur."

"What does that mean?" I asked.

"On a scale of 1 to 6, I'm hearing it's a 5," he said. Lifting the stethoscope slightly off David's chest he nodded to himself. "Can still hear it," he confirmed.

"What does that mean?" I repeated.

"I'm gonna refer him to cardiology, just as a precaution," he said, brusquely writing some notes in his pad.

"For the last time, what does that mean?" I asked again.

"Sorry darl' didn't mean to alarm you," he said, putting away his notepad and hanging his stethoscope around his neck. "A heart murmur may or may not be cause for concern. The one Dave's got sounds like a 5 on a scale of 1 to 6, with 6 being severe – I just need to have cardiology have a second look, hopefully it isn't cause for concern. Is he still a vegetarian?"

"Vegan," I corrected.

"Right. We'll have a look at his bloodwork too, see if he's anemic. Anemia can show a similar impact on the heart," he said. "I've been calling you Mrs David Davenport. I didn't catch your first name."

"Temwani," I replied.

"Teme," we both said in unison. I smiled at him and he

smiled back. "You're all he would talk about over the years. You ruined him."

"He's ruined me," I confessed.

"You're beautiful," he said, suddenly. "Do you have a sister by any chance?" he asked casually.

"Thanks for the compliment," I replied. "Matter of fact I do, but she's taken."

"Damn," he said, part joking, part serious. "The good ones are taken all the time."

"Making moves on my woman?" David said clearly as he woke. He tried to sit up then winced in pain as he stretched his abdominals.

"Told you he was a fighter," Edwards said. When David tried to get up again, Edwards placed a firm hand on his shoulder in an attempt to stop him from getting up again. "Easy old boy," he stated. "Take it easy, no sudden movements," he insisted.

"Who you callin' old boy, Lionel," David replied.

Lionel? I thought.

"No one's called me that for yonkers," Edwards stated. "I go by Edwards now."

"Hm..," David sighed, turning his attention to me instead. I quickly went to his side and embraced him as far as I could, without hurting him. "Everything okay with you?"

"I'm fine," I replied. "Just worried about you. How do you feel?" I asked, giving him the once over. He barely had a scratch on him. His hair was slightly disheveled, his face had colour and apart from the abdominal pain, he seemed the picture of health.

"Better now that you're here," he said, grinning from ear to ear. "How about some love?" he asked, beckoning me to kiss him.

"How about the doc sees how you're doing and we wait for a full recovery before jumping back into things?" I said, noticing the look of disappointment on his face which would soon turn to joy. "We're having a baby," I announced. Suddenly very alert, he frowned slightly as though he hadn't understood what I'd said.

"Rugrats on the way, mate," Edwards chimmed in, smiling sheepishly.

David and I finally caught on. "More than one?" David asked.

"Well, twins do run in the family," I stated, surprised and excited all the same.

He slipped an arm around my waist and pulled me near. "Babies?" His deep blue eyes danced with excitement that could not be contained. "How many weeks?"

"16 weeks give or take," I told him. "I truly did not know I was pregnant."

His smile further deepened as he placed a hand on my belly. I felt one of the babies kick, and so did he. We'd been so busy with life, we'd failed to notice the miracle of life unfolding within. I gushed with joy at the thought that we'd finally be having babies together.

Clearing this throat, Edwards mentioned, "I'd see one of the obstetricians before you leave just to be on the safe side. As far as I know, there isn't anything to be concerned about, other than the fact that you need to monitor the babies closely over the next few days and weeks as a precaution. Just in case we missed something." Putting David's chart away, he stated, "Obs are looking good, just the murmur I'm concerned about."

"I've had that since I was born, mate, hasn't bothered me any," David said.

"Just have a look at it will you, to be on the safe side?"

"Alright," David replied.

"Might have to start eating up on the ole red meat again," Edwards suggested.

"Not a chance mate," David replied, "Not a chance."

"Any chance of some red meat over dinner?" Edwards asked, looking at me.

"Inviting yourself over, now, are we?" David asked suspiciously.

"*We're* inviting him over," I clarified. He softened in response and nodded slightly to the affirmative, though clearly apprehensive.

As Edwards strapped a blood pressure cuff onto David's left arm, David stated, "Water under the bridge mate. Life's too short."

Slightly taken aback, Edwards paused, misty eyed. "I agree," he said, swallowing hard before putting his effort into pumping air into the cuff. Stethoscope on, he placed the dial on David's forearm. Releasing the valve, he took note of the measurement and nodded to the affirmative. "Blood pressure's looking good. Try to get some rest if you can. I'll get the nurse to change the dressing on your arm. Just a gash, nothing to be concerned about, though you might feel a bit of pain when the meds wear off. Then again you know this. You got this, doc," he said, winking at me as he turned to go. "I'll catch up with you both in a bit?"

I squeezed David's hand, grateful he was okay, and looking forward to the time he would take off from work. He'd given so much of himself to others the last few weeks, it was going to be good to see him take time off for himself to heal in more ways than one.

31

LINE RIDER

I loved the crisp morning air despite the cold. That morning, a little fog obscured my vision. After a moment of hesitation I decided to head out on my jog anyway. David was still asleep, as were the kids. It was 5 am, and they wouldn't be up for another hour or so.

David opened his eyes briefly after I kissed his cheek. Sleepily, he mumbled, "I love you," before turning to his side. I raised the sheet up the bed further to cover his well-toned torso which was exposed. My heart warmed at the thought of his love for me, my love for him, and our babies on the way.

Full of adrenaline and ready to go, I decided not to jog with music that morning. The fog would make it difficult to see, and I would need to rely on my sense of hearing to ensure I was safe.

As the sun came up, the fog gradually cleared. Midway through the jog, I paused for a breath. In my path, on the dewy ground ahead of me, lay a single stemmed red rose. *Strange*, I thought. I immediately thought of Daniel, the night we'd first met, and the rose he'd given me. Without further thought I bent down to pick it up. Raising the petals to my nose, the deep fragrance brought me to my knees as I remembered Daniel. For a moment I was lost in the memory of him. For a moment, I was spellbound on a memory, before I heard the crackling of leaves being trod on somewhere close behind me.

My first thought was it was some form of wildlife. A wallaby perhaps, or an echidna. Then I saw the boots. Adrenaline surged through me as I dropped the rose and ran. Heart thumping, heavy footsteps were not far behind me. Whoever it was, they were walking and not running. I ran towards a tree that had fallen in front of the path. Vaulting over the tree log, I underestimated the distance between the clearing and the tree and as a result, I fell to my knees. In that moment, the footsteps behind me suddenly stopped. Knee slightly grazed, I got to my feet. "What do you want!" I asked.

Silence answered me. Pregnancy had made me breathless, and it took a little while for me to catch my breath. Looking around me, I realized I'd strayed so far from my jogging path, and didn't know which turn to take to get home.

Not a moment later, I felt a hand cover my mouth and strong muscular arms pull me backwards. I tried to scream but my screams were muffled. I saw the ring on his middle finger first. My heart skipped a beat, and I remembered that Daniel had a very similar one. The one we couldn't find when we put together all his personal effects after the funeral. I then heard a voice that I knew all too well, and could never forget. "I'm fixin' ta take my hand off right now, don't scream," he urged. "Turn around slow."

I turned around to see Daniel, in a black cowboy shirt and hat, stone black jeans and cowboy boots, in the flesh, and very much alive. "I had to see you again sugarpie," he said, searching my face as though he wanted to emblaze it in his memory forever.

"Daniel?" I mouthed, in shock as I felt my knees get weak. My head was spinning, reeling at the sight of him. In an instant, I felt myself losing balance. He braced my fall.

"Easy now," he said, holding me tenderly but firmly. "Didn't mean to spring up on you like this and frighten the livin' daylights out of you, but I *had* to see you again," he stated. "I been fixin' ta see ya for a long time now. I missed you every hour and every minute and every second of every day but I had to leave when I did and stay away for as long as I did. Glad to see you found happiness," he said, just before I felt myself fall into his arms and lose consciousness.

In what seemed like hours later, I awoke with a start. I was in the bedroom, lying on the bed. David was kneeling at the end of the bed and greeted me with a nervous smile. I knew right then and there that he'd known about Daniel for a while now, if not, all along.

"Where is he?" I asked loudly and frantically.

David placed a hand on his lips as an indication not to talk.

My heart raced in anticipation. I needed to know why.

"You sprained your ankle on the jog," he started. "I'll take you in to the hospital on my way in this morning."

"You need to tell me where he is," I demanded.

"Babies are fine. Heart rates steady," he said. "No more early morning jogs alone," he said.

"Where is he!" I exclaimed impatiently.

"You'll see him when you settle down," he said.

I got up and nearly fell over. David braced me, pressing his body against mine to hold me steady. "Settle down Teme. You'll see him in a moment."

"I want to see him now!"

"Please settle down Teme," David urged. "Daniel's in the living room. I'll take the kids to Alana's. I'll be back in 10."

Getting up slowly this time, I made my way to the living room. Daniel stood there, leaning against the wall in his familiar cowboyesque pose. He had his hat in his hand.

I rushed towards him and poked him for good measure to see if he was really there in the flesh. My disbelief quickly turned to anger. "Why would you do this to me!" I exclaimed, fists balled, pummeling his chest. "How could you do this to us!"

"Come now, come now, sugarpie," he implored, tugging at my heart strings with his smooth and tender voice, taking my balled fists into his hands and pulling me in closer. "I did this to save you from me, and what a life with me would entail," he explained. "I did this because I love you and I want to protect you." Without warning, he planted a full kiss on my lips. Stunned, I stood there for a moment before resisting him.

"I'm not your wife anymore, Daniel!" I said, wiping the taste of him off my lips.

He smiled comfortably in response. "Oh, yes you are!" he stated. "You know as well as I do that your current marriage is null and void as the first one was not over when you tied the knot with David. Can't divorce a dead man who's come back to life, now can you?"

I slapped him hard across the cheek. "*You* did this to us," I said.

He winced in pain from the sting of the slap. "Baby, don't

get all excited. In fact, don't all welcome me back at once," he said. "I've been gone a while and all you can do is yell at me? Okay, I see I can still get you all fired up inside, but baby, this wasn't the homecoming I was expecting."

"Don't call me baby. I haven't been your baby for a long time. You left me. You left us!" I reminded him. "You faked your own death, I married your brother, and now you're back. What do you want from me! What will you have me do for you this time?" I questioned, angrily.

He paused for a moment before stating simply, "I didn't quite fake my own death...it's complicated. I'm sorry." His deep blue eyes glistening with tears, he apologised again. "I'm sorry."

As he stood there in the flesh, I knew I still loved him. I still wanted him. We shared a life together. A life that was cut too short. I still loved him, but this wasn't the time or place to rekindle old flames of love.

"I'm sorry," he said again. "Very sorry," he added. "It was all done for the love of you," he said. Stepping back, he held out his hand to take mine. I resisted at first.

"Sugarpie, please," he requested.

Reluctantly, I placed my hand in his. "Beautiful ring," he commented, examining the gold band with pink diamonds. "Pink diamonds? I see he spared no expense, yet again," he said. "I knew you'd be happy with him," he added.

"Really? You've come back to tell me that?" I queried. "How generous of you.

He ignored my attempt at sarcasm and instead offered a compliment. "Time's been kind on you, you're a sight to behold. You're still so damn fine," he said, bringing my hand to his lips for a kiss.

Though his kiss sent tingles down my spine, and sent my head into a tailspin, I took a step back from him to put some distance between us.

"You're complicating things, Daniel. I don't need things to be complicated right now."

"Sugarpie," he said, shaking his head. "I've been gone for so long. Is that any way to be with me? Where's all the *I can't live without you*, or *let's pick up where we left off*?"

"How dare you come here, asking me to pick up where we left off. You asked me to move on with David when you were gone. I've done that. I've...We've got babies on the way. I can't just walk away from him and onto you," I replied. "I can't do that to him."

"I see," he replied quickly, hanging his head in resignation. After some pause, he stated, "Okay, let's sit. I'll tell you blow by blow why I had to do what I had to do." Motioning towards the sofa, he implored me to sit with him.

In the half hour that ensued, he told me a sordid tale of lies, crime and revenge that left me shocked, angry, and sad at the same time. He knew better. *He should have known better.*

"So, if I hadn't gotten sick, my DNA might never have been linked to that matter," he said.

"It would have happened eventually," I conjectured.

"Maybe, maybe not," he replied. "I just know that I wasn't going to stand by and let things happen to you and the kids. You being with David and getting on with life with him, was my way out."

I nodded in response, starting to understand why he did what he did.

"I'm a wanted man," he said casually as though it were an ordinary, everyday thing. "I've been on the run for time now," he said. "I'm fixin' to turn myself in," he said. "Just tryin' not to take anyone else down with me. The Brotherhood needs to continue the good work it started."

"If it wasn't for the Brotherhood, you wouldn't be in this mess," I told him.

"If it wasn't for me taking matters into my own hands I wouldn't be in this mess," he insisted. "Don't blame the Brotherhood for this."

I nodded my head in response. I still had questions. "What about David? How far is he still entrenched in all of this?"

"He isn't," Daniel replied quickly. "That's all you need to know."

I didn't believe him. I looked him over, once more. He was here, in the flesh. The man I'd loved so deeply, the man who stirred me up the wrong way all the time, the man who did all he could to be protective of me, provide for me and shield me was here in the flesh.

"Look. I guess some part of me wanted to believe that you'd be alone for the rest of your life. Despite me pushing you to be with David, I'd hoped that what we shared would've been enough to last you a lifetime."

"I know, I hear you. I feel you. It took me a year to even consider loving someone else. Loving David happened so quickly mostly because I wanted to honour your wishes."

"Mostly," he said after me.

"Mostly," I repeated. "The rest was bound to happen," I said, honestly.

"I understand," he replied regretfully. "I guess my behavior when I was with you only drew you closer to him," he acknowledged. "Well, shoe's on the other foot for me now," he claimed. "I now know how David felt all these years," he said, in a forlorne and sad tone. "So much for forever, hey?"

I sighed in response before stating, "It would've been forever with you had you not left in the first place."

"I know, I know," he replied. "Look, for what it's worth, I'd much rather you be with him when it comes time for me to go down. I can't bear the thought of you being alone, raising the kids on your lonesome. I haven't been there for you like I promised I would the day we took our vows. I can't leave you alone."

"Daniel, if you'd told me all this instead of planning some elaborate skin game, I would have stood by you, you know."

"Skin game," he said, laughing in earnest, before replying on a serious note, "I'm not sure that you would've stood by me. Some things are beyond forgiveness."

"I would've stood by you," I confirmed.

"Yeah, I believe that," he said, with sarcasm, and unconvinced. "At what cost? Your career would be over. Life as you know it would be over. You might've even gotten booked for conspiracy."

"There's a ways," I replied in kind. "I would've stood by you," I said again.

David suddenly appeared at the open door and stood there for a moment before walking in. He wore a look of deep concern on his face. Barely looking at Daniel, he turned to me. "Everything okay?" he asked.

"Everything's fine," I assured him.

"*Right as rain*, she says," Daniel interjected. "This here situation is anything but fine," he stated.

"I figured that," David said protectively, searching my eyes for something that would betray me. He found nothing.

"Congrats on the babies on the way," Daniel managed.

"Josiah and Adalia must be chuffed," he added. "Speaking of which... where are they?"

"Out," David responded protectively.

"They are my kids you know, I need to see them," Daniel asserted.

"Seeing them would only complicate things," David stated.

"It's not as though I haven't seen them anyhow. I'm just asking to see them now, with you knowing," he confessed.

I felt fury rise within me, when I suddenly recalled how Adalia had talked about David and his cowboy hat. He didn't have one, so it was likely Daniel she'd been speaking about. "David, did you know about this?" I queried.

"I only just found out," he replied. Turning to Daniel he stated, "Kids'll be here in any minute. Time you made yourself scarce."

Daniel stood up abruptly. "I'm not going anywhere, mate."

I once again felt the tension in the air, the same old tension that would appear when the two were ready to go head to head.

"We had an agreement," David said. "I'm here now, this is my family you're talking about."

An agreement? I wondered.

"Last time I checked, Teme was still married to me and those kids are actually mine," Daniel reminded him.

I could see David was too overwhelmed with the changed circumstances to put up a fight. Still, he stood there, in silence, choosing his words carefully before speaking again. "I'm not fighting with you bro. You're going down eventually, and when you do, you won't take us down with you. I'm not fighting with you when we can be making peace with our choices. I'm not fighting with you when I stand to lose it all.

Teme and the kids are family to me now. *You've* always been family. I'm not fighting with you, when I could be making peace with you. The fighting stops now," David declared.

"Right. I believe you," Daniel said sarcastically, running a hand through his deep brown hair which was lightly peppered with a few strands of sunburnt auburn brown and grey hair.

"Look," David stated. "I'm *not* going to cuss you out. I'm *not* going to raise a fist to hurt you something pretty. I'm *not* going to hurt you with words. What I *am* going to do is I *am* going to give you a piece of my mind. I *am* going to ask for you to consider leaving things the way they are. I've loved this here woman for a very long time. I love your kids as though they were my own. I've worked hard to make things work and to keep everyone happy since you left. You coming back is not going to change things."

"That's a brave stance you've taken. Doesn't feel good now does it, shoe being on the other foot?" Daniel asked rhetorically.

"No, fighting with you and competing against you has never felt good. I'm happy you're alive and well, but changing everything now won't be good for anyone," David insisted.

"By anyone, do you mean yourself? Cause I can think of 101 reasons why I should stay," Daniel replied. "The kids and my wife being one of them," he said.

"You mean, my wife," David said firmly.

"If that's what you need to tell yourself to feel better about all this, that's fine. It's only a matter of time before things come to light," Daniel said.

Annoyed at the endless conflict, I asked, "What about your promise to let David and me be?"

Daniel scoffed in response. "I should've added a precursor

there. Everything I said then, was said before I realized how hungry I was for the life I had. The wife I still have..."

"Okay, that's enough Daniel," David said sternly. "The kids'll be back any minute."

"I'm not going anywhere," Daniel confirmed, taking a seat firmly on the chaise lounge.

David shook his head in annoyance. "You know, you taking a stance like that isn't helping. Kids talk, and it's only a matter of time before either of them says something to someone else."

"Well, if that's the price I have to pay, I'll take my chances," Daniel said.

Not a moment later, we heard the front door open and the children raced through the house. I got up to meet them, and David stopped me with a gentle tug on my arm. "If this is what he wants, let's give him what he wants. They're his kids too," he conceded.

I raised a brow in response and watched the kids as they bounded in unaware that their little worlds were about to change forever.

"Daddy!!!" Adalia exclaimed, running towards Daniel.

Josiah ran towards David, took a second look at Daniel and stated,

"That's not Daddy."

"Yes it is," Adalia said. "This is our Daddy who loves dress-ups!"

I rolled my eyes in response. Daniel had clearly been to see the kids before, and Adalia knew exactly what she was saying.

"Adalia," I called out but she cut me off.

"Mommy this is Daddy 1," she said quickly hugging Daniel.

"That's Daddy 2," she said confidently, before dashing to David.

David got down to his knees to be at eye level with her. "I might be Daddy 2 but I'm Daddy 1 at ticking you 'til you can't take no more!" he claimed, and she giggled in delight as he tickled her silly.

I sighed in relief. He always knew what to do and when to do it.

"Josiah," Daniel started. Josiah remained at a distance, apprehensive. "Hey buddy, come here," he said, trying to get to him. "How about I let you wear my hat?" he offered, taking his cowboy hat into his hands and tracing a finger along the brim.

Josiah hesitated for a moment longer, then approached. "You're not Daddy," he stated.

"Okay, that's enough Josiah," I stated, trying to avert a mini crisis.

"He's not my Daddy," he said again.

Daniel interjected. "Okay buddy, why don't you call me D? D for Daniel? D is also the first letter in the word Daddy."

"It's also the first letter in my last name. You're not my Daddy, D," Josiah stated, glaring at Daniel.

"Alright buddy. I'll take that. How about you try on my hat?" he offered again.

"No," Josiah said outright.

"Josiah, how about you go help Dad in the garden outside?" I suggested.

Josiah gave Daniel the once over before stating, "Okay," and running off.

Daniel sat with his hat in his hands, clearly disappointed.

"He'll know who you are, someday," I stated.

"I guess so," he said, running his palm along the mid line of his hat.

"You look exhausted Daniel, how about you get some rest while I make dinner?" I suggested.

He shook his head to the negative. "I've missed too many moments with y'all already. I don't want to miss any more," he said.

Dinner was a somber affair. Daniel kept mostly quiet as the kids chatted away about their playdate. David interacted with the kids, pausing every now and then to ask me if I was okay. My silence worried him, that much I knew.

Eating as though he hadn't eaten in a while, Daniel went for seconds then thirds. When he looked about ready to get his fourth helping, David stated, "There's more in the kitchen. Eat your fill."

Whether out of self-restraint or embarrassment, but more likely the latter, Daniel decided he'd had enough, and folded his fork and knife together on his plate, vertically. "Thank you for dinner, it was delicious," he said, before filling up on water instead. I gave David a disapproving look, as what he'd said had likely discouraged rather than encouraged Daniel to continue eating.

"Daddy!" Adalia asked, addressing Daniel, "Are you going to rock me to sleep tonight?"

Passing me a side glance before he answered, he replied, "Yes, baby, I will if you want me to."

David sighed in response. I could tell that his being a peace warrior was slowly wearing him down. Still, he offered, "How about you two give them a bath and I do the dishes?"

Daniel tapped his fingers lightly on the table. "Just as long as Josiah's happy for that to happen."

"No," Josiah said adamantly.

"Alright then," Daniel replied. "*I'll* do the dishes and you two can do the bath," he suggested instead.

"Aw... I wanted Daddy 1 to give me a bath. No fair!" Adalia exclaimed.

"Next time angel," Daniel assured her. "Next time. I'll be rockin' you to sleep tonight, remember?"

"Yes. And I don't want you to go away ever again," she said, breaking my heart and Daniel's too by the look in his eyes. Little did she know that her daddy was going to be going away for a long time.

"I'll do the dishes Daniel," I offered. "You look exhausted," I told him again. "The guest room is all set up for you to use." Despite his tiredness, I could tell that sleeping was the last thing he wanted to do. He nodded his head in agreement anyhow.

After their baths, I gave them some rice milk. David then helped them brush their teeth. Moments later, he read them a bedtime story in the living room. Daniel sat at the end of the sofa, observing the children with David. I could tell it was hard for him, but he had no choice. At some point during the story, Adalia jumped out of David's lap and into Daniel's lap. Wrapping her little arms around his neck, she listened intently to the story being read by David, and nestled her little head deeply into Daniel's chest.

Story done and ready to rest, Josiah grabbed the book from David and put it in the library bag. We'd made it a point every week to get new books to read from the local library, and he was all too happy to place them back in the bag once read, in anticipation of the ones yet to be read in the days to come.

"Goodnight mom," he said, bounding towards me and planting a kiss on my cheek. "Love you," he added.

"Goodnight Josiah, love you too," I said, planting a kiss on his plump cheek. He stole a quick glance Daniel's way before running towards David. "Goodnight Daddy," he said, giving David a hug and kiss on the cheek before running off to his bedroom.

Feeling his pain and very aware of the snub Josiah had given Daniel, David said, "Give it time. He'll come around eventually."

"Guess so," Daniel replied, not looking hopeful at all.

"I want to rest too, Dad," Adalia said sleepily to Daniel.

"Alright then. How 'bout you say goodnight to everyone else?" he suggested. She looked into him with her big brown eyes and agreed. Suddenly filled with energy, she got up and ran straight to David. He swept her into his arms and hugged her deeply. "Goodnight princess."

"Goodnight Daddy," she replied. She then ran towards me for a hug and a kiss, before going back to Daniel.

He took her in his arms, got up and paced the room, rocking her gently. "Hush a bye, don't you cry, go to sleep my little baby. When you wake you will have all the pretty little horses..." he sang. The beautiful and traditional lullaby, *All the Pretty Little Horses* was on point. We weren't sure how long he would be with us, but he would promise Adalia all the pretty little horses.

It didn't take Adalia long to fall asleep in Daniel's arms. He carried her to her bedroom and after placing her in bed, he came back into the living room to sit with me. Seeing the sadness in his eyes, I offered to show him some photos.

"Later," he said. "Can't do it right now."

I could see he was struggling to come to terms with things as they were.

"Do y'all have any beer, any alcohol?" he asked.

"There'd be something in the cellar," I said.

"Let's go down and have a look together, shall we?" he asked as a matter of factly.

I froze slightly, thinking for a moment that it would be a chance for him to make moves on me.

He read my mind. "Relax," he said. "I meant what I said earlier. I'm not here to start any trouble."

"Could've fooled me," I replied.

"I hear you, sugarpie," he said. My heart fluttered at the mention of that term of endearment. *Sugarpie.* Our days of loving seemed a world away. I realized then that I missed him deeply and still wanted him, but that there was no going back now.

"So, Adalia," I started as we walked down the stairs. "How long have you been visiting her without us knowing?"

"Not as often as I'd have liked," he said. "Mostly when David was away, but for quite some time now."

"And you being here in Aus, how did you manage?"

"I have my means. I have my ways," he said in deep thought. "If it wasn't for me being here, I would've had to give it up a long time ago, as in, I woulda been locked up a while ago."

And you're here, and we're harboring a fugitive. I thought.

We reached the cellar. Without hesitation, he opened the door and reached for a Riesling. Examining the year and make on the bottle, he asked, "Saving this for anything in particular?"

"No," I replied. "David doesn't drink, so the wine is mostly for guests and occasionally for me."

"Would this be an occasion for you to drink?" he asked.

"If I wasn't expecting, yes, Daniel," I stated.

"Sorry, that slipped my mind," he replied. "All the more reason for me to have a drink," he said, slightly under a whisper. Opening the cellar door again, he put the Riesling back and reached for a Merlot instead. "Guess I'm drinking alone." Closing the door, he stated, "I shouldn't have stayed away so long."

"No, you shouldn't have left in the first place," I said. "If you'd told me everything, I would've stood by you."

"So you say...," he acknowledged. "...but I saw how happy you could be with David so I made my mind up to keep you happy, no matter the consequence to me. I'm not gonna lie, it hurts me to see you with him."

I shrugged in response, and we stood there in silence, for a moment. "Should you be drinking?" I asked, recalling how he previously couldn't hold his liquor.

"I shouldn't be, no. But having a brew these days has kept me warm, it's kept me level, and it's kept me sane," he said. "We go back up?" he asked, changing topic. "Wouldn't want to give your new man the wrong impression."

"Sure," I replied, leading him up the stairs, all the while very conscious that he was watching my every move lustfully.

Upstairs, David was in the kitchen baking. He tenderly kneaded bread dough on the bench top, in a sea of flour, stopping to acknowledge me as soon as I walked in. He searched my eyes for something he would not find.

"I'm just in the living room with Daniel. Just hearing what he has to say," I offered.

"Good," he replied, surprisingly. "I trust you," he said. "I know where we stand."

"I love you David," I uttered.

"And I you," he replied.

"Join us when you're done?" I asked.

"Of course," he said, before planting a generous kiss on my lips. Playfully, he dabbed a bit of flour onto my cheek and nose and smiled gingerly in response to my reaction. Proceeding to wipe it off with his apron, he confirmed, "I'll be with you in a moment."

In the living room, Daniel sat waiting for me. Once I sat down, he poured the Merlot into his glass, and the grape spritzer into mine. I noticed his hands were calloused, rough and cut in places. He caught me staring at him, became self-conscious and stated, "Been doin' it rough sugarpie, been doing it pretty rough."

After handing me a glass, he raised his to mine for a toast. "A toast, to a new chapter."

Our glasses clicked then awkward silence ensued.

"I'm sorry I put you through what I put you through," he apologised.

"So you've said. Apology accepted, doesn't mean we can go back."

"No," he acknowledged. "We can't go back, you've made that clear to me."

More silence followed before I asked the obvious question, "When are you planning on heading back to Texas and are you planning on turning yourself in?"

"I'm not planning on heading back to Texas anytime soon, no, not unless I want to face the electric chair. I don't," he said. "I'll stay here for as long as I can, and try to avoid extradition for as long as I can," he said. "Maybe I'll get to serve my time here," he said wishfully, despite knowing the chances of that happening were pretty slim. "Jonah should really be serving time with yours truly, but I can't do that to him and Shania, I can't let that happen," he said. "They've got a young family, much like ours," he said. "I meant yours," he corrected. *He meant ours.*

"I would've stood by you," I told him again.

"I know that now," he said, deep in thought. "I know a lot of things now...hindsight is always 20/20 you savy?"

I agreed. His hands were trembling.

"Cold?" I asked, wanting to hold him when he wasn't mine to hold any longer.

"No, just the corticosteroids I'm on for the old asthma."

"You really need to look after yourself, Daniel," I urged.

"You know me. I'm trying the best I can, hasn't been easy."

"And your migraines?" The treatment he'd had meant the cancer was in complete remission and at bay.

"I have them every now and again, more now than before. Probably stress related," he concluded. "I get by," he assured me. "I'll have migraines over a tumour any day," he said.

"Well, you're here now," I replied, noting how different he looked from when I last saw him. No longer gaunt and clinging to life, he was muscular in physique but on the slender side. His skin was pale, likely from not going out too much in the day.

"You still makin' that yummy cornbread of yours?" he asked.

"Yep," I replied, remembering how much he loved it, and how much he loved food.

"And the sweet tea?" he asked.

"Yep."

"You happy to make them on demand?" he asked.

"Yep."

"You planning on giving me something other than one word replies?" he asked, setting his wine glass down on the side table to the left of him.

"If you insist," I replied.

"Hm..." he stated pensively. "I know we can't get back to what we used to be, but I'd like for you to tell me what I need to do to get right with you. For me to go on, I need to feel that you've forgiven me, and still hold me dear."

The nerve. "You're asking for a lot," I told him. "You've come back from the dead, you've asked for me to search myself to see whether there was any possibility of us being together again. You've asked for the kids to acknowledge you as Dad. You've pretty much picked up where you left off with David..." I broke off, as it became apparent that all I was saying was hurting him. "You're asking for something I can't give," I stated.

He pondered for a moment before he replied. "Right now I'm just asking you to forgive me. Forgiving me doesn't have to mean that we pick up where we left off. That'll be nice, but as I know now, that's not an option."

I sighed. "I would've stood by you had I known what you were up to. I wouldn't have condoned what you were doing, but I would've stood by you. Of course I forgive you," I said.

"Well, it doesn't feel like you have," he stated, knowingly.

How I wished he would stop trying to read my mind and second guess me. "Forgiveness is not just words. It takes time. What do you expect, Daniel!"

"Alright," he replied sharply, resigned to accept my response.

David snuck his head in the room in the knick of time. "Everything okay?" he asked, wiping his hands off on a tea towel.

I nodded to the affirmative.

"Okay," he said. "I'll be back soon enough, just finishing off in the kitchen."

"Alright," I said, wanting him to be back sooner rather than later.

"You haven't even touched your drink," Daniel noted, clearly disappointed.

I'm not in the mood. "You can have it too if you like," I replied.

Pouring it into his glass, he asked, "Those photos you mentioned earlier. Could I have a look now?"

I started from the beginning. Photos of the babies and us, three years ago, before everything changed. Looking at the photos brought him to tears. I felt for him. After all, he had a choice at the time. He chose to leave. He chose to walk away to protect us, or so he said. Now it seemed as though what he was trying to avoid by walking away, was going to happen anyway.

Wiping tears off on the cuff of his shirt, he took a moment to collect himself before continuing to view the photos. Hands trembling, he turned page after page after page. Tears streamed down his face and I wanted to hold him but I couldn't. I wanted to hold him but I didn't. The best I could do was to squeeze his hand. He squeezed back hard. "I feel I've missed a lifetime already," he managed, when he got to the last page of the album.

"There's still tomorrow," I said, in an effort to reassure him.

"Tomorrow isn't promised," he replied, closing the album. "I'm gonna head off to catch some shuteye," he announced, avoiding eye contact. "Thanks for letting me stay, after everything," he said, before abruptly getting up and walking towards the guest room. *Still getting up and walking away when the going gets tough. Some things never change.*

David came to join me on the sofa moments later. "You alright?" he asked.

"I'm fine," I lied.

"You're not," he replied.

"If you know how I am, why bother asking!" I retorted.

David paused momentarily before responding. "I ask because I care," he said.

"I'm sorry, David," I replied. "Sorry for being so short with you."

"Don't apologise," he said, "I know it isn't easy. I'm struggling to come to terms with the fact that he's back too, but I'm not worried. I believe what is meant to be will be."

"We're not properly married," I reminded him. "Technically, I'm still married to him."

"I know this," David said. "I also know that he still wants you," he said abruptly. "Look. I didn't want to tell you this just yet, but he asked me if he could have you back."

Incredulous. "What did you tell him?" I asked, quickly, as my heart fluttered at the thought of the man I once loved being so bold as to claim me as his own again.

"I told him about our babies on the way, I told him about our life together. I told him about the future we have planned. I told him about his little ones, who are my little ones now, and how hard it was for you and them to adjust when he left. I implored him to reconsider his request in light of everything.

587

I also said that the final decision ultimately lies with you. I'm surprised he hasn't asked you outright."

I sighed in response, overwhelmed with this new information. "David, you have the biggest heart," I told him.

Taking my hands in his, he stated, "It's no secret that I want you for myself. But I'll support you in whatever decision you make. And I'll be there for you no matter what you decide. I just hope that you've grown to love me enough to want to be with me and me only. I just hope that you choose me and only me, the way I chose you all those years ago."

I squeezed the strong hands that held mine so tenderly. Though I still loved Daniel, David and I had built a life together, and shared dreams and hopes together. After all the years he'd been in love with me, I wasn't going to be the one to bring it all to an end. He deserved better than that. Besides, we were finally having the children we'd prayed so long and hard for.

"I love you, David," I told him. "I didn't expect Daniel to leave the way he did, but he did, and that opened up the possibility of us being together. I'm not about to leave you now," I said. "Not after everything we've been through together."

"I know you still love him," David said, squeezing my hands back. "I'll stake my claim on you if I have to, but I just don't want you to feel obligated to me," he said. "Don't stay with me out of obligation," he stated. "You know me, I'll have you any way I can have you," he confirmed.

What did I do to deserve this man? I thought. "I'm yours," I replied, planting a kiss on his lips. Secretly I wondered about the nature of the conversation David had with Daniel, and how far Daniel had gone to stake his claim on me.

Lying in bed, unable to sleep, I heard Daniel come out of his room, likely for a glass of water. I remembered his midnight haunts fondly. With David fast asleep next to me, I decided to get up and out of bed. Looking at the time on my way out, it was 2 am.

Daniel sat in the kitchen, in the dark apart from the moonlight. The change of clothes David had given him made him look less like himself and more like David. "Can't sleep?" he asked.

I nodded in response.

"You and me both," he said.

He tapped the stool next to him, indicating for me to sit down.

We sat in silence for a moment before he spoke again. "So, what's it like, being with someone other than me?"

"That's a loaded question," I replied.

"It's a simple question, albeit loaded," he stated.

I hesitated for a moment before responding. "Well, being with someone other than you, is clearly different," I said. "There'll never be another you."

"I'm not sure if that's a compliment but I sure as Eve will take it as one," he said.

"What about you?" I asked. "You been with anyone else since me?"

"No," he answered quickly. "Just me, solo and my memories of you."

"We shouldn't be talking about this," I warned.

"You asked."

"You did too," I replied.

"Yes, I did. I *will* stop talkin about *this*, but not before I say what I have to say," he stated. Pivoting on his stool to face me directly, in a deep and commanding voice he said, "I know you remember me and how wildly in love we were." His fingers brushed mine lightly and suddenly my body was ablaze with desire for him again. "I know you remember me and those nights, and how we made mad passionate love not just once, but many times over. I remember every inch of your body. Every curve, every angle. I remember you and I. Say the word, and we can get back to it. Except this time, I'll be the man you need. I'll appreciate you and cherish you like I should have done when we were together. Don't tell me you don't remember me," he said.

I squeezed his hand gently. "I do remember you. But things are different now."

He sighed in response. "For you, yes. For me, no."

I expected him to dwell on things but he didn't. Taking a swig of his water, he changed topic abruptly and stated point blankly, "I need you to go to Switzerland with the kids. If they're coming for me, they'll come for you. Can't take any chances. Go there and get protected. Start anew," he urged.

I bawked at his sudden request. "You need to tell me a lot more than what you've told me so far, before I even consider doing anything like that."

Nodding his head in agreement, he stated, "Long story short, I've just caught wind that they're on my trail. A day or so from now, I'll be fixin' ta leave. Or else I'll be taken in. You won't be safe here, our babies won't be safe here, David won't be safe here."

Our babies. "They haven't been babies for a long time now."

"Yeah, yeah," he replied. "They'll always be babies to me," he said. "You'll always be my baby," he added.

"Yeah, yeah," I replied.

"Are we back to this already?" he asked.

"What, the fighting?"

"Yeah yeah," he said again.

"You're a trip," I told him in jest.

"Yeah, yeah," he replied. "You know, you still haven't told me just what it's like to be with someone other than me."

Wanting to put the issue to rest, I stated, "David's very conventional, which is different, but nice after being with you."

"Hm...tell me more?"

"You were a freak in bed, he's not," I said.

"Well, takes two," he said, giving me a wink. "I've still got the memory of us, which I replay when I need to."

"I didn't need to know that," I replied.

"Yes, you did," he offered.

I rolled my eyes in response. "Well, I'm with David now," I affirmed. "And I don't believe he would be as generous as you've been – allowing you to be with me again."

"I hear you," he replied. "He sort of made that clear to me from the get go," he said. "But you know me. I don't take orders from anyone."

"Don't I know that," I replied. "You still haven't told me the short and tall of the story of why you want me to take the kids to Switzerland, now."

"I will," he replied. "Soon enough. Get some rest now before David starts wondering where you're at. A lot of things done changed since we been together. I'm trouble now," he announced.

In a swift move, he got up, gently swept up the hair at the back of my head, planted a kiss on the nape of my neck and whispered, "Go to bed now, before you end up in a world of trouble." He then walked off without looking back.

I sat there in the kitchen for a lingering moment after he'd gone, exhilarated, yet at the same time feeling as though I'd been stripped bare, used and owned. I was with David now, but Daniel was still my lawfully wedded husband. On paper at least.

I needed to remind myself of how I felt and face facts. He'd left us, the children and I, to fend for ourselves. David had been there for us, and had been so good to us. Being with Daniel meant fire, passion and resignation to what he wanted me to be. Being with David meant constancy, reverence and freedom to be who I wanted to be. I knew what I needed. And no one could convince me otherwise. Or so I thought.

32

WUTHERING STORMS

"Look at this here buddy. Always take your hat off by the crown. *Never* handle it by the brim," he advised. An intrigued Josiah looked on. "Look here – take it off like so," he said, removing his hat by the crown with his left hand. "Now, try it."

My heart warmed as I watched them bonding. At long last.

That afternoon, we sat on the veranda, a pot of herbal tea between us. Just like old times. Storm, our Husky, sat there with us, at Daniel's feet.

"How'd you manage to get a Husky that looks just like Stormie?" he asked, referring to Josiah's stuffed toy. "The resemblance is uncanny."

I smiled, recalling Josiah's face when David and I had gifted him with Storm the Christmas gone by. "Dave and I searched high and low without any success, then one day we noticed an ad on Gumtree - you know Gumtree?"

"No..., but go on," he urged.

"Anyway, a young family was moving overseas and needed to give their puppy a home. The rest is history," I explained.

"Sounds like it was meant to be. Josiah must've been over

the moon," Daniel said, patting Storm on the head. He licked Daniel's hand then rested loyally at his feet.

"He's a pretty good dog - not a great guard dog, but he's been good to me. Loyal even."

"Yes, so I discovered. He was getting in trouble for disappearing for time. Little did I know he was keeping you company there in the woods," I said.

Daniel laughed heartily. "He even managed to sneak a chicken bone or two my way a couple of times."

"Oh no," I said. "Sharing his food?" I asked. "Do we need to think of de-worming you?"

He laughed again. "Probably." He wasn't joking.

"Yuck," I thought aloud. "He was getting into quite some trouble for snatching food off the bench. Now we know why."

"Yep, now you know," Daniel said, the laugh lines on his face and sea blue eyes warming my heart. I'd missed him terribly, and now that he was here with me again, I wanted to be back with him.

"Daniel, I wish you weren't out there on your own all this time. Four whole years. You could've come back to us earlier." I found myself softening towards him the more we talked.

"I could've," he replied. "But I saw how happy you were. Didn't want to take that away from you."

"You're saying that, but you're here now. Same thing, non?"

"Non, c'est pas la même chose. It's different now. I've had a long time to think about us, and I realised I can't live without you. Can't bear the thought of you being with someone else any more. I came back to show you how much I care. How much I truly love you, want you, and need you. Plus, we are still married."

594

"So you keep on reminding me."

"Well, that's facts. Look, I know this here situation is a mess. I wish it wasn't. I'm livin' each day as it comes, never knowin' when I'll be picked up or turned in...," he broke off, staring off into the distance. "I'm pretty tired of livin' on the run. Pretty tired of livin' my life with you and the babies at a distance. This is the closest I've come to bein' happy in a long time, and I have the feelin' it won't last."

"I'm sorry Daniel," I told him. "Sorry things worked out like this. If I'd just held off getting involved with David after you'd gone..."

"Don't apologise. You waited long enough to be with David. Didn't help that I was urging you on."

"I know. Why did you anyway? Seems counterintuitive if you ask me," I stated.

"Well, I wasn't in the right frame of mind when I was recovering from the tumour, and Craig made it seem like I'd never be able to return, so I just did as he said and stayed away. Up until I knew better, and found out I could return," he explained.

Craig. Hate was a strong word, but I was starting to hate Craig with a passion.

I listened intently, nodding on cue. *Husband.* I had to continually break gaze with him in conversation, since he made no attempt to hide the fact that he still lusted after me.

"Man I've hungered for you," he said all of a sudden, speaking what I already knew. "Since I've been back, have you been keeping your legs closed for me?" he asked suddenly. I gasped in shock, and he smiled wickedly. "It's a legitimate question. I'm back now, and only I have the right to be with you, as your husband," he insisted.

"Daniel, please don't talk like that to me, not now."

"You mean, please don't be honest?" he asked cordially. "Whyever not? We have a history together, we shared a life together, we got married and had kids together, I can't get myself to not want you anymore, just because of this here arranged marriage of yours."

I scoffed in response. "Arranged marriage?" I asked. "You have the nerve to come here, back from the dead, after pushing David and I together to suit your purposes, and talk pretty to me."

"Come on now, I ain't talking pretty to you. I'm fixin' ta talk dirty to you," he said.

I shook my head in response and got up to leave. He got up as well, and stood to intercept my path. "Look, I get carried away sometimes. Most times. You should know me by now."

"I thought I did."

"I don't mean you any harm. You know me, I've always been a jealous guy. I've always been a little bit selfish," he acknowledged.

"A little?" I asked, sarcastically.

He laughed in response. "Yeah, just a little," he stated. "You know, funny enough, though I hated it when we were together, one of the things I missed most about us being together was our daily banter."

"Banter, ha!," I replied. "Is that what you're calling it these days?"

"Yeah, banter. My memory serves me well. Rapartee, raillery, crosstalk, sallies, quips, ripostes..."

I giggled in response. "Okay, hold up Mr. Walking The-saurus. Hold up."

He laughed back. "You askin' an officer of the law to hold

up?" he asked. "Ain't nothing right about that," he joked, and ended up once again staring at me longingly. It was he who broke the gaze this time and took a step back. "Tu me manques, Temwani," he stated. "I really miss you like crazy."

An unexpected sigh escaped my lips before I spoke. "Daniel, I miss you too, but things are different now. We can't go back to what we were," I said. The look of disappointment on his face was apparent. "But you're here now. We can try to be happy somehow else. Are you happy?"

"What's it to ya," he replied, clearly hurt.

"You matter to me. Your happiness is important to me, and all you do and feel matters to me."

He hesitated before replying. "Happy, no. Thankful, yes. Thankful that we're here, talking. Thankful that I can finally spend time with our kids. Thankful that the tumour didn't kill me. Thankful but not happy. Happiness is relative," he claimed. "My happiness is tied to you, and your happiness is tied to him. So, thankful, yes. Happy, no."

"Daniel, you make it all sound very conclusive."

"Well, it is, isn't it?" he asked. "It's black and white, no gray areas. You're with him, not with me," he said. "That's facts. I had imagined a reunion that involved us getting acquainted with each other again. One that involved me demanding my dues as your husband. One that involved you enjoying me wholly and taking me back as you can't live without me. I imagined a lot of things, but I realize now that it's all fantasy. Turns out you *can* live without me. Problem is, I can't live without you," he said, wincing as though in physical pain. "It physically hurts being without you," he said, staring deeply into me. "I didn't know love could hurt this bad."

My heart hurt, and in that moment, I wished things were different.

Changing tone, he promised, "I'm not here to rain on your parade. I'm here to wish you well," he said.

"I find that hard to believe," I replied.

"I needed for you to see me again."

"I've seen you, you've seen me, now what?" I questioned.

"If I can't be with you, I'd rather be alone," he said.

"You're being dramatic Daniel. Of course you'll find someone else to love one day."

"I know I won't," he said. "Sugarpie, there are ways to be and there are ways not to be. This here is no way to be," he claimed. "But it ain't like I got a choice. I did this to myself."

"Daddy!!!" Adalia yelled, bounding towards us. Daniel immediately stood up and scooped her into his arms. I could tell just how much she loved being the centre of attention. "I bet she puts on this huge princess act, yet she's tough when it comes to her brother," Daniel guessed. "I'm betting she'd stand up to anyone who tries to mess with her brother," he said.

"Hm...," I pondered. He knew his daughter well. His statement made me think of all the people who'd violently opposed a union between David and I.

"You would've been proud to know you had a huge fan club – so many people stood up for you and opposed David and I being together."

"Is that right, now!" he stated, not sounding surprised at all.

"Yes, and in the end, it nearly never happened. Claudette would've made sure of it."

He laughed lightly in response, his smile widening by the minute. "Claudette, ey?"

"Yes, Claudette," I replied, not amused at his casual attitude where she was concerned. "I'm not sure I like her at all," I told him. "She doesn't appear to like me much either. I get the distinct impression she's judging me, all the time. Johnny later told me that you were keeping acquaintances with her before you left us. I wish you'd stay away from her, she doesn't appear to be good news."

"Don't mind her," Daniel said. "She's just a little overprotective," he claimed.

"Hm. I wonder why," I stated, knowing he was keeping secrets. My dislike of Claudette had markedly increased since the time she'd almost managed to convince me that David was making plans to be with someone else. Someone special. Little did she know, that someone special was me.

"She's a little overprotective of her brothers," Daniel said nonchalantly.

"Meaning?"

"Meaning just that," Daniel stated. "She's my baby sister," he confirmed.

I gasped in response and felt the babies within me kick hard. A kick was visible from the outside.

"Whoa," Daniel said, placing a hand on my belly, which he kept there for a while before letting go. "I don't mean to upset you," he said. "There's more."

I braced myself for whatever else he had to say. "Some of us in the Brotherhood – David, Jonah, Craig, Scott...we are all brothers. Duayne included."

I felt sick to my stomach at the mention of Duayne's name.

"That sorry excuse of a father was a busy man," he added,

by way of explanation.

My throat suddenly felt tight. "Does David know?"

"He knows about Claudette. I told him after his stint in the hospital. About the other guys in the Brotherhood, no. I figured Craig's the only one who knew this all along, that's why he made every effort over the years to bring us all together. I do plan to tell David the rest," he added. "Sooner rather than later," he promised.

The news hit me like a brick, and I took a deep breath as I tried to fully appreciate the gravity of the news. Meanwhile, Daniel carried on. "I owe a lot to Claudette, she's been instrumental in having a lot of things happen," he said. "If it wasn't for Claudette, I'd be even deeper up shit's creek than I am already. I'd be doin' it tougher than I already am, if it weren't for her," he said. "She taught me a whole lot about survivin' and livin' off the land. She's a force to be reckoned with. I learnt a lot about livin', and ways to be. If I knew her way back when we were together, she would've given me a good a talkin' to, and we'd still be together. So, next time you see her, try to make nice, will you?" he requested. "Do it for me, please," he added, sensing my reluctance.

I nodded and took it all in. "So, I have a sister in law," I stated.

"You'll probably find she's a lot more like a sister than a sister in law," he said.

I disagreed. "I don't know about that Daniel. She was pretty nasty when it came to me being with David."

He laughed briefly before stating, "Look, she's just got my back. She'd rather see you with me than with him. She knew I was still alive at the time – was only tryin' ta fix things up for me. Didn't work unfortunately," he said, regrettably.

"Hm..."

"She can't stand David's position of forgiveness when it comes to that man who unfortunately happens to be our father. So for as long as he continues to support Daddy Dearest, she won't have anything good to say to him."

"Well, David will be David," I stated. "He just so happens to have a big heart."

"Yep, Claudette and I are not so forgiving," he said abruptly. "Nor are any of the other brothers. Which is why I need you to get to Switzerland, now."

"David needs to know everything before any such plans are made," I warned.

"Right," he replied. I could tell that letting David know was the least of his priorities. He would have told him earlier otherwise. "Soon as he gets back, I'll talk to him," he vowed.

No such thing, when the time came. When David came home, Daniel was otherwise engaged, and avoided David like the plague. He seemed to constantly be in the business of avoiding David. I took the chance to call Shania. I needed to speak with someone. I needed to share what I was going through, but knew I couldn't. Still, speaking with her in general terms, would help.

Shania picked up on the first ring, as though she'd been sitting on the phone. I put her on speaker phone as I walked around the kitchen, preparing dinner.

"So, what's happening in your neck of the woods?" she asked.

"Well, we got that fireplace of ours working, finally. Chimney Sweep was here this morning, he fixed it good."

"Chimney Sweep!," she exclaimed. "Did you kiss him?"

"What?" I asked, hearing my voice echoing down the line.

"Did you kiss him! It's good luck to kiss a Chimney Sweep, don't you know?" she insisted.

I laughed heartily in response. "That may be the case, but it's bad luck to kiss anyone other than your significant other," I replied.

"Yeah, yeah. Coulda' done it on my behalf!" she insisted.

"Yeah, I'm sure your husband wouldn't have been too happy about that!" I said.

"Well, I don't think he'd notice to be honest. He's been rather distracted lately," she said. I could hear the concern in her voice.

"Distracted, how?" I asked. I was curious. Jonah, aka The Muscle, didn't seem the type to be distracted.

"I don't know. I can't put my finger on it. I've asked him and he doesn't seem to want to talk about it. It's like he's spooked or something."

"Hm...," I thought aloud as David walked in and sat at the kitchen bar. He'd caught the tail end of our conversation.

"Like, he should be excited we've gotten married, and that we have another baby on the way, but he's acting all scared and just...well, it's a little out of character for him. I haven't known him all that long but what I do know of him doesn't fit this behavior."

"I'll talk to him," David offered, clearly eavesdropping on our conversation.

"Hear that Shania?" I asked.

"Yep," she replied. "Thanks so much David, you're a standup guy."

"Don't mention it," he replied. "How's everything going with bub?"

"Sorry?"

"The baby?" David and I said in unison before smiling at each other. I was practically Aussie now.

"The baby is fine...," Shania broke off, in tears. He'd hit a raw nerve. "Baby is fine, I just miss my best friend," she said. Tears came to my eyes as I heard her break down over the phone.

"I miss you too, boo," I replied.

"Me three," David announced. "This here bestie of yours is a little lost without you," he said, beckoning me to sit with him. "So by default I miss you too." He placed a reassuring arm on my shoulder to comfort me.

Shania managed to laugh in response. "You only miss me 'cause you have no buffer now."

"I don't know what you're talking about," he joked. "No, seriously. Maybe we *are* due for a visit?" he asked, turning to me.

I nodded in agreement, though how we would manage a visit, I didn't know. Shania had no idea Daniel was still alive. Jonah most likely did. Maybe we *were* due for a visit. Then I thought of Daniel, and how he'd be alone in Tasmania. *He could always stay here while we were gone*, I thought. Now that he was back, I worried about him leaving again.

Squeezing my hand lightly to get me out of my thoughts, David said, "Shania, tell your man I'll be talking to him. And we'll be seeing you in a matter of weeks."

We said our goodbyes and ended the call. As I turned to put the phone back in its unit on the wall, I noticed Daniel standing there, leaning against the wall. "So, you'd rather go to Texas than Switzerland, ey?"

David looked at me, confused. I hadn't told him yet.

603

"Switzerland?"

"Yep, Switzerland," Daniel confirmed.

"What's this about?" David asked.

"Take a lucky guess mate. Don't act like you don't know what this is about. Goin' back to Texas now isn't a smart move," Daniel said sharply. "Y'all need to get to Switzerland, not Texas."

"You know, there's a relatively painless way out of this," David mentioned.

"Relative is the operative word. Enlighten me," Daniel challenged.

"Declan. You forgive him, apologise to him for what you've done, and he'll forgive you and drop all the charges against you," David suggested.

Daniel shook his head in response. "Are you for real? Oh man, he's got you wrapped around his finger."

David frowned slightly at the suggestion.

"After everything Daddy Dearest done did to you, to them, to us, you're on his side?" he asked, enraged. "Man, I never pictured you for such a wuss."

David let him have his piece. Daniel went on about Declan, his deeds and misdeeds. "The moment he found out I was on to him, he offered to pay me to go away. He offered to pay those women and girls to go away. Bad to the bone he is, and you're sitting here asking me to make peace with him? If I had to do it all over again, I would've shot him cold and dead. He doesn't deserve to live."

A chill ran down my spine as I heard Daniel talk about ending life as though it were not a thing.

"So, you're judge and executioner now, are you? Have you thought for one moment about redemption, and how it's not

604

up to you to determine the punishment?" David asked.

"Redemption? Ha!" Daniel scoffed. "I'm here worried about serving time for retaliating against him, while you're here defending him, saying he's redeemed, yet I see him walking free, I see him doing everything *but* act remorseful for what he done did in the past. He's the type of man who's sorry he got caught," Daniel alleged.

"No one's perfect," David said in response. "I understand your need for vengeance but that won't make things better."

Daniel laughed nervously, looking at me now. "Is he for real?" he questioned.

I shrugged in response. "He has a point."

"So do I!" Daniel insisted. "I can forgive a lot of things. But the things he did, I just can't. I can't bear the fact that I'm related to him. That he's my father. Our father."

"So, you'd rather do time than do as David's suggesting, and get him to drop charges?" I asked.

"I'd be doing time for a greater cause. I'm not bailing out on this here mission just because he's my father. In fact, because he is my father, I *will not* back down."

"Well, no one asked you to be a martyr," David said.

"No greater love," Daniel stated. "Isn't that what the Brotherhood stands for?" he asked. "Oh, no, wait. You don't care about the Brotherhood anymore. You're too busy livin' it up as a Rock Star Minister," Daniel claimed, clearly resentful.

"Okay, guys, you need to stop. You're not doing this right now. Cool off, and come back and talk," I told them.

"I'm not changing my mind over this," Daniel said, turning to go.

"You're setting yourself up for a lot of hurtin' then," David replied. "It isn't just you that you need to consider. You need to consider your family."

"My family?" Daniel retorted angrily. "You mean the family you now have? The family I *let* you have?"

"Your family." David replied calmly. "My family."

Daniel closed the kitchen door behind him. "He tried to kill you, you know? As if it wasn't enough to attempt to do it the first time, he had to go and do it again," he claimed.

"You're not making any sense Daniel," David replied.

"That truck, heading directly towards you, you think it was a coincidence? You, feeling out of sorts in the lead up to the accident, you think that was a coincidence? The kids talking about the nice man at school who gave them sweeties, you think that was a coincidence?"

"What nice man at school," David asked, absently. Stunned, I dropped the plate that I was carrying. *Declan. He'd been to the school. He'd talked to the kids without us being there.* Daniel quickly rushed to my aid.

"That can't be true," David said, clearly unnerved.

"Well it is," Daniel said. "Want to know what else is true? Jonah, Craig, Duayne and Scottie, we're all brothers."

David sat down again, this time head in his hands. "Why are you telling me this now? Couldn't you have told me the moment you found out?" he asked.

"I dare say Craig's known all along," Daniel intimated. "*He* could've told you at any time. And, by the way, Claudette's our baby sister," he added. I watched David's expression change from disbelief to shock.

"This is too much to take in all at once," David said, nervously stroking his chin which was peppered lightly with a day's stubble.

"Mate," Daniel said in an Aussie accent that was becoming

oddly convincing and natural to him. "The sooner you can build a bridge and get over yourself and him, the better."

"This changes everything," David said, ignoring Daniel's comment.

"Damn straight it does!" Daniel stated.

Rising to his feet with anger visibly surging within him, David exclaimed, "What the fuck is he doing at our kids' school when he was told to stay away!"

Raising a brow slightly at the sudden profanity, Daniel replied, "Your guess is as good as mine, brother."

"And what on God's green earth was he thinking when he decided to bed every woman he could?" David questioned.

"Probably fixin' to populate God's green earth!" Daniel said in jest. "But hey, look at the silver lining. Our mates are really our brothers. And sister."

"He best be staying away from our kids," David said.

"This is outrageous," I interjected, putting the bigger pieces of glass straight in the bin. Daniel reached for the dustpan to sweep up the smaller pieces. "He can't be turning up at the school, tryin' to get access to our kids...what are we going to do about this - this can't happen again."

"It won't," Daniel replied. "Not on my watch."

"I want in on this," David stated. "I want in on whatever you've got planned to set him straight."

"Good," Daniel said, managing a sly smile.

"Whatever you've got planned, I can't lose either of you," I insisted.

"I can tell you now baby girl, you won't lose him. I'll make sure of it," Daniel promised. "As for me, well, I'm the one on the run. I'm the one who's a wanted man. I'll do my best to be here for you. Might be tricky to do that being behind bars, but the best guarantee I can give you is my love, protection and devotion. I'm doing this all for the love of you. I'll do anything and everything I can to protect you." Pausing for a moment, hand on his heart, he added, "God as my witness, I'll make the ultimate sacrifice and give my life up for you and the kids. I hope you know that, Temwani. I truly hope you do."

I stood there, staring into the eyes of the man who loved me so much. The man whose love I paid no mind to when we were together all those years ago.

I stood there pondering the depth of his love before David interjected, "Daniel, you've given up so much already. Hopefully you won't have to make that sacrifice," he said coolly.

Despite what he'd said a day earlier about knowing where we stood, I knew it made him feel ill at ease to be witness to Daniel's repeated declarations of love and reminders of days in love gone by.

A warm breeze swept through that afternoon. "Storm on the way," I mentioned to Daniel, who was busying himself with the kids, finger-painting. They'd been on the swings earlier, then the bikes. I could tell they'd be tuckered out relatively quickly, and naptime might arrive earlier than expected.

He nodded in response. "At least I'll be inside this time," he said, making reference to the times he'd had to weather the storm in all its elements, outside.

After a hearty lunch which comprised of chicken kebobs, salad and spiced crinkle chips, Daniel put on a movie for the children to distract them while we talked out on the front porch. The children remained within earshot.

"Thank you for lunch, it filled a hole," he stated. "How are you feeling today? Any morning sickness?" he asked.

"Fortunately, no. A bit in the beginning, but nothing now." It seemed strange talking to him about the children I was having with someone else. Had he not left, we would have been talking about his children. Our children. He'd always wanted to have a "tribe" as he put it.

"Any idea what you're having?" he asked.

"David wants it to be a surprise, but you know me, I had to find out as soon as I could," I replied. "Please don't tell him," I begged. "We're having two boys," I revealed.

He dropped his gaze for a moment before turning back to me and saying, "Well, isn't that ironic. Congratulations!" he said with enough enthusiasm to convince me he was happy for me. "May I?" he asked, placing his hand on my belly as though it were a good luck charm of sorts. "Genie oh genie, grant me my three wishes," he joked.

I slapped his hand off in jest, and he laughed in response.

"Daniel, you're a trip," I said.

"I'm starved for compliments these days, so I'll take that as one," he said, placing his hand back on my belly. "It feels like it was just yesterday we were here, expecting *our* babies. But what with all the drama I caused, you weren't able to fully enjoy your pregnancy," he said. "I'm sorry for all that," he apologized.

"It's in the past, you're forgiven," I told him.

Out of the blue, he asked, "Does he give you a good foot rub the way I used to?"

I stopped for a moment and recalled us as we were, when I was pregnant with Adalia and Josiah. "No, I don't let him," I advised. "Reminds me of you," I added. "Anything that

609

reminds me of you is off limits for him," I said, slightly feeling sorry for David. Not many things were not off limit.

"I see," he said. He examined his hands, which were rough, slightly calloused and weather worn. "Can I give you a foot rub? Just for old time's sake?" he asked. "Ignore how my hands look," he said. "I'm pretty sure I've still got that tender touch that you loved so much."

I opened my mouth to protest but he was already on his knees. I felt my heart soar when he gently held my feet, rotated my ankles clockwise and anticlockwise, before taking my right foot in his hands and walking his fingers over the sole of my foot.

"I don't want to violate you," he said, pausing momentarily. "I don't want to do anything untoward, bearing in mind the fact that I'm no longer your man. We can't go back to the past, but I sure wish we could," he confessed. "I may not be your man any longer, but you'll always be my lady. You'll always be my woman," he declared.

I sat there in silence, searching for the right words to say. *I wish you'd never left*, I wanted to say, but I couldn't. My obligation was to David now, and there was no room for looking back into the past.

"Talk to me," he urged. "Sugarpie," he said, pulling at my heart strings. "Talk to me."

Tears threatened to fall, but I held them back when I heard the pitter patter of small feet making their way out towards us. *Josiah*. He was probably hungry and after a snack.

Somewhat surprisingly, he walked towards Daniel instead of me. "Can you come inside and watch with us?" he asked, sneaking a smile my way, and bounding over towards me to plant a kiss on my cheek. That done, he asked again of Daniel,

"Can you?"

Without hesitation, Daniel got up and replied, "I sure can." He gave me a tender squeeze on the shoulder before walking into the house with Josiah. I worried about the bond they were forming, and of how Josiah would cope when Daniel eventually had to leave.

We were still on the front porch enjoying our Sunday afternoon when the arrest happened. A crew of police officers appeared at our doorstep and asked to see Daniel. We all knew it would happen, it was just a matter of when. Storm howled wildly in the background, slamming himself against the screen door in an attempt to get to us. "Settle boy, settle," Daniel said in a firm but reassuring tone, standing up to face the policemen. Storm continued to howl, albeit, lower.

"Daniel Josiah Brennan, you're under arrest for the attempted murder of Declan Cooper, for the murder of Logan Archer, and for conspiracy to defraud the Commonwealth of Australia and the State of Texas in the United States of America. You have the right to remain silent, anything you say can and will be used against you in a court of law. You have the right to a lawyer. Should you not have one, a legal aid lawyer will be appointed to you."

"Just give me a chance to say goodbye to my kids. Please," Daniel begged, in a tone that was submissive and so unlike him. The officer in charge nodded his head in approval with the precursor, "Make it quick, mate." A younger looking officer followed Daniel and I in, so as to keep Daniel in his sight.

The kids were asleep on the couch. Daniel knelt down and gave them each a kiss on the cheek. I should have seen the next part coming, but I didn't. Standing up to face the police, he tipped his hat to me then took it off his head. "Take care of our family," he said, placing his hat on my head. I couldn't stop myself from crying. Gently cupping my chin in his hand, and wiping away a teardrop, he leaned forward and into me for a deep and imploring kiss.

"Hands up where we can see them mate," one of the officers called out.

His breath and my breath one, I didn't push him away when I should have. Instead, I stood there and let him savour me, in a brief moment that felt like forever. "Mmmm," he murmured before bringing our kiss to an end. Unabashed, he held my gaze. "Tell David I'm sorry," he said. "For the kiss, and for still loving you. You and our babies, it's all I've got now."

"A few steps forward mate, hands above your head," the same officer commanded.

Daniel did as was requested and walked towards them.

Making a quick turn back to me, he winked. "No greater love, baby. I'll be seeing you," he said, before confidently strutting up to the closest officer, hands above his head. He was cuffed instantly and read his rights again. I watched in slow motion as he was led out through the front door, silently, without words. He turned to look at me again, this time a little less confident than he'd appeared a moment ago, and mouthed, "I love you," before being roughly shoved into the back of the police paddy wagon.

I stood at the front door in tears as he was driven off. Hands shaking, I sat at the doorstep, not wanting to wake the children up as I cried. David pulled up not long after. He knew from the look on my face that Daniel had been picked up. He held me for a while, in silence, before asking where Daniel had been taken. "The Watch House at Lenah Vale," I replied, in between tears. Lenah Vale was also home to the only maximum security prison in the Greater Hobart and Southeastern Tasmania region.

"Okay, David said, thinking on his feet. "He hasn't formally been charged yet, surely there's a chance he'll be allowed out on bail?"

"Attempted murder and murder? Chances of that are pretty slim. The fact that he's been on the run indicates that he's a huge flight risk. It won't happen," I told him.

"I'll call Craig," he said immediately. "He'll know what to do," he said. Craig was the last person I wanted to talk to or hear from, but David was right, he'd know what to do. "I'll call Allistair as well," he promised. Allistair McQueen was a high flying criminal barrister, well known within local circles for his work with clients facing life sentences. "I'll also go and see him at the Watch House. You get some rest and together we'll work on getting him out of this mess," he promised, planting a kiss on my lips. For a moment, my mind flitted off to the memory of the kiss between Daniel and I. For a moment. I had to tell David sometime. *Just not now.*

"I know what he's like," David said intuitively, interrupting me mid thought. "I knew he couldn't resist," he said, gesturing at the camera overhead which I'd completely forgotten about. "I'm with you now, and that's all that matters," he said, slipping Daniel's cowboy hat off my head. "Let's go inside," he urged, protectively ushering me in.

"David, I didn't mean for it to happen..." I started explaining, wanting to apologize.

"Shhh," he said, silencing me with a kiss. "Already forgiven," he declared. "I know what I mean to you, and I know what he means to you. Most importantly, I know where I stand with you," he confirmed. "Water under the bridge. Let's not dwell on it. I'm with you now, he's not. He can try to stake a claim on you now, but he won't win, not while I'm here loving you, not while we're having children of our own," he promised, placing a tender hand on my belly. Our babies fluttered within ever so lightly.

I nodded to the affirmative, grateful for his big heart and his endless love for me. With Daniel being gone, I would've felt incredibly alone, were it not for David. So faithful, so constant his presence in my life was, yet deep down, I yearned for the familiarity, spontaneity and excitement that Daniel offered and the history we had together. Seeing him again, after losing him to a death that never happened physically, but to be fair, happened spiritually, forced me to recall the good of what we had and shared, and only the good. The children were a manifestation of our love, and if that were anything to go by, our love was true, and our love was beautiful.

Still, there were the issues we had in the past. The relentless fighting, and the tears. He loved me more when I fulfilled his desires, and when I answered to his every beck and call. Then again, what man wouldn't? A love with conditions of sorts it was, despite him trying to convince me otherwise. In the end, distance was probably a good thing. In his absence, he would get over me – he would get over us. I just wasn't sure if I'd ever get over him. David offered comfort in so many ways, but whether it would ever be enough to fill the void that Daniel had left behind, remained to be seen.

I slept fitfully that night, worried to bits about Daniel. The children were as restless as I was. I had no answers when Adalia and Josiah demanded to know where Daniel was.

33

SCHADENFREUDE

I refused to talk to Craig for days, which then turned into weeks. In the past, after the birth of the kids, then after Daniel had gone, he'd given me free rein to work from home if I pleased, and to take time off when needed. I used the authority he gave me then to avoid seeing him or talking to him now. Eventually I would have to talk to him, but not for the foreseeable future. I remained livid at the fact that he'd kept Daniel away from me, and had led me to believe that Daniel had passed on. I was in no rush to talk to him.

One morning, fed up with me not responding to his calls, texts or emails, Craig sent me a scathing text:

If you don't respond to my messages, I'm putting you on notice.

My response was, *If you don't stop harassing me, I'll report you to the Law Society of England and Wales, the Law Society of Tasmania, The Queensland Law Society, the American Bar Association and the Police.*

You wouldn't dare, he replied.

Watch me, I said in response.

You and David owe your happiness to me, he said.

Don't be ridiculous. You don't control everything, I told him.

I don't but I did. I made it possible for you and David to be together. You ought to thank me.

Incredible, I thought. I decided not to reply, which I was certain would infuriate him even more.

I was right. His next communication came through David, days later. One evening, David interrogated me. "Craig says you're ghosting him?"

I laughed at the suggestion. Typical of Craig to lay the blame on me and fail to see his contribution to it all.

"What's going on?" David asked.

"Craig is being Craig," was my reply.

"He's doing the best he knows how, cut him some slack," David said in his defence.

I was going to do no such thing. Craig had obviously known all along about Daniel's plan from the get go. All along. All this time. According to Daniel, the plan had been Craig's. He'd just gotten Daniel to go along with it. I tried to contain my anger at Craig when he turned up on our doorstep that day.

"How could you?" I asked immediately.

"Daniel insisted," he said. "He had his reasons. All of which I support."

"According to Daniel, *you* insisted. He was in no condition to disagree with you," I reminded him. "Some friend you turned out to be," I added.

"Well, I am a friend. One who cares for you and my brother here deeply," Craig explained.

"Could've fooled me," I replied.

"You'll thank me one day," he said nonchalantly.

"I highly doubt that," I replied.

"Look, I know you don't want to hear me out right now,

but you and David have a good thing going. I wouldn't have officiated your wedding if I didn't believe you two didn't belong together..."

"Oh, you mean the wedding you officiated which officially means nothing now? And as for being together, I took vows with Daniel. You know as well as I do that my marriage to David is not worth the paper it's printed on given Daniel and I are still married."

"Oh, but it isn't nothing. That's just it. It's what you make of it," he replied. "No turning back now," he said, adjusting his glasses.

"I don't get you Craig."

"You don't have to get me. You just need to know there was no malice or bad will intended," he said. "All will be revealed in time."

I was so angry at him I felt I would blow. Instead, I bit my tongue.

"I know you're not wanting to hear advice from me now, but one bit of advice I can offer you is guard your heart," he advised.

"Guard my heart?" I asked, shocked at his casual attitude.

"Yes, guard your heart," he repeated. "You've been through a lot. Your relationship with Daniel wasn't all peaches and cream. Don't forget that. You've forgiven him much. Don't let anyone guilt trip you into believing you haven't given enough. Don't let him guilt trip you into believing that you owe him anything. The decision he made was his alone."

"He was acting in accordance with *your* instructions, and given his state of mind at the time and his vulnerability, one could argue that it was all done under duress," I stated, boldly.

"I also understand that he was protecting Jonah," I said. "He at least deserves credit for that."

"Jonah didn't need protection," Craig said sternly. "If Daniel hadn't gotten involved, things wouldn't have turned out the way they did."

"I don't follow," I replied. It was clear he was going on the offence where Daniel was involved. No admissions, just offence.

"I haven't got time for this," he said sharply. I could tell that I was getting under his skin.

"So you say," I replied, with a view to enraging him further. *You're not going to get away with this.* "What makes you think I have the time to hear your excuses on why you took it upon yourself to lie to me all this time?"

He clenched his jaw in response and averted eye contact. "The Brotherhood was fine until Daniel came along. We did good, and we were good until Daniel and his ego came along trying to run things."

Pot calling a kettle black. Craig's ego was equally as large, if not, larger. Pity he didn't see that.

"You want to say something, say it," he challenged.

"No, I won't dare," I replied. "You'll only accuse me of being unfair to you," I conjectured. "What I will say is, the Brotherhood is anything but good. You can't rationalize what you do and assume you stand on the right side of the law. As it stands, you don't. You stand on the wrong side of the law."

"You're one to talk," he replied, angrily.

"What's that supposed to mean!" I asked.

"Well if you cared much at all about the right side of the law, your first port of call should've been to turn Daniel in. Obviously, you didn't. You can't pick and choose what side

619

you want to be on at whim."

"No, because only you can, right?" I asked, sarcastically.

He shook his head in response, then offered a disingenuous smile. "I always knew you had the mind of a prosecutor, yet the heart of a defense attorney."

"Whatever, mate," I said dismissively. "Meanwhile, you, as a defence attorney, and big brother, have no heart when it comes to Daniel."

"Don't judge me," he begged. "He should have left well enough alone. The Brotherhood could've done without his kind of help," he said. "Look, I know you're angry. I can only say I'm sorry." His apology sounded heartfelt this time, and I watched him adjust his glasses nervously. My heart softened slightly towards him.

I sighed in response. "Saying sorry won't fix this. Getting him out of this situation will," I advised.

Adjusting his glasses again, he nodded to the affirmative. "I'll see what I can do," he said. His phone rang vigorously several times before he decided to do something about it. "Gotta take this," he said. Turning away, he muttered something under his breath before stating, "Okay, London it is then. Anything leaving today is fine."

London. Of all places, and at this time. "London? You're helping Daniel by going to London?" I asked after he'd hung up.

"Trust me on this," Craig said, hurriedly getting ready to go. "David. You expecting him back anytime soon?" he asked.

"Not for another hour or so," I replied. "He's in town, busy with the street ministry."

"Hm," Craig said aloud, pensively. "Any idea what part of

town?"

"Clarendon area," I replied.

"Okay, I'll wait for him to get back then," he said, as I silently wondered how we would kill an hour together. I had so many questions about Daniel that I desperately needed answers to, but could barely stand to be in the same room with Craig, for fear I could not contain my anger.

"Why do you hate Daniel so much?" I asked candidly, hoping he would give me a straight answer.

"He's privileged. He's had every privilege one could want growing up. He lacked nothing," Craig stated.

"How do you figure that! You're making huge assumptions about a man you barely know."

"I've known him long enough," Craig replied. "If ever there was someone deserving of all he got, it was him."

"Craig!"

"He had law school paid for. Every whim catered for," Craig noted.

I tried to explain that Daniel had only had what he had as Jolène had insisted on it, and that their father, Pastor Declan, had paid only because his hand was forced.

Craig refused to listen, instead, seeking to annihilate Daniel with words. I waited until he was done with his tirade before I said anything.

"Daniel's had to struggle with the feeling that he didn't belong, all these years. You and the Brotherhood, well, you've had each other. Daniel's been alone in his journey through life in general. Growing up, Jolène might have ensured that his physical needs were met, but his emotional needs were neglected. You of all people should know that, and would've seen that. You and your brothers, you've been there for one another, you've supported each other. Then when he got sick he made the decision that he'd be better off dead than alive. You capitalized on his sadness and made things happen for me and David. If it wasn't for you, Daniel and I - we'd still be together. Maybe what happened with Jonah and Declan wouldn't have happened."

"You're reaching, Temwani. Reaching. You *chose* to be with David, don't forget, you actually made that choice." Craig replied.

"I wouldn't have made that choice if I knew Daniel was still alive!" I was crying now. "You've ruined him. You've ruined us all! When we ran out of money to fund Daniel's medical treatment you personally refused to step in. First you ostracized him. Then you tried to make out like it was him not wanting to live anymore. How dare you play God with his life! How dare you withhold your help from him, when it could've been the one thing that'd save him! How dare you!"

"Temwani, I had my reasons," he said firmly. "He didn't deserve to get sick, but he deserved to lose it all. He had the girl, the family, the career, the dream. He had everything, and he didn't know what he had when he had it. If I could do it all over, I would do the same thing again. He didn't know what he had 'til it was gone. If he was drowning I would *not* have lifted a hand to save him."

I sighed heavily before responding, "Craig, I never thought I'd say this, but I hate you."

"Hate's a strong word, Temwani," he said, shocked at my words.

"I *hate* you, Craig. I hate you for all that you've done to make it easy for you to stand by and let things happen to everyone else and not you. I hate you for thinking you can play God in our lives. I hate you for ruining Daniel's life."

"I didn't do that, he did that all by himself," Craig said haughtily.

He wasn't hearing me, so I commanded that he leave. "Get out, Craig, get out. I'm sorry I ever knew you."

Pain and shame was apparent in his eyes before he nodded his head in acknowledgement. As he turned to go, he explained, "For what it's worth, everything I've done has been for the love of the Brotherhood. Daniel included."

"Could've fooled me," I replied. "Get out," I commanded again.

"I never meant to hurt you," he said.

"Well, you did. Please leave."

"Guard your heart," he said again, then he turned to go, and I watched after him. When he reached the end of the walkway, he turned back and gave me a salute. I turned away, closed the door before I could see him drive off. Only a broken man would try to reap so much destruction on others. He seemed more broken than evil. I didn't hate him. I just wanted him out of my life for a time, and hoped that one day, somehow, he would realise the extent of his involvement in Daniel's downfall.

Jude called me that afternoon. He sounded rushed, and driven. After asking how the kids and I were doing, he advised, "We're not after Johnny. We're not after David. We're after Craig."

My heart skipped a beat. "Craig?" *Why was I not surprised?*

"Yes, the one and only," Jude confirmed. "A few things I need you to do, Temwani," Jude advised. "Firstly, the partnership you've got in place with him. Be prepared to turn over the books. Any clients he's recently signed on, any witness statements he's taken - I basically need you not to be anywhere near him when the proverbial shit hits the fan."

"That shouldn't be too hard to organise," I said, thinking of the way Craig and I had left things.

"Okay," Jude said. "Secondly, if you've ever entertained thoughts of a partnership with someone else, let's say, Johnny, now's the time to make it happen."

"He's still waiting to hear back from the Board," I explained.

"We're not after him. He's indicated a willingness to cooperate. We'll grant him immunity from prosecution in exchange for information. I'll even write a recommendation letter to the Board. As far as I've seen, he *is* a fit and proper person to practice as a solicitor," Jude declared.

"Lawyer. Attorney," I corrected.

"Yep, thanks for the reminder. I forgot which jurisdiction I was in for a moment. Speaking of which, about the UK, how much do you know about Craig's business there?" he asked.

"Only as much as he's told me," I said. "He's admitted as a barrister there, and that's the extent of it. I did look up some of his cases, he's quite the advocate."

"So is Ernesto," Jude pointed out. "So am I," he added. "We won't rest until justice is served and justice is done where he's involved."

"I don't know, Jude. Craig's pretty clued on, it's unlikely there's anything tying him to the things the Brotherhood has done. Last thing I want to see is Johnny and David getting caught up in the crossfire."

"No chance of that," Jude promised. "As I said, Johnny's

been given immunity against prosecution. David - well, it depends on the extent to which he wants to cooperate. Daniel, he needs to admit the truth and face the music."

I sighed heavily in response. "You're not making this easy."

"Teme, I'm looking out for you and your family. I wish it wasn't this way, but I can't turn a blind eye to any of this," he said. I knew then he was referring to Daniel and his whereabouts.

"I don't know what to say, Jude," I replied.

"Just say you'll heed my warning. I need you to act on what I've said. Don't hesitate," he advised. "About Daniel, he needs to do the right thing and own up to what he's done."

"Jude, you know as well as I do that Daniel can be a law unto himself."

"Yes, much like Craig. All for the love of power," he stated. "Alright, I must go now. I hope you know I only want the best for you. I'll fight to protect you come what may," he promised. "We're friends for life, and my love for you as a friend, is unconditional," he stated, catching me by surprise. "Keep this conversation to yourself please. Take care for now."

Before I got a chance to reply, he had hung up.

34

SOMETHING BEAUTIFUL THIS WAY COMES

I couldn't bear the thought of Daniel being alone and behind bars. I knew what David would say, but I did it anyway. I snuck out that night to see if I could see Daniel in prison.

The car was already out in the driveway. A cool mist had formed over the windscreen, and I knew it would be ice cold inside. Hoping the sound of the ignition wouldn't awaken David, I sat at the wheel, contemplating the decision to drive out to Lenah Vale at that time of night. By the time I got there it would be close to 5 am, and I'd be there with only an hour to go before visiting time commenced.

Light rapping on the window startled me. It was David. Rather than open my door, he made his way over to the passenger side of the car, opened the door and got in.

"Baby," he said. "Won't you come back inside. We can go see him first thing."

I shook both from the cold and from sadness. Tears fell.

"You're not in this alone," he reminded me. "I know how

you feel about him. I know that you still love him. You should know you're not in this alone. I'm not about to walk away from an opportunity to show you how much I love you, in spite of him. Won't you come inside now. Please," he pleaded.

We made our way back upstairs, and in bed he held me in his arms, to comfort me, though I was convinced it was partly an attempt to ensure I remained where I said I would remain.

True to his word, we drove to Lenah Vale early the next morning. Both kids were being looked after by a friend, so there was no need to rush the visit.

We both got out and stared at the expansive white gates and barbed wired fence. "You'll be okay?" David asked, leaning against the car door. I realised then that he wasn't coming in with me.

I nodded in response, unsure of what to make of his stance. It seemed as though everyone was distancing themselves from Daniel when he needed them the most.

"Before you do," he started, approaching me. He traced a finger along the outline of my lips, then placed his strong hands on my shoulders. "Remember how much I love you. Remember how much I cherish what we have and how much I adore you. Remember that I'll support you in everything, and will be with you 'til the end."

"I love you too," I told him, leaving him in the car, my heart and mind already with Daniel in the walls of that prison.

I showed the guard my prefilled visitor's form, and he let me in through the initial security gate. I walked a few metres with a guard before I got to the sliding door entrance of the prison. Inside, I was directed to a legal conference room. I sat on one side of the glass, waiting for Daniel to be ushered in.

Moments later, he was brought in. His face showed signs of strain, his eyes a turbulent sea of blue. Seeing him behind glass, in his prison jumpsuit, brought tears to my eyes. Holding the phone in his hand, he motioned for me to use the one on my end. I picked it up, and placed the receiver against my ear, tears falling down my face.

"Don't cry, beauty. I'm fine," he said.

You're anything but fine, I thought, knowing he was being stoic and brave.

"Sugarpie," he commenced, and I managed to laugh in between tears.

"You don't get to call me that anymore," I said.

"I will, if it'll make you smile," he advised. "How are you?"

"I'm managing the best I can," I told him. "I didn't realise how much I'd worry after you."

"You miss me?" he asked abruptly.

"Ask me something else," I told him.

"Why're you here?" he asked. "Is this a welfare check?"

"Daniel, we were married once. This is more than just a welfare check," I replied.

"We're still married," he corrected. I nodded in response. *Not for much longer*, I thought.

"I'm doing okay, just trying to keep my head above water," he said. "Is David not here with you?"

"He's in the car," I advised.

"I see," he said pensively. Leaning forward, he mentioned, "Those divorce papers you wanted signed, I left them in the top drawer, guest room," he advised. "I owe you that much," he stated.

The timing was all wrong. He, behind bars, me, no longer

one foot out the door but still full of love for him. Love hadn't ended. It had been arrested. Despite everything that David was to me, and he was everything, I longed to go back to where Daniel and I had left off, as it felt we hadn't concluded in love. I longed to go back to the moment that he'd decided to leave, except he wouldn't leave this time. I would will him to stay.

Daniel rapped on the glass. "Hey." As he stared straight at me I noticed the deep sadness in his eyes, but I knew that he would not dare cry. "I'll always love you, but it's for the best. David needs you now more than ever," he stated. "File those papers, and you're free to marry him, just as soon as you've had the babies," he said.

I stopped for a moment, puzzled. "What are you talking about? Why only after I've had the babies?"

"Texan law dictates that you can't get divorced while you're expecting, whether or not the child or children are from the current spouse," Daniel explained.

That was news to me. I knew instantly that David would be disappointed.

"There's no doubt that these babies are his," I stated, removing any shade he'd intended to throw my way.

"How can you be that certain?" he asked to my surprise.

What? "I know who I slept with if you know what I mean," was my abrupt response. I was livid at the suggestion that I might have slept with someone else.

"Well, it was a miracle you got pregnant with David, given his - well, his condition. Even more of a miracle that you're carrying twins," Daniel stated. I frowned slightly, puzzled at what he was getting at.

"The doctor wasn't wrong about your due date," he said

into the phone, in a mysterious and cryptic manner. I sat there for a moment in silence, trying to figure out what he was trying to say. "*You* weren't wrong about the date of conception," he added.

"Daniel, will you stop beating around the bush and just say what you want to say?" I asked.

"Alright," he said, shifting slightly in his seat. The guard to the right of him motioned for him to wrap things up. He nodded in response. "I recommend you order a DNA test of the babies as soon as they're born. I have reason to believe they are yours and mine, not yours and his," he said.

I tried to hide my shock, but couldn't. "That's impossible," I suggested.

"Is it now?" he asked. "You wanted it as much as I did that night," he stated. "I didn't violate you, you gave me your consent."

My mind flitted back to the night when I believed the babies were conceived. David had said he'd be doing a 12-hour shift at the General Hospital that night, and I'd been surprised to find him urging me to fall into his arms in the early hours of the morning. At the time, I'd thought it quite unusual that he was so filled with energy after such a long shift. The love that we'd made had been passionate, voracious, explosive and very much like the love Daniel and I used to make. When I mentioned this to David the following morning, he put it off to it possibly being a very lucid dream. Only, it was no dream, as I came to realise now, following Daniel's confession. *It had been Daniel in the flesh, all along.*

"I can't believe this Daniel," I said, angrier than I was before, but now crying. "How dare you violate me."

"You wanted me as much as I wanted you," he said in

justification. "I didn't violate you."

"I didn't know it was you."

"I was and still am your husband," he said. "I didn't violate you."

"Time's up," the guard announced sharply.

"I do love you Teme. You can be with him now, just like you've always wanted to. Just not until after the babies are born. I didn't make the law," he said.

"No, but you took matters into your own hands and made decisions to suit you – you became a law unto yourself," I said, in between tears.

"It wasn't all about me. I did it for the love of you," he explained. "I was all alone and I needed you. I know you needed me too."

I shook my head in response, a sinking feeling in my stomach. *David will be devastated.* "How can I be with David now, in all good conscience, after everything you've told me? How is anything ever supposed to go back to normal..."

"Visiting time is over," the guard announced, ignoring the fact that Daniel and I were still talking.

"I love you," Daniel mouthed, pressing two fingers on his lips then onto the glass. Obediently, he got up, to presumably avoid trouble for himself later on. Shifting awkwardly due to the chains on his feet, he offered his hands up to the guard. The guard gruffly cuffed him and led him down the hall. I watched after him for a while until his silhouette was gone. *David will not just be devastated, he'll be heartbroken to find out that the babies might not be his.* I sat there in front of the glass moments after Daniel had gone. Overwhelmed with emotion, I cried.

When I got back to the parking lot, David was restless. I could tell that the time I'd spent seeing Daniel had him on edge.

"How is he?" he asked immediately.

"As well as can be," I stated, not wanting to talk, and just wanting to cry.

"How are you?" he asked, tracing the outline of my face with his fingers. "You've been crying," he noticed.

"It's..." I started, before breaking off. I wasn't quite sure what to say and when. "He wants to see you next time," I managed.

"I figured so much," he replied. "I just couldn't bear to see him today. Part of me wishes I was in there instead of him," he stated. Searching my face for anything that would indicate that I'd made a choice between him or Daniel, he found nothing. Apart from the tears of sadness, I'd found a way of disguising my emotion with him. For a time anyway.

We sat in silence for a moment before he spoke again. "I'm feeling pretty helpless right now, there probably isn't anything I can tell you that'll sway you either way. I can tell you're conflicted," he said, sighing heavily before stating under his breath, "He wasn't supposed to fall for you in the first place," he said, referring back to the job that he'd ordered and the request he'd made for Daniel to save me all those years ago.

"So much for the best laid plans," I thought aloud.

"Well, I guess with the babies I'll always be in your life," he hoped.

The bad feeling in the pit of my stomach grew. *They may not be your babies.* I wanted to tell him, but I couldn't. Not just yet anyway. Instead, I stated, "David, you know it isn't just about the babies. It's about the bond that we have. The love that we share, and so much more."

He took my hands in his. "I know. But I just can't shake the feeling that we're loving and living on borrowed time," he said worriedly. "I know what I said before about being okay with whatever decision you make, but the more I think about it, the more I know that I won't be okay. You're my first love. I've loved you way too long to go back to living without you," he said, exhaling deeply as though he were taking a final breath before dying.

"David, he signed the papers," I said, my heart skipping a beat as I spoke those words. *He'd decided to let me go.*

David's eyes lit up instantly. "That's awesome...," he started, stopping short before searching for the right words to say. I knew the news of Daniel having signed the papers was good news to him. Instead, he paused further before asking, "Is this what you want?" I shrugged in response.

"We can file them but I won't be divorced from him until the babies are born," I told him. He seemed a little shocked.

"Why not?"

"Law of Texas," I said. "If the woman is pregnant, whether or not the kids are from the marriage or not, she cannot get divorced until the babies are born."

"Some law," David said. "Why do I get the feeling there's more?"

I held my silence.

"If there's more to this, you need to tell me now," he requested.

Heart pounding so much so that I could hear it in my ears, I decided to tell him to save delaying the inevitable discovery. "I don't know how to tell you this, but the babies may not be

633

yours. They might be his."

I watched the colour drain from his face and my heart sunk.

"But how is that even possible?" he said aloud, despair and anguish clear in his voice. "How can this be?"

"Remember how I tried to convince you of the night that I believed the babies were conceived, and you put it down to a lucid dream? Well, according to him, it was no lucid dream. It was him."

David's face turned red with anger, and he slammed his fist against the top of the steering wheel. "Damn it," he swore angrily.

"I'm so sorry David," I apologised.

"Don't," he said. "Don't apologise. This is all him. I know you well enough to know you wouldn't do this to me willingly," he stated. "Man, this is just beyond belief. Nice guys do finish last, I guess," he said, furious. Breathing heavily, he yanked open the car door and paced alongside the car. Apart from the day Daniel and David had had it out on the veranda at our cottage in Nambour on the Sunshine Coast, I had never seen him this angry. I sat in the passenger seat, waiting for him to cool off. I needed to give him a moment. He needed a moment to come to terms with what I'd said. I needed a lifetime to come to terms with what Daniel had said. Eventually, he yanked open the door and got into the car, still livid.

"I'm so sorry David," I said again.

"Again, don't apologise," he insisted. "This is all his doing."

"Where do we go from here?" I asked.

"I say we go home right away, and I lay you down and make love to you. He's back. What we have will be over soon enough, if he has anything to do with it. I want us to focus on the here and now. So if you're asking me, I'm asking you for permission to make fervent love to you when we are alone, tonight."

I blushed at the suggestion. Before I even had a chance to reply, he stated, "Tomorrow's tomorrow. We'll deal with tomorrow, tomorrow. We still have tonight," he said, leaning in to give me a passionate kiss before starting the car. *He's never kissed me like this before*, I thought, the sense of urgency and fervour in him making my senses reel out of control.

"If what we have has to come to an end, I'll give you something to remember me by. Something to miss," he vowed.

That evening, David stood against the bedroom wall by the bed we'd shared as husband and wife. By the bed he'd built when there was only ever the possibility of us being lovers in some distant time in the future which would eventually came to pass. By our bed of dreams, wants and desires.

"You coming to bed?" I asked.

"Not just yet. We need to talk," he said, not moving from where he was, standing up against the wall.

"Okay," I replied. I knew by his tone it would be one of those serious conversations.

"Darlin' this won't do," he stated. "I know what I said earlier, but me wanting to have you while you're still married to him - that won't do," he said. "I'm an ordained minister now. I need to do better than to give in to my emotions. I need to do better than to lead you down a path that'll surely cause you to sin. Now that we know he's back, and I've known for a while now, we need to do the right thing. We know better. I know better."

"I hear what you're saying David. The issue is, we took vows to each other. I promised to love you to the exclusion of all others," I reminded him.

"Yes, you did. We both did. That was before we knew he was still alive..." he reminded me.

"We might not be legally married, but my heart is with you," I declared.

"Is it now?" he asked.

"It always has been David. You shouldn't have to ask. After all this time, and what we've been through together, what we've shared, you should know it is."

He shrugged in response. "All I know is I've been loving you a long time and I never thought I'd be without you in the end."

"This isn't the end," I told him.

"Oh, but it is," he replied. "I know you still love him. I know part of you still wants to be with him, to rekindle what you had. If he hadn't gone away, you might've still been together."

"Might've. Not if you had anything to do with it."

"True," he agreed. "But you made a decision in the end. You chose him. You're choosing him now."

"David, it's more complicated than that..."

"It isn't," he insisted, "You know, I know you better than you know yourself sometimes, just as you know me inside and out. It isn't complicated. It's a matter of love, loyalty and honour. I've always been here for you, and I will always be there for you. I just know we can't continue to ignore the fact that he's back. This is adultery," he stated, point blankly.

"Dave, your argument has a lot of holes in it," I said.

"Right. How so? How 'bout you school me then, Counsel-lor?"

"Okay, for one, you've known Daniel was back for time. How long have you known?"

"A few weeks now."

"How many weeks?" I asked.

He pondered for a moment before stating, "Well, he's been back since Adalia's birthday."

"That long?" I asked.

"Yes, I'm afraid," he said. "Look I'm really sorry I didn't tell you earlier. I just couldn't bring myself to give you up that soon."

"Okay, so you've known since June. I found out in or around July."

He nodded in response.

"So the argument about us committing adultery now, is really about us committing adultery then as well, since you knew he was back, and technically he and I were still married. What about the times before we got married, when he and I were still together, and you literally committed adultery just by thinking of me?"

"I know," he said somberly. "I just think that now we know he's back for sure, and you're still officially married, we shouldn't be doing anything to get in the way of a future between you and him."

I shook my head in disagreement. "I wish you'd fight harder for me David."

"Please don't say that. I've been fighting for you all these years. Trying not to get in the way, waiting for you to take me on. If I had his balls and his guts, I would've spoken to you all those years ago, and you and I would be together. No doubt. But I'm just not like him. I can't..."

"David, no one asked you to be like him."

"No, but being like him would've gotten me a lot further with you than where I am now," he alleged.

"David, I fully enjoyed the time we shared together, and I can say with a full heart, if he wasn't around, I would be with you, forever," I declared and felt my heart sigh at the mention of the fact that forever with him would only exist if Daniel were not around.

He left his post on the wall and joined me on the end of our bed.

"Look, if the chance comes again that he isn't around, I'll be here for you, waiting for you to take me on again," he promised. Stroking his chin as he did when he was anxious, he added, "I love you so much, Temwani. You truly are my best friend and my other half. Lost without you is what I'll be, but I'll try to get by," he said sadly.

I pulled him into me and hugged him with all my might. I felt his tears fall onto the nape of my neck before he pulled back, embarrassed. Wiping his eyes brusquely, he turned away and said, "Me being this emotional isn't such a good look. Wish I wasn't such a mess, but my heart is breaking right now and I can't really keep it all inside."

"You don't have to keep it inside," I said, tears rolling down my face.

"I'm not sure I can do this – letting you go," he confessed.

"You don't have to. I can file those papers once the babies are born. We don't have to let what we have come to an end."

"We do," he insisted. "We don't have a choice about it – you were married when we got together, Daniel was still alive. I won't be the man that tears apart what the Lord has brought together."

"Do you really believe that?" I asked. "Wasn't it you that brought us together? You trying to save me, you enlisting Daniel to come to the rescue, you trying to comfort me when we thought we'd lost Daniel, wasn't that your doing? God might have had a hand in bringing Daniel and I together, but..."

"You're confusing this," he interjected. "None of that matters now. It's pretty simple. You're still married to Daniel. I can't be with you."

"David, he's given me the go ahead to file for divorce once the babies are here."

"That doesn't mean much in reality, especially when the babies are very likely his," he said.

"Do you even want to be with me?" I asked, getting annoyed at him. "It seems like you're coming up with every excuse under the sun as to why this cannot work, yet we've been getting by fine before now."

"Of course I want to be with you, Teme," he replied hastily. "I've spent a great part of my adult and teenage life doing everything I can to get with you. Please don't diminish what I feel for you. Of course I want to be with you, but the circumstances will not permit," he advised.

"Okay," I replied.

"If the circumstances won't allow us to be together, I'm committing myself to Ministry one hundred percent," he added.

The notion that he would give up the search for love and become married to the Church was romantic, but I didn't think he was being realistic.

"That sounds drastic. Do you think that's the right thing

to do?" I asked.

"I've thought about this for quite some time. Not everyone can or should marry," he said. "If the Apostle Paul could do it, so can I," he said firmly.

You're not the Apostle Paul I thought to myself but I knew better than to argue with him anymore.

"What if the babies are mine and yours?" I asked.

"They're more likely to be his and yours."

"What if they are mine and yours, David? *What if.*"

He paused as though carefully considering not only his response, but his preferred course of action. "That would change everything," he said.

"How so?"

"I wouldn't let another man raise my kids," he said.

"So, you'd say bye bye to singledom then," I summarized.

He hesitated again, then stated, "Yes, I guess I would have to. Reluctantly of course," he joked.

"Can you be single tomorrow then?" I asked.

"What?" he questioned, not understanding my proposition.

"Singledom can wait," I clarified. "Can you not be single tonight?"

My proposition caught him off guard and he laughed suddenly when he realized what I was suggesting. "You're quite the temptress," he remarked.

"Is that a yes or a no?" I asked. "One night is all I'm asking for," I told him. "Just one night."

"I can give you that," he said. "But it stays between us," he stated, both of us pretty certain that if Daniel caught wind of this, there'd be hell to pay.

"Of course," I said, ready to receive all he was willing to

give, and to give him my all, if only for one night.

Four o'clock in the morning and my phone rang.

"Hello?"

"Craig here."

What? "Craig?" I was surprised to be hearing from him at all, after the way we'd left things days ago.

"I've only got a few minutes," he said, his voice strained. The line sounded slightly muffled. The murmur of a crowd spoke in the background.

"I need you to file those historical charges against Duayne to facilitate a swift extradition back to Texas," he said.

"Craig, I'm not about to reopen old wounds and humiliate myself over him."

"It'll help Daniel," he said firmly. "He can argue psychiatric injury as a secondary victim. He can also try to argue self-defence over retribution. Generally, violence in defence of another can be justified more easily than violence in defence of oneself."

I held the phone in silence before I responded. "Why are you so keen to help Daniel all of a sudden?"

"Daniel doesn't deserve to be where he is," Craig stated.

Someone in the background called out, asking him to hurry up on the phone.

"I need to go now," he said. "I know it'll be difficult, but please bring those charges forward."

"Craig..."

"For what it's worth, I'm sorry about the things I said about Daniel. I was wrong and out of line," he stated.

The phone cut and I sat where I was, contemplating what he'd asked me to do. Filing rape charges against Duayne meant going back to Texas. I knew David wouldn't be too keen on the idea. I knew how important the ministry he was running was to him. Asking him to part ways with it to move halfway across the globe wouldn't be an easy task. I then contemplated Craig's sudden change of heart where Daniel was concerned. I wondered what had brought it on. *Perhaps Jude and the District Attorney's office had started their shake up of the Brotherhood?*

I broached the idea of going back to Texas with David when he woke up.

"I'm thinking of going to Texas, for a while."

"Texas - why now?" he asked.

"Do you even have to ask?"

"Right," he replied, somewhat disappointed. "You know I'm in the middle of the Sermon on the Mount series. Then there's youth camp. Besides, Daniel warned us off going back there anytime soon."

As much as I supported him in everything he did, it hurt me that he would choose to remain in Tasmania at such a pivotal time, choosing ministry over us. Then again, I hadn't given him much to be loyal to. I knew he was hurting over the fact that the babies I was carrying may not be his. I could tell he was having difficulty forgiving Daniel for having laid with me at a time when he and I were supposed to be married. I knew his heart was breaking over the fact that our relationship had to come to an end.

"Why the sudden urge to go to Texas?" he asked again.

"Craig called. He suggested I file charges against Duayne to help Daniel somehow."

"Craig?" he asked, slightly shocked. "He's in prison, you know?"

I couldn't hide my surprise. "Prison?"

"Yep. In the UK," he explained. "Something to do with Duayne."

The thought of Duayne having something to do with it sent a chill down my spine. The thought of Craig being in prison saddened me. I couldn't be certain about the reasons why he was in prison, but the one thing I did know was that someone was well and truly on the warpath.

"Daniel's insisting I go to Switzerland, Craig is insisting I go to Texas."

"I'm not liking the thought of you and the kids going anywhere without me, let alone back to Texas," David said firmly.

"The kids and I can go on our own," I told him.

"I don't like that idea, not one iota," he said. "You're 32 weeks along, how are you going to manage on your own?"

"I won't be on my own," I told him. "Jonah and Shania are still in Texas, I can call on my sister who's in California now..."

"I mean day to day," he clarified. "I don't like the idea of you being there on your own."

"I won't be on my own. Not if you come with me," I replied.

He sighed heavily in response. "I'll give it some thought," he said. "Worst case scenario, I'll join you afterwards," he promised. "For a time."

I nodded in reply, knowing that at this point in time, ministry mattered more to him than anything to do with the Brotherhood, or anything else for that matter, our family included.

Daniel had lost a considerable amount of weight when I

saw him again. Concern and worry filled his eyes.

"How are you?" he asked, speaking deeply into the phone on his end.

"We're all okay," I told him. "As best as we can be without you."

I noticed he had fresh lacerations on the palms of his hand, part of his arms and wrists. I gasped in alarm.

"Shivs. Improvised knives," he explained. "I had my hands up shielding my face and got my hands slashed as a result."

My stomach sunk. "Daniel..."

"I'll be fine," he told me. "I'm a big boy. I'll manage." After a slight pause, he said, "They be fixin' ta extradite me back to Texas next week or so. I can't go back there to face trial and the inevitable capital punishment," he said. "I'm not sure I can handle solitary confinement for months on end in a room with no windows. I'm certain I can't deal with going back to Texas now. I really need for you and the kids to not go back there either," he insisted.

"Craig is insisting..."

"Well, you know what I think about Craig," he replied.

"It's for your benefit, apparently."

"Right, more like for *his* benefit," he said. "I wouldn't trust him as far as I can throw him."

The animosity between the two of them was now legendary, but I felt compelled to do as Craig had asked. Duayne was bad news, and any opportunity to make him pay for what he'd done to me all those years ago would be one to take, especially when there was the opportunity to help Daniel.

"Jonah and Shania. How are they?" he asked.

"Good. They're both in Geneva now."

"Good," Daniel stated. "Jonah needs to keep well away

from Texas."

"And why's that?" I asked.

He couldn't tell me without talking in riddles. "He's the reason why I'm here," he said bluntly.

It took me a moment to understand what he had said.

"Better me than him," Daniel said.

Shock washed over me. "You mean to say...all this time..."

"They have another baby on the way, and this is a chance for him to make a clean break from the Brotherhood."

"Daniel..."

"I made the decision with my eyes wide open. The only regret I have is seeing you and David living the life that was meant for me, but this is outweighed by the fact that you're happy," he said.

Why hadn't I considered the possibility that Daniel might be innocent before? Of course Daniel would never be guilty of murder or manslaughter. He was a stand-up guy. Such a standup guy he was, that he had taken it upon himself to take the fall for a crime that Jonah had committed.

"I'm not going back to Texas," he vowed. "I also know you're not listening to me. So, when you do go back to Texas, keep safe. Don't stay any longer than you have to. Link in with Colleen. Touch base with Jolène if you can. Tell her I'm safe, and that despite the way things went down in the end, I *am* grateful to her. She raised me after all."

"Okay," I told him. "Will do."

"If you're going to Texas, do it now," he suggested, with a sense of urgency about him, which I would only begin to understand later, as time went on. "Lastly, remember how much I love you," he added. "Remember how much I want you. Remember that wherever you are, I'll find you," he promised. Getting up to go, he pressed his fingers on his lips for a kiss, then on the glass. "I'll be seeing you sugarpie."

I called Jude that morning to let him know of my plans to return to Texas. He wasn't in his office, so I left a message.

Halfway through the staff meeting at the community legal centre, my phone buzzed incessantly. Should've turned it off, I thought, then the thought struck me that it could have something to do with the kids.

Pulling my phone out of my handbag, I realised it was David. It wasn't usual for him to randomly call me at work, unless it was an emergency. I excused myself from the meeting and stepped into the corridor to take the call.

"I need you to meet me by your car. I need you to come down as soon as you can," he said.

"Okay," I said in response wondering about such a cryptic command as I immediately resolved to go to my car.

David was leaning against the car door, sunglasses on.

I greeted him with a kiss on the lips, and he held me firm, returning the kiss with passion and abandon. "You didn't come here just to do this now did you?" I asked.

"Let's talk in the car?"

"David..."

"In the car," he commanded.

I unlocked the car and sat in the passenger's seat. He quickly walked over to the driver's seat, shut the door then took off his sunglasses. "Sugarpie..."

My heart skipped a beat. "Daniel?"

"The one and only, baby."

A million thoughts raced through my mind at once. *Daniel,*

646

not David.

"Daniel, where's David!" I asked, panicked. He was wearing the clothes David had worn that morning.

"He's in Lenah Vale. Had to do what I needed to do. He'll be alright. He'll be out of there in no time," he said with certainty.

"Daniel!" I exclaimed, frightened and fearful for David, yet even more so for Daniel, now that he was on the run. *Again.*

"Try not to get too upset about it all. He'll be alright. Mates inside will make sure of it."

"Daniel! What were you thinking!"

He tenderly placed a hand on my belly and replied, "I was thinking of you, I was thinking of our babies. I was thinking how I got myself into this here mess in the first place, I was thinking on how things would be so different had he never turned up. I was thinking that I won't have my goals my plans and my dreams deferred any longer, that I won't be the one to lose this time. I can't be without you any longer. I needed to come home. I was thinking of you."

I sighed in response.

"Right now, I need you to help me out. We need to leave now. Me, you, the babies, we need to leave here tonight."

I shook my head in response. "Daniel you won't be able to pull this off. They'll be on to you in a heartbeat if they're not already looking for you."

He half smiled. "*We will* pull this off. Think positive baby," he said, leaning across to get to the glove compartment. He pulled out the owner's manual. Within the pages of the manual, he'd placed his Zambian passport. I'd applied for it not long after we'd married, with the help of my parents, who were all too happy to welcome him into our family. Whether

647

they'd feel the same now was questionable.

"Leave work now, get the babies organised and we can go. Flight leaves at 6. First Captain Musonda's piloting the flight. Here to Perth, then Lusaka via Joberg."

All I could think about was David.

Daniel read my mind. "David'll be fine," he said again. "Stop worrying about him. Now's as good a time as any to come correct where we're concerned."

"I can't leave like this, Daniel, I can't leave here with everything, and leave him with nothing."

"Oh, but you can," Daniel argued. "The babies you're carrying, are likely ours. And if by some bizarre twist of fate, they aren't, I'll raise them as my own."

I paused for a moment before I replied. "You say that now Daniel, but I know you."

"Hm...well if you know me, you'd know I'm not letting go of you this time. I'm willing to do anything to keep you with me," he replied.

"Then let me say goodbye to David. I need to know he'll be okay," I told him. "Then and only then will I go away with you. For a time."

"I'm not needing you to go away with me for a time. I'm asking you to lay low with me until I can clear my name. However long that takes. I'm not asking you to go away with me for a time. I'm asking you to leave with me, and be with me, forever."

"Let me say goodbye to him," I insisted.

After a momentary pause, he stated, "Alright." Slipping his passport into the inner pocket of his bomber jacket, he added, "Offer still stands. We can leave tonight, and never look back."

I was tempted, but leaving with him meant saying goodbye for good. There was no telling how long it would take for his name to be cleared. He certainly wouldn't be helping things if he insisted on being on the run. Things could get complicated.

"Talk to me," he requested. "I know you have a million and one questions, so talk to me. Tell me what you're thinking."

"I don't know where to start Daniel," I said. "First, I'm so happy to see you, out from behind bars, but I'm worried about David."

"Stop worrying about him."

"I can't help it. He's not as strong as he lets on," I said.

"He's stronger than you think."

"Then, me leaving with you. We won't stay under the radar for long. Being in Zambia won't make it any less likely that you'll get caught."

"No, but at least I won't be facing lethal injection or the chair," he said.

I sighed in response, unsure of what to say next. My silence was unsettling to him.

"Temwani, I'm drowning here. Throw me a lifeline, give me something. Anything," he pleaded.

I felt for him, but felt I couldn't and wouldn't allow myself to fall for him yet again and leave David in the lurch.

"You know, it's only ever been you for me. It's only ever been you," he said, tugging on my heart strings with his every word. "Here I am again. I'm alive baby. I'm here to hold you and love you whole, yet you hesitate...don't you love me anymore?"

"I love you very much," I replied. "I just... I don't see myself being on the run with you forever."

649

"It won't be forever," he promised. "What about South Texas? Me, you - it was okay then, what about now? Why is it not okay now?"

"So much has happened since then," I told him.

"This I know, but my love for you hasn't changed," he replied. "If anything, it's gotten stronger."

"I hear you baby," I told him.

"So, what d'ya say to taking a chance on me again? What d'ya say to taking a chance on our love again?" He didn't wait for me to respond. "I know you're worried about David. He'll be fine. I had to do what I did, for if I didn't, I wouldn't be here with you now. I don't expect you to bail on him straight away, but I'm hoping you'll be with me soon."

"I'm not planning on bailing on him," I replied.

"Okay," he replied, resigned to accept my position. "I'll be around. Wherever you are, I'll find you."

I shrugged in response.

He leaned back into the driver's seat, his shoulders heavy with an invisible weight I could not carry.

"So, is this it? Is this where our story ends?" he asked. "In my heart I feel this is not the end. You're still my wife. I'm still your husband. We *were* supposed to get through anything and everything together. My heart won't rest until I'm back with you. I've wanted you from the start. I...," he said, his voice cracking slightly. "I will love you always, Temwani."

The tears fell down my face unabated.

He hated to see me cry. "Sugarpie, I'm sorry. I can't just be without you and the kids. Not now and not ever. Without you, effectively I'll have nothing."

I wiped the tears off my face with the back of my hand.

"I'm sorry for all of this. All I've put you through, and all I'm putting you through," he said, raising my hand to his lips for a featherlight kiss.

In that instant, my phone rang. *Jude.*

"Temwani. Let me speak with him," he said immediately, shocking me.   *Jude knew where he was.* I handed the phone to Daniel, who hesitated initially, before putting it on speakerphone.

"How far are you willing to go to protect your family?" Jude asked.

"To the ends of this here earth," Daniel replied without hesitation. I sighed inwardly, thinking of all the things he'd already done in the name of protecting our family.

"You need to come back to Texas then," Jude advised.

"No chance of that," Daniel replied.

"If you don't come back to Texas there'll be hell to pay," Jude warned.

"I'll take my chances," Daniel said, hanging up the phone. Jude called back immediately.

"Let it ring," Daniel requested, and I did.

I had a million and one questions on my mind. *How did Jude know Daniel was with me? How did...*

"Watch out for your friends," Daniel warned.

"Sorry?"

"Ernesto. He's as dirty as they come," Daniel stated.

"I find that hard to believe," I replied.

"Watch out for your friends," he warned again. Slipping his sunglasses back on, he stated, "I'm hitting the road now. I see you're not planning on coming with me now. But I know you will be, soon. So, I'll be seeing you," he stated assertively, giving me a quick kiss on the lips before abruptly opening

651

the car door and walking off.

I wanted to run after him but I didn't. I owed it to David to stay behind. As Daniel turned to slip into an alleyway, he gave me a salute, his lips mouthing the words *I love you*.

In the interim, David's stint in jail lasted 48 hours. He was released without charge, since the playback on the video footage showed he was an innocent party, and had known nothing of Daniel's plans to escape.

On his release, I found that on the contrary, he *had* known.

"I knew he was up to something," he told me. "I just didn't know what. When has he ever really wanted to see me in person? I wasn't born yesterday."

"If you knew what he was up do, why didn't you stop it from happening?" I asked. "Things could've ended badly for you."

"They could have, but they didn't," he rationalized. "All's well, ends well." After an audible pause, he stated, "I know he came to you."

I felt my heart sink at the thought of his heart hurting over me. Yet again.

"I'll stand by whatever decision you make, but I won't fight the fact that he's still your husband. The only way I can be with you is if he lets you go. Somehow, I don't see that happening any time soon," he said, stroking his lightly bearded chin. "However, if by some miracle of fate he agrees for us to be together, and I then have to choose between being with you and having him in the background doing everything he can to win you back, I'd choose to dedicate myself to God and ministry, entirely. I'm not sure I can take losing you again."

I loved David more than I cared to admit, and my heart hurt more than I thought it would when it came to him. David and I had shared something special. He'd loved me all those years, and a love like the one only he could give felt pure and unadulterated. Still, I understood his position. If he couldn't have me, he'd rather be alone.

In the days that ensued, he went to great pains to avoid being alone with me. We'd have dinner together, but once the kids were asleep, he would be in the study, out, or anywhere other than where I was. His avoidance of me hurt deeply, and it was in those moments alone that I wished I had left with Daniel when he'd asked me to.

Still, I remained patient and stayed there with David. Josiah and Adalia loved him, and I saw no withdrawal of his love for them, only a deepening of his devotion to them, and through them, me. What hurt the most was letting go of a love that was meant to last.

We talked very little about our future but spent the next few weeks preparing for the babies to arrive. The big elephant in the room was the paternity of the babies. CVS sampling was possible, but David was not prepared to take the risk; he preferred to wait until after the babies were born. In the end, we agreed on having the testing done, and would wait until after the babies were born to read the results. With Daniel's whereabouts unknown, David promised to stand by me, regardless of the outcome of the test. Being the man that he was, he vowed to raise the babies as his while there was no clear idea of when and how Daniel and I would be together again, as a married couple.

As weeks went on and the prospect of welcoming the babies

became a reality, we finally sat down and talked at length about plans moving forward, with him being in my life, and I being in his, though not as husband and wife.

"So, I guess you'll be dropping my name?" he asked. "Going back to being Mrs. Daniel Brennan?"

"Out of respect to him, yes, but I hope I can keep your name – I could just hyphenate it – Davenport-Brennan."

"Oh, I can tell you right now, he's not going to like that at all," he predicted, knowing Daniel all too well.

"Just a thought."

"What would be the point?" he asked.

"The kids," I said a little too quickly. "Changing it all up now complicates things," I said. What I'd meant to say was I was trying to hold on to him and any evidence that we'd been one. I didn't dare tell him this. Not now anyway.

"I see," he said, sounding hurt, as though he were hoping I'd keep his name for other reasons. If only he knew the real reason why I wanted to hold on to his name – I wanted to remain tied to him in some way.

"You've been the one for me," he said suddenly, touching my face and tracing my cheek with the back of his finger. "You've been everything for me. You'll always be the one for me," he said sadly, before turning away and bringing an end to our conversation.

One afternoon, David sat me down and told me things he had not told me before.

"I have to tell you something Teme," he said, trembling as he spoke. "Some things."

I sat up, alert.

"I couldn't tell you before, but now I have to," he said, with much difficulty. "What I have to tell you could save Daniel, but it'll implicate me. It'll implicate the Brotherhood."

I listened as he spoke through pursed lips, his tone terse and weary. Declan. The common thread that bound them all. Declan. The source of so much pain. The Brotherhood. The Healer. The Priest. The Muscle. The Judge. The Juror. The Knight. The Gatekeeper. The Marksman.

I'd heard enough.

"I'm going away for some time to serve as a missionary. I'll be back before you know it. Daniel's on the run. He wants to meet up with you eventually. I can't do anything to stop that, but I can do my best to protect you. You being on the run with him is not something I'd support. I accept you cannot be with me now he's back. However, I won't accept you being put in the path of danger. I'm laying down plans to keep you safe," he promised.

I'd heard enough. "You know what? I've had enough of you all planning and plotting and scheming around my life. You've known all along that this stuff with the Brotherhood would come to a head. You've put me in the middle of it all. Jude knows this. Jude won't stay silent."

"I'm sorry Teme. None of this was meant to happen this way," he admitted.

So we parted ways for a few weeks. My heart bled for David. I imagined him all alone, lonely, without anyone to call his own. I imagined him longing after me, I imagined him hurting over me and the fact that he'd loved me all those years, we'd finally gotten a chance to be, and now we were no longer together. I imagined him praying that the babies I was carrying were his. I imagined him crying over the fact that

655

Adalia and Josiah would now only know him as uncle when he'd previously been known to them as Dad. I imagined him still very much in love with me that being with anyone else was out of the question.

Though David didn't like the thought of me travelling so far into the pregnancy, I decided to take the children to visit my family in Zambia, by way of Texas. Travelling to Zambia would be the first solo tip to the motherland, and my last before the babies were born. David would not be accompanying me immediately – apart from the missionary work, he'd commenced a prison and street ministry which was in full swing. Apparently, it needed him more than I did. In my heart of hearts, and in my plans to head to Zambia, I hoped I would see Daniel again. Whether I'd see him again depended on whether or not he was able to get in.

Adalia and Josiah were on their worst behaviour that afternoon as we sought to check in to the flight heading for Texas.

"You're going to have to check in your pram now," the air hostess insisted.

"I was told I can keep it with me, that it could be put in the cabin hold so I could use it to travel through the gates..."

"I'm not sure who told you that but..."

A gentleman at the check-in point to my right interjected, "I can accompany you to the gate with the children, you can check the pram in now."

I was convinced that his generosity would come at a price.

The man stepped into my lane, placed a carry bag similar to mine immediately in front of the counter, on the floor and mentioned again, "I'll help you with the children, you are

SOMETHING BEAUTIFUL THIS WAY COMES

free to check the pram in now." He seemed familiar to me, up close. "Juan. Te recuerdas? Me conoces?" His eyes. The same sky blue. The Brotherhood.

"Si," I said in response. "Te conoce."

"May I?" he asked, lifting my suitcase onto the carousel.

"Okay, just a few security questions. Did you pack your own bag? Are you carrying any prohibited items?" the air hostess asked.

I glanced over at the bag Juan had put onto the carousel. It looked exactly like the one I had.

The bag I brought to the airport, I packed myself. "No... I mean, yes, I packed my own bag."

"Gate 53, boarding at 10.50pm," she announced, handing me the tickets.

I quickly glanced at my ticket before putting it in between the pages of my passport. Hobart to Melbourne, Melbourne to Lusaka. *Lusaka?* What happened to going to Texas? This was some sort of a mistake. Before I had a chance to turn back to the stewardess, Juan stated just above a whisper "Aguas."

"What?"

"Aguas. Something bad is going to happen if you go back to Texas now," he warned.

The children's terrible behavior seemed to peak at that very moment. Juan reached into his pocket and produced some lollipops. "Adalia and Josiah," he said smoothly, kneeling down to be at eye level with them. "Which one would you like? Red, orange, green?"

Having Juan with us on the journey from Hobart to Melbourne, then Melbourne to Lusaka via Abu Dhabi was a blessed relief. The children were reasonably well behaved on the journey, with occasional bursts of sadness. Adalia struggled to come to terms with the fact that her father had gone away on a long trip. I felt for her. Josiah missed David terribly, but I was certain that in time he would be fine. I resolved to keep them very busy when away, so as to not have them notice the absence of Daniel or David too much.

A few weeks into being in Zambia, and I realised how well loved Daniel was when everyone who knew me asked after him. He'd set quite the impression on my family and friends. The support was overwhelming. Offers to help with the children and offers to prepare meals were plentiful.

Inside, I still thought of David constantly, wondering about him, worrying about him. Despite what he'd said, I knew he was cut. I knew there would be more to him letting me go than he let on. The love he felt for me would not just dissipate. It was destined to grow and reshape into a different mold, perhaps one stronger than the former. Still, I had to let him go.

He had planned to join us in our last week in Lusaka, but changed plans at the last minute. I was heartbroken, as I'd hoped it would be one last occasion for us to live the fantasy – that he was mine and I was his. One last chance to be with him again. No such luck, David was not joining us.

A few days before we were scheduled to fly back to Australia, the decision was made to go to Livingston Lodge, a Safari park just a few kilometers out of Lusaka. Heavily pregnant, the trip was going to be the last before the babies were born. The trip planned by my family was an attempt to take my mind off the stress I under. The possibility of the children being Daniel's was not raised at all. Though they all knew Daniel was still alive, there was no reason to not assume that the babies were David's.

The day we arrived, the children busied themselves with all the available activities – swimming, pony riding, bike riding. I opted out of everything except for the Safari drive which would commence at dusk. As I stood in line waiting for the 4WD to arrive at the Safari pickup point, a familiar voice and touch on my shoulder caused my heart to flutter.

"Sugarpie," the voice said, and I turned around to face Daniel. "So good to see you again," he stated. His deep blue eyes beheld my gaze and I fell for him all over again. His skin was heavily tanned, evidently from days out and under African skies. Though it had been only a few weeks since I'd seen him last, he looked older. Streaks of auburn red hair merged with grey and deep brown hair. He traced my face with his fingers as though he were imprinting and committing a visual of me to his memory forever. In that moment, I was his, once again. I embraced him fully and wholly, not wanting to let him go.

"Let's lose this crowd," he urged, just above a whisper, sending tingles through my body. "Wife, lover, friend, it's good to be here with you again, beholding your beautiful face, your beautiful body, your mesmerizing eyes, your warm and generous heart, again," he said, planting a kiss on my lips. "Let me show you just how much I've missed you," he urged. I felt my body melt in response to him, and I let go of all my defences. In that moment, what David and I shared was far from my mind. In that moment, I only had eyes for Daniel.

"Ba Boss," the safari guide interjected turning to Daniel. "It's only the two of you remaining now. Can we put you on the next ride? The one before is fully booked."

"Shall we?" Daniel asked, slipping a hand around my waist.

659

I nodded to the affirmative. I needed to sit down, gather myself and get over the fact that he was here with me, again. "Yes, we'll go on the next one," he confirmed on our behalf.

"Okay, Boss, the driver will be here in a few minutes," the tour guide said. "I'm Melvin by the way," he stated.

"I'm Daniel. This is my wife, Temwani," he said in response, beaming from ear to ear.

"Temwani, one of ours," Melvin noted. "Welcome back to Zambia," he said, cordially.

"I'm Zambia's latest son," Daniel stated.

"Welcome to Zambia Boss," Melvin stated, shaking Daniel's hand. "Anything you need while you're here, just let me know," he offered.

"Cheers, na totela," Daniel replied, thanking him. They engaged in small talk in Bemba before Melvin walked off to respond to the call on his walkie talkie.

I had a million and one questions for Daniel. "Since when do you speak Bemba? How did you know we'd be here?" I asked. "How did you get here?"

"I told you I'd find you wherever you are," he reminded me.

"About how I got here, there's ways. The important thing is that I'm here with you now. Me you, the kids, we're finally together again."

My heart leapt at the thought of him with his children again.

"Let's do all the talking we can do now," he said. "Something tells me there'll be a lot less talking and a whole lot of action later," he joked. I laughed heartily in response. It had been a long time since I'd felt so happy.

"Well, not too much action," I warned, hand on my swollen

660

belly. "Not trying to bring on labor early now are we?"

"I guess not," he stated. "Still, there's a whole lot of other ways I can love you down," he asaid, kissing me firmly and pulling me into him. Arms around me, he held me and we stood against the backdrop of the expansive blanket of purple orange sky.

"I've longed to hold you again, and here we are. I'm a wanted man, but I'm free here with you. Let's enjoy every moment. Let's try to make it last. There's gotta be a way for something so meant to be to last."

"I truly hope so," I said, longing for more moments with him to last forever.

"Let's not worry about tomorrow," he insisted. "Let's focus on today. Me, you, our babies, something beautiful this way comes."

EPILOGUE

I woke to a sudden start that night. Daniel stirred next to me in his sleep. I gazed at him for a moment, filled with so much love and desire for him. I wasn't sure how long this would last, but we wanted to make it last for a lifetime. Still, I wondered after David and hoped he would find happiness.

My mobile phone buzzed several times on the bedside table. I checked the time. 1.20 am. A message had just come through on WhatsApp, from David.

Call me when you can. I'm in Livingstone.

My heart sunk. He was but a few hours away. He'd be crushed to see me back with Daniel, so soon.

Call me please. I know you're with him now but no matter. Call me. It's urgent.

I hesitated for a moment, considering the fact that he knew Daniel and I were together again, yet he still wanted me to call.

I dialed his number and he picked up on the first ring. He spoke first. "Teme."

Hearing him say my name sent shivers down my spine. The effect he still had on me. If any two people were meant to be from the start, it was he and I. Only circumstance wouldn't permit.

"I've missed you so much," he confessed. "I should've come with you and the kids in the first place, but pride got

662

the better of me," he claimed. "I hope you'll forgive me."

I sighed loud enough for him to hear. "David, you don't need to ask for forgiveness. You've been through a lot with me, I'm hardly in a position to dictate how you should behave."

"Okay. As long as I'm alright with you. That's all that matters to me right now. How are you?" he asked. "How are the babies, and our kids?"

"I'm okay," I replied. *Our kids.* He still thought of Adalia and Josiah as his own. "We're all fine."

"Teme, before I tell you what I have to say, I need your forgiveness for breaking a promise to you." My heart sunk. *More lies?*

"David, whatever you've done, I'll forgive you. I forgive you," I told him.

"Okay. You know my mate Lionel? Dr. Edwards?"

"Yep, I remember him." No longer distant, they'd grown close. As I came to find out, Daniel also held him in high regard.

"Well, he helped me gain access to the CVS sample results."

I had to sit down to brace myself.

"I promised I would wait 'til after they were born, but I just had to know now," he admitted.

"David!"

"Teme, I'm sorry. I know, I promised. But things change. Now that I know, it's all become clear to me what has to be done."

"David, you had no right!" I exclaimed.

"On the contrary Teme, I had every right."

My phone buzzed again as another message came through.

"I've just sent you a copy of the results," he said. "I wanted to wait until I saw you, face to face, but his being there with you now made me finding out all the more urgent."

Daniel will be disappointed.

"Something's gotta give, and this time, it won't be me and my love for you," David said, determined.

"So, the results are final?" I asked. It was clear from the way he was talking that the babies were his.

"As accurate as they can be," he replied. "One baby is mine, one baby is his."

"What?" I asked, gobsmacked.

"Yes, you heard me. One of the babies is yours and mine, one is yours and his."

"David, that's not possible."

"Oh, but it is. It's rare, but not impossible," he claimed.

I felt like crying. *How did things get so complicated?*

"Teme," David asked, "You okay?"

"Not really," I told him, for want of something better to say.

"I love you Teme, I always will."

"David, I never stopped loving you. I just feel you shouldn't be settling for crumbs. You deserve more than I can give you. Now with one of the babies being yours..."

"Teme, I have nothing else apart from you. Ministry is ministry, but you're my everything," he professed.

"David..."

"I'll even be your second husband," he said, in a desperate tone that surprised me. "Modicum, morals aside, I'll risk eternal damnation just to be with you."

"Come back to bed," Daniel sleepily called out in the background, making me jump.

"I have to go, David," I whispered into the phone.

"Okay," he said. "Take care of yourself, take care of our kids," he added. "I'll be here in Livingstone, on mission, for another few weeks. I'll get to you as soon as I can," he promised. "I'll be seeing you shortly."

Immediately our phone conversation ended, I opened the message he'd sent me with the DNA results. There was no doubt that the babies were from two different fathers. Daniel Brennan and David Davenport.

"Bring your beautiful body back over here," Daniel insisted, startling me while I was in the process of reading the results. I didn't know how to tell him. "What are you doing out of bed at this time anyway?" he asked.

"David called," I told him, sliding back into bed.

"And?" he asked, rubbing his eyes in an effort to wake up.

"He's gone and accessed the DNA results."

"And?"

I swallowed hard before replying, "One of the babies is yours, one is his."

He shook his sleepy head in response. "What?"

"Only one of the babies is yours."

"Like, how is that even possible?" he asked.

"It's rare, but apparently, it does happen. Two separate eggs, two separate..."

"Spare me the science," he said curtly. "I don't care what the results say. I'm not letting go of you again."

"Neither is David."

"Here we go," he said, suddenly bolting up and out of bed, completely naked. He stood there in front of me, tall, bronzed, his body perfectly crafted, looking more like a mythical god than the Daniel I once knew, who was so insecure and so afraid of losing me. This Daniel wasn't afraid

665

of losing, he was ready to win. "Show me the messages," he ordered.

I handed him my phone, notwithstanding the fact that he would see the other messages David had sent.

Scrolling through the messages, he laughed haughtily. "Second husband? He's dreaming. I'm not giving you up, and he's not going to have a piece of you. I appreciate your right to choose. But I'm your husband. Always will be your husband." Handing the phone back to me, he announced, "I'm not going to stop him from seeing his child, but if he doesn't back off, *c'est la guerre*. All's fair in love and war."

www.ingramcontent.com/pod-product-compliance
Lightning Source LLC
Chambersburg PA
CBHW032249020726
47495CB00001B/32